THE MINING MEN

THE AUTHOR

Otis E Young, Jr., who makes his home in
Tempe, Arizona, is an historian who has spent
many years in research on the mining era in the
West. He is probably the most knowledgeable
writer on the subject today. He is the author of
many articles and books on mining in the West,
among them *Western Mining* (Norman, 1971).
He has long been absorbed by the diversity of
men who contributed to the mining era.

THE ARTIST

Tom Phillips, who provided the sketches for
the book, is a well-recognized artist of the West.
His book, *The Sketches of Tom Phillips,* was
published by The Lowell Press in 1971. His work
here makes Young's characters come alive, as he
vividly portrays an era when gold fever ran ram-
pant.

THE MINING MEN

BY OTIS E YOUNG, JR.

ILLUSTRATED BY TOM PHILLIPS

THE LOWELL PRESS/KANSAS CITY, MISSOURI

OTHER BOOKS BY OTIS E YOUNG, JR.
  THE FIRST MILITARY ESCORT ON THE SANTA FE TRAIL
  (GLENDALE, 1952)
  THE WEST OF PHILIP ST. GEORGE COOKE (GLENDALE, 1954)
  HOW THEY DUG THE GOLD (TUCSON, 1967)
  WESTERN MINING (NORMAN, 1970)

Printed in the United States of America
Library of Congress Catalog Card No. 74-15158
ISBN   0—913504—18—1

THE MINING MEN

DEDICATION

We ourselves count mining amongst the honourable arts, inasmuch as it promotes wealth by good and honest methods. Who can fail to realize that mining is a calling of peculiar dignity?

Georgius Agricola
De re metallica, Book I

CONTENTS

PREFACE &
ACKNOWLEDGEMENTS

This is not exactly the way it was, but it is an honest attempt to show things as they could have been. The backdrop persona, institutions, and events are historical. They flourished at the times and places given. On the other hand, the foreground actors are completely fictitious, and no resemblance to actual persons is implied or should be inferred. There was no Rocky Mountain Territory, there was no firm of Huggins & Casey, and there was hardly a placer or mineral district in the West that did not have a Molly Pitcher location recorded.

With the exception of the Cornish and the Irish miners' dialect, the conversation approximates reasonably modern English. The speech of the period was so stilted and occasionally so larded with contemporary slang and hyperbole as to create the effect of burlesque should a serious attempt be made to imitate it. For that matter, it is highly questionable whether the mining men of nineteenth-century America really did speak as Bret Harte, Samuel Clemens, or William Wright appeared to quote them.

In their day the mining men walked the earth as giants. Their contemporaries regarded them with awe and listened to their opinions with respect, an accolade seldom popularly bestowed upon technicians. For two generations they were folk heroes of the American people, and it was not until the general debasement of the arts with the rise of mass-entertainment media that they were displaced in the popular imagination by the cowboys of the open-range cattle industry.

Even such a minor celebration as this could not have been written without the ungrudging assistance and cooperation of scores of knowledgeable professionals. Old-time miners, modern mining engineers, officers of mine corporations, professional historians, employees of state bureaus of mines, archivists, librarians, and personal literary associates contributed unstintingly of their time and knowledge. To list every name would be to retrace ten years of research. Special mention must be given to my associate and technical collaborator, Robert Lenon, P.E., of Patagonia, Arizona. Bob worked with the old-timers and knows as much about this nearly vanished breed of miners as any person can. Without the assurance of his aid and expertise nothing could have been attempted.

I am obligated also to my friend of twenty-five years' standing, Dr. Richard E. Buckingham, of Bloomington, Indiana, for professional services rendered herewith; to Dan Mathisrud, of Lead, South Dakota, a gentleman and scholar who earns his living at the end of a Joy air-leg machine; to Ross Thomas, of Dolores, Colorado, who in his time used a doublejack and hand steel; to the state mine inspector of Arizona, who, as I write this, is engaged in an attempt to rescue two miners trapped on the twelve-hundred-foot level of a copper development not too far from where I sit at my ease; to various gentlemen on various levels of the administrative staff in the institution where I work, who have turned the blind eye and extended the helping hand, thank you all, very much.

I wish to express the gratitude of Bob Lenon and myself to Dr. Doyce B. Nunis, Jr., for permission to include a modified version of the article, "Big John Tretheway: a Day in the Life of a Western Miner," published in the 1974 *Brand Book* of the Los Angeles Corral of the Westerners.

TEMPE, ARIZONA   OTIS E YOUNG, JR.

ix

CHAPTER 1

1871
MATT WHEELER

H E WAS STARING DOWN into his prospect pan, frowning in puzzlement. At length he gave the drag another swirl, peered again, and then remarked conversationally, "Now you see it, an' now you don't. I be goddamned."

Rosebud broke wind loudly.

"I feel the same way," Matt Wheeler agreed. Groaning as he straightened his painfully hunkered legs, he waded two long steps to the edge of the little watercourse and sat down on the bank. Rosebud decided that nothing more of interest would happen for a while and that the bunch of grass a few feet away might repay investigation. She sauntered over, dropped her nose, and began tugging at the brown clump.

Wheeler removed his battered slouch hat to reveal a shiny pink skull scantily fringed by long hair whose iron-gray color matched his untidy beard.

"I be goddamned," he repeated, and then looked up slantwise at the sun. "Too late to go on today." He paused as if to listen to an exchange of views inaudible to anyone but himself. "No wheres else *to* go. Best get to it."

He made camp under a small cottonwood with the deceptively-

Tom Phillips

casual speed of long practice. One side of Rosebud's neatly stowed packsaddle lying on the ground gave up a bedroll and a jute sack of cooking supplies. Wheeler shook his head pessimistically at the withered folds of the flour sack and the slender end of a side of bacon. "Too bad burro ain't fitt'n for nobody but a Messican to eat," he remarked, with a leer at Rosebud. The jennet paid this the attention it deserved.

Wheeler collected wood and lit it with a sputtering sulphur loco-foco. He sliced bacon into his frying pan and, when it was mostly done, fished it out of the grease. Keeping one eye on Rosebud, whose unabashed lust for bacon was but one of her many failings, Matt next made a thick flour-and-water paste, which he dropped into the hot bacon fat. He presently turned it, finished it, and lifted it out with the point of his knife. The flapjack and the bacon would constitute his evening meal. Rosebud sidled over, snuffed hopefully at the empty frying pan, and then returned to the bunchgrass.

His back against the cottonwood and with a tiny scrap of cut plug in his cheek, Matt gave himself over to a review of his professional findings of the day now so nearly done. Two months ago, while moving south in the basin country, Matt had observed a small notch bisecting the low range off to his right. He had reason to believe that the country beyond was mineralized, and the mouth of the gulch looked inviting. He had borrowed a meager grubstake and slipped quietly out of Bancroft at midnight, ten days past. Such secretiveness was essential; he had learned long ago that, when a prospector openly left camp on business, two or three loafers would often follow him in the hope of horning in on whatever he might find. Sometimes they horned in with rifles— and sometimes with lawyers, which was worse. Rifles might miss their mark, but lawyers never did. Matt earnestly consigned the whole tribe of smooth-talking, black-coated vultures to the devil, who, to the detriment of his reputation, had proverbially fathered them.

It had taken him more time than he had allowed to find the notch again; it was visible only from the northeast. But there was vegetation at the bottom, indicating water higher up, and Matt's first inspection of its outwash fan had revealed a promising variety of rock.

"Now, cut that out!" he cried, emerging from his reverie and shying a handy stone at Rosebud, who was getting ready to assay his bedroll. The jennet snorted and minced away haughtily.

"Durn females!" Matt commented. "The second a man tries to do some thinkin', they start in foolin'."

Rising, he sidled in a crabwise fashion to Rosebud, planted a foot on her trailing halter rope, and hauled himself up to her. He untied the rag that muffled the clapper of her neck bell. Rosebud shook her head, producing a rapid series of "tonks." Releasing her, Matt returned to the cottonwood and resumed his introspections.

"Wush old Hank was here," he mused. Hank Heintzendorfer it was who had taught Matthew Wheeler to prospect in hard rock, back in 'Fifty-five after the Californy diggings had begun to play out. All that Matt had known previously was placering, but Hank had been a miner back in the Old Country.

"Und where is placer goldt, is someblace up der river ein goldt lead," he had lectured Matt. "Or silber or *kupfer* or somedink. Always. *Vielleicht,* not much but ve go look."

They had never struck it rich or made at best more than grub, but Matt had learned volumes while following the long-bearded old Saxon. Hank Heintzendorfer was now long gone, dead of the black lung fever in the Bodie excitement, and Matt, who by now was not as young as he had been, had buried him in their prospect pit. It was the only open ground in that frozen country and hadn't had much in it anyway. Matt often wondered whether Hank had left anyone in Saxony to whom word could be sent, but Hank had never mentioned any names. Maybe he, like a lot of people, had gone to Californy to get away from something or someone. If Hank were still alive, perhaps he could make sense out of this confounded valley.

The issue was gold. At the point where the narrow notch opened into the basin country, Matt had dug his first prospect pit. A shovelful of sand and gravel taken from next the shallow bedrock, a quick dip and swirl in the water, and Matt had begun to claw pebbles and sand out of the pan. More water, more flipping swirls, and in the end there reposed a streak of fine black sand in the drag. Glinting within the black band were a few tiny yellow points of light. However, if Matt had two bits for every time he had panned out *some* colors, he would be richer than Commodore Vanderbilt, he reckoned. The trouble was, the colors were small and few and spotty in their distribution. The next mile upstream had taken days to traverse, what with putting down a prospect pit every furlong. From the sands at the bottom of some pits Matt had recovered gold; from as many more, nothing. Never had he found more than a few cents' worth, and more than once he would have given it up had not the black iron sand persisted.

"Gold rides a h'iron 'orse," he had heard a hundred Cousin Jacks swear, and old Hank, too, had been powerful fond of black iron sand. Yet, scan the widening valley sides as he would, Matt had nowhere observed any outcrop trace of black or rusty red or limonite yellow. The country rock appeared to be only a commonplace granite, which failed to account for the variety of the stream gravels. He must press on, he had decided each dawn.

About noon of this last day Matt had come upon a small waterfall, above which was a diminutive pool. Beside it a number of cottonwoods had taken root. Such places were formed by natural rock sills, along the upstream foot of which gold dust might be concentrated by water action. With some sense of excitement Matt had put down his last pit here but had found nothing of moment. Now he must positively decide whether to push on or turn back. His grub was already too low for his peace of mind, and the extension of one more day would cut things mighty close. Maybe he would end by eating burro meat anyway, for all the cranky fondness he had for Rosebud. In this country in the olden days, he had heard, the mountain men had eaten worse than burro—much worse. The worst meat there was, for a fact. Matt thereupon made up his mind. He would sleep on the decision.

He prepared for bed by having a drink at the pool, making a return present to it, covering the fire, and then flipping the top half of his bedroll over his legs. He pulled his hat over his face. Rosebud was invisible, but an occasional distant "tonk" told him that she was not far off. Burros liked company, and she wouldn't stray far. Indeed, he would be lucky if sometime during the night she didn't put a hoof in his belly. Matt relaxed, but beside him under the blanket and tarp his old carbine lay at hand, a cartridge in the chamber. This wasn't such bad Indian country any more, but . . . . He fell asleep swiftly and easily.

Sometime during the night his hat fell off his face, and Matt awakened to feel his nose numbed by the predawn chill. A glance at the stars confirmed the hour. He quietly slipped out of the bedroll, still holding his rifle, and eased over some yards to a clump of boulders he had marked while making camp. They formed a reasonably defensible breastwork, and from between two he could observe anything moving over the light sand of the creek bottom. This was the hour when he always wished earnestly that he had held onto that job of teaming in Tucson. The Old Pueblo was a hellhole, but at least it was warm there most of the time. As he shivered, he persecuted himself with memories of Señora María Concepcíon García, a widow—courtesy of the Apaches—with whom he had had a domiciliary understanding. María was no spring chicken, but, being a widow, she was her own boss in the curious way the Messicans had, who otherwise guarded their womenfolk like hawks. And, he reflected, she had a mighty light hand over the cooking fire.

This led to fond memories of María's succulent goat-cheese enchiladas, her fiery but delicious tamales, her *salsa pura,* until Matt's empty stomach rumbled loudly enough to wake the dead. At night she warmed the blanket like a coal stove. Matt's teeth chattered. He would have been indignant had someone told him the plain truth about himself, but María had sighed as she watched him go, whispering "loco" to herself. As a woman and a Spaniard, hence doubly a realist, she knew that men of Matthew Wheeler's kidney could not be restrained by chains of iron or even *chilis relleños* when the itch to go forth came upon them. Matt Wheeler shuddered violently, cursed himself vigorously, but kept his station. Discomfort was better than risking a Ute haircut.

The sky paled with false dawn. The air grew colder. Then the sky began to lighten, and after a while it was dawn. Matt still held on but, after allowing another ten minutes, relaxed. The time of danger had passed. Up the valley he heard one "tonk." Shuddering, he dug out live coals from his fire, piled on dry sticks, and warmed himself back to life before the blaze, his blanket hanging over his shoulders. He drank hot water (the coffee beans were long since exhausted) and felt himself begin to limber up. He prepared and ate a breakfast identical to his supper except in greater frugality and then started up the stream to hunt out Rosebud. Just as he came up to the jennet, Matt was astonished to see a mule deer lowering its nose to the water. He eased behind Rosebud, rested his gun across her neck, and carefully squeezed off a shot. The old carbine bellowed. Rosebud squealed and bucked, her ears flat against her neck. White powder smoke obscured his view for a moment, but when it cleared, the deer was lying on the sand, its head in the water.

Matt smacked his lips. He could now have three or four good, belly-bursting meals, make some jerky, and be able to extend his trip for four more days. He spent the rest of the morning butchering out the deer, his work broken by pauses to gorge himself on the stick-roasted meat. Rosebud's pack line was pressed into service for jerky hanging.

During one trip to the creek to wash his knife and hands a curious incident occurred. Matt stumbled over an angular, mud-brown shard of rock, kicked it from his path, and was surprised to hear it fall with a clear, bell-like musical chime. "What in hell . . . ?" he asked, as he automatically picked it up. Aside from its musical proclivities it proved hardly noteworthy. The color was unpromising, its weight unfavorable, and it appeared to contain neither quartz nor anything else of interest. He tossed it away, heard it chime again as it struck, and then noted that the creek bed contained a large number of its fellows. Wheeler decided to ask an assayer some time what the peculiar stuff was and so, picking up another fragment, tucked it away.

He was feeling so good at noon that he even dug a prospect pit in the bank where the deer had fallen, thinking it a good omen. He did not feel so good when the drag of the pan washed clean. There was not even black sand in it.

"*Also,* Matt, ven die colors run oudt, ve chust passed der lead. So—go back, *jetzt.*" Matt could almost hear old Hank saying it. Yet a careful scanning of both sides of the valley showed neither promising shades of mineralization nor the snagtooth of outcrops. Just then his eye fell on the cottonwoods fifty yards downstream where he had hung his jerky line. Matt bounded forward, splashed through the stream, and dashed toward his camp. As he pounded up the gravel, Rosebud raised her head from her illicit meal of jerky, snorted, and started to move away. Matt bent over, grabbed a hand-sized rock, and hurled it at her hindquarters with venomous force and aim. Rosebud recoiled and headed for the higher brush, the meat line dragging behind her. Matt threw another rock, and another. His voice rose higher. (He had once worked a rocker at French Bar in partnership with a retired Marseilles stevedore, and some of his words would have made an Old Port trollop widen her eyes in admiration.)

At last, gasping for breath, Matt sat down, letting his last missile slide out of his fingers. As it rubbed his fingertips, he felt a rough sandy texture—not at all what one would expect from stream-worn granite. He looked down at it and then brought it close to his eyes. At first he thought that the fragment was sandstone because of its sugary surface and feel, but a close study showed him that the glassy grains were tightly cemented together and that many were broken through the middle.

"Quartzite," he said, nodding. The specimen was a bleached light brown in over-all appearance, but here and there a thread of darker red-brown was visible. Matt tossed it up and down in his palm, Rosebud's pilferage momentarily forgotten. His eyes went blank with concentration. Looking again at the rock, he verified his first impression that, although it was weathered, it had not been appreciably rounded by stream action. "I jest wonder . . . ," he muttered.

Shovel in one hand and carbine in the other, Wheeler headed purposefully up the moderately steep rise to the east. He soon left the creek-bottom vegetation and was ascending a dry grade composed of thin, crumbling soil. Innumerable glints of light reflected the sun into his eyes. Matt examined a pinch of the soil and verified his estimate that it was composed of a mixture of clay and mica. So intent was he upon his examination that he nearly fell into a brush-filled depression. It needed but a glance to tell that it was artificial—and old.

"Somebody's been here afore," he concluded glumly. His rising hopes fell considerably. If the slope had been prospected before and then abandoned, there would be little use to press on. Nevertheless, his streak of stubbornness drove him to clear the brush out a bit and to attempt a prod or two with his spade. At his second swing a yellow-brown spherical object broke out of the dirt and rolled off to one side. It lay there, looking vacantly at Matt's boots with eyeless sockets. Matt regarded it quizzically. "Still here, too," he remarked.

More work with the spade revealed long bones in reasonable order and the ruins of a spine and a rib cage. Between two vertebrae a much-rusted triangle of iron was deeply embedded. Pursing his lips, Matt rolled the skull over and found, as he had expected, an ugly pattern of radiating cracks on the right temporal bones. Matt's inquest was concluded. The big, sound teeth hinted that his predecessor had been a young Mexican *gambusino* whose luck had run out here. The arrowhead clearly showed how and why: the Mexican had first been shot in the back, and then, as his legs went out from under him, he had been finished off with a stone-headed club. The brush growing in the pit suggested that the incident had happened some years previously, perhaps as far back as Mexican times in the territory.

"Let's see what you found, partner," Matt said. Moving the bones no more and no less carefully than the coarse scree, Matt gophered away in the pit. With each inch of depth the soil became harder to dig, changing swiftly from the clay-mica mixture to black chips of rock so coated and spangled with mica that they glittered as though newly immersed in water. Now and again Matt came upon a relic: a horn button, a corroded iron bar point, the remains of a hide water bag. Matt was finally reduced to using his hands to collect samples, which he placed on the blade of his spade. By now, he reckoned, he was in virgin dirt; poor Pedro hadn't gotten this far before he was gobbled. Probably he was used

10

up by one young buck, eager for a scalp to prove his manliness but not so eager that he didn't wait until Pedro was bent over and helpless; there were not enough arrowheads in the bones for it to have been done by a war party.

Balancing the spade and its contents in one hand, Matt tramped downhill to the creek. He tilted the dirt into his pan, hunkered down over the water, and began washing. After a time he raised the pan, swirling and tilting it expertly to catch the late-afternoon light. One, two, three . . . fifteen gold colors in plenty of black sand, he noted, the colors ranging from fine dust to one pretty respectable fleck. Not quite enough to save, he decided, and let the left edge of the pan trail down into the water.

Matt calculated that, with one partner and a rocker, he could take enough gold out of Pedro's pit to just about starve to death in a month. But the trail was definitely starting to grow warm. Tracing the hillside lines of wash, Matt noted wryly that Pedro's pit was the merest trifle downstream from the rocky sill that had pent the creek into his campground pool. No wonder he had found nothing above the sill.

Reasonably sure of himself now and too experienced to go running over the hills in late-afternoon shade, Matt resumed his housekeeping labors. He found the jerky line, now sadly chewed and tangled, repaired it, tied it up well out of Rosebud's reach, and went back to the mule-deer carcass for another load of meat. He gathered wood, inventoried his possessions, and arranged matters for a stay of several more days. Fried venison and a very small flapjack constituted his dinner, the smell of which lured back an impenitent Rosebud. The jennet hung around until she was certain that no scraps were coming her way and then moved off into the bottom to secure her own meal. As a last thought Matt walked back to Pedro's pit before dusk and made shift to provide the bones with passably decent burial. Into the small mound of scree Matt jammed a rough cross of twigs. He felt that some sort of prayer would be in order, but his prayer lode was in *borrasca* except for the dimly recalled childhood, "Now I lay me down to sleep . . . ." At its conclusion Matt crossed himself as he had seen María do and considered that these rituals ought to hold Pedro.

As the sunlight touched the western ridgeline the next morning, Matt was finishing his breakfast. He felt so good that he let Rosebud clean up the frying pan for him. Shouldering the carbine, he tramped upward to Pedro's grave, scanned the ground to find the lines of wash, and began following them uphill at a steady, climbing pace. The going underfoot was difficult, slippery even though dry and seeded with sharp angles of schist chips. Matt kept his eyes to the ground, looking for quartzite float. Now and again he came across such a piece, and his satisfaction increased. The quartzite was not easy to pick out from the mixture of granite and schist scree, but Matt's eyes were keen, and the bright sunshine was of great assistance to him. After perhaps a quarter mile of trudging he came to the foot of a low, dilapidated natural wall, or sill. It was no more than a yard or two wide and a foot high at most, but it extended laterally some distance on either hand. From his camp down by the creek it must have been invisible, screened from view by the cumulative effects of five hundred yards of scrubby growth.

Matt used his boot to scuff at the forward edge of the low wall. Schist. He stepped over the wall to scuff again just above. Granite, beyond doubt. He leaned forward to brush and puff away the layer of sandy dirt atop the wall itself. It was clearly quartzite and identical in all respects both to the float on the hillside and to the piece he had nearly flung at Rosebud. Sighting along the sill, he estimated that it was by no means truly vertical but tended to emerge from the ground at an angle so pronounced that its uphill corner merged evenly into the granite country rock.

Wheeler grimaced. At this orientation to the compass the wall should have cast a decided shadow early in the morning, and *would* have done so, making a dark, linear, and eye-catching display, but for the fact that the ridge beyond to the east blocked the rising sun until it was so high that the sill's shadow would be only an inch or so wide. Mother Nature had been at some pains to conceal this sill, and, but for Rosebud's greed and his own experienced fingertips, Matt would probably have never suspected its existence.

The old prospector wandered back and forth, eying his find. Matt was hoping to locate some segment of the sill whose color or texture hinted that it was more heavily mineralized than the average. From time to time he also poked about its forward margin where it lay in contact with the schist, hoping to stir up some surface gold colors. Having no luck either way, he finally fastened at random upon a small block of the stuff and with some effort got it away from the point where it was embedded. Turning it over to inspect the comparatively unweathered surface, he observed dozens of tiny spots of natural rust scattered with fair uniformity across it.

Altogether, the block seemed unprepossessing, but Matt happily took it in the crook of his left arm, picked up his carbine, and began to make his way down toward the creek. He started to sing tonelessly:

> Oh, what was your name in the States?
> Was it Jackson or Williams or Bates?
> Did you take a man's life
> Or another man's wife?
> Oh, what was your name in the States?

Back at his campground Matt unrolled a neat bundle that had heretofore remained lashed to the off side of Rosebud's packsaddle. The canvas revealed a curious assortment of ironmongery, most of which suggested correctly that it had been reclaimed from rubbish heaps and quartz-mill junk piles. Matt picked up a four-pound hammer, selected a large, flat boulder, placed the boulder upon the canvas, his block of quartzite upon the boulder, and with his hammer began systematically pounding the block to fragments. He used some care in this process and then, choosing a number of pieces at random, began reducing these fragments to still smaller fragments, until at last nothing remained above the size of a grain of Indian corn. Discarding the boulder-anvil, he poured an inch of his produce into a squat iron cup, hacksawed from a mercury flask whose disappearance from the Golden Belt Quartz Mill had momentarily troubled the storekeeper thereof. It made a tolerable and convenient mortar; the pestle was a foot-long length of drill-steel stock, and the hammer clinked cheerfully against the steel as Matt systematically worked down the quartzite to dust and powdery, fine sand.

It took the remainder of the morning and part of the afternoon before Matt was finished with this tiresome but not particularly demanding work. In view of the fine size of his placer colors, he decided to reduce his sample to as small particles as he could, and this required much hammering, sifting, and rehammering. He accompanied himself by song and verse—or as much of both as he could remember—some of his renditions were highly sentimental, and others were of a nature to make Rosebud cough and turn away in shame. At length the work was finished, and Matt was able to contemplate a cone of approximately one-half pound of quartzite dust. From the opposite sides of this cone he carefully extracted two measures of the dust, using a heavy glass one-ounce container whose disappearance from the Grand Oriental Saloon had momentarily troubled the bartender thereof. These two ounces of pulverized rock—as near the formal "assay ounce" as one could expect—went into his pan.

Matt next produced a small druggist's bottle whose ground-glass stopper was carefully wired to the neck. Opening it, he decanted a brief dribble of heavy, silvery fluid into the small pile of rock dust and then poured in a half cup of water and a dash of table salt. He slowly and methodically stirred the puddle with his finger, rubbing, stroking, heaping, flattening, and rubbing again until he felt reasonably certain that the ounce of quicksilver had been brought into intimate contact with every part of the dust.

He interrupted his work long enough to build up his campfire and, when the embers burned down to coals, placed his shovel blade upon them to heat. When the shovel felt moderately warm to his hand held an inch above it, Matt took his pan to the creek and swiftly washed away the quartzite powder. A small pellet of quicksilver the diameter of a five-cent piece remained in the drag. Matt rolled this in a scrap of paper, twisted the ends tightly, and placed the small packet on the heated shovel blade. Testing the direction of the slight breeze, he carefully removed himself to the windward side of the fire, for only a fool put himself in the way of mercury vapor, however little of it there might be around.

When the paper showed signs of charring, Matt removed it

with his knife point, allowed it to cool, and then very carefully dissected the brittle, carbonized mass. His search was not at first successful, but he went over the paper remnants again and again until, with a sigh of relief, he located a remarkably small sphere. It was little larger than a grain of millet, and he worked carefully lest he lose it, but after painstaking rubbing between thumb and forefinger, he peered closely at its surface. Small as it was, it glowed golden-yellow.

With extreme care Matt transferred the tiny bead to his tongue and pressed two teeth hard against it. The ease with which it flattened indicated that it contained little in the way of silver or base metals. Tongueing the resulting disk upon a finger, he reinspected it with the experienced eye of a placer man accustomed to dealing with and valuing natural dust. Matt judged that he might have, including losses in the panning (which would be about half of the sample's content), ten cents' worth of gold.

He was not handy at ciphering, but, with a twig for a stylus and a flattened stretch of sand for a writing surface, Wheeler commenced figuring. Use of the "assay ounce" reduced his labors considerably, so that he soon was writing "$600." Past experience made him reduce this to an even $500 gold per ton. Not bad! Of course, the surface outcrop was usually much richer than the ore a little way down, and there was no way yet of knowing that the entire outcrop would go as much as the grab sample he had taken at random, but still . . . .

Matt eased his back and stared skyward. Had he, after all these years, finally struck it? Prospector's optimism warred with the caution of age and disillusionment. He mentally balanced the poor placer showing of the creek against his rough field assay of the lode and concluded that he had better take another day or two to be sure.

Knowing with a fair degree of certainty what had to be done, and knowing of old exactly how to do it, Matt Wheeler engaged in a disciplined fury of activity for the remainder of that day and the two days succeeding. He paced out the visible strike of the quartzite outcrop and took small surface samples along it. Another field assay of the average whole gave up a gold bead approximately the size of the first, a hint that the gold values were distributed through the outcrop with fair uniformity. Matt bagged the fragments of his samplings to take back with him for the attentions of a regular fire assayer. He next paced out two five-hundred-foot locations, built location cairns, and in the central monument that divided the two locations placed a hastily filled-in printed location notice. Lacking any regular writing instrument for this purpose, he shaved down the point of a carbine bullet, the soft lead making a tolerable substitute for a pencil. Nor did he neglect to pace out and similarly locate a mill-site claim down by the stream.

Halfway through his labors the flour sack gave up its last contents, but Matt scarcely noticed the fact. To make his location good for a year, he still had to sink ten feet on the ore, and he had settled on the schist footwall as the least of three evils. The granite hanging wall was impossible and the quartzite lode itself worse, but the schist might yield to his pick. While he was engaged in this work, he bagged another set of samples composed of equal parts of schist and quartzite where they touched the side of the pit and each other; it was more than possible that the schist contained some values which had (he would have said) leaked out of the lode sideways. This was all very laborious work, and the deer carcass was little more than bare bones upon its completion.

Upon the fourth day Matt rose with his tough old muscles aching but easy in his mind. His work was done. It was time to make a beeline for civilization, and he knew that the way going home was always faster than the way coming out. There was some aggravation with Rosebud, grown fat and insolent, but the sun was scarcely above the eastern ridges before the subdued jennet was packed and was picking her way downstream at the end of the halter line. Matt strode along at a ground-devouring pace, yet with attention to his footing; it would never do now to break an ankle on some stream cobble, spend a week eating burro, and then have to hobble seventy miles on a crutch, starved down until he looked worse than poor Pedro. In a way Matt was perversely glad that his find was so low tenor; had it been chock-full of native gold, he would have been sorely tempted to stay longer, load up Rosebud until her knees buckled, and so make his return trip far more difficult. A good marching pace would help keep him warm down in the windy basin country; as matters presently stood his pants and hickory shirt were fluttering tatters, his boots wrecks, his coat as thin as paper, and in general he looked like the beggar coming to town.

Matt was actually in sight of the throat of the valley, through which he had a glimpse of the gray-dun basin country beyond, when his nose detected one tiny acrid whiff. He stopped so abruptly that Rosebud poked her own nose into his back. Matt's eyes darted right and left, and his grip on the old carbine tightened. Then, dropping the halterline, he moved swiftly and noiselessly as a lizard into the jumble of fallen boulders which lay close to the edge of the stream. Rosebud tried to follow him but, making poor work of it, took the opportunity to grab a mouthful of greenery. Matt continued to scan the stream as he worked out possibilities. Indians never built fires while on business. Therefore, one or more white men were about and had extinguished their fire with water, which no honest men would do. Furthermore, they were lurking in an ideal ambush spot while the sun was high, instead of going about their lawful occasions, whether travel or prospecting. It did not necessarily follow that the party or parties unknown were laying for Matt himself, but it was a fair presumption until proved otherwise.

Had they seen him? This was the puzzler. Where were their animals? Another puzzler. Which side of the valley were they on? Matt's ability to follow up small bits of evidence with rough-hewn but sound logic stood him in good stead. Up ahead, on his side of the stream, a sizable promontory forced the water to make a detour to the left. Presumably the reception committee and its animals were behind the nose. In the normal course of travel he himself would ford the stream on the near side and continue down the broad shingle on the other bank, thus giving the waiting parties an excellent chance to back-shoot him. They wouldn't even have to post a lookout—just loaf around sunning themselves until Matthew Wheeler appeared, going more or less on a tangent away from them. Then they could in leisurely fashion shoot him down, rifle Rosebud's pack, and go on upsteam to see what Matt had

17

found. A slight change of location notices, and all his work would be theirs.

Completing this train of thought made Matt's knees go watery. Retreat was out of the question for want of supplies, as was the hope merely of waiting out his possible assailants. A man of enterprise and a degree of ruthlessness could well turn the tables on the lurking party; the valley wall on the right was not so sheer that he could not quietly ascend it, turn the flank of the ambushers, and shoot down most of them without greater difficulty than the physical effort involved. Matt understood this. He also realized that he simply was not capable of it. Never noteworthy for displays of courage even in a bad cause, Matt always preferred flight to fight when given the choice. It was this very streak of easygoing acquiescence which had strongly impelled him to seek the distant climate of California. Not to put too fine a point on it, Wheeler was too weak even to cheat a trollop, let alone bushwhack suspicious characters.

In something akin to despair Matt's eyes fell upon a tall, slender pinnacle of rock which soared upward from the nose of the promontory. He automatically classified it as granite and noted that it was naturally fractured into polygonal blocks which merely rested each upon the next. If it were not so sheer and shaky, it could have served admirably as a lookout station for his presumptive enemies. Shaky! His mind began to function despite his terror, and he was encouraged to note that between two of the lower blocks was a linear cavity, ideal for what was beginning to shape in his mind.

Quietly turning Rosebud around, Matt retreated up the creek until he was hidden from sight. He tethered the jennet, loosened her cinch, and tumbled off her pack and saddle. He burrowed frantically in the packs until he found what he sought—two flat tin canisters of blasting powder and a hank of safety fuse. Slipping them inside his shirt, he took several empty sample bags to the stream, where he filled them with damp sand. Draw tapes tied to draw tapes, he pulled them around his neck and shoulder like a bandolier. He checked his match safe and cartridges and then began to work forward with enormous caution. He reached the side of the promontory and softly ascended it, trying always to keep himself hidden among the rocks but angling steadily upward and leftward toward the base of the tall pinnacle.

After a seeming eternity of what was, toward the end, some fair mountaineering, Matt was finally able to inch his nose forward and peep down the reverse slope of the abutment. He saw three men and three crow-bait horses scattered in a little sandy cove by the stream. The horses were saddled, and he suspected that they had not been unsaddled for days—their backs must be one great collective sore. Their frowsty and neglected condition was a fair match for the men. Two of them were playing cards in a patch of shade, while the third was slouched nearby, keeping one eye on the game and the other on the stream bank opposite. Their campsite was strewn with excrement and empty whisky bottles, enough of both to suggest that the length of their stay had about equaled his own. Matt was puzzled. How had they known to follow him, when he himself had no concrete idea of what he was seeking? Had he dropped an unguarded word, or had Henry Wilson, the grocer at Bancroft who had grumblingly grubstaked him, been garrulous? Probably the latter, for Wilson was as free with his mouth as he was tight-fisted with his stock.

Matt froze as the men beneath him stirred about, but it was soon evident that they were merely rearranging themselves. The watcher took a hand in the game, and one of the players went on watch. As they moved, Matt recognized two of them. One was Little Noah, last name unknown. The other was Stink-Finger Jack Conners, renowned for the fact that he never removed his index finger from a nostril except to eat—and not always then. Both were natives of Bancroft, notorious for their persistence in cadging whisky and boasting about their facility in wickedness. The third man was unknown to Matt, but he doubted he was Senator Gwynn.

When the men had resettled themselves, Matt went to work. He thrust the first powder canister into the granite crevice as deeply as it would go. The second canister he uncapped and then paused in confusion. How could he ensure that the end of the safety fuse remained embedded in the contents? Inspiration smote him. He rummaged for a cartridge—the one whose point he had sharpened to write his location notice—tied the fuse end firmly about it, and pushed it into the neck of the can. He worked it around until it was caught sideways, like a toggle, across the base of the neck. Now the second canister went into the crevice. It was followed by the sand-filled sample bags, each pressed and pushed into place as firmly as possible. Matt fished for his knife and matches, retreated a foot, and then split his fuse. As it began to sizzle, he scrambled sideways as rapidly as he could. The pinnacle might not drop at all (it was far more massive than it had appeared at a distance) or, worse, drop the wrong way. If it dropped on *him,* Matt Wheeler would take no further interest in the proceedings.

There was a muffled thump. Looking up, Matt saw the pinnacle shiver. There was a startled yell from the other side of the crest. To his inexpressible delight the pinnacle bowed slightly toward the far side of the ridge and then separated into its component blocks. They disappeared from sight like a swarm of bumblebees. A moment later they drummed against the flanks of the promontory. A cloud of dust rose into view. The drumming persisted. By now, Matt reckoned, the boulders must be jumping through the camp like a herd of toad-frogs! He was so exhilarated that he risked another quick look over the ridge but was rewarded by little but the sight of dust and the whinnies of badly frightened horses.

Matt waited longer before peering again. The dust was thinner now, enabling him to observe Little Noah and the Senator trying to control the frantic horses. They seemed determined to depart as soon as their affairs permitted, for in a moment each swung up on a horse and started down the gulch with more speed than dignity. It looked to Matt like a dandy way to break a horse's leg, but the third horse evidently disagreed with him, for it too jerked loose and followed its companions. Jack Conners was nowhere in sight.

The weak, to survive, must learn patience. Matt had no intention of walking boldly down to the camp and possibly right into the muzzle of Conners' gun. Therefore, he backed down the promontory, circled its point, and cautiously protruded both nose

Tom Phillips

and carbine around its corner, careless of the cold water that wet him to mid-thigh. The little cove was now littered with boulders, each at the end of a deep rut in the sand. Then Matt's eyes widened. From beneath one such boulder two boots protruded. Matt turned away sickly. This he had not desired. All he had wanted to do, he told himself, was to frighten them away. He was desperately sorry; he nearly wished that he had allowed himself to be killed instead. Now he was a murderer, and unless he made tracks, he would be hanged or, worse yet, caged for life, never again to roam the hills.

A counselor might have attempted to comfort Matt by pointing out that he had some arguable justification for what he had done. That Conners' gruesome end was an unpremeditated accident. That a wise judge and a knowing jury could probably be persuaded that Conners had digged himself a pit and had fallen headlong therein. In Matt Wheeler, however, cold fright was reinforced by bitter realism. Little Noah and the Senator would join forces to swear his life away, while up at Empire, the county seat, folks would positively relish a hanging day as the occasion for a public fiesta. It would give them something to look forward to and something to talk about for months after. If a lawyer (assuming Matt could get a lawyer) could argue that Conners was acting suspiciously in dangerous country, a prosecutor—and there *would* be a prosecutor, never fear—would ask him to prove it. Even Wilson, who had grubstaked him, would have an interest in seeing Wheeler hang or go to territorial prison, for then Wilson would be in position to take over the whole location.

Matt first thought of turning north the moment he left the throat of the valley. This, upon reflection, would not do for the same old reason—lack of food. There was no settlement to the north until one got to the Salmon River. He would starve long before then, even assuming that he ate Rosebud first and then was able to fell one of the remarkably scarce buffaloes still remaining in the range country for each of the four cartridges he had left. Due east was as bad or worse. West was impossible. Then an idea came to him. Instead of walking into the lion's mouth at Bancroft, he would march southeast, strike the railroad, and go directly into

22

Empire before anyone at Bancroft thought of sending to the sheriff there. He would register his locations, have his samples assayed, and borrow another grubstake, then instead of hanging around, depart by night to the south. With supplies in Rosebud's pack he could get to the Colorado and ultimately to Tucson. There were always the Apaches to consider but at the moment they represented by far the lesser evil.

With his mind made up, Wheeler wasted no time. He repacked Rosebud, took up her halter, and got out of the little valley as rapidly as he could. That night he camped far out in the basin, gnawing half-jerked deer meat in preference to lighting a fire. On the second dawn he began curving to the southeast. In the middle of the third day he struck the rusty iron of the railroad and after dusk on the fourth slipped into Empire. He spent the night on the outskirts of the ragged little community and, as soon as people began to move around in the morning, went about his business. He deposited his samples at the assay house, hunted up the claims office, and registered the location as hurriedly as the slow-moving official would go.

"What name you giving it?" that worthy asked.

"Uh—the Rosebud," Matt stammered.

The official thumbed through a battered ledger. "Can't," he announced. "Already spoke for."

"How about Monarch?"

Another deliberate thumbing. "Taken."

"Jesus Christ!" Matt cried. "I'll have anything!" His mind drifted back to the lonely prospect pit and the pitiable bones he had reburied there. "How about Lost Pedro?"

More thumbing. "That'll do. Hell of a name. That'll be two dollars, cash money."

Matt produced the money in five- and ten-cent pieces from a greasy buckskin pouch, and with much deliberation and lead-pencil licking the claim was recorded.

Matt returned to the assay house. The youthful assayer, Ben Roderick, was an old acquaintance of Matt's, on the strength of which Ben had put through Matt's samples with his first batch of the morning. Roderick greeted him, filled out a certificate, and

23

said, "Two dollars first, Matt."

The buckskin poke gave up only one dollar and eighty cents.

"Oh, hell, that'll do. Here." Roderick slid over the certificate.

Wheeler glanced at the document and cried out in indignation, "You made a mistake! This-here says two hundred and fifty dollars in gold! I run a assay myself out there, and it went a hell of a lot closer to twicet that!" The old prospector was near to weeping from frustration, fear, and hunger. "I know gold, and I know I done it honest, and I know it ort to be four hundred, five hundred dollars. Here, look at this!" He fished in a pocket, producing a scrap of thin leather. Unwrapped, it gave up the tiny, tooth-flattened gold bead he had first recovered. "Now, goddammit, I got this-here out of a shade less'n two assay ounces of that outcrop. Sampled fair, coned, and quartered. That's a good two-fifty *there*. You know as well as me you lose half in the pan."

The big assayer took the bit of gold and looked closely at it. He weighed it on the tip of a finger. He frowned. Rummaging in a drawer with his left hand, he sorted among a number of similarly flattened beads contained in a pen-nib box. Selecting one, he placed it beside Wheeler's on his fingertip. They seemed of equal size. "You're right," Roderick agreed. "Just a minute." He went back to his balance room, soon reappearing with a third bead. "This is what I got from your samples." It was a fair match for its two companions.

"Well, I be goddamned," Wheeler admitted in bafflement. "Maybe I hit a extra-rich spot—no, I done it honest like I said. Have I been salted some way?"

"I don't see how." Roderick was equally puzzled. "I washed your samples well before I worked them down. A man won't go to salt himself, that's for sure. Now tell me exactly what you did. Go over it step by step."

Wheeler obliged, pausing between each part of his narrative. At every pause he looked hopefully at Roderick, but the assayer shook his head. "An' then I roasted the quick off, an' that's what I got," he concluded.

"What did you roast it in? Not part of your gold-dust poke?"

"No, hell no! I ain't no idiot. Just a ordinary piece of paper."

Roderick asked one more question. Had Wheeler previously worked up any metallic gold or very high-grade ore in his mortar? No? "Then," he concluded, "I can think of only one thing. Where did you get your mercury?"

"My quick?" Wheeler cocked his head as he searched his memory. "Bought it off a feller placering down on the lower Gila. He hadn't done no good and needed some money. So he sold me a bottleful for a dollar."

Roderick pounced on the point. "Was it new mercury or had he had it in his rocker already?"

"Lessee. Didn't come out of no flask. No, he poured it for me out of a beer bottle."

"Then it *could* have been in his rocker?"

"Could of, yes. I s'pose. But, hell, Ben, if he hadn't done no good with it . . ."

"Bring it in and let's see."

Wheeler darted outside, soon returning with the quicksilver bottle. He accompanied Roderick into the laboratory, where the assayer poured a generous measure into a small porcelain saucer. With a glass rod he stirred around the two tiny silver inquart needles he dropped on the surface of the fluid.

"These go one five-hundredth of an ounce apiece," he explained. "That's to give us some bulk to grab onto."

When the silver had been amalgamated, Roderick placed the saucer carefully in a moderately hot section of his furnace's oxidizing deck. Presently the mercury was gone, leaving a very small pellet in the saucer. Seizing the bead with a long forceps, Roderick waved it gently until it was cool. Still holding the tiny bead, he went to his small balance room and laid it on one pan of the balance. With the forceps he nudged the small sliding weight back and forth until the pans hung level. He inspected the index pointer of the weight.

"There," Roderick announced. "Look for yourself."

Matt squinted sagely but was not up to interpreting the scale. "Tell me."

"Together the two inquart needles add up to two five-hundredths of an ounce. That's four one-thousandths. That weight

25

shows the pans balanced at over five one-thousandths. Where'd the extra weight come from?"

Matt scratched his head. "Out of the quick?"

"Right. Matt, you *did* salt yourself. The gold is in the mercury you bought. That placerman may have thought he wasn't getting any cleanup, but there was enough gold in his sands to salt the mercury he sold you. Sorry. It would have been a real fancy location at five hundred dollars. As it is, and considering all the pyrite and other junk I noticed in it, you'll get something but not as much."

"Thanks, Mr. Roderick." With dragging feet Matt left the office, the certificate still clutched in his hand. He put his arm around the neck of Rosebud much as a child will slide his arm about his mother's neck when he feels miserable but has been informed that really big boys do not shed tears.

"Well, look who's in town!" a familiar and hateful voice grated in Matt's ear. Matt pressed his eyelids tighter together. His cup of woe, brimful to that moment, had just slopped over. Of all the people who had to be in Empire . . . who had to see him at this minute . . . .

"Hello, Mr. Wilson," Matt replied in a soft voice.

Leering at him was a humanoid whale. The groceryman-cum-publican of Bancroft must have weighed over three hundred pounds composed equally of fat and meanness. The smile on his multiple-jowled countenance would have done discredit to an Indian Ocean shark. "Why, Matt, ain't you got nothing more cheery than that to say to your own true partner after coming out of the assay office with a big strike?" Reaching swiftly, Wilson plucked the assay certificate from Matt's hand. He scanned it. "Two-fifty a ton. I seen worse. How big is it?"

"Big," Matt replied numbly. "No more'n two-three yards wide on the outcrop, but maybe a quarter mile long or longer." He was trapped and knew it, but Wilson continued to gloat. Tucking away the certificate, Wilson removed the artificial smile and replaced it with a more natural-appearing glower. "I come over here special to talk to the Sh'urf on business. But maybe it'll wait. For a spell."

"If'n I don't get me something to eat, I'm just going to lay down here in the road," Matt protested. "I ain't had nothing for two days, and before that only green deer meat. I got to have something to eat!"

"I ain't standing in your way," Wilson snarled.

"I ain't got no money. Spent my last dime recording the location and paying for the assay. Mister Roderick even excused me twenty cents."

"Looks like I got to feed the whole starving country," Wilson grumbled. He propelled Matt to the nearest saloon, sat him down, and told the bartender, "Give him something to eat. Nothing over two bits. I'll be back in a minute." By the time Matt had wolfed stale bread and tough beef, Wilson had returned in company with two street characters. He flourished a printed paper under Wheeler's nose. "You sign right here," he commanded, pointing. "Here's a pencil."

Matt looked at the paper. It was a standard quitclaim form, assigning all right, title, and interest in the Lost Pedro location to Henry Wilson, his heirs and assigns. Matt looked up pleadingly.

Wilson's piglike eyes narrowed even more. "Sign, or maybe I'll remember quick what I come here to do. Them boys told me all about it when the two of them got back to Bancroft."

Wheeler slowly scribbled his name. Wilson strode to the bar, changed two cartwheels to quarters, and threw three of them on the tabletop. "For one dollar and other valuable considerations," he quoted. "Six bits and the sandwich. Here, you two, sign for witness." The men stepped up, signed, and received a quarter apiece. After the men had departed, Wilson carefully tucked the quitclaim in his wallet and slid the wallet into the pocket of his bagging, tentlike pants.

"Now listen, you old bastard," he grated to Wheeler. "You get out. Out of Empire, out of Bancroft, out of the whole damn territory. And stay out. I don't want to see your face no more."

"I'd get out and glad," Wheeler replied docilely, "but I ain't got no money, no grub, nothing. Could you stake me at least ten dollars?"

Wilson laughed with heavy sarcasm. "That's your lookout. You can always eat that woolly jackrabbit you got tied up outside." His voice lowered. "I meant every word I said. If'n you ain't gone in one hour, I go to the Sh'urf. May go anyway. The territory'd be better off if old farts like you was hanged out."

"Mr. Wilson," Matt said with pathetic dignity, "You ain't a Christian man. You ain't even much of a human bein'."

For reply, Wilson slapped him across the face and turned and stumped out.

A few minutes later Matt Wheeler was slowly untying Rosebud from the hitch rail in front of the assay house when Ben Roderick looked up from his office desk. "Going to sell your location, Matt?" he asked cheerfully out the open window.

"Done sold it," Matt muttered.

Something in his tone brought Roderick outside. "Sold it in half an hour?" the assayer asked. "For how much?"

Wheeler silently produced the three quarters, then recollected himself. "I owe you twenty cents," he said, picking up one of the coins and holding it out.

Roderick did not reach for it. "Who did you sell it to?"

"Mr. Henry Wilson."

The name was not unfamiliar to Roderick. "And now where are you going?"

"South, I reckon."

Roderick's eye drifted over Rosebud's pack—too small to contain much of anything in the way of supplies. There was a great deal of nothing to the south of the railroad, and a man could starve to death very readily in it.

"Could you hold on a bit, Matt?"

"Mr. Wilson gave me one hour. I think I best be going."

"Just a minute." Roderick stepped back into his office and reappeared with three eagles in his hand. "Here. This is a grubstake. Go get some supplies and meet me back here before you leave."

"I'll take it, Mr. Roderick, and thank you, but to be honest I ain't got much in the way of prospects."

"Never mind. Buy that grub." Once Matt and Rosebud had ambled off, Roderick did some thinking. He had had no traffic with Wilson nor desired any but knew him by reputation, which was not good. What was the fat, money-hungry brute about, buying the half of a pretty tolerable location for seventy-five cents and then forcing the seller out of town? For that, forcing him to almost certain starvation? What hold or leverage did Wilson have over Wheeler? Roderick finally concluded that it was sheer brutality: the ability of a bully to smell out and systematically torment a victim of no visible courage. Matt was likable if weak as dishwater, and Roderick felt a certain bond of professional kinship with him. Now, here came Wilson himself! The fat hulk turned into the assay office and sat down, the chair creaking ominously under him.

"Good day, Roderick, good day!" Wilson puffed cheerfully. "Just bought a prospect and came in to check on it."

"I know," the assayer replied in a neutral voice. "The lode is quartzite, carrying about two hundred and fifty dollars' gold in pyrites. Some of the values go into the schist footwall. If it is as big as reported, it should be a fair proposition for someone."

"No chance of its being salted er nothing, is there?"

"I doubt it. I washed the samples carefully and have reason to believe that those values are both genuine and pretty uniform in the outcrop."

"Thank'ee, thank'ee! Now I'll be going. Got to send a telegram."

"That will be thirty dollars," Roderick continued in the same voice.

"Oh, go on!" Wilson affected to laugh. "Always havin' your joke."

"Thirty dollars."

Wilson grinned unpleasantly. "Won't pay it. I didn't ask you for nothin'—you volunteered."

"Thirty dollars, or there will be a sheriff's attachment filed against the location in one hour. It will cloud the title. A buyer wouldn't like that."

"I ain't a-goin' to pay thirty dollars for a mouthful of words!" Wilson bellowed in anguish.

"Take your choice."

As the fat man considered which of the two alternatives was the less painful, Matt Wheeler and Rosebud reappeared. Rosebud's pack was as round as Wilson's belly but was carried with considerably better grace. Glad of a more vulnerable target, Wilson rounded on Wheeler as he entered. "Goddammit, I told you to get gone a half-hour ago!"

"I'm leaving now, Mr. Wilson."

"Your time is up. I'm a-goin' you-know-where as soon as I leave here."

Roderick stood up in intervention. Since he was nearly six feet, four inches tall and proportionally broad in the shoulders, his rise was impressive. "Hello, Matt. Where are you heading out to?"

"Tucson, Mr. Roderick. I got a friend there."

"Have a good trip. Hope you find rich float down in the Santa Ritas."

"Thank you. Thank you kindly, Mr. Roderick. Guess I'll be going."

"Well, I ain't done with you by a long chalk!" Wilson roared.

Roderick appeared to take no notice. "Goodbye, Matt. Oh, incidentally, that piece of musical float you showed me is called phonolite. Interesting, but worthless." He turned back to Wilson as old Matt quietly slipped out. "As I was saying, you owe me thirty dollars. You will pay me before we leave this office. Then you and I will go down to the livery barn and you will get a rig and go back to Bancroft. And you will stay in Bancroft hereafter and not sully this community with your presence."

"You ain't givin' me orders," Wilson demurred.

"Or I will drag you out there in the street right now and personally beat two tons of blubber off you in public. Now, get up the money!"

Wilson produced it from a greasy leather snap purse.

"Now, let's go."

"I got to send a telegram!"

"Give it to the liveryman." As they approached the barn, Roderick seized Wilson above the elbow in a painful grip. "Let me give you a parting word of friendly advice, Wilson."

"I don't want nothin' more from you!"

"This is on the house. Some day, Wilson, you're going to try your tricks on a man who's tougher and smarter than poor Matt Wheeler there. I don't know what you did to him except cheat him out of everything but his immortal soul. However, that still leaves him better off than you. As I said, a tougher and smarter man will come along, though you'll be too stupid and avaricious to recognize him. I hope he breaks your greedy hand for openers and then runs you out like you ran out Wheeler. Now, get that rig and get the hell out."

With a final push Roderick shoved Wilson forward, turned on his heel, and walked back to his assay house. "Total profits for the morning, a dollar-eighty," he said to himself. "I'd better get to work, or the whole day will be wasted."

CHAPTER 2

1871-1872
COLONEL FRANCIS R. M. CASEY

IT WAS OPPRESSIVELY QUIET in the Louis XV drawing room of George and Cecelia Huggins' Nob Hill mansion. The sleek society doctor had arrived an hour ago, put in his head to crack a time-worn joke at the expense of the unhappy George, and gone upstairs trailing a comet's tail of every unengaged female on the premises. Seated in a corner where he could keep an eye both on George and on the big hall clock was Frank Casey, business partner and friend of the family. A family that it was hoped was to be very soon increased, although the way George was behaving it was worse than a cross between a bank panic and the deliberations of the jury in an apex suit. Casey found himself wishing that George would either let the rye alone or else go out for a walk and let him, Casey, do his indoor fretting for him. It was very hard to affect the proper degree of calm and friendly concern.

To take George's mind off both the decanter and what was happening, or not happening, upstairs, Frank attempted to start a conversation about their affairs. Huggins responded absently, lit yet another cigar at the gas wall sconce, and let the subject die. Cecelia's horse-faced French maid, Marie, scurried down the

stairs. George was instantly at the hall door. Marie shook her head and went on about her errand with the insolent assurance that all women projected at such times. "Oh, dammit, Frank!" George groaned again. "How I envy you—just sitting there able to take it or leave it alone." He strode purposefully toward the sideboard again.

"Better not for a while, George," Casey warned. "I haven't been keeping count on you, but you want to be bright-eyed when . . . ."

"Oh, shut your fool mouth!" Huggins snarled.

Casey looked away. George was certainly taking it hard. Trying once more, Casey remarked, "I got the week's report on the Molly Pitcher today. Penrose has hit the orebody at fifty feet and says it's holding good at that point. He'll be ready to start crosscutting pretty quick but says that the quartzite will chew up the steel like Turkish delight."

"Fine." Huggins' voice was devoid of any enthusiasm. He sat, stubbed out four inches of cigar, and reached inside his coat for a fresh Havana. "Please, Frank," he pleaded. "Don't try. Just let me suffer, will you?" He wrung his hands.

Casey settled in his chair, allowing his mind to wander. This had all begun to come together last July, on what had started as a perfectly ordinary day at the Fremont Street offices of Huggins & Casey. Well, not quite ordinary. It was Thursday, and a premiere performance was going to be given that night at the San Francisco Grand Opera. Casey had come in about nine, nodded to the clerks in the outer office, turned left, and unlocked the door to his personal office. The massive furnishings, deep-pile Brussels carpet, heavy velvet drapes, and bright-polished spittoon bespoke the lavish bad taste of an up-and-coming hive of San Francisco finance. As always when entering his domain, Colonel Francis Raschid Mohammed Casey wished to himself that the money had instead been invested in sound 8 per cent securities. After settling himself in an overstuffed and tufted throne of a chair, however, he would grudgingly admit that Huggins was right—the effect was worth the ferocious cost. Confidence was what made the public cough up, and what could convey confidence better than this haven of conspicuous consumption? Even Boston Yankees slightly relaxed their grip on their moneybags in such surroundings, while Britishers became downright human. Particularly after a few snorts had loosened them up.

In the adjoining room Huggins was hard at work, to judge by the confusion of rasped orders and scurrying of office boys to and from the telegraph office. Casey could relax for the moment; his half of the partnership consisted in letting people come to him, whereas George had to get out and scratch gravel. If half-overheard words were any indication, George was busy floating the Golden Midas footage and blessedly having more trouble cooling out the penny-ante purchasers (who always carped about assessments) than he was in attracting interest of the big-money boys. But then the Golden Midas was a good development. It might even show a long-term profit, although the firm of Huggins & Casey intended to be over the hills and far away before that question ever arose.

The two partners had been among that number of 'Forty-niners who had taken one look at the diggings and decided that San Francisco offered a better game. Huggins had begun by selling whisky at five dollars the pint out of a barrel set on two sawhorses in the open air; at night he had slept under his inventory for a number of reasons. Casey had not had as smooth a start. After stevedoring for a while he had taken his savings and talked a ship captain into selling him a crate of pit sawblades. Up in the diggings (where plank sold for one dollar a board foot) they brought him one hundred dollars apiece, with the sawyers calling down blessings on his head. Both men invested their gains judiciously and widely so that fire, panic, or the depredations of the Sydney Ducks could not deal their capital a mortal blow. By the time the Comstock excitement began, they were ready to go into the market.

Since both were temperamentally inclined to be bearish, Casey and Huggins had first met in a hotel room where the latest bear raid was being concerted. They had taken a liking to each other, joined forces, and discovered that first impressions had served

35

them well. Huggins represented the moneyraising side of the partnership since he could sell overcoats to Sandwich Islanders or—what was infinitely more difficult—coax money out of Bostonians who regarded dipping into capital as the eighth mortal sin. Casey was the money spender, finding in himself an unexpected talent for smelling a rat before the rat could smell itself. Perhaps his half-Levantine blood accounted for it, he didn't know, but whether the proposition was a trumped-up bull market or a mining prospect that was not what it should be, he could somehow *tell*. He had made mistakes of course, but Huggins hadn't resented it as long as his coups outnumbered his bad guesses.

What had kept them afloat when bigger men sank right and left in the panics of 'Fifty-five and 'Fifty-nine was a degree of what could be called intellectual humility. Neither man scorned genuinely expert advice. They might not act on it if instinct bade otherwise, but within the growing caste of western mining men, bankers, and working railroaders Huggins & Casey had the reputation of listening with care, weighing the odds, and, best of all, paying generously for professional opinion rendered. Also their word was considered their bond to the extent that the age understood business ethics. This began with the failure of a deep-laid market shenanigan, when Casey had refused to deal with, or even listen to, a shabby clerk who professed to have inside bull information that he was willing to sell. Casey chuckled at the memory. The business world had ascribed this refusal to sanctimoniousness. In fact, Casey had remembered seeing that same clerk two days previously, dressed considerably better than the threadbare suit in which he had appeared in this office. A genuine traitor turns his coat after, not before, he has received the reward of his villainy.

Casey tinkled the bell on his desk. Willie Byers, his personal clerk, popped in. Good old Willie, Casey thought. Looked like a Presbyterian missionary, had the memory of an elephant for details, and spent all his pay on the "six-bittee" girls of Chinatown, whom he could not seem to stay away from. Casey liked to know the vices of the employees who were in position to get a view of his affairs; it had cost him something to hire a private detective to follow Willie around for two weeks, but it had been a good investment. Chinee sing-song girls could hardly be put up to pumping one of his men, seeing as how none of them spoke any more English than was necessary to do business.

"What's for today, Willie?" he greeted his clerk.

Willie closed his eyes and began to reel off a string of duties, obligations, and details, most of which he was hired to shelter his boss against, and was so instructed. "And I'm to remind you that you are to escort Mrs. Huggins to the opera tonight. It's something Eye-talian."

It was always something Eye-talian, Casey thought. "Pick up three tickets for my box. Send a messenger to tell Mrs. Huggins' butler that I will be honored to come by her home at the usual time." At Casey's nod Willie departed.

Casey smiled thoughtfully to himself. George Huggins loathed all forms of music from street organ-grinders up to the socially obligatory opera. Therefore, eight months ago—on November 27, to be exact—Casey had cried, "Deep enough!" when George began lamenting again about having to dress up like the corpse at a funeral and sit sober through four hours of screeching. Something prompted Casey to offer himself to take Cecelia, properly chaperoned, of course. Although Casey was not enamored of operatic bellowings, he would have crawled to Carson City on his knees for any chance to be with Cecelia Huggins. He had been desperately and silently in love with her ever since he had first seen her at her marriage to George eight years before. Just touching her hand gave him the chills and fever. George agreed heartily to the suggestion, especially since, knowing that his wife was stowed securely away for the better part of five hours, he would have a clear track to Belle LaFourche's place. There he could whoop it up and yet be innocently asleep at home before the music lovers returned. Why a man who was married to Cecelia would even think of visiting Belle's house was beyond Casey, but marriage sometimes did peculiar things to people.

So Huggins felt that Casey was doing him a double favor and was suitably grateful. Casey replied something about, "Any time, George," having received elsewhere a princely reward for his services. That evening—how every detail stuck in his mind!—he went up to the second floor of George's mansion to change from dinner to opera dress. His suspenders were dangling around his knees when an inconspicuous door opened, and Cecelia herself walked in with the graceful swing of a tall, self-confident woman. She was wearing something loose and feathery and came right into his arms, murmuring his name. Casey was too stunned with delight even to think to lock the hall door, but Cecelia herself did so in a businesslike way before returning to him, her eyes shining. He couldn't even remember the name of the opera, which afterward he sat through in a total daze, Cecelia beside him and grim old Mrs. Gregory scowling in the seat behind them in the box. Thereafter opera nights became a regular institution with the firm of Huggins & Casey.

Casey had heard it said that the best cure for love was its achievement, but in his own case this had not been true. The more he learned of Cecelia in those stolen half-hours when she was supposed to be primping, the more he respected and loved her. Once he had whispered something about divorce, but she had put her finger over his lips and said, "Don't be silly, Frank." And it had been silly, but she had seen it instantly, whereas he hadn't. Since it would never do, even in tolerant San Francisco, for a lady to accept any gift from a man not her husband, the best Frank could do was write an annual check for ten thousand dollars to the opera subscription committee. He received and treasured a cool little note from 'Celia herself as chairman, thanking him for his contribution, which would help assure the continuation of the fine arts in San Francisco.

These musings, which would have been of deepest interest to George there in the next office, were interrupted by Willie's reappearance. "Telegram for you, Colonel," he said, dropping it on his desk. Frank opened the yellow envelope and scanned the message. It was from somebody in some place called Bancroft out in the Rocky Mountain Territory. As best he recalled, Bancroft was the end-of-track of the Independence, Ft. Riley & Pacific, a miserable line which had not seen better days because it had had no better days. The message read:

Offer you first chance at big gold strike seventy miles north of here stop   Big outcrop of quartzite assays at 250 dollars stop   Double discovery location and mill site on water stop   If interested send agent stop   Henry Wilson

The message was interesting as much for what it did not say as for what it did. It evidently had not been written by an experienced mining man. It did not say what kind of country constituted those seventy miles—a matter of great moment. "Big" was subject to many definitions, and the assay valuation could be taken with a grain of salt. Two hundred and fifty dollars at the surface was not much, considering that the ore would probably decline sharply in tenor at depth. In addition, development costs would be tremendous during the early, and otherwise most profitable, stages. At first glance the offer sounded merely like a way to lose money, and better opportunities to do that were both more numerous and closer to hand. Casey decided that a reply could wait. All he could think of at present was how to kill the rest of the day as rapidly as possible.

He rapped on the door to the adjoining office and stepped through. George looked up from the mass of papers over which he was dropping cigar ash.

"Opera tonight," Frank said with studious calm. There was a pause while each man thought his own thoughts, and then Casey continued, "I'll go to a Turkish bath and lay up in my room the rest of the day." He paused. "It'll be a long performance— *Rigoletto.*"

George nodded, removed the cigar from beneath his graying moustache, and in a neutral voice replied, "You'll look after 'Celia tonight—as usual?"

"As usual, George."

"See you at dinner then."

Frank Casey stepped back into his own office, shrugged on his light overcoat, and left. The clerks in the outer office noticed that he was whistling softly. One nudged the other. "The Colonel sure likes opera, don't he?" he observed. Willie Byers would have reprimanded him for wasting time, but he himself was rapt in thought of a girl whose very inappropriate name was "Fat." A

39

mindreader, had one existed, would have been greatly puzzled by the vibrations emanating from an office ostensibly devoted to the single-minded pursuit of lucre.

Casey felt remarkably pleased with himself that evening as his team of four matched bays was finishing the climb up Nob Hill to the Huggins mansion. He told himself that he could even endure the scowls directed at his shoulderblades by Mrs. Gregory during the opera. His coachman pulled the team under the porte-cochere, tied the reins to the brake handle, and hopped down to open the carriage door. Casey was admitted by Sweeney, who relieved him of his cloak, cane, and tile and ushered him into the drawing room, where George and Cecelia were waiting. Mrs. Gregory hung in the background, neither flesh, fowl, nor good red herring, but contriving to look dour as George ordered a drink for Frank and himself. It was evident as the conversation went along that the drink had not been George's first of the evening, nor even his third; he was obviously priming himself for his visit to Belle's place.

Dinner was gotten through somehow. 'Celia excused herself to dress while the men lingered over brandy and cigars, Frank contenting himself with a small one and feeling as though the beating of his heart ought to be plainly visible through his vest. At long last he was free to saunter up the wide staircase to the room where his evening dress had been laid out by Sweeney. Once inside, he locked the door, took off his coat, and tapped with his fingernail on the door to 'Celia's room. It opened an inch and 'Celia whispered, "Go ahead and dress. I'll see you when I'm finished."

So that was the way it would be! Frank was bitterly disappointed, but 'Celia had had what women called "the vapors" once before. Now he wished he had taken a larger brandy. He dressed glumly, hunted all over the floor for his front collar button, made a sad affair of his cravat, and cursed the white vest. Then he had a prolonged wait, which he improved by pacing up and down, occasionally glancing at his watch. Finally the door opened, and 'Celia swept in, looking very regal in a blue Worth gown, plumes, and a cascade of evening jewelry. Despite himself, Frank bowed to her and smiled. "You're very beautiful tonight, 'Celia."

Cecelia was not displeased. She returned his smile, looked at herself in the pier glass, and raised her eyebrows. "Thank you, kind sir," she said curtseying. "Do you see anything different about me tonight?"

Frank ran his eye appreciatively over her hair, jewels, the new blue gown, mentioning each hopefully. Then 'Celia laughed softly and put her fingertips on his shoulders so that he was virtually forced to slide his hands about her enticingly narrow waist. "I'm not wearing my stays," she prompted. Frank's hand confirmed this, but he wondered what she was up to. No lady would appear anywhere in public, including her funeral, without her corset. Women's ways were inscrutable to him. 'Celia was trying to tell him something, but what?

"And I won't be wearing them again for quite a long time," she breathed.

"Oh?" Frank asked in interest. Then it hit him, solidly, like a boot during a waterfront fight. "Oh!" he gasped in comprehension. Then, "Oh, *George!*"

"Sit down," 'Celia said firmly, leading him to a chair. "You look terrible. Frank?"

Shaking his head to clear it, he looked up at her with mute appeal.

"George will be pleased as punch after all these years," she declared. "Let me handle George."

"You're sure?" he pleaded.

"Quite sure." 'Celia now had a gaminelike smile. "It took you long enough. I was beginning to lose hope."

"I don't think I can face George," Casey mumbled. "I mean, congratulations. Congratulations to both of you—us—oh, Lord!" He shuffled his feet and looked with interest at his right shoe. "I've never been a father before. What do I do?"

"First," 'Celia said crisply, "you go down to the drawing room and have another brandy with George. Any excuse or none will serve. Then I will send Marie down with word that I don't feel well suddenly, and you will go home to that hotel of yours. For you certainly don't look capable of an evening at the opera. Then, if a lady may suggest it, go out of town for a few days to hide your guilty face. Is there any place you *can* go, by the way?"

"I don't know. Yes, maybe there is. Yes, there's a gold prospect out at Bancroft. I can go look at that."

"Then, go!" Cecelia said, giving him a playful push on the shoulder.

As she started back to her room, Casey looked mournfully at her—she was *so* beautiful, and he was beginning to suspect that for all practical purposes circumstances were dropping a permanent barrier between himself and the woman he was so hopelessly in love with. " 'Celia," he burst out in despair, "I love you!"

"And I love you, Frank. Now go down and have that drink." She waved her folded fan at him and closed her door.

Somehow he made his way back down to the drawing room and collapsed into a chair. George was putting the stopper back into the decanter. He looked at his partner with the faintly owlish expression of a man comfortably feeling his liquor. "You look like hell, Frank," he observed brightly. "You all right?"

"So-so, George. Yes, thanks, a short one."

Marie, Cecelia's maid, appeared and spoke her lines, giving Frank time to sip his drink and try to pull himself together. When Marie had departed, George said ruefully, "There goes my evening out. What do I do?"

With sudden insight Casey knew that George would have enough to do presently. "I'll go back to my hotel," he replied. "And—uh—why don't you go up and hold 'Celia's hand or something? Sweeney will see me out." He stood up in decision. "I got word of a prospect at Bancroft out in the territory today. I'm going to go look at it, tomorrow or the day after. Tell 'Celia I hope she feels better soon. Wire me at Bancroft if there's any need." He started for the hall and then looked back. "Take care of her, George. Take good care of her. Please?"

"I'll take care of her. Bring us back a gold mine, Frank."

Despite his intention to go to sleep early, Casey spent a restless night and helped Willie Byers open the office at seven the next morning. He gave Willie little rest thereafter. Telegrams were sped east, north, and south—east to Bancroft; north to the Golden

Midas to summon John Trego, the development boss; and south to the C.P. yardmaster to get the firm's private car ready to go. A stock car would be coupled behind to hold six horses, together with saddles, supplies, and a store of civilized food and drink. The hotel was summoned to have cook, hostler, and housekeeper packed and paraded. Since Casey had gone forth in such wise before, Willie was able to get matters organized with tolerable precision, but by noon he had reported with two pieces of annoying information. John Trego had firmly refused to march; his shaft sinkers had unexpectedly started to cut heavy ground, and he dared not leave at such a critical moment. The other was that the C.P. positively could not accommodate his car until six o'clock the next morning. Casey would not fight Trego and could not fight the Big Four. But he had to have a mining man, therefore had to get a substitute, therefore had best consult George Huggins on the matter.

George was wearing a very peaceable expression when Frank walked in, but Casey found it better to look out the window while he outlined the problem.

"Got anybody in mind?" Huggins asked.

"John Mackay—over at the Kentuck mine in Virginia City. He's a first-rate man and might be able to shake loose for a few days."

"I've heard of Mackay. He'll do."

"Fine, then." Casey started to leave, but George intercepted him.

"Here—have one," George said, waving a cigar under his nose.

"Just finished one, thanks."

"Have it anyway." George was beaming. "You know why 'Celia didn't go with you last night? Well, after you left, she told me. I'm going to be a father."

Casey did not have to feign surprise. "Really? Congratulations!"

"After all these years!" Huggins positively strutted. "Guess there's some fire in the old stove yet." He draped his arm over Casey's shoulders. "You wouldn't know, Frank, being a bachelor, but take it from me there's a lot of disappointment when you think you can't have kids. Then when you strike it . . . . Makes you feel

43

like a young man again."

"Hope it's a boy," Casey said lamely.

"You'll stand godfather? Promise?"

"I promise."

Huggins was strutting again, thumbs in the armholes of his vest. "I'll call him William Francis Huggins. William, that was my father's name. And Francis for you."

Casey closed his eyes momentarily. "Thanks! How did 'Celia go for it?"

"Oh, 'Celia liked it fine. Said it was real appropriate. If it's a girl, we'll call her Alice Frances. Alice for *her* mother, and Frances for you again. 'Celia sure sets store by you, Frank."

Casey fled, pausing in his office only long enough to dictate an offer to Mackay, telling him that if he accepted to catch the private car at Reno. Then he almost ran down to eat his noon meal. Halfway through, he pushed his plate aside and laid his head on his forearms. He was glad he had a private dining room—if he were seen this way by anyone, the news would affect the market. Finally he straightened his back, blew his nose, and started on his plate again. He wondered how old a child would have to be before it would be safe to give him a pony cart.

Returning to his domain, Casey grappled briefly with his last decision. Legal counsel would have to accompany him against the faint possibility that the location might be worth optioning. In ordinary circumstances such a routine bit of work would fall to the most easily spared of the firm's junior attorneys. That would be Everett Beecher Ward, a pillar of State-of-Maine probity and dullness whose very presence set Casey's teeth on edge. However much the dreamy Celt and the steppe raider might clash within Frank Casey's soul, both halves of him detested Ward's pious snufflings. Nothing would have done Casey's heart more good than to drink poteen from a cup fashioned of Ward's skull.

But if he did not take Ward, then he must take Dick Jellison, even though the young Philadelphian was nearly indispensable to the smooth operation of Huggins & Casey. No question that he would be a far more entertaining companion. The detective-agency folder on Jellison was very interesting. Despite his legal education and family antecedents, Dick gave every sign of being an enthusiastic and dedicated sinner, specializing in contriving the downfall of women. The agency noted in mitigation that Jellison was fastidious in the selection of his victims, that they seemed to cooperate heartily in their undoing, and that few or none appeared to nurse resentment when Dick kissed them and went his way.

Aside from this personal shortcoming, if shortcoming it was, Dick was loyal to his employers, imaginative in his briefs, and not possessed of any habit likely to interfere with his work. Casey's heart warmed to the boy. Dick had the instincts of a true buccaneer, tempered by cynicism—or was it instead that he merely saw things as they were and was amused by the sight? Taking Dick to Bancroft would inconvenience George Huggins greatly. But Casey hardened his resolve. He had already inconvenienced George more than George would ever know, he hoped, and in addition to this . . . . For some time Casey had been trying to convince Huggins that the firm badly needed a third partner, trained to the law and equipped with a gentleman's manners. Would not absence make the heart grow fonder?

"Willie," Casey announced to his factotum, "step down and tell Mr. Jellison to pack for this trip. He's to meet me at the depot at five-thirty tomorrow morning."

In a few minutes Willie was back, looking puzzled. "Mr. Jellison says, aye, aye, sir, but that pillows will be wet with tears while he is gone."

"Tell him it's a good excuse to be out of the city for a few days. He'll understand. Five-thirty sharp, or I'll leave him here to work for Ev' Ward."

Five days later Frank Casey swung down from his railroad car to cast an eye upon the fair city of Bancroft, R.M.T. One glance was more than enough. Bancroft consisted of a rusty railroad wye, an off-plumb general store and saloon, a few rickety shanties, and some patched tents. The private car undoubtedly more than doubled the city's tax rolls during the ten minutes it took to get it spotted and uncoupled. Civic activity seemed minimal. If a gold excitement was in progress, there were few signs of it. John Mackay's boots hit the ballast beside Casey, and the two men stood together in silence. Jellison remained in the car. After a time a grossly fat man in a dirty storekeeper's apron waddled from the saloon and made for them at a joggling trot. He exuded sweat, unction, and the manners of a tin horn.

"I'm Henry Wilson," he panted. "You gentlemen Colonel Casey's agents?"

"I'm Casey—this is Mr. John W. Mackay," Frank said.

The fat man's piglike eyes opened wide as he pumped hands. "Proud to meet you—proud to meet you! Got your telegram last Friday." He looked about with theatrical furtiveness. "Anywheres we can talk private?"

Mackay and Casey exchanged glances. The mere presence of a private car proclaimed the business at hand to every pair of eyes within twenty miles. Wilson was evidently a dunce as well as personally repugnant. Bowing to necessity, Casey invited him into the car, introduced him to Jellison, gave him a drink, and asked him to open the negotiations. In many, many words Wilson told of grubstaking a prospector, Matt Wheeler, who had actually made the strike in question. There had been some trouble . . . . At any rate, after registering the discovery locations and mill site, Wheeler had sold his half interest to Wilson and left Bancroft. He was not expected to return.

"So you gentlemen see," Wilson concluded, "that all you have to deal with is one party."

"You," Casey remarked flatly.

"Me." Wilson beamed greasily, actually rubbing his hands.

Mackay had been stirring restlessly during this recital. Now he began to question Wilson about the nature of the outcrop, its extent, its dip, the country rock. The fat man professed utter ignorance. "I figured you-all would go out and see for yourselves," he replied unhappily. "All I got is the assay certificate and some of the rocks old Wheeler brung in."

"Go get 'em," Mackay commanded. While the storekeeper was gone, Dick Jellison completed his examination of the grubstake agreement, the claims registration, and the quitclaim. "They're more or less all right, on the standard printed forms," was his opinion. "If Wilson can produce the quitclaim witnesses, they'll stand up."

"Last of our problems right now," Casey intervened. "Good title to a bad location is worth less than cloudy title to a good location."

Wilson puffed his way into the car carrying a canvas sack. Before he could open it, Casey snapped, "What's the country like between here and this location?"

The fat man pointed out the car windows. They followed his gaze across dreary basin land sprinkled with sagebrush. At one sector of the horizon a dark line marched. "Flat as this nearly all the way. That there is the Mineral Mountains. Just follow them north seventy miles, to where there's a little creek coming out. Go up that creek a mile, maybe. Wheeler said you couldn't miss it."

"Flat like this *all* the way?" Mackay demanded.

"He said. 'Cept for the last bit up the creek. I ain't never been up that way myself, so I can't swear, but Matt warn't given to lying about things like that."

Young Jellison intervened. "You implied that he *might* lie about some things. And what was this 'trouble' you mentioned and said no more of?"

"Well, he'd tell some stretchers when he was feeling his liquor. And the trouble . . . . Three of the boys followed him up there, for a prank maybe. Two of them and the third one's horse come home. Matt was in a hurry to sell out, like I said. Nobody's said nothing, but I can put things together."

Mackay was fingering through the contents of the canvas bag. "Most of this stuff's quartzite," he said. He fished out a flat, shiny chip. "Schist. The one's porous, the other's full of cracks. Easy to salt."

Wilson's voice rose defensively. "It ain't salted. I asked the assayer, special."

"What assayer?"

"Ben Roderick, up to Empire. He warshed 'em good first, he said."

Casey made his decision. "Dick, you stay here and see that the telegraph instruments are hooked up. Wire Colonel Huggins that we'll be here—um, five or six days. Mr. Mackay, you feel like a

47

ride out in the country?"

"I ain't going," interjected Wilson, who had not been asked. "I got a store to keep." But his mind evidently turned to the fare of men who could afford a private railroad car: quail on toast, caviar, champagne . . . . "Course, I *could* just close up for a few days," he concluded optimistically.

"I don't have a horse that would carry you, Mr. Wilson," Casey stated. "We're going to ride hard. The sooner gone, the sooner back. Thank you just the same." He rose, pointedly terminating the interview. "Gentlemen, I think I'll stretch my legs while there's still daylight. Dick, would you also ask the hostler to put together a trail outfit for Mr. Mackay and myself? We'll leave at first light."

During the long ride north Casey and Mackay said little to each other. Their silence was companionable rather than hostile, but mining men do not as a rule talk greatly about professional concerns. They had few mutual friends, although Casey knew Bill O'Brien, a San Francisco speculator with whom Mackay seemed to be having some dealings. That topic exhausted, they rode steadily on, the string of pack horses and remounts being handled turn and turn about. Mackay once observed, "You haven't gotten fat and hog-lazy like most big operators, Frank. You doctoring?"

"I've seen too many men eat and drink themselves to death once they made enough money to afford to," Casey replied. "I just go light on both. Besides, I may lose it all some day and have to go back to work."

Mackay laughed. "Any time you want a job mucking at the Kentuck, tell the timekeeper I sent you."

Two men, traveling light on good horses, can swiftly cross a great deal of ground, so that the afternoon sun was still high upon the second day when they rode up the outwash fan of the creek and entered the valley. A half mile in, Mackay pulled up his horse and pointed to the left. Across the creek in a little boulder-strewn cove a raven was at work on something. Rising in his stirrups for a better view, Casey saw two ragged boots. "The third man," Mackay remarked. "No wonder that prospector sold out and left.

How did he put that rock on top of him?"

"Those old boys have their ways. Live out in places like this long enough, you learn the tricks or die."

Still farther in, Mackay said, "I see another prospect pit. And there's his mill-site monuments. The outcrop must be nearby. And there's a good place to camp. We're here, Frank." They had a good, lazy evening before the fire, and Casey unbent enough to confide to Mackay that a bit of personal embarrassment had sent him out of San Francisco. "Not that this is purely a snipe hunt," he concluded. "And your fee was settled. But if we don't find much, don't think I'll be disappointed or mad at you."

"I wish everybody was like that," Mackay nodded, poking at the fire. "Usually when I turn in a bad report, you'd think I did it just for spite the way they carry on. But I'd still feel happier if you'd brought along one of these professors who knows the theory of geology. I know all about the Comstock there is to know—and," he added obscurely, "more than most who think they know it all. But this is strange country to me, and I may end by telling you to get a real expert after all."

"Fair enough, John." Casey looked above at the stars. "Let's turn in. We'll have one whole day to look around and get our own samples, but I bet we'll be done before ten tomorrow morning."

He would have lost the bet. At mid-afternoon Mackay had filled two horseloads of sample bags and was bemoaning their failure to bring a wagon. "For it's a big one, Frank," he said, mopping his forehead. "Wilson wasn't lying. A mining man's dream, if it doesn't pinch out two feet down."

Casey, who had been sacking and labeling samples, snapped the perspiration off two fingers. "Any guesses about that?"

Mackay creased his forehead and pulled at the end of his moustache. "The granite looks solid. But underneath? A professor might guess, but I can't. Yet it's many a timber I've leveled by eye, and I would swear that that outcrop looks just the least bit wider in spots where the ground falls away. No promise, y' understand. And the gold in it is thin, but if it runs all through it . . . . I just wonder now where the tailing would go in this narrow valley. Put in a big dam higher up, I guess, and use the mill water to pipe them down to the flat like we do at Virginia City." He leaned on his pick, musing, in an attitude that one distant year would be carved by a sculptor.

"A bonanza?" Casey asked.

"No, Frank. Just a good, sound investment. Yet if I'm right, the grandsons of the Cousins who first come in here will still be going to work at the headframe." He swept his eye up and down the valley. "Th' mood is on me, Frank. There'll be a nice little camp here. A school and churches and young folk growing up. What would you be after naming it?"

Casey noticed that Mackay's brogue had imperceptibly broadened as he spoke. "The prospector Wheeler registered it as the Lost Pedro for some reason. I'll call it the—," and he clamped shut his mouth. No, he thought, the Cecelia would be a bit too much. Too many people would ask why and begin to speculate. And what if little William Francis came into the world with a set of dark brown eyes, while both George and Cecelia had blue eyes?

"I'll give it thought," he said lamely. Shouldering the cluster of sample bags, he led the way down to the little grove of trees. When he was halfway down the slope, his eye caught a low mound surmounted by a rude cross. He gestured with his chin. "There's Pedro. That grave is new, though."

Mackay absently picked up a chip of rock and tossed it on the mound. Then he picked up another and stared at it. "But this land is old . . . old," he reflected. "I'll be interested in reading your professor's report when you get around to it."

As they started the ride south on the next morning, Mackay asked, "You will buy it, won't you?"

Casey grunted affirmatively. "I'll make an option offer to that hog. He'll squeal, but he'll take it. I wish I could have dealt with the man who found it. In that case my offer would be just double what I'm going to give Wilson. I'd admire to meet a man who could put a boulder that size on anyone."

Thereafter Casey questioned Mackay steadily and relentlessly. To many of his questions Mackay returned a blunt, "I don't know, and nobody will until they get down to see," but to others he responded at length. Since the back trail is always the short trail, they were in Bancroft by mid-morning of the next day, and after baths and meals Wilson was summoned. He came in hot haste with visions of wealth.

Casey cooled Wilson off rapidly by telling him that he would option the location without waiting for the assays, the price to be twenty-five hundred dollars, to be placed in bond until the assay reports were in. As he had predicted, Wilson screamed like a pack peddler cheated of three cents, but Casey was adamant. "That's probably ten times what you bought the quitclaim for," he growled, and enjoyed seeing Wilson's jowls droop. "You won't get a dime more from anyone else. All the venture capital is going into Sutro's tunnel at Washoe or into the Northern Pacific. Twenty-five hundred will get you out of this hellhole and buy you enough stock to go into business where you'll have a chance to make money. Take it or leave it." He laid his open watch face up on the table. "In five minutes the offer will be withdrawn."

Well within the time limit Wilson was signing the documents that Jellison was dealing to him like a poker hand.

As soon as Wilson had departed, Casey called Jellison back. "Sit down," he commanded the young attorney. "And don't look so nervous; this could be good news. When we leave, you can stay here. Where I don't know, but that's your concern. You've been with us for five years now, and if you're ever going to amount to anything, this is the time to give you the chance. I'll put you in here as general manager. Your drawing account will be one hundred thousand dollars in the Hibernia Bank. That's the limit, so stay inside it. When I get back, I'll send you a good development boss. . . ." Casey's voice trailed off, and he turned sideways. "John, would you try it? I'll double whatever the Kentuck is paying you."

Mackay shook his head. "Thanks. But I can't leave Virginia City right now. I have something going there."

"Fair answer. All right, Dick, I'll give you a few parting words. Don't buy new what you can buy secondhanded. Don't buy secondhanded what you can lease. Don't become dependent upon anyone just because he shaves a few cents off his bid. Pay top prices for men, timber, and rope—and be sure you get what you pay for. Don't skim the cream off the orebody in the hope of making yourself look good, for we have to make our profit by selling it. And listen to your development boss and your men." He pushed a sheet of paper across the table. "This is what I want for my money."

Jellison did not pick up the paper. "May I ask a question or two? What if I refuse? Or what if I make a mess of it?"

"Then you'll probably stay a hired attorney the rest of your life."

"And if I succeed?"

Casey grinned. "Within two years you'll be coming in to George and me looking pious as hell. You'll lay it out for us. A junior partnership or your resignation, because you couldn't walk a block down Fremont Street before another firm grabs you."

"Some of the firms blacklist men who do that."

"And those firms shortly go broke because they can't get good men once the news gets around."

"This is my big chance?"

"You'll never have a better. You're young enough to be a driver but old enough to weigh the chances. Now or never."

Jellison turned to Mackay, who had been listening without appearing to. "What should I do, Mr. Mackay?"

"Hell, son, I can't tell you. Nobody can. But either you have the nerve or you don't. If you don't, you ought to go back to Philadelphia. Mining is no game for a man who doesn't like to take a chance."

"Philadelphia is very dull," Jellison mused. "If I don't try, I'd always wonder about myself, the rest of my life." He picked up the sheet of paper with a decisive movement. "Thank you, Colonel Casey." He extended his hand, and Casey took it. Behind Jellison's back John Mackay nodded solemnly at Casey.

Jellison had hardly time to get his valise before the rusty, steam-leaking special engine sent out by the I.F.R.&P. was groaning around the wye to pick up the car. The last Casey saw of him he was standing beside the switch, valise in hand and a mixture of bewilderment and determination on his face.

The car jarred and jolted over the track for nearly two days before transferring to the slightly better Transcontinental roadbed. In another two days they were approaching Reno. Casey was waiting for Mackay, and as they pulled into the depot, he produced a check. "Thanks, John," he said extending it to Mackay. "It was a good trip in good company."

Mackay made no move to accept the check. "Could I take it out in trade instead?" he asked. Reaching into his coat, he extracted a list of mining stocks. "I'd like whatever that would buy me of these. At the lowest possible price."

Casey looked at the list. "These are all cats and dogs. Worthless. Better take the money."

"I'd rather have those."

"John, take my word for it. They're not worth a dime and never will be. You ought to know that. Most of them—yes, all of them—are in that dead ground between the Ophir and the Gould & Curry."

"I do know." Mackay's face set stubbornly. "And you're trying to do me a favor, Frank, and I appreciate it, but I still want those feet."

A fool and his money, Casey thought, but at least I tried. "I think I can get you a lot more than by open trading," he said. "Most firms on the street have feet like this tucked away in their strongboxes. One foot of Golden Midas at an inside price will swap for over a hundred feet of this junk. What will you call it when you get it all together?"

"The Consolidated Virginia," Mackay replied equably.

A light brightened in Casey's mind. "I bet you'll threaten to sue the V.&T. Railroad for trespass or something if they don't buy you out at your price. Their yards would be right on top of you then. But be careful—Bill Sharon won't like it, and he fights dirty."

Mackay smiled faintly. "Glad you think so. Can I sell you some Consolidated Virginia when we have it organized?"

Casey laughed heartily, clapped Mackay on the shoulder, and waved as he picked up his valise and took the long step down. The engines blew down their mud, tooted, and gathered themselves for the big pull up the snow-shedded pass. Reno slid backward, and

John W. Mackay was lost from sight in the crowd.

Once back in San Francisco, Frank Casey wrestled with a decision as he cleaned up outstanding business. Two mornings later he walked into George Huggins' office to announce, "I'm leaving."

George nearly lost his cigar. "You mean leaving us—the firm?"

"Sorry—didn't mean to startle you. No, I'm going to Europe. Paris, if they get that war over quick, London if they don't. I have to get away for a while, George."

"If I didn't know you better, Frank, I'd swear from your tone you had woman trouble. Certainly. Just answer one question if you please. I don't like that name Lost Pedro for the Bancroft location. And I'll be having the certificates engraved before you get back, maybe. What should we reregister it as?"

"Ask Dick Jellison. He's in charge now. Or pick one yourself."

"Well, it was your baby . . . . What's the matter? Did I say something?"

"No, just woolgathering."

"How does Molly Pitcher strike you?"

"Fine. Anything's fine," Casey rose. "Say good-by to 'Celia for me, will you? Tell her . . . tell her I'll miss our opera nights."

Huggins beamed fatuously. "She won't be going to the opera while you're away. But I'll tell her. When will you be back?"

"When's the baby due, George?"

"January sometime, she says."

"I'll be back for Christmas then." They shook hands, and Casey left to summon Willie Byers.

So now, London was a memory instead of a vision. And George was sprawled, snoring and shoeless on the divan, a pitcher that had gone to the decanter once too often. In the hall the clock showed the time to be nearly two in the morning. Casey was dozing lightly when a hand on his shoulder roused him. It was the doctor. Frank looked up in startled concern, but the doctor smiled. "Mother and son doing well," he nodded. "Shall we tell Colonel

Huggins he survived?"

They tried to rouse him, but George had passed out beyond recall. "He'll have a headache in the morning," the doctor pronounced. "Common among males following parturition. They recover eventually."

Casey hesitated. "Could I see Mrs. Huggins? I could tell her he went for a walk and can't be found."

"Very diplomatic," the doctor nodded. "Go right on up."

Cecelia had been prettied up and was resting with her eyes closed, a lace-wrapped bundle beside her. Frank tiptoed closer. He was regarding 'Celia quietly when she turned her head and opened her eyes.

"Where's George?" she whispered.

"Out for a walk. We couldn't locate him."

'Celia smiled, a bit sadly. "You mean he's on the divan, full of whisky. Thank you for the kind lie, Frank. And for coming to see me. Are we alone?"

Frank looked around the dimly lit bedroom. "Yes."

'Celia opened the bundle. Inside was something small and very red and very wrinkled. "William Francis," she said.

"William Francis," Casey repeated slowly.

"William Francis Huggins," 'Celia said, with a flash of her old firmness. Her right hand drifted over and seized Casey's briefly, strongly. Then she closed her eyes. Casey left as quietly as he had entered.

CHAPTER 3

1872-1873
RICHARD DREXEL JELLISON

DICK JELLISON EXPERIENCED a twinge of panic as the caboose of the special pulling Casey's private car lurched slowly over the uneven track and began to rattle down the right of way. He desired very much to swallow his ambition, run after the crummy, and be on his way back to civilization. He might even have done so had not the portable telegraph sounder, sheltered within a wooden crate nailed to the terminal pole, begun to click. He cocked an ear. The telegrapher up the line at Empire was asking if the special was going to leave soon. Jellison slid the switch across and tapped the key. "Spcl now lvng."

"Hoo u?" the brass pounder up the line asked.

"Nu man. Dick J."

"O.K. 30."

At the time of his employment by Huggins & Casey, Jellison had observed the volume of telegraph traffic that accompanied mining promotion and finance and had concluded that it would be no bad thing to learn the art. It might draw favorable attention to him at a critical moment, or, contrariwise, since it was a sealed book to nontelegraphers, a man who knew Morse but kept quiet

about it might be able to profit in many ways, not all of which would fall in the line of duty. He had hired a down-at-the-heels Western Union night man to tutor him in the early evenings at his boardinghouse. It was hard work but no harder than absorbing the law of contracts, and although he had grown a trifle rusty, he was now very glad that he was not totally out of touch with the world.

Jellison continued to rub off the rust during the next week by talking frequently to the operator up the line. There was simply nothing to do in Bancroft but get drunk at Wilson's doggery, a form of entertainment that he avoided. There was nothing to read, nobody with whom to carry on a conversation above the level of half-wittedness, nowhere to go, and nothing to see. He began to understand why rural folk became the way they were. The isolation and boredom were mind-rotting. Only an imbecile with no interests beyond bad liquor and the one or two hideous and undoubtedly diseased females in evidence could endure such conditions. Therefore, he stayed out by the terminal pole during most of each day, trading gossip and stories with the equally bored Empire operator and hoping passionately that a message of recall from Colonel Casey would come in for him. When a message at last arrived, hope fled:

Captain William Penrose hired as development boss for location stop   Arriving within week stop   Casey going to London six months report to me stop   Huggins

He did not see how he could endure another week. When in an excess of zeal he tried to rent a horse to go look at the location, he found that there was none to be had for less than twenty dollars a day—to him. His wretched shakedown at Wilson's saloon and three meals, or what passed for three meals, cost him five dollars a day. He wondered how soon he would be charged for the air he breathed by the avaricious Wilson. Jellison divided his time between punching the telegraph key and kicking jackrabbits out of the sagebrush. Tossing about at night, he devised ingenious new methods of putting Wilson to a slow and painful death. Many of these methods hinged upon breeding a giant and extra-voracious strain of bedbugs. Try as he might, he could think of nothing constructive to do for the plain reason that he lacked the smallest idea as to how one went about developing a mine.

He had abandoned both hope and attempts at personal cleanliness by the time the weekly freight wheezed in, groaned around the wye, and halted for a drink in the manner of a dragon dying of senility. Jellison watched with lackluster eyes as a gang of men appeared from nowhere, fell upon the boxcars, and began leading off horses, rolling out wagons, and unloading lumber. He doubted that people used much lumber in mines; they did not build houses underground, did they? A stocky, white-whiskered figure detached himself from the throng and strode over to where Jellison sat cross-legged beneath the terminal pole in much the fashion of a starving Hindoo mendicant at the foot of a roadside shrine to the local devil.

"You Jellison?" the stocky man demanded, regarding him with remarkably bright blue eyes.

"Yes."

"I'm Bill Penrose. You been on a drunk or something?"

Jellison wearily explained his plight. He described his sudden marooning, Wilson's malevolent extortions, the loneliness, the execrable food, the legions of bedbugs. No, he had not been out to the location. No, he had made no arrangements for freighting. No, he did not know even the trail. Pleading *nolo contendere,* he threw himself upon the mercy of the court.

The leathery-faced development boss nodded. "Y'know," he said in a not-unkindly manner, "we got a new lieutenant once in the Ninth Michigan. He about busted a gut until a corporal finally showed him where to go to let down his pants. Then he saluted the corporal. You know what his mistake was?"

"Saluting the corporal?" Jellison inquired dully.

"Goddammit, no! His mistake was thinkin' that because he was a officer he ought to know everything about soldiering, whereas he didn't know a Springfield from a Napoleon."

"Neither do I, Mr. Penrose."

"Let's try again," Penrose recommenced patiently. "They'd

told him to go and soldier, but they forgot to tell him about sergeant majors. You see, when he come into camp he should have told the sentry, 'I want to see the top soldier,' an' he'd of been took to the top soldier. Then he should have said, 'Sergeant, I'm here. What orders do you want me to give you?' That way, someday he would have known what orders to give without asking first."

"I think I get the point," Jellison said, rising to his feet. "And how did that lieutenant do once he found out all this?"

"Last I heard he was a major." Penrose, in charity, did not add that the major in question had gone and got himself killed at Chickamauga, this being one of the few things sergeant majors cannot do for officers.

"Well, then, Mr. Penrose," Jellison said, and smiled for the first time in over ten days, "I am very glad to meet you. And now you are here, what orders do you want?"

"That's the idea," the powerful old man nodded. "Well, I got two carloads of lumber there for a warehouse. That bunch of . . . ," his profanity was startling, "will knock it together and build a little corral. We'll load it full of supplies and stuff—mostly lumber—then freight it out to the development. To build a warehouse *there*."

"To store the gold?"

"No, son. Mostly to hold more lumber."

Jellison raised his eyebrows. "It must take a great deal of wood to mine gold," he ventured.

Penrose laughed. "That young lieutenant after his first week told me that it took an awful lot of paper to fight a war. You're both right. Now where can I go to send a flock of telegrams?"

"I can send them for you here."

"You? I be goddamned! All they told me you could do was sign the checks."

His world beginning to come back into focus, Jellison stepped to the instrument crate and requested a through circuit to Meade. Once he got his GA, he asked, "Name your pleasure, Mr. Penrose."

Penrose dictated telegram after telegram to various supply houses near and far, reeling off huge quantities of mysterious items. Dates for delivery were included, and Jellison, working the key industriously, noted that the dates appeared to fall into sequence. It seemed that the development boss knew not only exactly what he wanted but when he wanted it and that certain items must not be shipped until others had been received. Very little seemed to have anything to do with mining as Jellison understood it—but then, he understood very little. Once or twice he asked for the spelling of a word, but Penrose waved it off. "They'll know what you mean. They've got orders spelled worse before and done all right."

As the last message went out, a rough-looking man came up to the development boss. He filed a very short brief. "The old hog in there," he said, jerking a thumb toward the saloon, "is trying to ask a dollar cash money for a drink."

"That's Wilson," Jellison volunteered. "Colonel Casey wouldn't pay him a fortune for the location, and he's trying to make up the difference by profiteering. I told you about what he charged me."

"Any law here?" Penrose asked.

"I haven't seen any signs."

"Go reason with him, Bert," Penrose commanded.

The man strode away. Soon there were loud noises from the saloon. Wilson shot out the door horizontally and feet first. One or two other locals departed in the same manner. Penrose watched complacently. "I hired a tough bunch," he said, with a touch of pride. "Construction men, not miners. They get het up easy. Can't keep them away from whisky and don't try."

"Suppose you gave them an order they didn't like, and they tried to reason with you?" Jellison was moved to inquire.

Penrose made no reply to what Jellison suddenly realized was an indiscretion. After a prolonged pause Jellison asked meekly, "Do you mind if I ask a more sensible question? Since this is desert country, why do you go to all the trouble of building two warehouses for supplies like lumber?"

"If we didn't, that whole pile there would be gone by morning. Same in camp. People would steal the headframe if there wasn't a night watchman and it bolted down to boot."

Despite the intermezzo at the saloon the crewmen were

61

working with speed and dexterity, their hammers making a mighty clatter. Almost as Jellison drew two breaths, a section of wall framing rose and then a second at right angles to the first. Before the last wall framing had been erected, roof joists were being slid up and nailed into position. To one side a tent mushroomed out, a stovepipe slid into view, and woodsmoke started to curl upward. The clamor of hammers never slowed its pace. Eying Wilson, who was now crawling unsteadily about like a bear coming out of hibernation, Penrose asked, "Suppose that hippo is well enough now to tell us where this location is?"

"I can tell you." Jellison pointed across the basin country. "North seventy miles. Up a little creek coming out of those hills. Wilson said you couldn't miss it, and Colonel Casey and Mr. Mackay apparently rode right to it."

"John Doubleyou himself? Well, now. Glad you kept your ears open, Mr. Jellison."

"Thank you, Mr. Penrose." Jellison's tone, while not precisely humble, was respectful, for it had begun to come to him that some very good men wore hickory shirts and dusty boots and were perfectly at home in strange lands to which he himself was a naive and rather simple-minded newcomer.

The education of Richard D. Jellison progressed notably thereafter. Penrose was garrulous and seldom minded giving an explanation for whatever seemed incomprehensible to his ward. Jellison learned the rudiments of haulage-road scouting and improvement, the negotiation of teaming contracts, and insight into the dark ways of railroad freight agents and hay ranchers. The day arrived, much sooner than he had anticipated, when he, Penrose, and a small crew armed with empty whisky bottles first entered the little valley leading up into the Mineral Mountains. Preceded by boulder rollers, they worked their way upward. Periodically at a nod from Penrose a construction man clutching four bottles dropped off the rear of the wagon.

"What are we doing?" Jellison inquired.

"Locating mining claims," Penrose replied. "Every foot of this creek clear up to wherever the outcrop is will be located and registered. Those bottles hold the location notices, all filled out."

"But there's no mineral . . . ," Jellison mused. "Then what?"

"Then when I pay off these boys, each sells his claim to Huggins & Casey for one dollar and other valuable considerations, meaning he doesn't get his head knocked off."

"But that's illegal!" Jellison cried, his attorney's instincts aroused. "That's collusion! Conspiracy to defraud! I don't know what-all!"

"Sure, sure," Penrose soothed him, as a mother her fretful child. "But look at it this way. Suppose we or somebody else wants to run a railroad up this way some day. And suppose a somebody like that Wilson meantime slips out here and locates a claim or homestead square across this valley while nobody's looking."

"You can't deny access to a mineral claim."

"Sure you can't. But how do you go about making it stick?"

"Why, any court—"

"How long would it take to go to court to get it? How much would it cost?"

"I don't know."

"Make a guess. Suppose some hungry shyster hooked up with Wilson while Huggins and Casey started hollering for that railroad right *now.*"

"Well, they could delay things if they wanted to. I'd settle out of court—pay them two or three thousand."

"That's right. Two or three thousand then. But three dollars and four whisky bottles is what it costs right now. I thought Casey told you to do this cheap?"

"He did."

"Then we'll do her cheap." And for good measure Penrose had a townsite and a damsite and additional mineral locations at the ends of the discovery location pegged.

Although he had the feeling that he really ought to do more looking and less talking, Jellison could not resist commenting on the unambitious dimensions of the projected crib-and-boulder dam that Penrose designed and surveyed, using only a pick and half an hour of his time. "Shoot, son, we want some water, not Niagara Falls," was the comment. "In this country you get your water toward the end of winter and early spring. We want enough to

63

use, so we put in a dam. But once in a while you get a real ripsnorter of a cloudburst coming down on you. It'll take out any dam that's less than solid stonework and wash everything you have clear to Yuma if you build her too big. Time comes we need a high dam, we'll build a high dam and do it right. Meantime, we don't want no more water'n we know what to do with on a dark and stormy night." As always, it seemed logical when explained.

Penrose's apparently casual, one-step-at-a-time methods presently began paying ample dividends, as demonstrated by the uninterrupted flow of materials coming to the camp. The I.F.R&P. regularly brought three cars a week, whose contents were stored in the warehouse at Bancroft. From there contract teamsters moved the supplies to the location, taking a week with Sundays off for the round trip. The warehouse at the camp receipted, ingested, and disgorged the materials, which for long consisted of lumber for the housing and food for the feeding of the hard-working and heavy-eating crew.

"Some companies try to save money on rations," Penrose commented, plowing into the food that he and Jellison were eating in the transplanted mess tent, "but it don't pay a cent. You want your men to work hard, so you can't starve them. A hungry crew wastes more time grousing and playing sick and quitting on you than any saving is worth."

"Colonel Casey said not to skimp on men, timber, or rope."

"Colonel Casey told you the truth. But you look like you're troubled by something."

Jellison drew his fork across the oilcloth that distinguished the executive table in the mess tent. "We've done all this work, set up the camp. . . . When do we actually begin mining?"

"Getting worried?"

"No, just curious." Jellison looked off and continued, "I've learned a lot, and the biggest lesson has been to get the best development captain you can find. Yet I feel I owe it to Colonel Casey to get started as soon as we can on this Molly Pitcher mine. He's losing money, principal and interest every day we delay—if it *is* delay."

"You think a lot of Casey, don't you?"

"He and Colonel Huggins took me in when I was green as grass and about to starve trying to run my own law practice. Now they're giving me a chance to move up. I'm not burning to run things. I don't know enough yet to come in out of the rain. But I would like to know what's coming next so I can fit it together in my mind."

Penrose nodded. "First you have to have a place for your miners to eat and sleep. Next you need equipment and supplies for them to make a start without interruptions waiting for something they have to have but hasn't come in. We've moved right along on quartering them, a lot better than in some boom camp, where you have to fight for every stick of wood and pay five cents for a pint of water, with the squitters thrown in for free. A boom camp is heaven for gamblers and hookers, but it's hell for working men. When winter comes, it's worse than hell. Cold. Snow. Lung fever. French diseases. You name it. Here, now, we're about set. Food laid in, men under cover, and if the trail to Bancroft gets bad, that's the contract teamsters' problem, not ours."

"You make it sound easy."

"Compared to what I've heard of 'Forty-nine in California or the winter of 'Fifty-nine in the Comstock, it *is* easy. Or, for that, you should have seen the old Ninth Michigan trying to muster in, drill, and stay alive without food, tents, or anybody knowing how to requisition them. Matter of fact, I'm about ready to pay off half this crew. We'll keep the carpenters and a few dumb ox's for road building and wire John Doubleyou that we're hiring on shaft sinkers. You've ordered a lot of lumber and nails. Soon you'll be ordering drill steel and powder." The old man raised his white eyebrows. "You don't by any chance know how to survey as well as telegraph, do you?"

Jellison shook his head. "Never occurred to me I might need to."

"We'll need a surveyor first of all to lay out the shaft, stake a flume line from the dam, peg out the site of the mill we'll build next spring, and so on."

"Which reminds me," Jellison interrupted. "The—the outcrop is right on top of the ground. Why do we need a shaft? It seems to me that the easy way would be just to go straight down into the ore."

"It is the easy way. Done more often than not, especially if the ore is rich and the people mining it don't have too much money. You work in the open air, save a lot of cost, begin milling right away, and less aggravation all around."

"But we aren't doing that."

"Because the ore is *not* rich, we do have the money, and, when you mine open-cast like that, you can't know what's an inch farther down and no way *to* know till you get there. You're working blind. Now, we're here to develop a mine for sale. Could you sell a pig in a poke like that?"

"*I* wouldn't buy it."

"Neither would anybody else who's smart, and somehow in this wicked world the smarter men seem to end up with the money. No, the shaft is to help us explore and block out the ore. That's to say, we have to have some idea how big the orebody is, how the values run through it, how it dips—a hundred things. It's like selling timber land when you can see only the trees at one edge of it. You have to cut trails through, at least far enough to get some idea of what you're selling. Along toward next spring, though, we'll build a little mill, learn how to concentrate both the surface and the development ore, and maybe even get back a little of the money you've been spending. Then Huggins & Casey can go to work and say, 'We got a mine for sale,' and sell it."

"That's a great many 'if's'."

"That's mining. Hell, the outcrop could thin down to nothing or pinch clear out four feet down. With a shaft we'll find out in a hurry. In that case we skin off the pay ore in the outcrop, mill it, and call the old hole deep enough."

"Even so, we'd take a loss."

"But we wouldn't have lost so much."

Jellison smiled wryly. "And I would go back to being a junior attorney for the rest of my life."

Penrose rapped his knuckles on the table top. "Do you think Huggins and Casey are fair-minded men?"

"Yes, I think they are. They've always treated me fairly, and they have a good reputation."

"I think so, too. Now, Dick, they'd get vexed at you for hiring on more men or less than we need or buying some patent mill process that don't work or building yourself a big, fancy house to live in here or some jackass trick like that, but they won't blame you for what the lode does or doesn't do."

"How about quarreling with you?" Jellison grinned.

"Faster'n anything else. But you ain't hot-headed nor bull-stubborn like some of these Scotchmen the British companies send over to be managers, Sandies who don't know mining from playing the jew's-harp but won't admit it. Fact is, you're right easy to get along with as general managers go—you don't ask me if something is *really* needful more'n four, five times a day." Penrose used his trousers legs for a napkin and threw his leg back over the bench. "Let's us go visit the big, sinful city of Bancroft tomorrow, if they didn't go to spit and the hogs ate them while we was gone." And outside the mess tent he hunched his shoulders to the evening wind blowing down the valley. "Winter's coming on. Gets cold early up in this country. I'll tell the boys to start cutting cordwood while we're away—something I can count when I come back so they can't loaf on me. They can use the brush to build a stable, too. Animals get cold same as people."

During the three-day journey Jellison rode with Penrose in the back of an empty freight wagon. Two months had produced notable changes in the dandified young legal meteor of Fremont Street. Jellison's hair and moustache were considerably longer than San Francisco fashion dictated, and his Napoleon goatee had thickened out into the beginnings of a beard. A valiseful of city clothes was gathering dust under his bunk, and he went about in the costume of the country: hickory shirt, suspendered woolen trousers, rabbit-eared knee boots, and slouch hat. He had not yet come to carrying a pistol or a Bowie knife in his waistband, but since Penrose did not, he would not. A degree of hard work and much outdoor life had considerably reduced his waistline and browned his face and hands. And while he could not keep pace with even the weakest member of Penrose's crew, he no longer lagged ludicrously behind at the work to hand. Jellison improved the journey by attending lectures given off the tail gate by Penrose, one such having been set off by his comment: "I think I heard you say something about learning to mill our ore. I thought you just milled it the same everywhere like gristmillers do with wheat."

"Thunder, no!" Penrose exploded, appalled at such ignorance. "Every ore is different, every mine is different, and there's a hundred mill processes, some of which work, but most of which don't, though they try them anyway. In the Comstock they use the old Mexican system. It don't take any fuel or flux but uses up a power of quicksilver. Over to Colorado they smelt. In California they amalgamate. Down in Arizona Territory they use the Freiberg process, which is a kind of morphadite. Gold ore is different from silver, and silver from copper, and copper from quicksilver. There's three different kinds of gold ore, speaking generally. And the gold is all mixed in, often as not, with base metals all the way from lead, which is good, to arsenic, which isn't. Lord Almighty, I doubt any two mills in the Republic do it the same way. What I got in mind is to dump our ore in a little jaw crusher, then run it under California stamps. That breaks the quartz free from the mineral itself. Then we'll concentrate it—let the dust flow in a stream of water down a slanting table with a lot of low rifflebars on it. The quartz will keep right on going—the water buoys it up, so to speak—but the values will be trapped, most or all of them, behind the rifflebars. Every so often you scrape them out—that's concentrates—bag them in hundred-pound sacks, and ship them to a smelter. Let *them* worry about it, then."

"Doesn't sound too hard," Jellison ventured, following the process mentally.

"Isn't, unless any one of two million things goes wrong. In Colorado at first they put in the California system, and it didn't work *no* way. Then Professor Hill hired a bunch of Germans to come over, and they learned how to smelt the ore. Even if our way sounds the easiest, don't forget the smelter takes a big discount for its trouble. I've seen smelter checks returned made out for zero dollars and nought cents. Discount ate up all the values. But smelter men got to live and buy coke, too."

It seemed to Jellison that there was absolutely no end to what one could learn about this business. In its way it was the complete antithesis of the practice of law, which, he privately admitted, once learned was thereafter 90 per cent fairly dull repetition. On the other hand, a man could spend a long lifetime in mining and still not have the opportunity to master every aspect of it that required his attention. While laboring on Fremont Street, Jellison had got the impression that mining consisted chiefly of buying a desirable property and then turning around and floating the shares at a considerable profit. In between there was something called "developing," which you told somebody to do and wrote the checks for, and presently it was done. Obviously he had missed out on a great deal. Did George Huggins and Frank Casey know anything of this huge encyclopedia of knowledge that he was beginning to stumble into? He suspected that they did, and his admiration for his employers was increased to the same extent that his own self-esteem diminished. "We live and learn," he nodded dangling his booted feet over the end of the jolting wagon.

Bancroft, unlov'liest village of the plain, rather surprised Jellison, who had not laid eyes on it for more than six weeks. During his isolation at the Molly Pitcher the old hole had changed. Whether the change was for the better was arguable, but changed it had. For one thing, the influx of business from the Molly had attracted a new blind pig. More shanties and tents were visible. There was a new hay barn, a larger corral, a farriery, and (he was shortly informed) three ladies of evil reputation and worse aspect, who had set up shop for the relief of suffering teamsters. The I.F.R&P. had installed a tool shed and a loading platform. Penrose regarded the scene mordantly. "All it needs now is a preacher to tell them what's sinful and a pimp to sell it to them," he observed.

The first telegram Penrose dictated was somewhat alarming to Jellison, but he dutifully tapped the message to Moses Finkel & Sons Mine Equipment, Salt Lake City:

> Need complete oufit for fifty-foot shaft and exploratory crosscut Molly Pitcher mine shipped via Bancroft RMT stop Invoice Hug-

gins and Casey stop　Need surveyor two weeks work now and good blacksmith soon stop　No Irish need apply stop　Bill Penrose.

"It's sent, but is this some kind of joke?" Jellison asked.

"Only the 'no Irish need apply' part. Old Moses runs the best second-hand mine-equipment yard in the West. His sons are mostly always out, buying from mines that are closing down. I've sold stuff to Mose, and I've bought from Mose. He's outfitted half or more of the mines in the country. You just tell him the depth you want to sink, and he'll send everything you need from the whim to miners' lights and candles in one shipment. I've seen him walk through his yard, tell his hands, 'Dat, dat, and fife of dis,' and not had to special-order one single thing."

Jellison noted the point mentally for future reference. "What's the joke, then?"

"Oh, those Mormons there say the Indians are the Ten Lost Tribes of Israel, so I told Mose that since he didn't look like no Indian, he must be an Irishman in disguise. Kind of weak, but jokes are hard to come by in Salt Lake. They say the Gentiles there stand around watching mud puddles dry up for lack of anything else to do."

"Have you tried Philadelphia?" Jellison inquired softly.

The second telegram was to Mackay at Virginia City. It asked him to spread the word that the Molly was hiring shaft sinkers and could use two crews, starting at once. "The Comstock is slowing down," Penrose commented, "and some good men will be glad to come. John Doubleyou will pick them for us. Ordinarily I wouldn't pester him, but since he took an interest in this location, he'll do it as a favor maybe."

"You think highly of Mr. Mackay, don't you? I'll admit I didn't know his reputation when I met him, but he seemed like a gentleman."

"He is a gentleman. And probably the best mining man there is today, though some of those professors wouldn't admit it. He'll be a millionaire some day. What is that thing saying?"

The sounder had started to click, and Jellison got busy with his pencil:

> Mr. William Penrose, Molly Pitcher mine, care Bancroft,
> RMT For you I make a real bargain stop Surveyor and equipment
> loading tonight stop No Cousins need apply neither stop Moses
> Finkel

Penrose laughed heartily and began counting on his fingers. "Leaving Salt Lake tomorrow. Two days to the junction, then two days to here. That's four, call it five, with being side-tracked half the time. The shaft sinkers have a longer way to travel, but they'll ride side-door Pullman and not be held up by schedules. Shoot, son, if we went back to the Molly, we'd just have to turn right around and come back here. Let's fix us a place to bunk in the warehouse, and I'll learn you to play buck euchre. Also you want to telegraph for some coin to pay off the men I'm sending out and to get passes for them on the freight. So what'll it be, buck euchre or looking at sagebrush for six days?"

"Do I have a choice?" But Jellison estimated that the time would not be wasted by any means. He attended to the bedrolls, while Penrose went out to give orders to the teamsters. Fortunately, those in transit could pass instructions—provided they were simple enough—to each other, considerably easing the task of mobilizing transportation. The wagons presently leaving Bancroft would unload at the Molly and pick up the men being laid off. Then the construction men would be paid in Bancroft and loaded on the same freight that brought in the shaft sinkers and the mining equipment from Finkel. Jellison had ample time to draw up his payroll and wire for the cash to the bank at Meade; the pay sack would be on the same train. Another lesson learned: close attention to transportation schedules could save many days of idle waiting while workmen loafed around and ate their heads off at company expense.

"And," Penrose concluded, "I will not be letting those men hang around here and lose all their money. Give each man a dollar to buy whisky. Not a cent more until they're on the train. Then you pay them their time right in the cars. Some won't get past Empire before it burns a hole in their pockets, but at least they won't be idling around here, broke and getting into trouble."

"What about food while they're on the cars?" Jellison asked.

"They can look out for themselves, provided they sober up enough to get hungry. Did you never hear of Mulligan stew? All you need is engine-tender coal, an empty can, and a farmer who has some chickens or a smokehouse and a garden patch. Fit for a king and free as the air to boys who know how to walk lightly at night."

The six days were filled with more instruction, buck-euchre lessons, and bits of company business. Only once was other recreation provided. The sound of a shot caused Dick to lay down his card hand and lean back to look out the warehouse door. A man ran out of Wilson's saloon, looking back over his shoulder. He was followed by a second man. Both were obviously drunk and quarrelsome. The man in front stopped, turned around, and extended his arm. White smoke jetted from his hand, followed by a loud pop. The pursuer did the same. When both the guns had been emptied, the men advanced cautiously on each other, talked a minute, and then walked back into the saloon together.

"So Bancroft has its man for breakfast," Jellison remarked sourly, picking up his cards. "Comes from that trash drinking their breakfasts. Can't even shoot straight." He did not reflect that a similar affair witnessed three months before in San Francisco would have provided him a day's worth of excitement.

"Ever really want to kill a man," offered Penrose, who had not even deigned to look out the door, "use a shotgun. Better yet, shoot him in the back, close up." He produced a card. "High, low, jack, and the game."

"Jack o' diamonds, jack o' diamonds, I know you of old," Jellison sighed. "If they put Socrates to death for corrupting youth, they ought to hang you twice."

"Who was that—some restaurant Greek in San Francisco? I thought you Frisco people was *born* corrupt. Quit taking my mind off the cards and deal."

The whistle of the approaching freight ultimately put an end to the sabbatical. Bancroft's population was temporarily doubled as the construction men, incoming miners, and teamsters in congress assembled, mingled and milled about. Penrose bellowed instructions, ordering all hands to load the freight into the line of waiting wagons. The sight of his shopping list coming forth did not cheer Jellison. Everything appeared rusty, crippled, remarkably ill-used—an enormous hurrah's nest of tangled and confused iron-mongery. Three great iron buckets were half-filled with bolts, nuts, plates, bits of wire. There were a huge leather bellows, a battered anvil, shovels, scoops, sledges, steel. Some were wired together in lumpy bunches, while others were piled carelessly in splintered wooden boxes. A great spool of greasy wire rope was rolled out, accompanied by something that looked like an uprooted ship's capstan.

Clutching the many pages of invoices, Jellison eased up to Penrose. "Sign for it?" he asked, extending the file.

"Sign for it."

Jellison signed. He also signed for the small but remarkably heavy canvas sack the conductor produced from a caboose locker. "How long you going to hold us here?" the conductor complained. "We got a time card, you know."

"I know, I know," was Jellison's reply. "You have to get into the siding before the midnight mail comes through. Then that will be *two* engines this broken-down streak of rust owns—provided you call that thing up front an engine."

"And I ain't carrying that bunch of apes, neither," the conductor continued.

Jellison looked the conductor straight in the eye. "Do you want to tell them that, or shall I?" he inquired softly.

The conductor grabbed a lantern and left the caboose without further comment.

The wagons were moving out one by one as their loads were completed. "Construction men, over here!" Jellison shouted. Loads were dropped as the men in question converged about him, all looking thirsty. Jellison told them the news. "Put your blankets in the cars. Each of you gets one dollar—one dollar only—to spend here."

"Hell, the girls charge that much," someone complained.

"And spend it quick because not until every last one of you is aboard do you get your time. Now form a line." As each man filed

73

by, Jellison slapped a silver cartwheel into his hand. The men scattered for the saloons, from which they soon emerged, uncorking flat bottles. Many tossed the corks away. They piled into the boxcars. Fortunately there was a uniform payroll; every man now had $119 coming to him—five double eagles, one eagle, one half-eagle, and four cartwheels. Jellison quickly got it down to a system by putting the various gold denominations in different pockets while doling out the silver from the bank sack. Also fortunately money and men came out even. Dropping down to the ballast, Jellison waved to the conductor. "All done! Get 'em out of here!"

The conductor waved his unlighted lantern in a wide circle. The engine tooted twice asthmatically, and the conductor swung up into the caboose as the train rattled off. Penrose was sending off the next-to-last wagon, laden with mess-tent supplies and a party of miners who would take turns walking and riding. "You done pretty good," he commended Jellison. "Fast as a Chattanooga hooker and pretty near as slick. Have you seen our surveyor?"

Jellison looked around as though hoping the surveyor would rise from the ground.

"No? I fear our friend is likely in Wilson's, lining up his instruments or something. Let's go get him—the last wagon's about loaded, and we don't want to miss the picnic tonight." Side by side they strode into the gloomy fug of the saloon.

At the bar a bloated-looking man with reddened eyes and a thin, scraggly beard was gesturing for Wilson to pour again. The elongated instrument case on the floor beside the rail was sufficient identification. Penrose walked up to him and clamped a hand over the mouth of the glass. "Come on, friend," he said firmly. "We're about to pull out."

The surveyor drew himself as erect as he could. "One for the road," he wheedled. "Dry as dust fr'm the steam cars." He plucked at Penrose's hand as though to dislodge it. He had no success. The man looked at the hand, at the bottle, licked his lips. "Landlord," he complained to the glowering Wilson, "you going to let your guests be badgered this way? What kind of a place are you running here, a man can't be allowed a sociable drink or two?"

"Leave him be," Wilson commanded.

Penrose's eyes went to the saloon man's enormous belly, which seemed to lie over half the width of the bar top. "When you going to let that baby you're carrying down and walk?" he inquired conversationally.

The remark ignited a spark of fury in Wilson. Stumping out from the end of the bar, he thrust a hand under his apron and pulled a revolver. Aiming it squarely at Penrose, he shouted a stream of abuse, its tenor not improved by the shaking of his red-mottled jowls. His real or imaginary grievances had obviously been festering within him for weeks, redoubled by Penrose's canniness in sending off the construction men to have their spree elsewhere. To the startled Jellison the man appeared half-insane and on the verge of shooting Penrose as soon as he had worked himself up to a sufficient pitch. Penrose was taking the verbal filth quietly enough but was in an awkward position—too far away to grab at the gun but too near to attempt escape.

Seeing that he himself was being ignored, Jellison began to move very slowly. He cautiously flexed his left knee until he was balanced wholly upon that leg. He eased his right foot back, an inch at a time. In San Francisco he had seen some of the French 'Forty-niners while in wine, kicking dexterously at each other. Perhaps he could do something similar. Wilson was short, and the elbow of his extended gun arm appeared nearly within range. At that moment Penrose shuffled back a step as if in fright. Wilson advanced upon him. Hoping for the best, Jellison flung wide his arms, kicking high and hard. He felt his instep connect jarringly with gratifying results. Wilson's arm was struck up, and the pistol fired harmlessly into the exposed rafters, the bullet bringing down a cloud of dust. Penrose took two steps forward and sank his left fist into the center of Wilson's belly. The man retched and started to double forward. Penrose hit him squarely on the ear with his other fist. Wilson was flung sideways to the floor.

As the fat man floundered about, still grasping the pistol, Penrose drew back a boot and kicked him almost delicately on the side of the wrist. The gun skittered across the floor, and Wilson rolled, screaming in a high voice. Ignoring Wilson now, Penrose reached for the bar bottle, took it out of the surveyor's hand, and cracked it sharply across the edge of the bar. Glass fragments and whisky spattered. "Get out of here and put your traps in the wagon outside," he commanded. The surveyor scuttled away. Then Penrose turned to Jellison and said, "Thanks. For a moment there I thought I was a gone coon."

Jellison's eyes drifted to Wilson, who was now kneeling, bent over and clutching at his wrist. "You going to slice him up with that?" he asked, seeing the broken neck of the bottle still in Penrose's hand. Penrose looked at the bottle neck, laid it on the bar, and, reaching down, gathered a handful of apron and shirt, bringing Wilson's face up to his. "Now you listen good to me, you tub of hog guts," he announced. "You're done here. Next time I come back to this rotten hole, I want to find you gone. If you're still here, I'll break both your legs." He shook Wilson like a child. "Do you hear me?"

"Y-yes! Yes!" Wilson whimpered. "Oh, my God! My arm!"

"Stick your arm up your arse and tickle your liver." Penrose opened his hand and let Wilson sag. "Come on, Mr. Jellison. We've got to get that surveyor before he finds there's another saloon here."

The surveyor was sitting meekly in the wagon, however, his bedding and instrument case beside him. Penrose ignored the man, and Jellison thought it best to do likewise. "Try to catch up with the food wagon if you can," Penrose instructed the teamster, "but don't make no race of it. We have a couple of hours." Jellison glanced at the sky in puzzlement. It was mid-afternoon, and they ordinarily did not camp until dusk. What would happen in about two hours, and what had this to do with the food wagon?

As the sun began to approach the horizon, enlightenment came. The surveyor had gradually become increasingly restless, moving his head about, mumbling to himself, and fumbling ceaselessly with his instrument case. At length he held his hand closely to his eyes and announced, "There's hair growing out between my fingers." He waved the hand around, looking about brightly for confirmation. Jellison could see no hair. Penrose did not even look.

"Ho, the wagon!" he hailed ahead. "Hold up and give us a hand!" The lead wagon halted, and a number of the miners trailed back. "We got a case of the horrors here," Penrose told them matter-of-factly. "Now don't nobody give him whisky. Help me get him down out of here and into his blankets."

By evening Jellison had been treated to a short lesson on the camp care of delirium tremens. It consisted of little more than tying the patient securely into the cocoon of his blankets, keeping an eye on his thrashings, and turning the deaf ear. During moments of lucidity the surveyor was given water into which the juice of a wrinkled lemon had been squeezed. The miners seemed unperturbed about the incident and needed little coaching in their duties. After the evening meal the miners grouped together about the fire and began to sing. The songs were Old Country hymns, unfamiliar to Jellison but delivered in part harmony that sounded even to his ear good enough to charge admission to hear. He sat entranced and during one pause whispered to Penrose, "They're *good!*"

"They're Cousins. Back in Cornwall they sang in the wheals, in the ships, walking the roads. Then they really sang in chapel on Sundays. A Cousin is born with a pick in one hand and a hymnbook in the other. But don't never make them perform for company like they was a bunch of trained bears. They sing when they feel like it, never on orders."

"What about that poor devil back there?" Jellison jerked a thumb at the feebly moaning caterpillar-like object on the ground.

"He'll either die or get better. Probably get better this time around."

"Wouldn't it be best to take him back to Bancroft?"

"We need a surveyor. I had a fair idea we weren't going to get no bargain."

"Why did Finkel send him?"

"Probably the best of a bad lot. A good surveyor holds a steady job. One you can hire for two weeks' work likely has something wrong with him. I'm just surprised he hadn't sold his instruments. Probably did, and Mose lent him a set so he could take the job.

And gave him enough money to stay drunk on during the trip so he wouldn't sell this set."

"Then we pay Finkel back, deducting it from this man's wages?"

Penrose shook his head. "About all Finkel will get is satisfaction. At least while this pilgrim is working for us, he'll stay sober. And he'll stay sober because nobody in the camp will give him a drink, no matter how hard he begs. And because seventy miles is just a bit too far for him to walk for his dram. Then if he's sober, maybe he'll have some appetite, and we'll feed him up a little."

"What when he's done at the Molly?" But Jellison did not require any prophecy about what the surveyor would do the moment he was within reach of liquor and had two weeks' pay and a case of instruments in his hand. "Why?" he asked helplessly.

Penrose shrugged. "Sometimes I think God just has it in for some men, like these predestinarian preachers say. I bet when he comes out of the horrors you'll find he's a pretty nice man. Soft-spoken, maybe educated some. What I can't understand is, if he wants to die so bad, why don't he take a gun and do it quick and clean?" The development boss shook his head then changed the subject. "Speaking of which, I ain't thanked you proper for what you did today."

Jellison felt faintly embarrassed. "No thanks due. Besides, where would we be if you were laid up hurt?"

In the morning the still-incoherent surveyor was bundled aboard the wagon and the party set out again. Occasionally far ahead of them they could see dust rising from the preceding wagons. By the time they were turning up the outwash fan to the valley on the third day, the surveyor was rational, if weak. Thankfully remanding him to the cook, who doubled as the camp's Sanitary, Jellison returned to the parked freight wagons. Penrose was directing their unloading, snapping decisions about what cargo would go to the warehouse, what dumped on the spot, and what left in the wagon beds to be dragged up the hill and unloaded near the site of the future shaft. In this last process something like a trail began to be agreed upon by the teamsters, whose broad steel wagon tires soon eroded a trace into the hillside.

Jellison bore a hand while trying to note what went up and what stayed down. He could not put a name to most of the objects, but the huge buckets going up evidently were buckets, and Penrose referred to them as "buckets," which was good. However, one of the miners looked straight at one and said, "Kibble," and Dick's heart misgave him. Either there was something he could not see that distinguished it from its two companions, or else (nearly as bad) there could be two or more different names for things.

During one interval while Penrose was away shepherding the ship's capstan he called a "whim" up the hill, one of the miners dragged a horrid object off a wagon bed. As it fell with a thump, Jellison's eyes widened. He stalked over, staring down with disbelief. It was nothing less than a great, heavy coil of wire rope, sketchily tied together with bits of dirty hemp line. It was rusty beyond description. Broken wire strands stood out every-which-way, bristling like the hair on the back of a frightened dog. Even to Jellison it was rope long past all hope or caring. He would not have hoisted a litter of kittens with it if he cared for the kittens. Through his mind ran Casey's admonition, "Never skimp on men, timber, or rope."

"Damn!" Jellison said experimentally. The ice broken, he said, "Goddamn!" in louder tones. Miners nearby paused. Jellison inflated his lungs and started to shout. He abused Finkel as a thieving disgrace to the Tribe of Israel. He cursed the wretched coil to perdition and back. "How in the name of blue hell," he demanded of the world in general, "can I develop a mine with this rotten, bastard cross between a porcupine and a red octopus?" The miners were now grinning openly and nudging each other. Greatly encouraged, Jellison was taking breath for a formal excommunication, anathematization, and casting-out when Penrose reappeared.

"Easy, easy!" the development boss said solicitously. "Did it fall on your foot?"

"Look at it! Just *look* at it!" Jellison demanded, hopping about in rage. "What did we pay for that worthless, man-killing ton of turkey dung?" And he was off again, using language more suited to the Embarcadero than to the Main Line.

79

One of the miners muttered to his mate, "H'education 'elps greatly when h'a man be letting h'off h'a bit o' steam. 'E ain't said two bleddy words h'alike, but h'if h'I was they rope, h'I'd be 'iding me face h'in shame."

The other was also listening with intent appreciativeness. "Cheer op. H'at least 'e cares h'about h'it."

Penrose waited patiently and then informed him, "We paid a dollar or two—no more."

Jellison was in no mood to be mollified. "We paid the freight on it, didn't we? If Finkel gave it to us free, we were still robbed. I wish that rope was around his neck and six mules on the other end of it!"

"I ordered it," Penrose injected casually.

"You what?"

"Leastwise, it was part of the order. Now, hold on! It's for a blasting mat."

"A what?"

"A blasting mat. When the lads start blasting, there would be pieces of rock flying around. They'd cut up our headframe, ladders, and shaft collar, not to mention going through a roof and maybe hurting somebody. So they'll weave a mat out of that junk rope and lower it over the rock just before they shoot. What gets through will be too small to do any harm. You wouldn't use good rope for something like that, now would you?"

Jellison thought it over. "I guess I just made an ass of myself, didn't I?"

"Not altogether. The men will think you were refusing to make them hoist with junk rope."

"Well, I was!"

"Then they'll appreciate it and think the better of you. And something else. What *is* the offspring of a Cairo camel-bugger and a one-piastre Port Said *bint?*"

"I thought it was Moses Finkel, but I was dead wrong."

It took an afternoon of grinding labor to get the mining equipment unloaded and properly disposed, but finally it was done. While the teamsters went into bivouac, the Molly Pitcher's management and labor lined up by the stream to wash off rust and grease. There followed a general stampede when the cook hammered the dinner bell, a large piece of boiler plate. Penrose strode to the head of the line and shouted, "A good spell! Take the rest of the day off. Wash your shirts and get settled in. There's a privy—*use* it! Any man who makes a nuisance in the camp gets docked one dollar. Tomorrow we start work."

And after the meal Jellison asked, "What now?"

"Now we start mining. Tomorrow we begin to sink a fifty-foot shaft to hit one side of the orebody. That'll give us lots of information right there. Then we drift a crosscut at right angles to the strike, always sampling as we go. I mean—we drive a long tunnel sideways from the foot of the shaft, parallel to the line of the outcrop. The tunnel stays in the ore on the fifty-foot level, more or less, with the bottom just touching the contact between the lode and the footwall."

"Till we come up in Empire?"

"If the values persist, till we come up in San Diego. Actually, until the orebody either narrows down or gets too poor to make it worthwhile to go farther. The assays will probably tell us when. Then we stop and drive up a raise at the other end for ventilation and safety."

"Like a gopher going down, digging along, and coming up?"

"Right! Then we or somebody else can do a lot of different things should the ore hold good. For instance, we can sink an inclined exploratory drift at right angles to the crosscut, slanting it down to follow the dip of the lode. If all goes well, they can extend it back out to surface, put a steam hoist on top, and develop the orebody deeply with drifts extending out to either side of that incline. If *they* show pay ore, we start stoping out, that is, removing the ore in large masses by extending those drifts upwards, and sideways until they run into each other."

"Who decides all this, Penrose?"

"The board, on the recommendation of the superintendent. Or, if he's in doubt, they'll bring in an expert to look it over. Either way it's something of a gamble, though the idea is not to risk too much on one throw. Do a little, see if it will pay, do a little more, and so on, always figuring things so the work you did just before that won't be wasted."

"And if things go wrong?"

"Stope it out to surface and call it deep enough."

"You lost me there."

"Pull all the ore that *will* pay, then let it go."

Jellison's eyes were unfocused as he concentrated on the picture. "Tell you what. I'll draw a diagram of what I *think* you just told me, and you see if I have the idea."

"Fine. We'll pick out a point for the shaft tomorrow, and while the miners start work, I'll have the carpenters start on the headframe. Just four good trees, trimmed and bolted together like a tripod, with their butts held in hitches—holes, sort of—in the rock. We hang the sheave for the bucket rope from that and hoist with the horse whim. Cheap and quick for Colonel Casey. Since we're sinking only fifty feet or so, no need for anything fancier. Time for fancy will be after the orebody is developed."

"How can I make myself useful?"

"Do your paperwork, sign the checks, then come around and watch. But don't get in the way. And if you hear somebody shout, 'Fire!' run off about a hundred feet and get behind something solid. That means they're blasting." Penrose buttoned his coat. "It's getting cold, evenings, now. I'll be glad when we're underground and out of this wind."

In the morning Penrose led Jellison up to the outcrop and there introduced him to Hector Grenfel, a wedge-shaped individual who would be in direct charge of shaft sinking and related matters. "Take Hector around," Penrose said with a smile, "and show him the best place to put the shaft."

Dick followed the shaft boss past the unknown's grave and waved his hand vaguely. "Here it is, Grenfel. Take your choice."

The big Cousin looked keenly about, walking this way and that. "Schist footwall . . . granite hanging wall," he muttered to himself. "We'll sink in they granite." He sighted along the outcrop and then paced some distance uphill. "Fifty-foot shaft h'ought to 'it 'er h'about 'ere." He kicked a depression with his boot heel. He walked parallel to the outcrop until he was amid the heap of equipment on the downstream end. Stopping short, he bent over and squinted to line himself up with his previous mark. He kicked another shallow hole. Cutting and sharpening a wrist-thick stake, he thrust it into the thin soil. " 'Ere," he proclaimed. " 'Ere will be she shaft. Us'll call 'er they Penrose."

CHAPTER 4

1873
BEN RODERICK

EN RODERICK SAT IN THE OF-
FICE of his assay house, listening to the wind blow, a jobber's
invoice under his hand. Both were depressing. The December
wind in the high, cold basin country was bad enough by itself,
driving strong men to drink and dutiful wives to hysterical
nagging. The invoice was modest as such things went. In a neat
clerk's hand it listed "6 doz. crucibles, 10 lbs. refined borax, 50 do.
best assayers litharge," and so on. With express charges prepaid
and 10 per cent discount for thirty days' cash, it came to a shade
under two hundred dollars. The problem was that Roderick's total
liquid assets amounted to seventeen dollars and—he counted his
pocket change—twenty-two cents. On paper he enjoyed accounts
receivable of better than a thousand dollars. In fact they were
worthless—two dollars here and ten dollars there owed by
prospectors who, whatever their intentions to pay someday, had
even less money than Roderick. When, he asked himself, would
he ever learn to harden his heart and demand the cash in hand
before he parted with an assay certificate that showed, probably,
five dollars in silver, twenty-five cents in gold, with small
percentages of lead and copper?

It was not, he told himself, altogether his own fault. The prosperity back East was humming along. Good news for the East, however, was bad news for western assayers in places like Empire. When men were making money in Pennsylvania, there was no compelling pressure for them to rush out to mineral excitements the way they had stampeded to the Pike's Peak fiasco in 'Fifty-nine, when the panic came. Also, there had been few excitements at all since the South Pass rush in 'Sixty-eight. Roderick had opened his house in Empire in 'Seventy-one, following discovery of some silver-lead lodes in the district. The I.F.R.&P had built in for the same reason. Now both of them were sorry. The lodes were of the sort that miners said lay "big end up"—a few cubic yards of high-grade ore at grass roots, rapidly and disastrously playing out a few feet down. The Empire balloon had swiftly busted.

Instead of pulling up stakes at that point as a sensible man would, Roderick had hung on at Empire for all the world like those scarecrow denizens of a hundred riffled-out placer camps. Like them he was eking out a bare living in the hope that revival must somehow come to the district. Then he would be in on the ground floor. For six months he had run custom assays for prospectors like old Matt Wheeler. It made grub, but it did not pay expenses, as witness this invoice! The development at the Molly Pitcher had at first given him some cause for optimism, but the people at the Molly were not throwing business his way as they should. Now and then they sent Roderick a few samples to run but by no means the number he needed or they should have. For some reason they expressed as many or more directly to Kellogg, Hewston & Company in San Francisco at what must have been considerable cost in time and money. Not that Ben Roderick went out of his way to pry into other peoples' affairs, but in a place like Empire it was impossible for anyone to mind, or keep to himself, his own business.

Now winter had set in. Prospecting had ceased. What little custom Roderick had enjoyed was therefore gone. He was even now warming himself with expensive assaying coke, not wanting to lay out money even for stovewood. He could pay his board and room for four more weeks with what he had in his pockets. Then he could sleep on the office counter and eat odds and ends for a while. But what could he do after that? A rapid canvass of possibilities showed that he could sell his pan balance locally for perhaps five dollars. It would buy him a ticket to somewhere. Then he could lock his office door and walk away. On second thought, why even bother to lock it?

The bell tinkled as the office door in question opened, admitting a lot of wind, a little snow, and a man in a hurry to get out of both. The man was so muffled in buffalo robe, overshoes. and scarf-tied hat as to be unrecognizable. He headed for the office stove, pulling off wolfskin mittens. After warming his blue hands, he started skinning off the layers one by one. "Cold day," he said conversationally.

"Going to get a sight colder," Roderick agreed in the time-honored ritual. He still did not recognize his visitor but hoped from his manner and appearance that he had come with intent to exchange money for services rendered. Certainly he was neither a prospector nor a supply-jobber's drummer.

"How's business?" the man asked.

"Rolling along," Roderick replied untruthfully.

"If you're busy, I'll come back. But I had a proposition for you."

Roderick was intensely interested in any conceivable proposition that did not require a cash investment. "Go ahead," he remarked as casually as he could.

"I'm Jellison," the man said, thrusting out his hand. "General manager at the Molly Pitcher."

"Glad to meet you. Ben Roderick. I've heard of you—you've been shaking the bushes up that way."

"We try, we try. I'll not waste too much of your time. Bill Penrose, our development boss, told me that assayers always have eighteen things going at once and can't afford to stand around and gossip."

Roderick looked hard to see whether his visitor was being sarcastic. Apparently he was serious. The man looked typical of the breed, perhaps somewhat younger and less muscular than usual, but more weather-beaten than a mere mahogany miner. "Today's a little slow," Roderick admitted. "Cold weather keeps people in."

"Wish *I* could have stayed in. But the train runs only one day a week. Now I'll have to hire a livery team to get back and pay some yahoo to go along to bring it back *here*. Of course there was no fire in the stove of the caboose, and I'll freeze to death. Anyway, Mr. Roderick, I'll start by saying that we've heard some good things of you and learned some more. To be frank, we sent out some split outcrop and sinking samples—half to you and half to Kellogg, Hewston in San Francisco. Then we compared your work with theirs. No offense, but there's a lot of men doing privy-hole assaying."

Roderick was not greatly offended. The term had originated in the story that some assayers merely threw the samples down the privy-hole and then wrote out the certificate in a way that would please the customer. Temporarily. In any event, splitting samples in this manner was an accepted way of finding out whether an assayer was doing his job well and conscientiously.

"I wouldn't be here if your work hadn't compared well—very well."

"Thank you," Roderick nodded, beginning to see the light ahead.

"You even threw in a little extra for good measure. We asked only for a gold-silver report, but you gave us manganese, too."

"Oh, that. I was trying out an idea I had and had to make a manganese wet determination, so I just reported it."

His visitor appeared interested. "Indeed? None of my business, but would you mind . . . ?"

"No, not at all. I started wondering over a year back why these lodes around here produced such poor placers. Didn't seem right somehow. I had my figures on a good many of them, so I got them out and looked to see if they had—or lacked—anything in common. I finally decided that all of them had a certain amount of manganese in the outcrop. Of course, outcrop was about all most of them were. Any way, I checked out the Molly samples, too. By the way, *are* there many placer colors in the sands down-

88

stream from you?"

"Matter of fact, no. Some of my crew did a little panning, evenings. 'Chloriding' they call it for some reason. They didn't have much luck."

"Good! I mean, too bad for the men, but good for my idea. That supports my notion that manganese in the ore somehow makes for poor placers."

"H'm." Jellison was evidently digesting the idea. "Proving—what?"

"Well, that just because your placer color is thin or nonexistent, it doesn't follow that there's no mineralized lode to be found."

"Can you tell easily if manganese is present in such a lode?"

"Oh, yes. The outcrop tends to be a dead midnight black in spots. A velvet black. Prospectors love it."

"Let me get this straight," Jellison said, ticking off points with his fingers. "Absence of colors does not exclude lode, because of manganese present. You check for this manganese at the lode by observation. Therefore, if you see manganese in the lode, you know why you didn't find colors to lead you there. Right?"

"Right!"

"But your argument is circular. The whole object of your investigation was to find a lode in the first place. If you find it, you now know why you did *not* find it. But this is excluded, too, because you *had* to find it to prove your contention."

Roderick's mouth opened. "You're right," he said weakly. "You should have been a lawyer."

"I *am* a lawyer."

"I thought you were a mining man."

"Thank you," Jellison smiled through his neatly trimmed beard. "Perhaps some day, given great good fortune, I may yet be one. One more point, though."

"Oh, no!"

"The Molly ore is *not* dead-black, any part of it."

Roderick sighed in relief. "Well, the manganese *you* have is rhodochrosite, not the usual black oxide of manganese I mentioned. I saw very small crystals of it under my microscope in the samples of sinking ore."

"What is rhodochrosite?"

"A different compound of manganese. When massive, it is very beautiful—a pale, warm pink. Some miners call it "pink spar," but it's not, really. A fine, large piece is a semiprecious stone. Can be made into jewelry."

Jellison abruptly changed the subject. "These are your books," he observed, fingering their spines. "Quite a few, and they seem well worn. I was under the impression that most assayers learned by apprenticeship and that if a man was able to do some simple calculations he needed little more education than that."

"It is mostly learned by apprenticeship. I myself was taught by Melville Attwood at Placerville."

"The name's not familiar, but I can tell that you respect him."

"He was a fine man."

"And the books?"

"He also taught me to try to learn a little more than just the bare bones."

Jellison stood up. Rather formally he said, "Mr. Roderick, I would like you to be the mine assayer for the Molly Pitcher. I'm afraid that all I can offer you is one hundred dollars a month and found."

Roderick was unable to speak.

"Oh, very well. One hundred and twenty-five dollars, and that's my limit. We'll transport your equipment, and we'll buy you supplies upon request. Will you consider it?"

"Yes! I mean—as soon as I wind up my obligations here."

"We allowed for that. We'll move you out about April first."

"Uh . . . ." Roderick thought desperately of some way to save face. He could not go into hibernation for two months, desirable as it might be. Jellison had been honest with him, he decided, and he could do as much. "The fact is that I'm almost broke and can't even pay that jobber's bill there. Is there any way I could start sooner? Even as a laborer?"

Jellison smiled sympathetically, "Mr. Penrose told me to listen for your furnace when I first came in. He said a roaring furnace means a busy assayer. If his fire is out, he's in difficulties."

"Very true, I'm afraid."

"We really can't use you full time until we start crosscutting. And the weather is holding up work on the shaft. But you come out as soon as this cold moderates—I'll send a teamster and wagon to help with your laboratory. For the time I can use a warehouse assistant; Penrose drives me pretty hard. We'll get along, I think—I tend to cotton to men who want to know more than just enough to get by." He extended his hand again. Roderick took it firmly. "Now where's that livery barn? I want to be in Bancroft before dark."

Roderick began packing, a process that required a good many days. Some chores that required two men he deferred until the arrival of the teamster. He gave notice at his boardinghouse and wrote a letter to Kellogg, Hewston imploring a brief stay of execution in the matter of their invoice. He passed the time afterward warming himself with his accounts due and writing a short piece intended for *Mining and Scientific Press.* This San Francisco weekly, to which he subscribed when he had any money, was bought, borrowed, lent, sneaked out of other men's mailboxes, displayed on office desks and waiting-room tables, and read on the privy by every mining man who professed any degree of scientific literacy. Because of the isolated situation of so many of its subscribers it carried a page of world and national news, but not even the death of a crowned head rated as much linage as the editor would give to a new patent concentrating table. The letter, "Influence of Manganese on the Formation of Placers beneath Lode Outcrops," summarized Roderick's observations and conclusions in fairly turgid prose. He carefully refrained from any suggestion about what the new crumb of knowledge might be good for and hoped that this omission would also escape the busy editor's attention. If it ran, it might constitute good publicity.

Upon a day there duly appeared a teamster at his office. The man seemed subdued for his kind and made no demur at helping skid the furnace up to the wagon bed, dismantling soot-filled stovepipe, or even shoveling assay coke from the bin into sacks. The man pumped easily; in fact, Roderick soon regretted priming him. He talked steadily for the whole day it took them to get to Bancroft. "That 'ere Mr. Jellison is a hard man, Mr. Roderick," he was saying, "and Mr. Penrose, he's harder. Looky there . . . ." They were rolling past a pile of wood ashes and crumpled, smoke-stained roof tin.

"What am I supposed to see?"

"That 'ere was Wilson's store and saloon," the teamster proclaimed, brandishing his whip.

"They didn't burn the old hog out, did they?"

"Pret' near. There was some trouble. They say Wilson pulled a gun. Mr. Jellison, he kicked the immortal hell outta him, and Mr. Penrose, he stomped him. Broke his arm and run him out. Old Henry loaded up his stock—*had* it loaded up, ruther—then come back and opened the coal-oil bar'l and burned her down. Then got on the train an' left. It's said around that Mr. Penrose told him if 'n he ever come back they'd get rough with him."

"Broke his arm! My Lord! I wished it on him, I guess."

"Don't wish nothin' on me, then. Old Henry was a sight. I never seen a man *so* fat get *so* poorly *so* fast."

"Maybe because he couldn't eat so much with only one arm," Roderick replied, as they turned in to the warehouse corral for the night. Nonetheless, he wondered what he was getting into. Jellison had seemed citified and pretty pleasant when he hired him, but the teamster made the manager and the development boss sound worse than the proverbial bad combination of a New England skipper and a Liverpool mate.

Peace was restored to his soul on the following day as they began the long trek to the Molly. Riding along was one John Trewartha, late of Truro, the Keweenaw, Grass Valley, and other parts devoted to mining. He had a heavy Cousin accent compounded by a jaw alarmingly swollen on one side. It took Roderick a while to catch on to what he was saying, but it developed that Trewartha had a 'ollow tooth that had started to trouble him. The camp cook had applied the standard remedy, a pair of machinists' pliers, but had succeeded only in breaking the tooth off short. Wherefore Penrose had sent him to the farriery in Bancroft, whose resident was a tooth drawer of renown. The farrier had fixed the miner up good and for good measure had trimmed his hair with the horse shears.

"Croust be good," Trewartha deponed. "Not Cornish, but plenty h'and cooked well h'enough. Penrose works usn's 'ard but feeds we like noble bleddy lords. Grenfel be shaft boss. 'E knows ore. Jellison, 'im h'I don't know too good, but they say 'e'l do. They Molly be small, mayhap, but 'tis steady work h'and no dirty business. Do she 'old h'up, h'I'll send fer me wife h'and nippers."

"I was told," Roderick hinted, with one eye on the teamster's back, "that Jellison and Penrose rubbed out and scalped that Bancroft saloon man."

" 'E needed h'it," Trewartha replied, with perfect calm.

And so, like certain other pilgrims, they entertained each other with tale and reminiscence until they arrived at their destination. Roderick was billeted by Jellison in his capacity as quartermaster, being assigned a new bunk in the bachelor officers' quarters of the warehouse and a seat at the head table. A partitioned space behind office and quarters had been set aside for his laboratory. But when it came to the furnace, both men shook their heads.

"Won't do," Jellison agreed firmly. "This is a fire trap, and I worry about our heating stove as it is. Could you make do, for a while at least, with a separate shanty for your furnace? I know it will be inconvenient, but you won't be that busy until warm weather. Then you may be glad it's out from under this roof. I'll have the carpenter put up something, and we'll take the wagon over there to skid it down when he's ready. Fire is the curse of mine camps."

Time passed, Roderick entered upon his new duties and was outwardly content. Upon a vile afternoon in early February a blue-faced teamster dropped a packet of mail at the mine office and went off to care for his head-hanging team. Roderick was too engaged to pay attention and seldom received mail in any event. Jellison quickly sorted the small stack, proceeding more by experience than by perusal. Telegrams (there was one) and business-sized envelopes were his portion. Pencil-scrawled letters on cheap gray stationery were personal mail for the crew. Printed material was Roderick's. Anything else went into the jackpot. Jellison opened the telegram first. He read it twice over and then laughed heartily. "Roderick!" he called. "Are you too busy to go up the hill and ask Penrose if he can come down? Tell him it's not trouble, but get him if you can. You come back, too."

Shortly the top managerial and scientific echelon of the Molly Pitcher mine was assembled around the office stove, Penrose tucking snuff into his lip and Roderick filling his pipe. Jellison waved the telegram. "Attention to General Orders Number One!" he announced, and began to read aloud:

> January 31 Colonel and Mrs. George Huggins became proud parents baby boy William Francis seven pounds eating like a shaft sinker stop   When are smelter returns going to start stop   Wire congratulations and tonnage on dump or everyone fired stop   Frank Casey

After the general laugh Jellison remarked, "Casey is sure worked up. But he has a point. Spring will be here before we know it, and we have to start thinking about the concentrator. Penrose?"

The development boss settled his snuff and spat a few stray crumbs onto the stove. "We're here to develop for sale, not to stope it out. But Casey wants some interest on his outlay. I'd say, . . ." he calculated silently, "twenty tons a day. That's two Blake crushers, ten stamps, and about seventy-two square feet of concentrating table. One medium-small Comstock rake settler for the tails. About a ten-horse-power engine."

"Roderick?"

"Sounds all right to me. But I'd add one amalgamation table at the head of the line for each battery. Some of the gold will mill free, and we can make more money selling it as amalgam than shipping it all in concentrates."

Jellison, making notes, nodded. "I've been reading in your books, Ben, that even waste and mill tailing carry values that might interest a buyer. Penrose, where could we dump our tailing close by—where it could be impounded out of the way, but got at easily?"

Penrose reflected. "We could put in a wooden launder to run them down to Boot Cove—you know, the little place where those boots were sticking out from under that boulder when we came in here. Put a log breastwork across the open side for a dam. It'd do."

"Do you suppose there's actually someone in those boots, or were they stuck there for a joke?" Jellison asked idly. "Maybe we could look sometime. Everybody goes past in too much of a hurry to wade the stream and find out. Now, the other thing. Ben, we're going to need a millman. Want to take it on?"

"I can't set up a mill!" Roderick protested.

"Know you can't. When I buy it from Finkel, I'll ask him to send along the men to set it up. You can learn from them and then run it when it goes on line. Give it a try?"

"Thanks. Yes. But no promises. If the men are like that poor surveyor you told me about, they may be too busy fighting off green spiders."

"He was a poor specimen," Penrose nodded, "but God pity him in weather like this. He may be lying in some alley right now, freezing to death. But don't worry about the millwrights. They move around all the time. My only worry is getting them. 'Course, if we bought everything spanking new from the Union Iron Works or Risdon, they'd send along millwrights with it. But you know what our motto is ——."

"Quick and cheap for Colonel Casey!" Jellison and Roderick chanted in unison.

"For some reason, that reminds me," Roderick said in a serious tone. "While I was up the hill fetching you, Mr. Penrose, I was standing by a headframe leg—the downhill one of the pair to the west. I heard it creaking a little, a sort of ticking noise."

"Wood'll do that when the strain comes on. You ought to hear a wooden ship when it goes about in a seaway."

"But you weren't hoisting then. That's why I asked."

"Ah?" Penrose's forehead wrinkled. "Lots of reasons. The cold weather freezing green wood. Them trees was growing one day and working in a mine the next. I'll bear it in mind, though. This cold plays hell on us generally. Drill steel breaks easier. Chippings

95

freeze in the blast holes. Takes a man four times as long to do anything. Powder loses its strength. And—the lads are getting restless."

"What's eating them?" Jellison inquired.

"The Old Adam, mostly. Solid family men, most of them, but after four, five months you miss the wife and nippers. Especially the wife. Me, I'm beyond that, damn it! What they really need is a few drinks and a long night at home, and they'd be bright-eyed and bushy-tailed tomorrow."

Roderick, who tended to be rather prim, pursed his lips in disapproval of such sentiments, but Jellison, remembering the gamy and available delights of San Francisco, sighed audibly. "We bring in all their other necessities," he complained, "But I could just see what would happen if I wrote a check on Huggins & Casey—'To transportation and pay one dozen light ladies, necessary for exploratory drifting.' "

"Them as live by a river don't understand thirst," Penrose philosophized, ignoring Roderick's pointed departure from a conversation that was rapidly becoming lewd.

"I always wondered how isolated men did," the general manager sighed again. "And the answer is, they don't. Now help me get this telegram to Finkel in shape."

In the assay laboratory Ben Roderick was gritting his teeth. As a boy he had sniggered at his older sisters' blissful sighings over sentimental novels of unrequited love. Now in the trap himself, he found laughter about such matters in extremely poor taste. He had feebly hoped that his self-exile to Empire two years before would make Sue Ann Villanelle realize that the apple was bobbing out of reach. She would come to her senses, fly to his arms . . . . Instead, she had calmly married Tom Weatherbe just as though Ben Roderick did not exist. And who could blame her? Weatherbe had dark good looks, money, and the unconcerned attitude that somehow got the girls more interested than did any amount of solicitous and gentlemanly attentions. Now here was Dick Jellison, another Weatherbe come to persecute him with his very presence. And Jellison, too, had the looks and the ease of manner that indicated that he would be perfectly at home with either genuine or imitation ladies. (At that moment, for natural reasons, Roderick's mind persisted in dwelling the more upon the inferior imitations.)

A dispassionate observer of Roderick's envious writhings might have noted that, since one love is the antidote for another, Ben's flight to Empire tended to be a trifle self-defeating. He might have hinted that Roderick's attitude was founded chiefly upon his ignorance of women—sad to relate, but not unusual for the age, Ben Roderick's total experience of the fair sex had been gained at no distance closer than three feet. With women this is as good—or bad—as three miles. Roderick was not in love with Sue Ann Villanelle; he was in love with a combination of dreams and the rising sap. The observer might even have suggested (provided he was powerful enough to defend himself) that what Roderick required second-most was a good kick up the behind. Following the advice of improving books, Ben Roderick decided to bury himself in work. Therefore he opened the copy of *Mining and Scientific Press* that had just come in. Turning to the regional development news, he read that a new combine calling itself Consolidated Virginia had organized in Virginia City and was calling for bids on various development projects. He dismissed it from his mind as probably another piece of stock-jobbery. Everyone knew that the Comstock was playing out.

As the days lengthened, so did the crosscut. The ore dump on the hill grew larger. After several warm cloudy days a freshet broke up the ice in the pond, overtopped the dam, and sent big plates of ice crashing down to the creek bed. There was just a hint of green out in the basin country. On one warm, bright evening Jellison rode up the valley at the head of a wagon train. In the wagon bed behind him was firmly chocked and chained a diminutive steam boiler and its smokepipe. Other wagons followed with firebrick, mortar, yards of odorous leather belting, piping, ironmongery, world without end. In the last wagon sat three derby-hatted wise men, the steamfitter, the millwright, and the master mason. They carried their bags of personal tools with the air of Edinburgh surgeons summoned to attend the sick cat of a wealthy dowager. Men who had erected one-hundred-stamp mills

97

and Washoe mullers whose girth exceeded a steamboat's paddle wheels, laid foundations of granite masonry forty feet deep, and installed steam engines of 250 horsepower were not likely to be greatly impressed by the Molly Pitcher job.

The magi were greeted personally by Penrose, whom they treated as craftsmen will treat a respected colleague who is down on his luck. They were at pains to be civil to the respectful miners and carpenters. Even Roderick, as practitioner of an art and mystery, they admitted to their presence. They were curt only to Jellison, since custom insisted that pen pushers (even if the pen in question made out their checks) were men of straw, not iron. The magnates were housed with care, their personal and professional needs were instantly catered, and the camp turned itself inside out for them. As a matter of course the cook fed them at the head table, ladling out special tidbits with an anxious eye. During this royal progress Penrose kept one eye on Jellison and was relieved to see that the general manager smiled and smiled and played the villain.

Everyone turned out early the next day, with the exception of the steam fitter and the millwright. These worthies occupied themselves with a deck of cards, while the master mason fell to upon the footings and foundations. The modest size of the prospective concentrator and its machinery much speeded this work, whose end a few days later was signaled by the boss mason himself, who with his own hands inserted the machinery hold-down studs into the mortar-filled holes that the miners had drilled into the granite blocks. He nudged, tapped, and twisted by eye alone and then gave his benediction. "There, now—that ought to hold the sonsabitches. Don't tighten up on 'em till the mortar's set good, or you'll pull the bastards right out of the holes." The mason then took over the steamfitters's hand in the euchre game with the air of Cheops just come into the house from finishing the Great Pyramid.

As the work progressed, the miners were returned to the crosscut. On the morning of April 20, Penrose stretched his gnarled arms upward, snuffed the air, and, heading out the office door, proclaimed, "Hot weather! It's good again to be alive!" He paused and said, "I believe I'll have a look at the face, if Grenfel will let me in the drift." He glanced at Jellison. The latter, buried in a payroll, waved his pen at the development boss and resumed his labors. In the assay laboratory Roderick could be heard bucking down a sample. Still Penrose lingered and then pushed open the door and was gone.

Perhaps ten minutes later both Jellison and Roderick heard the sound of splintering wood and falling timbers, accompanied by shouts of alarm. Both dashed out the door toward the headframe, each realizing at the same moment that it was no longer there. Its components lay across the shaft platform in an ugly tangle of wire rope and wood. A group of men were gathered, peering down the mouth of the shaft.

"What's up?" Jellison panted. "Anyone hurt?"

"Gallows-frame leg snapped," someone said. "On a full bucket. Some 'un be h'under h'it—h'I 'eard 'im cry h'out."

"Jesus Christ!" Jellison exclaimed. "Si-*lence*!" He looked at the confusion of material and men. "You—unbolt that sheave! Quick! The rest of you—horse one of these legs *across* the shaft mouth! Roderick! The ladder's smashed! Fetch a lot of hemp rope from the warehouse and some chain. At least four feet of as heavy chain as you can carry!"

As Roderick ran off, he heard another shout from Jellison. "You on the whim! Start getting the slack out of that hoist rope!"

By the time Roderick had returned with his burdens, one of the sound headframe legs had been dragged by brute strength over the shaft. A miner sat astride it, his legs dangling. The miner was given the end of the chain and with some help draped it over the log. Men grabbed the two bights of hoist rope and used them to lower the massive sheave so that the rider could feed a chain end through its eye. The two ends of the chain were quickly tied with hemp, but Jellison shook his head. "Won't hold. You! Get a one-foot bolt and bolt those chain-end links together! Got one? Good—do it! Take up some more with that whim!"

In a few moments Jellison cried, "All clear! Hoist man—raise the bucket ten feet and *lock* it!" The hoist rope creaked and then slowly began to rub heavily over and cut down into the platform

99

planks. When he saw that his arrangement was going to work, Jellison tied an end of the coil of line securely and tossed the coil into the shaft. "I'm going down. I want—," his eye drifted over the group. "Roderick, follow me down. You men here—get a wide six-foot plank and get a lifting line on one end. We'll tie him to the plank, and you raise him. Let's go." He lowered himself slowly out of sight. Roderick felt a qualm but suppressed it and followed as soon as it seemed safe.

Halfway down Roderick heard a sound of anguish from below. When his feet touched rock, he turned and to his dismay saw Jellison kneeling beside Penrose. The old man's eyes were bright, and he was speaking quietly. "Hit me in the small of the back and nipped my arse and legs. What happened up there?"

"One of the headframe legs broke. Right in the middle. Oh, *Bill!*" There was wild grief in Jellison's voice.

"Nay, nay! You're taking it harder than me. I don't hurt much at all."

"We'll get you on a plank and out of here." Jellison turned his head. "Roderick, keep an eye peeled for it." Roderick dutifully looked up but shuddered at the sight of the bucket dangling just above their heads. It moved slightly, malevolently, like something alive. There were, he saw, dark stains on its bottom.

" 'Ere come they plank!" said a voice from above. It came swaying down.

"Give me a hand here, Ben."

"Easy, lads," Penrose cautioned. "I'm leaking somewhere inside. I can feel it."

Working carefully together, they slid Penrose onto the plank and lashed him fast. Roderick did not like the feel of Penrose's legs. They seemed mushy and dead. There was blood on the hemp before they were done. "Hoist away—carefully!" Jellison cried. The plank upended, and as his weight came on the lashings, Penrose cried out and fainted. Just at that moment the face crew came charging out to the shaft. They saw what was going on, looked at the bucket, and retreated into the crosscut.

"Lower the bucket now! Slowly!" As the two men stayed well back, the thing inched down and crunched to a stop.

100

Jellison tied a double bowline to his own line, stepped into it, and ordered, "Hoist away, here!" The line tightened, and he rose from sight. Presently the line came down, and Roderick was summoned. Up top to his surprise he saw Penrose still secured to the plank, lying on the platform in the sunlight. Jellison sat beside him holding a tin cup of water. Jellison's face was drawn, but Penrose's was deathly pale, and there was yet more blood on the platform. Roderick felt hope ooze away.

"Ye'll do, Mr. Jellison," Penrose whispered. "You used your head and got me out of there as fast as any Cousin could. Like you used your head with that hog in Bancroft."

Jellison pulled himself together with an obvious effort. "Is there anything we can do? Anyone we can write to?"

"They'll have forgot me back 'ome. And the Ninth Michigan was mustered out. No, I don't recollect anyone. Give me another drink—I'm thirsty." He sipped more from the cup and then looked to his left. "Plant me over there—where the old grave is. A good spot. Gets the evening sun." Penrose gargled, turned his head to one side, and pumped blood in astonishing quantities from his mouth. When the flow had subsided, his white beard was red about one side. He spat feebly. "Mr. Jellison, we'll make a mining man of you yet." He closed his eyes and appeared to rest for a while. All at once he said casually, "My light must've blown out. One of you Cousins lend me . . . ." Penrose's head drooped over, and he lay still. After a moment Jellison released his hand and fumbled in his pocket for a handkerchief. Unfolding it, he laid it gently over Penrose's face.

The next morning they buried William Penrose in the fashion he had desired. His cortege would have been considered honorable even in Virginia City. Jellison, in his capacity as general manager and chief officiant, led the procession, accompanied by Roderick. Behind came the coffin. The millwright, steamfitter, and master mason assisted by Grenfel and the two leading miners, were the pallbearers. The shaft sinkers attended as a corporate body, as did the carpenters. The cook walked alone, followed by a ragtag of teamsters. There were no flowers but the springtime wildflowers on the hillside, no muffled drums but the steady crunching of

101

hobnailed boots. Upon the waiting mound of schist chips and soil lay a carefully wrought wooden cross.

When the coffin had been lowered, Jellison stepped to the head of the grave. For a minute he quoted what he could remember of the words of resignation and acceptance. "Man's days are grass. . . . He is born to trouble as the sparks fly upward. . . . Where the tree falleth there shall it lie, but generation succeeds unto generation . . ." He paused and then continued, "Oh, Lord, forget not Thy servant, William Penrose. We pray for him and for us, and for all miners, sailors, soldiers, lumbermen, railroaders, and those others who labor at the cost of their lives so that city men may sit at their ease. We commend him to Thy light and Thy peace, for he was a good sergeant-major and a first-class mining man, and of such is the kingdom of Heaven. Jesus Christ said, I am the resurrection, and the life: he that believeth in Me, though he were dead, yet shall he live. Now let Thy humble servant depart in peace. Our Father, . . ." and the little crowd of men joined with him in the final prayer.

There were two inquests. The first was brief. The boss carpenter bent over a badly-splintered headframe leg and pointed. "Rotten. Rotten half-way through. How it lasted long as it did, I dunno."

"Could you have told it?" Jellison demanded.

"If we'd barked it and sounded it, maybe. But Mr. Penrose said not to fuss."

"Let me look at the butt and the top end." The butt, heaved free of its stone hitch-socket, was clear, sound wood. In the sheave end there was a small, insignificant-looking brown check.

The carpenter fingered it. "I bet water leaked down through there into the rot and froze. That'd weaken it even more."

Jellison nodded slowly. "Don't see how you can be blamed." The carpenter's face cleared. "Well, set up another one. We have to have ore for that mill."

The second inquest was formal. It was held in an Empire saloon. Jellison was the only witness. When the testimony was finished, the coroner returned. "Nobody at fault." As Jellison turned to go, the coroner coughed. "Custom here is to treat the jury f'r their time and trouble." Jellison dropped two cartwheels on the bar of justice and strode out rapidly. Roderick, waiting outside in case his testimony would be needed, looked at his face and refrained from comment.

Toward the end of May, upon the evening of one of many pleasant spring days, the three wise men were in the mess tent, making way with boiled beef and potatoes. Jellison admired their dexterity—the ends of their hash knives disappeared in and out of their throats as though they were amputating their own tonsils. With the flesh restored, the millwright brushed his luxuriant moustache free of crumbs, looked significantly at his confreres, and asked, "You feel like the free trip to the menagerie tomorrow?"

"Is he trying to tell me something, Ben?" Jellison asked Roderick, who was looking pleased.

"Yep," the millwright interposed. "Pat says the engine is ready, and I got the last of the stamps stood today. Tomorrow we're going to put 'er on the line. We ort to be ready to go if nothing shakes loose and if you really got some values in that ore dump of your'n."

Jellison produced a toothpick and finished his meal. "Lead the way, boys. Ben, do you have a helper lined up?"

The millwright grinned. "We learned him a thing or two. Got one of your Cousin miners to break the ore and feed the crusher. I'll start the stamps and show you how it's done. A sickly baby could rabble the concentrates—don't take any sense. Since this man of yours is already a assayer, he knows how to handle the amalgamation tables. Nothing to it in a little mill like this-here." He turned to the steamfitter. "You going to hire on here and run that Corliss Giant, or you got somebody can tend the teakettle without blowing the place over to Bancroft?"

"Ah, I wouldn't be stayin' in this hole if the law was lookin' fer me," the steamfitter replied, with the hauteur of a man who had the blood of kings in his veins. "One iv th' carpenters knows which end of a stick ye throw in the fire, and him I learned a bit. He'll give ye the steam."

The master mason sealed the discussion with a vast and juicy belch that reminded Roderick of a drift round being fired. Smacking his lips several times appreciatively, the mason frowned. "*I* might be tempted to stay f'r the food, were it not that I had a job to do in Sant Louie." He allowed the remark to sink in and then pursued it. "Jim Eads has run into trouble on his west pier and is wanting a good master mason." This effectively upstaged his colleagues. The Eads Bridge would be one of the wonders of the world, if it was ever finished, and any man who had half a hand in it would drink free on his reputation for the rest of his life.

"That's it, then," the millwright concluded. "Come over when ye hear the whistle blow, and we'll start up the peanut roaster for ye."

Long before the whistle tooted, Jellison and Roderick were in the concentrator building, following the millwright intently from point to point. "Remember, oil here," he was saying, "up there on both ends of the line shaft, and *here* twicet a day. You want to hire on somebody who knows belting. That's good belt, but it won't last forever. Hey! There she goes!" As he spoke, the line-shaft pulleys began to turn. Belts whirled, but nothing of moment seemed to happen. "Let's go up on the ore platform first and follow 'er through."

At the high side of the mill a miner was leaning on a sledge. A scoop lay at his feet, and a substantial pile of broken ore was in sight on the platform. Satisfied, the millwright pulled a lever. At the lower end of a short, tapering wooden chute, something began to open and close silently like the mouth of a hungry beast. "Put about five-six scoops down now," the millwright ordered, "and when I yell, start feeding her steady." The miner reached for his scoop, ore shot down the chute, and was followed by a crackling, crunching sound accompanied by vibration underfoot.

"Come on, now." Inside the mill the wright tugged upward on a wooden slide. As it eased up, water gurgled, and soon the surfaces of the tables began to gleam. He inspected the sheet of water, dribbled a handful of fine stream sand across the high end of the table line, and followed its progress closely with his nose almost buried in the water. He opened the slide an inch more, tested again, and at last produced a pocketknife. With it he incised a small notch on the edge of the slide to indicate the correct degree of flow.

Leading his flock up a short flight of wooden steps and along a small railed gangway, the wright contemplated the big, silently spinning cams of the stamp mill. He listened intently, felt a bearing, and made a small adjustment. He pointed to the motionless stamp rods. "Them's one, two, three, four—over to ten on the right. I'll go down now and make sure there's ore under the stamps. When I sing out a number," he said, as he put his hand on the bank of wooden levers, "ease that lever back toward you. That releases the stamp. Got to have ore under it, or it'll crack the die and maybe the battery. *Never* run no stamps on a empty battery, or they'll pound it to pieces before you can get them hung up again." He brushed past them and vanished. Peering down cautiously (Roderick had no desire to catch one of the big cam ears on his forehead), he saw a wooden stick spreading crushed ore around in the massive iron trough below.

"Start feedin'!" came a bellow. The crusherman outside responded, vibration built up again, and soon a stream of crushed ore started to spill into the battery from the uphill side. The stick worked itself around again. "Drop number two!" Roderick pulled on the lever. The stamp rod moved, was caught by the ear of the cam, raised, and dropped free to fall with a metallic thud. The thud was immediately repeated, over and over. "Number four!" Another stamp began to pound. "Number one! Keep the hell feeding!" Soon the whole building was filled with a pounding chant that beat out a nerve-tingling rhythm. The millwright reappeared, leading the men away by gestures.

At the tables Roderick found himself staring at the battery screens above the silvery mirrors of the amalgamation plates at the head of the lines. A gray powder was beginning to work out of the sheet-iron screens. It spilled into the water, which seized it and carried it downward, the water turning milky with its burden.

"Nothing to do now but wait a while," the millwright commented above the continual pounding. "Everything's working good." From time to time he inserted his finger delicately into the opaque water and at last said, "Ha!" explosively. He took up a peculiar tool—it resembled a tiny garden hoe with an overlong wire handle—and gently pulled through the water with it. As it approached the near side of the table, it was evident that it drew a burden along. The small load, perhaps a quarter-cupful, dropped with a liquid "splat" into an open-ended wooden trough. The millwright repeated the process farther down the table, and then again. When he was done, a line of brassy-black powder, touched by glints of blue and green, lay in the trough.

Jellison stared at the material as water drained from it. "What is that?"

"Concentrates," Roderick replied in fascination.

Jellison touched the material, examined the few flecks that stuck to his fingertips, and then carefully brushed them back into the trough. "For that . . . ." he said slowly. "For that . . . ."

"I want to run an assay on it," Roderick declared. He looked about, seized a nearby cup, and half-filled it from the trough.

"Hey, you two!" the millwright intervened. "Quit dreamin'! Help me shut her down."

"Why?" Roderick demanded with sudden belligerence.

"Hell, she works, don't she?"

Roderick grinned widely—the first spontaneous smile Jellison had ever seen on his face. "Damn right she works!" he yelled. He stalked forward, rabble in hand, and began to clean the second line of tables. "Nothing to it." The big young assayer ran toward the back, thrust his head out the rear door, and bellowed, "Keep feeding!" He laughed and danced a hornpipe in front of the chanting stamps.

"What's got into him?" Jellsion asked.

"Mill fever," the millwright replied equably. "He may get over it. Best let him be—I'll see he don't hurt himself."

Roderick returned, babbling demands. He wanted a regular crusherman, cordwood, a table cleaner, concentrate sacks. A powerful surge of excitement had him in its grip, so that he barely acknowledged Jellison's patient, "We'll see—we'll see." Roderick ran out the back, ran in again, cleaned the tables a second time, and shouted in glee as the line of mineral in the launders grew fatter.

106

"What'll it take to shut *him* down?" Jellison asked.

The millwright was regarding Roderick's antics with the patient eye of age and experience. "He's like a kid just found out what girls are really good for. He won't stop till he's got that ore dump of your'n worked down. Then cut off his boiler cordwood afore he starts milling them stream rocks. Well," he concluded, turning away, "I guess I'm finished here."

"I have the feeling we all are," Jellison replied. "Will you take a telegram for me when you go out? Just give it to the conductor—he'll send it on."

Four days later Frank Casey and George Huggins were reading the telegram:

> April 30 concentrator went on line stop   No trouble stop   Daily output estimated quarter ton concentrates fifteen ounces gold balance quartz and pyrites stop   Amalgam cleanup not determined yet stop   Losses eight per cent gold in tails stop   Hiring more men to push crosscut mill and work outcrop stop   Shipping first concentrates Pueblo June fifteen stop   Jellison.

"Well, George," Casey remarked with satisfaction, "he fetched her through. How's the stock going?"

"Just dandy, Frank. This telegram will move the final lot. Then whoever's got her can have her. Want to know how we did?" He produced a sheet of paper. It showed total expenses at a touch over $125,000 and stock sales, at about $250,000. "We doubled our money. And that carload of concentrates will bring, h'm, twelve thousand dollars. Near ten per cent interest on our money. Sure you don't want a few feet for yourself?"

Casey did not reply. He was drafting a telegram to Jellison:

> Molly Pitcher changing hands about July 1 stop   Terminate all contracts and operations that date stop   Turn over property records and equipment to new owners agent thereafter on demand stop   Lay off crew offering jobs to good men our Montezuma location Mono County stop   Return San Francisco soonest thereafter for personal report stop

He paused, considered, and added another line:

107

Tell crew congratulations on good job stop   Give all men railroad
passes and bonus one week pay stop   Frank Casey

Upon a day in midsummer Willie Byers thrust his head into the
office of Frank Casey, who was contemplating a large painting, so
newly hung that the smell of linseed oil and varnish was still
evident. "There's two mining men outside want to see you,
Colonel. They won't tell me their names, but they say it's about
company business."

"Bring 'em in."

There presently entered two bearded young men wearing the
clothes associated with the headworks employees of working
mines. One was darkhaired and gave the impression of lean
strength. The other was big enough to be a top mucker.

"I don't believe I know you gentlemen," Casey said, as they
stared about at his surroundings.

"I believe you do, Colonel, nonetheless," the slighter of the pair
replied. "Do you remember a junior counsel of this firm—Dick
Jellison?"

"Yes, but he's—Dick!" Casey's eyes protruded. "Welcome
back!" They shook hands warmly. "Who's this giant you brought
along with you?"

"Our assayer and mill superintendent, Ben Roderick. Colonel
Casey—Mr. Roderick."

Introductions performed, Casey shouted for Huggins and said,
"Have seats. Tell me all about it."

When Huggins had entered and been surprised and similarly
introduced, Jellison made a brief verbal report, summarizing the
year's work. "Ben has plans that necessitate being here, so I
brought him up to see the office. He's a country boy and doesn't
know that city men put it in spittoons. Could he see yours, Colonel
Huggins?"

Huggins led the men to his office and displayed its glories to
Roderick's wondering eyes. Jellison found his attention drifting
away from the conversation. Back of Huggins' desk hung another
new painting. It was a portrait of George himself and of a beautiful
woman in a white dress holding a baby. Evidently this was Cecelia

Huggins and young William Francis. It was also noteworthy that the painter had made George somewhat more slender and a touch less gray then he was in the flesh. What was Casey saying?

"Sorry about Bill Penrose. How did you get along personally?"

Jellison looked down at the carpet. "He was one of the best. It was like losing a father. He died game as hell. We buried him where he requested."

Jellison's distress was so evident that Huggins changed the subject. "And what are you going to do with this grizzly bear you trapped and tamed?"

Roderick blushed faintly. "Mr. Jellison has talked me into matriculating at the Columbia School of Mines. I had nothing to keep me back there, so I took him up on it."

"Takes a lot of money," Huggins calculated.

"Dick's grubstaked me. Also he promised me summer work to help out."

Casey looked at Huggins. Huggins, affecting to draw on his cigar, winked one eye. "Well, you both have considerable back pay coming to you. I guess you'll want to get some civilized clothes and food. And you'll want your old desk back, Dick."

Jellison sat more erect. "I won't mind the back pay, no. But I think I'm finished with paper shuffling here. Once you've seen the elephant . . . So much to learn. So *damn* much to learn. And it's all so interesting. The responsibility. Something new all the time. No, I don't think I do want that desk back." w all the time. No, I don't think I do want that desk back."

Casey returned the wink now. "We forgot your bonus. You stayed a little under that hundred thousand we allowed you. Not much, but some. About twenty-four or twenty-five hundred, I think. It'll be added to your check. Complements of Huggins & Casey."

"Thank you very much."

"Now while you're here, would you two step back to my office for a minute? There's this gold property down in Arizona we're interested in, and I'd like a rough estimate of the cost to get it in shape."

As soon as Jellison and Roderick had closed the door, Casey turned to Huggins. His voice dropped. "Sink or swim, George, and by thunder, he swam. God rest Penrose, he did a good job with that boy. We'll have us a junior partner yet."

Huggins smiled. "Another uncle for little William Francis."

"Er—yes. Of course."

"Think he'll bite on it?"

"He's as good as in Arizona right now. Hope we can get that big boy he's got with him. We'll need a real engineer."

"You're always harping about never skimping on men, timber, or rope."

In the next office Jellison was staring at the other oil painting, the one he had first noticed. He had remembered it as a duplicate of the one in Huggins' office, but it was not. It was Cecelia Huggins by herself, holding the baby in the same pose. In this version she was wearing a blue opera gown, plumes, and evening jewelry. Also her expression was slightly different. Beautiful pictures, both of them, and very expensive, but Jellison felt that somehow he would do better not to mention them. He and Roderick were bending over the maps and assay reports when Casey re-entered the office.

"Well, now," Jellison said expansively, as he and Roderick walked out into the afternoon sunlight. "You're on your way, and I'll be on mine. Write me and tell me all about little old New York. Care of the office here; they'll forward it. And I'll write to you and send it out by smoke signal or whatever they're using in Arizona Territory. Now let's go to the bank and get barbered and washed up and into some city clothes and I'll take you out to . . . ." His voice trailed off. Ben Roderick was not there.

Turning around, Jellison saw his companion rooted to the sidewalk, facing the other direction. He was in contemplation of a saucy little bustle, waggling enticingly away. Roderick's face had an expression that needed no interpreter.

Taking him firmly by the elbow, Jellison turned Ben around and got him started again. "As I was saying, we'll try the sea-food."

"What?"

110

"Then we'll see . . . ."

Six hours later two young San Francisco dandies were debating, just a trifle thickly, while a bored horsecab driver recalculated his fare for the fourth time. "Social presence!" Jellison was insisting. "No way to learn it but by experience. Absolutely necessary for a college man. Suppose you go to a tea at the dean's house. Want to eat like those roughnecks at the Molly? No, hell no!"

"But *now?*" Roderick asked plaintively. "My train leaves tomorrow afternoon. We've had a good time tonight, although I can't get the hang of those oysters. Do we *have* to?"

"We have to. Out!" Jellison paid the cabbie and shooed him on his way. They were standing in a dark, quiet residential street at the foot of Telegraph Hill. In front of them was a large, staid-looking mansion, a match for its neighbors to right and left. Jellison steered Roderick up the steps and, guided by the glimmer of a small doorway lantern, pulled a bell cord. After a short wait a pretty young Negro girl in maid's costume opened the door.

"Yes, gentlemen?"

"We wish to pay our respects to Mrs. LaFourche if she's at home to us, miss."

The girl inspected them and then stepped back. "Mrs. La-Fourche will be down very shortly. Please have a seat in here." The girl led them to a small sitting room and closed the door.

"I don't want to make any social calls," Roderick complained. "I want to see some more of the bright lights, Dick. Balancing teacups for two hours and eating cookies and talking about the weather. . . ."

"Now, Ben. You want to be an educated man. There is more to education by far than books. Do Huggins and Casey want to have a learned fool on their hands? Or a boorish bookworm? The social graces, man, the social graces. Now, Mrs. LaFourche is one of our most respected San Francisco institutions. No gentlemen would leave San Fran——ah!"

Both men rose as a gray-haired, severe-faced *grande dame* in somber black bombazine entered the sitting room. Jellison bowed and was imitated by Roderick. "Mrs. LaFourche, may I present a good friend and associate, Benjamin Roderick? Ben, Mrs. La-

111

Fourche."

"I am delighted to meet Mr. Roderick." Mrs. LaFourche's voice was soft and more youthful than her appearance. "And I haven't seen you for ages, Mr. Jellison." She extended her hand, palm down, to both, who bowed over it again.

"We have both been totally isolated in a mining development in the Rocky Mountain Territory. I for nearly a year. Mr. Roderick, here, for over three years."

"Hein?" The lady raised her winged eyebrows. "This is indeed deplorable! Even sailors are not at sea so long any more." She looked at Roderick's size, as though in estimation. "Your companion is a very large man . . . ."

"But very *spirituel,* Mrs. LaFourche. He isolated himself as the result of an unhappy affair of the heart." Jellison seemed somewhat affected by his hostess's manner, Roderick noted, becoming rather Gallic himself. Perhaps Jellison was right; he might learn something here.

"I shall see what I can do. And for yourself?"

"Journeys end in lovers' meetings. I am a man of settled habits."

Mrs. LaFourche rose from the settee where she had been seated, her back as straight as a grenadier's. "Will you gentlemen accompany me, please?" In the hall she said something in a low voice to the waiting maid. Ben Roderick, at the tail of the procession, followed them through the well-appointed hall, up carpeted oak stairs, and to a carved door on the second-floor hall. Mrs. LaFourche opened the door. A blaze of light flared out. "Make yourselves at home, gentlemen," she said, ushering them inside. "The champagne is *there.* It will be a moment or two longer." Then she was gone.

While Jellison applied himself to the champagne cork, Roderick looked about. The room was large and expensively decorated. In the center were soft settees upholstered in bright pastels. There was a large, low table occupied by a champagne cooler, glasses, a cigar box, more champagne bottles. At each end of the room was a large, comfortable-looking four-poster bed, equipped with tied-back hangings matching the rest of the décor. There seemed to be

a profusion of mirrors, doubtless to augment the illumination of the numerous candelabra. For that, Roderick saw himself reflected in a big mirror *beyond* the four-poster he was looking at.

"Dick . . . ." Roderick began.

"Wait." The cork popped, and Jellison was pouring champagne into—what was this—*four* glasses? "Here, Ben." Jellison handed Roderick a bubbling glass.

"Dick . . . ." Roderick's voice had sunk to a whisper. "Dick, is . . . is this a w——?"

"It is. And we are. And you shall."

"Oh!" Roderick looked about again, somewhat wildly.

"Here, now! A toast!" Jellison extended his glass. "I give you education—and the benefits it confers upon our youth, the hope of our fair Republic!"

From *The San Francisco Call,* June 10, 1874:

HUGGINS & CASEY CO.
NEW GOLD VENTURE

We are pleased to inform the public that the well-known firm of Huggins & Casey, 117 Fremont Street, announces it has acquired the property of the defunct Molly Pitcher Gold Mining and Milling Company, the mine being at the camp of Phonolite, near Bancroft, R.M.T. Huggins & Casey has announced its reorganization as the Molly Pitcher Mining Company, and is presently floating an issue of first-mortgage 8½% bonds, par value $1000, for certain surface capital improvements. We are given to understand that the bulk of the money realized is intended for construction of a narrow-gauge railroad from Bancroft to the camp of Phonolite. Despite the present tightness in the money market, Col. George Huggins anticipates no difficulties disposing of these obligations.

Our Fremont Street readers will recall that the original Molly Pitcher Company was first organized less than a year ago. Inadequate capitalization and the recent money panic which caused default on levied assessments among other things led to its precipitate failure. The first president, Col. J. S. Bloodworth, is now awaiting trial upon certain charges, following which the previous footage holders propose to have at him in the civil courts provided this turnip should prove worth the squeezing.

Cols. Huggins and Casey, whose firm originally bought and developed the Molly Pitcher location, have proposed to put Humpty Dumpty together again, having a higher opinion of him than did the discouraged friends of Col. Bloodworth. They state positively that no feet whatsoever are for sale. They offer only the above mentioned bonds and state that if the investing public does not care for their proposition, Huggins & Casey will lose no sleep over the matter. Seldom has this journal heard the clarion of wealth sounded so moderately. Our own inquiries reveal that the better-situated members of the Fremont Street brotherhood are reaching for the Molly Pitcher bonds faster than the Celestial reaches for his rice, they being already privately quoted $120 above par. A few persons, we hear, were "let in" at par, and we wish that we were as good friends to Cols. Huggins and Casey as these favored Elect.

Toward the end of our interview, Colonel Huggins gave us a brief look at the examination report on the Molly Pitcher, submitted by Prof. J. M. Dawson of Denver. The professor writes in moderate prose as befits a man of his eminent position, but he makes it clear that Huggins & Casey have acquired a bargain.

Finally, we were introduced to Mr. Richard D. Jellison, just admitted to a junior partnership in the firm following a sojourn among the Apache Indians who make the Arizona Territory so interesting for visitors. Mr. Jellison informs us that Arizona is full of copper, Gila lizards and deserving Rupublican office-holders whose room the National Administration prefers to their company in Washington City. He expressed the opinion that the Territory may have a great future, provided only that enough water and good people can be introduced there. Mr. Jellison, who appears to be a wit, refuted as slanderous the story that citizens of Yuma Crossing refuse to attend Divine Services, in the assurance that the Wrath to Come will prove cooler than their present circumstances. He states positively that the whole body politic of Yuma Crossing actually removed there, seeking a cooler climate than the ones they had left at home.

CHAPTER 5

1876
ARAPAHO CHARLEY SMITH

ITH THE COMPLETION of the narrow gauge to Phonolite the fair city of Bancroft took on new or enlarged functions. It became a rail transshipment point employing transfer men, clerks, and carters. The I.F.R&P. constructed a depot and freight houses and announced plans to build on westward—to where, exactly, the directors were vague. A hotel opened its doors: eight rooms, two beds to a room, two or more men to a bed, and all you could eat for fifty cents provided you weren't particular. The livery barn moved over from Empire. What gave Bancroft its biggest economic boost was a number of hog ranches occupied by people who would have fainted in shock had a pig actually entered the premises. These were frontier institutions of the sort that prevailed outside army posts and inside cow towns, dedicated to the proposition that a man and his money wanted to be parted as rapidly and efficiently as possible. Although the proprietors were prepared to use any device from cajolery to bung-starters to this end, their old reliables were faro, whisky, and girls, in that order of importance. The girls softened up the customers for the whisky, and the whisky softened them up for the faro bankers. On a good night when everything was running

smoothly, they could clean out a week's paycheck in one hour by the clock.

The basis of this hive of industry reposed on the fact that Phonolite, the cornucopia from whence these blessings flowed, had been decreed a "family camp." This was something rather less than a company town, something considerably better than a wide-open boom camp. The board of the Molly Pitcher had laid it down that Phonolite must be a decent place in which to bring up children. This meant no banked games, no girls, no short cons, and absolutely no exceptions. The rule was enforced by Police Officer Willard Ames, a company hireling who was vigorous in his duties, if not up to the last subtleties of constitutional due process. Faro bankers who tried to open a layout had their cases broken over their heads. Girls were treated with more civility but no less firmness. Itinerants who demonstrated no legitimate business were dealt with according to Ames's lights, ranging from a meal to a night in the one-room lockup. In any event, all were aboard the next train pulling out for Bancroft.

This is not to say that a tooth-gnashing Yankee Infant Damnationist would have equated Phonolite with Braintree or Concord Village. Some concessions were made by the board, but only of the sort that steady bachelors or settled family men could enjoy without remorse or too much wifely harping. Phonolite had two saloons. The Miners' Rest catered to the Cousins, and the Shamrock to the denizens of Corktown. These were quiet, club-like refuges devoted to political debate, saloon mining, and research into the laws of statistical probability as defined by the rules of draw poker. This last was a western institution so respectable that neither the Reverend Algernon S. Parley nor Father Aloysius Feeney ever dreamed of assailing it. The free lunch was nutritious, and the whisky, if not Kentucky's finest, was potable. And no lady, wife, or female had ever intruded upon the premises of either stronghold since their doors had opened, or ever would.

Phonolite had two competitive general stores, a respectable millinery shop, a boarding hotel, a one-room school, a volunteer fire department, two churches, and the above mentioned lockup.

Its civic policies were established by four aldermen and by the mayor, who doubled as police magistrate. If the aldermen were on the Molly's payroll and the mayor owned one of the general stores, then everyone in Phonolite, for that, was directly or closely dependent upon the Molly Pitcher. (An organizer from the Western Federation of Miners was to come through in the middle 'Eighties, take a look around, say, "Oh, hell!" and depart of his own volition. Phonolite clearly was unripe for the Revolution.) It should not be inferred that the camp was heaven on earth. No place housing over a thousand human beings could be. Hell, however, was not permitted to obtain an organized foothold.

Behind the peaceful façade things went on which even Officer Ames could not prevent. Father Feeney shook his head at some of the confessions he heard at Saint Barbara's. The Reverend Mr. Parley often sought strength and consolation in prayer. Husbands beat tired-out wives for announcing another pregnancy. Wives wept, surrounded by murmuring women, over coffins screwed shut before they left the mineyard and kept shut thereafter. Some women betrayed hard-working husbands, spent more money than they could afford, nagged, slapped their children, and deliberately stirred up trouble. Men got drunk at the Shamrock and the Miners' Rest, stole, sought out other men's wives, fist-fought, beat their children brutally. The children . . . were children. That is, the adults sighed at their behavior, predicted that no good could come, and were thankful when the sins of their offspring were not made public. Young people complained that there was nothing to *do* in Phonolite. More often than not marriages were celebrated hastily. Perhaps these last two issues were not unrelated.

However much the management desired otherwise, it was obligated to hire a certain number of social misfits who happened to be very good—some of them superb—at their work: tramp miners, itinerant railroaders, timbering crews, mill hands. The Molly required, directly or indirectly, fifty highly skilled trades. Such men, if competent, had to be taken on when there was need. Since these wanderers came and went at short intervals (barring those who hung around until the "Wanted" posters could age a little), there existed in Phonolite a floating population of over two

119

hundred hard-fisted, hard-working, hard-living sinners. They ranged the spectrum from violent youth to evil old age. On tally-and-pay night they required something more heady than the quiet calm that prevailed at Jack Spargo's Miners' Rest or Brendan Finnegan's Shamrock.

Therefore, clutching their pay envelopes, they made a wild dash from the headworks to the narrow gauge, just then pulling out for the evening run to Bancroft. To be sure, seventy miles back and forth is one hundred forty miles, but the narrow gauge was fairly dependable as such railroads went, and the prickings of the flesh made light of the distance. In a pinch—usually meaning a derailment—the train men could count on the enthusiastic assistance of a hundred hard cases capable of lifting the miniscule engine back onto the rails with their bare hands. Should the difficulty be more complicated, the revelers merely got off and walked, pushing ahead over the sagebrush flat to the bright lights, the shrill laughter, and the flat voices of the faro bankers.

The train puffed down from Phonolite more or less at 7:00 P.M. By 11:30 it was clicking over the switch points outside Bancroft. Despite the hour Bancroft would be alit and waiting. At 6:00 A.M. the next morning the train would return to Phonolite with most of the revelers aboard, dead beat, dead broke, and dead to the world. Now and then one of the returnees would be merely dead. It is a tribute of sorts to the skill and address of the Bancroft folks that they always returned Phonolite its corpses, though never the contents of their pockets. From time to time the superintendent of the Molly would complain hotly to the board about the Social Evil. Nothing was done or even proposed about it. As one board member remarked, "If we hired Bancroft wiped out tonight, there would be a worse gang there tomorrow."

Reasonably enough, the business community of Bancroft armed itself against reproaches with an ancient and effective set of rationalizations. "We're businessmen, same as any other," proclaimed Sweet Charley Smith, recognized as the leading pimp. His compeers, listening in sympathy, needed little convincing. "We sell service. Nobody's forced to come here. Nobody's, by God, forced to deal with us. It's a free country, and they can take it or leave it alone. We sell for cash, and we deliver the goods or we go out of business. Right? So these holier-than-thou tightwads say we ought to be run out. Why, if we was to go, there'd be a new gang here tomorrow night, and the place would prob'ly get a bad name." There were nods all around. The address was so well received that Smith wondered momentarily whether he ought to go into politics.

In this address, as in most self-gratulatory lectures delivered to appreciative gatherings of businessmen, there were elements of those half-truths which, accurate so far as they went, went only so far. In actuality Smith provided no direct service to the ultimate consumer; he left that up to his string of girls. He had confidence in their talents; otherwise they would not be working for him. His own contribution was managerial, albeit remarkably complex, demanding a recondite mixture of talent, intuition, and clinical experience. "Pimping ain't a skill, it's an art," Smith insisted. "A good pimp is born that way. All you got to do is set him on the right path and give him a few tips. A man ain't a born pimp, why he could work a hundred Kansas City girls and still go broke." There was much in what Smith said.

A pimp must, first and essentially, have a dark view of humanity in general and a despicable view of women in particular. Indeed, it helps greatly if he is just a touch attracted to his own gender. He must be vain as an actor, cold-blooded as a surgeon, mendacious as a diplomat, and self-righteous as a United States senator caught soliciting a bribe. Yet withal he must be sensitive to psychological need, capable of sensing the right moment to say the kind word, pat the back, or administer a black eye. His labors are dreary to a degree, for he must listen for hours to the most dismal feminine drivel without betraying boredom. Yet even then he is deprived of the consoling thought that each passing minute puts a dollar in his pocket. Worse, he must face his communicant directly, unable to snooze behind a notebook or close his eyes as if in appreciative contemplation. He must know when to dole out money (an act he hates), as well as to lay hands vigorously upon it (an act he loves, if he loves anything). He must never display hesitancy or lack of total self-confidence. Finally, he must be physically strong, mentally awake, and capable of preserving, protecting, and defending his string of girls against the wheedlings or blandishments of his colleagues.

His business rests firmly upon the axiom that women are a subhuman species good for only one thing, if, indeed, any are good even for that. Like other domestic animals bred to brainlessness, they must be managed for their own, as well as his, welfare. He fleeces them at regular intervals, moved by the thought that the possession of money only makes women restless and unhappy. He tends their fleshly and spiritual needs, herds them to fresh pasture, stirs them up when they require exercise, and chastizes them when they are unruly. Like any conscientious herdsman he must continually add fresh stock as he ruthlessly culls out the aged and worthless. His difficulties are multiplied by the customer, or John, who tends to be coarse, violent, rough on the merchandise, loudly critical, and prone to beat his bills. The John must then be soothed, intimidated, diverted, or cold-caulked as circumstances dictate. The pimp fights singlehandedly against a host of predators, all of whom are intent upon taking the bread from his mouth and the gold fillings from his teeth. If he has any potential ally, it is a tough, no-nonsense policeman who will stay bought. Unfortunately, even this costs him money, since a policeman will take out only so much in trade. He tells himself that he earns his living the hard way, and what politician could say him nay?

These lucubrations were occupying the mind of Sweet Charley Smith upon a Friday evening in Bancroft. Business was dull. He sat alone at a table in the Giant Powder Saloon, nursing a small beer and absently watching the bartender polishing and stacking six-ounce glasses—a Bancroft specialty. These glasses, into which the standard drink of fifty-cent bar whisky was poured for direct consumption, were especially molded for the trade. They looked and felt like regular six-ounce glasses, but their bottoms were so thick and were curved upward so cunningly that Mr. Jack Daniels himself could not push more than 3.5 ounces into any one of them. The whisky itself was compounded on the premises from an old family formula featuring renatured industrial alcohol, water, flavoring extract, and coloring matter. Lye soap was stirred in to

122

impart an attractive bead. The cost of this refreshment was the same as the real whisky available in Phonolite in full measure, but distance always lends attraction to the eye of the consumer.

Sweet Charley bent a lackluster gaze upon the bartender, who was now working up the free lunch for the evening to come. Charley wrinkled his lip in disdain. The ham was so green and the cheese so old and dry that the slices of each were almost indistinguishable. Twenty-six hours' further exposure to the air and flies would not improve them. Charley took it for granted that the boys from Phonolite had iron stomachs or that the bar whisky and the free lunch somehow fought each other to a standstill. He himself would not touch either, being a man of great concern for his own welfare. He caressed his gleaming silk cravat, fondled his massive gold watch chain, and gazed down with regard upon his tailor-made suit and hand-sewn, one-size-too-small patent-leather boots. Were it not for his coiffure, he might have been mistaken for a banker, and his fingers sensuously stroked the silky nap of the hundred-dollar John B., which he had removed after sitting down.

He reproached himself for idling away the hours. He had to make a decision now concerning the senior member of his troupe, Dirty Della. She said that her last name was LaFleur, but all the girls prettied up their names when they went on the turf.

Item: Della has been hitting the bottle even more than ever of late, and is suspected of working with her head in the bag, a practice strictly forbidden by Charley. Item: she is getting neither younger nor prettier, and there have been reproaches on both scores from Johns who ordinarily regard these considerations as secondary. Item: she is therefore not turning as many tricks as she ought, a serious matter. And item: she has developed the Old Joe again but will not follow the orders of the clap doctor Charley engaged for her at some expense. Conclusion: Della has got to go. Corollary: in what fashion and by what road?

Charley is here on firm ground. He must act tonight, for Della will expect him to wait until after tomorrow night's rush, and therefore be on her guard then. In about (he glances at his expensive hunting-case watch) two hours she will have finished

123

her nightly bottle and be out like a light. He will slip the barman and the bouncer a dollar apiece to swing her into a wagon, drive the wagon to the depot, and insert her into an empty boxcar. The I.F.R.&P. will pull out at 4:10 A.M. By the time Della wakes up, they will be rolling into Meade. Are there any flaws in the program? Charley cannot think of any. Della will not be put off the train prematurely by the shacks, since she can pay her fare with the same old ticket, and brakemen are not at all particular. Since Charley will have gone through her garters before departure, she will have no money to come back on and make a nuisance of herself. Where she will go from Meade is no concern of his. Smith nods. Foolproof, quiet, and easy, the way he likes things to run. "Hey, Billy," he calls to the barman, "another short beer here!"

The object of his thoughts, Dirty Della LaFleur, born Schmitzer, was at that moment regarding the last two inches of whisky in her quart bottle with the enormous clarity lent by alcohol. She had started drinking that evening to drown her growing apprehensions in regard to Charley. He hadn't been too kind to her recently; she sensed that she was not pleasing him as much as were the rest of the girls. But she resolved to do better tomorrow night, win back his favor, and therefore turned her mind as she always did at this stage to a minute review of her past. Her objective was to discover some point in her thirty-odd years where, had she done something different, things might have changed. Not that she was particularly unhappy with her life and vocation—just curious to determine whether she could have been somewhere else at this minute but in a crib in Bancroft.

Della had been born to the Schmitzer family on a southern Illinois farm. The people thereabouts had a saying, "There's scrubbing Dutch, saving Dutch, dirty Dutch—and Schmitzers." Well, her Pa hadn't been overfond of work, that was for sure, and her Ma was a match for him there. The worst house Della had ever worked in was a model of cleanliness and thrift compared to the old home place. Ma and Pa seemed to be good at only two things, drinking schnapps and whomping up kids in their old bed. Della was the fifth or sixth (she wasn't sure) of a dozen by the time she left home. Not good at housework, not smart at school, and already showing strong promise of her present homeliness, Della hadn't amounted to much until she blossomed out good when she was about fifteen. It was Ma who put the idea into her head to try for old Hunsecker, a well-to-do farmer who'd just buried his second wife. Della did her level best, and it worked real good. Up to a point. At that point, she found out why the Schmitzers were poor and old Hunsecker was rich.

"So," he'd said to Pa, "your daughter's bigged up. Why come to me?"

"You done it—you got to marry her," Pa had replied, with Ma nodding her head beside him, all ready to move in on Hunsecker.

"Now you listen to me," Hunsecker snarled. "First of all you can't law me—the age of consent in this state is fourteen, and she's fifteen. I checked up. Next, maybe I done it, and maybe I didn't, but my hired men will all swear that they had a run at her, too. And I wouldn't marry her even if she was smart, clean, and hard-working—which she ain't—because she is *so* goddamn ugly. So both of you can just quit making plans to turn this place into a hog wallow like the one you come from. One hog wallow in this county is enough. Now you get out of here before I kick all three of you down them steps."

Then, as they started to leave, Hunsecker changed her life, since otherwise Della would just have gone home and had the baby. "Here," he said, holding out a ten-dollar gold piece to her, "go to Chicago with this and get yourself fixed up or something." Surprisingly, Ma and Pa had let her go. Ordinarily they'd have taken the money and drunk it up. Maybe they were tired of looking at her.

In the Chicago depot, she'd not gone ten feet before she was gathered up by Auntie Aiken, who made her living casing the trains for fresh fish like Della. Knocked-up farm girls landing in Chicago were Auntie's business. She gave Della a meal, easily gained her confidence, and wormed her story out of her quick. Then she changed the subject slightly. "You love him?"

"No," replied Della. "He was old and smelled bad."

"You like what he did to you? How it felt?"

Della shook her head. "Didn't feel like much, one way er the other."

"You know that good-looking men pay money—for doing that with girls?"

"Honest?" Della gaped. "I'd sure like some money. I ain't got much."

Auntie Aiken deposited Della on Big Bill Bowler, chief whoremaster of Chicago and points west. "You won't believe this one," Auntie remarked, discussing Della as though she were a crate of eggs. "You won't even have to break her in. Dumb an' willing."

"She's got a bun in the oven," Bowler objected.

"Sure she does, but she can work for a while. Then we'll see."

"Here, you," Bowler said to Della. "Lay down over there and pull up your dress."

Della did it.

Bowler walked over. "Jesus, she's dirty!" he said in some disgust. Going back to his desk, he reached into a drawer. "Here, Auntie."

"Thanks, Bill." The old woman started out, looked over at Della, and said sharply, "Pull yer skirts down—ain't you got no shame?" Della did as she was told.

After that Della started work in Miss Willadee's house near the stockyards. She caught on soon and did what she was told although she did not care for the constant washing. After a while, when she got too big, she laid off but stayed on at Miss Willadee's. She had a baby but never saw it. Miss Willadee told her it was taken to an orphanage. Della didn't care much, one way or the other. A few other things happened. She was taken up by her first pimp. She got her first dose of the Old Joe.

"Cheer up, honey," said Lucille, her best friend. "It'll get better. You ain't really a working girl till you've had it three times."

"I wisht I didn't have it *once,*" Della snuffled. "It hurts like hell."

126

"A girl gets it good, she prob'ly won't catch another kid," said Lucille, pointing out the silver lining.

"Wouldn't mind that none. That hurt even worse."

Lucille went away, and Della missed her. Then she learned another lesson. Whisky soothed the cares away and let you sleep soundly. It made you feel good while you were awake, and you didn't get bad dreams toward morning. Della began to sop it up.

One day Miss Willadee sent for her and said, "I've got good news for you, Della. You're going out to work in a nice parlor house in Kansas City."

"Where's that, ma'am?" (Miss Willadee always insisted that her girls be polite.)

"Out west. Lots of free-spending cowboys go there. You'll like it. Hard work but good pay."

"Yes, ma'am. What's a cowboy?"

"You'll find out. Lord, you'll find out! They're all from Texas, and you can tell them by their great big belt buckles and little bitty tools. Now get packed."

"Yes, ma'am."

"You've been a good girl, Della," Miss Willadee said. "If only you wasn't so goddamn ugly. . . ."

Kansas City lasted a while. Then she went to Dodge. Then the places sort of blurred together. Now, she was—where? Della wasn't sure. "Make any dif'rence?" she mumbled, pulling up the soiled blanket. She decided it didn't, and let the soft darkness wash over her.

Back in the Giant Powder Saloon, Sweet Charley Smith looked at his watch again. Time to see Della aboard her side-door Pullman. As he reached for his John B., a muscular young man with a sharp face and sandy hair marched into the saloon. He spoke to Billy at the bar while Smith sized him up. By the dress, a mine worker from Phonolite, come in on the evening narrow gauge. By the face, one of those Missouri boys, tough and dirt-mean. Unlike most miners they had no compunctions about using their knives, front or back. The boy wheeled around and started in Smith's direction. Coming up to the table he stood spraddle-legged. "You

127

Smith, the pimp?" he asked in an ugly manner.

"What's it to you?" Smith replied. He eased back in his chair and tapped sharply three times on the table with a coin.

"I'll tell you what's it to me!" the boy snarled. "I went with one of your rotten whores last pay night, and she give me a dose, that's what!"

Smith stalled for time; in response to his signal Billy was coming, a sawed-off pool cue in his right hand. "My girls are clean," he said piously. "Must have been someone else's."

"I got it off that old sow Dirty Della," the boy pressed. "I learned you're her pimp. So I'm gonna stomp the liver out of you, and then I'm gonna stomp it outta *her!*"

Smith pulled his coat gun and leveled it at the boy. "Drop that knife!" he commanded. The boy did so. "Now, pick it up!" As the boy leaned forward, Smith let him have the side of the revolver along the skull. The boy dropped like a stone. Billy, seeing that everything was under control, strolled back, while Smith automatically leaned forward to go through the boy's pockets.

"Did I just see you lay that rascal out?" demanded a new voice.

Startled, Smith looked up. He blinked his eyes and looked again. Since he did not believe what he saw, he looked carefully a third time. Before him stood an apparition wearing a huge, silver-embroidered Mexican charro hat, so wide he would have to take it off to see what the weather was like. A pink-striped shirt and string tie were obscured by a beaded buckskin jacket whose innumerable long fringes made it look like a haystack in a storm. Striped city pants and elaborately tooled Texas boots reached from the jacket fringes to the sawdust. The apparition's hair was of womanly length and carefully curled, the mark either of a kill-crazy gunman or a certain notorious cavalry officer. In front of the face was a waxed Napoleon moustache and goatee. And around the waist of the jacket were belted two ivory-handled, nickle-plated pistols. Butts *forward,* for God's sake!

Recollecting his own pistol, Smith tucked it away. "Huh?" he asked.

"I just saw you buffalo that man!" the apparition said with

enthusiasm. "Neatest job I ever witnessed. Congratulations!" He thrust out his hand, which Smith automatically took. "It's fast-thinking men like you are making the West a fit place to live in. I'm Prong-Horn Arly Baker. Glad to meet you. Yes sir, I'm editor and owner of *Baker's Illustrated Weekly and Sporting News.*"

Smith relaxed somewhat. Baker's weekly was not unknown in the West wherever train butchers, barbers, billiard parlors, and the sporting element prevailed. It ran a cover illustration and story each issue, titled something like "The James Boys' Big Train Robbery, or the Detectives' Greatest Case." Inside there was more of the same, while the advertising columns ran heavily to gold chloride kidney medicines and remedies for Diseases of a Private Nature Stemming from Youthful Excess. Baker babbled on excitedly. "Are you the law here?" he demanded. "I didn't catch the name."

Smith thought that one over. Bancroft had no law as such, although codes of behavior were rigidly enforced by those whose business it was to see to them. To this extent he could correctly

assert that he was. But it did not seem quite right, somehow, to admit to being known as "Sweet." Thinking rapidly, he replied, "Yes, I'm the law. They call me Arapaho Charley Smith."

"I thought so," Baker bubbled on. "I have to get your story. Tell me how you came here. What you did before that. How many men have you killed?"

This was familiar ground to Smith. Johns were always asking his girls how they happened to go on the turf. Each girl had a story, calculated either to speed the John on his way or to work him for a tip. Well, if his girls could, he could. "I was just a farm boy," he began, "when I learned, kind of by accident, that I could *not* miss with a gun. Not even if I tried." He sipped his beer. "Then when the Quantrell gang came by our farm, during the war . . . ." It went on and on, but Baker was absorbing it without difficulty, not even diverted when Billy dragged the fallen boy out by the heels. There were Johns and Johns, Smith reflected, and this Baker was a John after his fashion, too. "So after I killed *him*," Smith concluded, "I had to lie low. It was self-defense, but he had too many friends. I came here—and here I am."

"You're wasted here!" Baker exclaimed. "A man with your nerve and record ought to go where the towns need taming. What ever happened here in Bancroft?"

What indeed? Smith thought.

"I have good friends in Hays. I'll wire them about you tomorrow. They'll put you up for a star there. It's a tough town—full of gamblers and Texans and bad women. They have a man for breakfast every morning."

Was this man serious? Smith asked himself. But the possibilities were enticing. All those gamblers and painted women would pay very well for some official protection. Very well indeed, especially if a man who knew their businesses inside and out was doing the protecting. "I admit I'm restless," Smith said reluctantly. "You sure they could swing it?"

"Sure, I'm sure. They need a good man. A man good with a gun."

Another problem. Smith was not at all good with a gun. Then he reflected that people and whores were much alike. One good lesson was what it took, like the way the girls quieted down after he had worked one of them over a little. Obviously he must kill a man or two right off to show he meant business. Given the right management, it could be done easily and in fair safety. Then the rest would know he had sand in his craw and conduct themselves accordingly.

"Shake on it, partner," urged Baker.

Their hands clasped again in the brief, firm grip that is the mark of the silent, courageous frontiersman.

"Now I'm going back to that flea trap and write up your story while it's still fresh in my mind," Baker said, rising. "Good night. I'll see you here in a day or so with the good news." He marched out as though preceded by the entire Sioux nation with war bonnets and tom-toms.

Wonder if he means it? Smith asked himself. He really hoped so. But in the meantime there was business to attend to. He walked over to the bartender, beckoned to the bouncer, and as their heads came together said, "I have a little job for you boys tonight after you close it up. You know Dirty Della? Now, here's what I want you to do. . . ."

Many, many years later the author Harold L. Butterworth (formerly of the *New York Evening Herald*) concluded the opening chapter of his classic biography, *Two-Gun Galahad: Arapaho Charley Smith, Law-Man Extraordinary,* with the ringing words:

> Thus, a chance meeting in a Bancroft bar-room set Smith's feet on the trail to Hays, Kansas, and to eternal glory. Fearless, considerate to the weak, relentless to the vicious, Charles Andrew Smith was now to begin a long career of imposing six-gun justice on the violent Old West. Hays, Abilene, Deadwood, and Tombstone would learn to fear—yes, and respect—this man of steel-blue eyes and chilled-iron nerves. Although to his credit he actually killed few men outright, he put the fear of God into many. The West would be a better place for Smith's work, which he himself regarded not as glamorous but as merely necessary. When he finally hung up his guns to write a little daily column for the *Denver Sun,* he often remarked, "A peace officer was only a kind of businessman. We gave the people service, and we delivered the goods or we went out of business." A refreshing thought from a courageous and unspoiled man.

131

CHAPTER **6**

1880
JOHN TRETHEWAY

MRS. TREGO KNOCKED FIRMLY
on the bedroom door, calling, "Wake 'ee, wake 'ee!" Leading
miner John Tretheway groaned, sensed the chill on his face, and
shoved an elbow into the ribs of his fellow boarder, Penhallow.
"Op, Ge-arge!" he commanded, swinging his legs out and feeling
under the bed for the vitrified bedroom companion. It was
pitch-dark in the room and colder than Presbyterian charity, and
the union-suited Tretheway did not delay unnecessarily in sliding
into his hickory shirt, pants, brogans, and blanket-lined jumper.
While Penhallow had his turn at the pot, Tretheway stumbled out
the door into the warm kitchen, where Mrs. Trego handed him a
pitcher of hot shaving water. There was a delicious smell in the air.
Mrs. Trego had been up for two hours, building the men's
croust-time pasties, which were now baking in the oven of the
kitchen range. Gulping a cup of scalding tea, Tretheway took the
water back to his and Penhallow's half-room. Penhallow had the
candle lit by now, and the two of them lathered up to shave elbow
to elbow, grimacing before the scabrous mirror and ignoring the
upper lip completely.

Back in the kitchen, Tretheway and Penhallow were joined at

132

table by the two other boarders. One was young Polwheal, American-born, whose broad shoulders marked him as a promising miner. The other was old Uren, ancient of days, pumpman at the Molly Pitcher. Uren had learned his trade at Deep Pool a generation past and had tended pitwork everywhere from Cuba to Italy without becoming in the slightest degree assimilated. The men gabbed away—Cornishmen were never noted for taciturnity—but Tretheway observed young Polwheal and Mary Trego occasionally exchanging glances. Poor Dick Trego had been killed a year ago when his machine man drilled into a missed hole; the machine protected the driller somewhat, but Trego was forward of the Burleigh as chuck tender, and the flying muck cut him to pieces. The Odd Fellows gave Dick a fine funeral to be sure, but that was poor consolation to his widow, who was left with three young'uns and no income. Mary Trego turned her three-room "shotgun" dwelling into a boardinghouse, taking the four miners into a divided bedroom while reserving the kitchen for herself and the front room for her still-sleeping sprats. With hard work she was making ends meet. She was still young (though a bit tired-looking), Polwheal wanted a wife, and Tretheway half-suspected that come the spring there would be a wedding at the Methodist Church. Then it would be time for him and the others to look for other lodging should they still be working up on the hill behind Phonolite.

The four men plowed swiftly through a hearty Cornish breakfast and a gallon of tea, while Mary Trego poured more tea into the tank-like lid compartments of their lunch buckets and drew the four sputtering pasties from the oven. These were oval-shaped meat-and-vegetable pies. One to a man, they would be popped into the bottom of the buckets and later consumed with hands and teeth during the thirty-minute croust break at the level station. Since it was going on 6:00 A. M., the four men rose, slid into fleece mackinaws hanging inside by the back door, pulled on stiff felt hard hats, and clattered in hobnailed brogans down the wooden back steps. Three headed for the mine road through the windy, arctic dark; Polwheal joined them after a few paces, having lingered for a swift kiss behind the kitchen door. Tretheway frowned in disapproval. These young folk had little shame! It was probably the influence of American ways, for there was a more becoming modesty in courtship back in Dolcoath, as he remembered it.

The frozen ruts of the mine road, coming to be named Casey Street, accommodated other small knots of men. Those coming down off the night shift walked silently with the flat-footed gait of fatigue. The upward-bound groups were soon augmented by a noisy procession trooping in from the path from Corktown, above which loomed the steeple of Saint Barbara's, the largest building in Phonolite. Tretheway overheard fragments of their conversation. "Home rule," "Gladstone," and "Hancock" predominated. He shrugged. He was a Garfield man himself, as were all the other Cousins in the camp. The men ahead of him veered unexpectedly to the right, paused, and then marched on. Tretheway wondered what had excited their curiosity. Ten yards farther on he saw in the ditch a nearly naked human body. He also stepped out of the rut, but one glance at the ragged breechcloth, the tattered blanket, and the empty bottle told their own story. Somehow one of the handful of Indians who hung around the camp begging had managed to get some whisky. Fresh off the boat, twenty years ago, Tretheway might have thought of offering help. Now he too stepped back in the road and continued upward.

Through the gate, past the incline headframe and the office buildings, over the gravel of the mine yard Tretheway made his accustomed way. The yard was full of activity, conversation, and light—all of it so familiar that he paid no attention to anything but his own business, that being to load an empty mine car with necessary equipment and get it and himself to the shaft headframe in time to avoid a bad mouth from the dayshift cager. So intent was he that he nearly walked over the boy Albert Bolitho, newly added to his crew as tool nipper. The lad was gaping about entranced. His nostrils were twitching from the wood smoke from the pump, compressor, and hoist boilers mingled with the spicing of steam cylinder oil and a whiff of coal smoke from the blacksmith shop. He seemed dazzled by the glare of boiler fires as they were stoked and was staring in fascination at the high upcast column of white

135

vapor rising above the shaft platform. " 'Ere, lad," Tretheway beckoned. " 'Op h'over to they magazine h'and fetch one box h'of machine powder. Bring 'er 'ere. Then go back h'and get . . . ." The boy nodded and made off, followed by Tretheway's injunction to tell them buggers Riley and O'Leary to get wedges and lard oil before they met him at the shaft platform.

Taking an empty car spotted near the smithy, Tretheway pushed it over to the racks of newly sharpened drill steel, protected from the weather by the smithy's overhanging eaves. He helped himself to starters and changes sufficient for sixteen holes. "Eh, Ephraim," he greeted the boss smith inside, a large man tying on his huge leather apron. "They damn machine be right?" This question was in reference to the level's Burleigh drilling machine, a comparatively new invention that had begun to eliminate the hand drilling that had so broadened the shoulders of hard-rock miners everywhere. Ephraim, a transplant from rural Vermont, nodded. "Ay-yuh." After this outburst of conversation, the smith turned away to the pile of dulled steel dumped by the night shift, slid the bit ends of several steel into the forge, and nodded to his helper on the bellows. Tretheway was somewhat, but only somewhat, relieved. Hauling a repaired machine down to the face was hard work, but he also knew that if the machine had not broken down during the night shift it would probably do so during his own, perhaps losing the crew an hour.

Men began to congregate under the headframe. The day-shift boss was circulating, counting noses and making reassignments to fill in vacancies of the crews. Tretheway's men drifted up one by one. Bill Bolitho, chuck tender and father of the tool nipper, handed Tretheway three candles and a glassed lantern. Tretheway knotted the wicks of two through the buttonhole of his jumper pocket, lighted the third at a lard-oil lamp, and inserted it into the lantern. A sound overhead indicated that he had a few moments yet, for there came to his ears a soft rustle as the hoist man began a test run of the empty cage down to the sump and back—his first duty when coming on shift. He then had to lower three other crews to deeper development levels before it was Tretheway's turn. Therefore, John walked over to glance at the board displaying the drift assays of the previous day. Strictly speaking, this was none of his business, but the more a miner knows the better it is for him. Although Tretheway was barely able to write his own name, he quickly found the assays for the three-hundred-foot level. As he had suspected, samples taken from the left side of the heading were distinctly leaner than were those from the center and the right-hand side. This meant that some adjustments in his drilling pattern would be needed. The shifter would confirm, but it would be best to be set up for it before his arrival.

Out of the corner of his eye Tretheway saw old Uren working his way around the pump engine with an oil can. It had stood idle during the night, but the Molly had apparently made enough water in the last twelve hours to require a start-up. Uren threw a few sticks of cordwood into the firebox, opened the damper, and checked the boiler gauge cocks. He nodded his head in satisfaction as water spurted steaming from the third-lowest. The night man had been on the job, keeping the boiler full and steam up. Uren put away his oil can and cracked the throttle. There was a soft clink and hissing from the valve gear. The walking beam inclined, and the flywheel began to turn, ever so slowly. As more steam was admitted to the vertical cylinder, the flywheel speed increased, although Tretheway could still follow its spokes around with his eye. The large bull gear rotated, and the triangular bob hanging over the pump compartment started to tip upward in a dignified manner. Uren was content but kept his hand near the throttle while rising mains and valve casings filled solidly with water. The huge timber pump rod hanging from the nose of the bob slid upward, paused, and then eased down. After a dozen strokes—perhaps two minutes—a gush of water could be heard entering the wooden flume that led it away from the vicinity of the headframe. Uren adjusted the throttle, caught Tretheway's eye, and pointed significantly to the shaft platform. Tretheway turned back, his hobnails ringing on the sheet-iron flooring.

Car, crew, and cage were about ready. John glanced into the car, making a final check of its contents. Drill steel, lunch buckets, a burlap sack of timbering wedges, a wooden case of dynamite, a reel of safety fuse, and a small, innocuous-looking box containing fifty blasting caps were mingled with a miscellany of other items. Tretheway fussed with the box of caps; he had seen much and heard more of what carelessness with that little object could do. "Damn 'ee, h'Albert!" he reprimanded the tool nipper, " 'ee forgot they dirt box. 'Op to h'it!" The tool nipper rushed back to the secluded region where empty candle boxes filled with dirt were provided to be carried down to the level station for the accommodation of occasions of nature. Turning to the toothpick-chewing toplander, Tretheway remarked, "H'after croust, usn's'll be wanting h'a set h'and collar braces. H'I'll send yon lad to 'elp 'ee." The toplander nodded, letting it go in one ear and out the other. Tretheway made a mental note to fire a shot under the worthless, ten-day clot when the shifter came down; the lander was a lazy bugger, always having to be told everything twice.

A distant bell tinged, and the cage rose six more feet. The cager stepped out from the lower deck. He was given a hand to push the loaded car onto the stub tracks of the deck. Then the cager reached over and pulled once smartly on the bell cord adjacent to the shaft framing. The cage eased down until the upper deck was again level with the platform. Riley, O'Leary, and Bill Bolitho stepped on, turning like soldiers right and left to face the timber guides. At that moment the tool nipper stumbled up, clutching an odoriferous wooden box. His father beckoned to him, putting an arm about his shoulders. Tretheway entered, executing a shuffling right face. Last came the cager, who lowered the safety bar and in the same moment grasped the bell cord. In the distant, darkened hoist house two bells struck, then one more, calling the three-hundred level. Then one bell, and Tretheway took a firm grip on the cage stanchion as the deck seemed to fall away from beneath his feet.

Instantly it was all windy, rushing darkness, illumined only by the flicker of the single candle protected by Tretheway's lantern. Free fall clutched at his stomach, but was ignored. The smells changed as abruptly as had the transition from light to dark. There was moist warmth, the acrid taint of dead powder smoke, rock dust, and over all the indescribable dry odor of fungus-dripping timber. Tretheway carefully catalogued them with his nose. All were familiar and consequently of no moment, but mine fires usually start at shift end and gain momentum disastrously in the hour when the workings are relatively deserted. He sniffed gently for the deadly scent of wood smoke. There was none. To that extent then he could relax.

The deck of the cage pressed against the crew's feet as the hoist man far above eased on his brake. The dim light of a station oil lamp appeared. The cager lifted the safety bar for the crew to shuffle into the station. They produced iron candle holders and got a light from the oil lamp, but Tretheway preferred the old Cousins' method of fixing his own candle to the front of his hard hat with a lump of sticky clay. The cager brought up the equipment car, which was dragged out onto the turnsheet flooring the station. Lunch buckets were removed. In the station was a plank from which several round palisades of drift pins protruded. Snuffs, or half-used candles, would be lit just before croust time, fixed in the center of the rings of spikes, and the top sections for the tea of the lunch buckets set atop the nailheads in the manner of a chafing dish to warm up the contents. The powder and blasting accessories were carried to a dry niche in the wall to await their time. Hand tools and the Burleigh and its column, left in the station by the night shift, all went in the car. Mackinaws and jumpers were discarded, hung high on convenient nails. The cager and cage departed. It was time to go to work.

Two years before, the Molly Pitcher had shown signs of dying on its feet as the better ore near the surface was exhausted, and some small exploration had found only low-tenor sulphide ore below. Huggins, Casey & Jellison had then brought in young Wilbur Smith, a brash but well-trained engineer, who had proceeded to rejuvenate the dying after the gospel preached in the *Bergakademie* at Freiberg. He had abolished hand drilling and brought in the new Burleighs. He had sold off the old concentrator and demanded an assessment to install an up-to-date concentration mill. Exploration had revealed a series of sulphide orebodies which were now being developed enough to pay current expenses while Smith planned ahead to stope it out as soon as he knew for sure what the Molly had and where it was. Tretheway was grateful that life was being breathed again into "his" mine—he and thousands like him had been forced to leave Cornwall, where the adventurers preferred to close the tin setts rather than invest new money in new methods.

The four men took turns, two by two, pushing the car down the drift, while Albert Bolitho walked ahead to give them some light. The smell of dead powder grew stronger. Iron pipe hung from the timber sets, the pipe bottoms seeming to display drips of water miraculously petrified; actually this was silica gel, deposited by the evaporation of slow seepage through the granite hanging wall. Tretheway paid no mind to this phenomenon but a great deal of attention to the tunnel sets as they passed by each. The Molly was in sound country-rock, granite above and schist below. Nevertheless, air slaking or blast vibration could insidiously loosen a wedge-shaped block of granite, which, if not restrained temporarily by the sets, might fall without warning. Before it went, however, it would bow the cap timber downward, the wood popping or knocking at measured intervals as the stress came on. Sight and sound were enough to give warning well in advance of the fall, provided one was careful to check daily. Likewise, big lateral ground movements, often initiated by incautious stoping elsewhere, first gave notice by throwing the post timbers out of alignment. Like the hoist man's preliminary trip of the empty cage (another way of detecting such trouble, for a cage that sticks in the guides indicates moving ground in a shaft) a degree of forewarning enabled the miners to prevent worse things: once the ground starts to move, it is very difficult to stop it. And Tretheway had not mined—and lived—for the past twenty years by neglecting small details.

The fifty-yard length of the lateral drift ended in the working chamber, the left side of which was encumbered by a large pile of shattered ore lying upon the iron muck sheet. The crew pulled the car forward off the tramming rails and began unloading, while Tretheway went forward to inspect the effects of the last drift round. After a careful examination he nodded in satisfaction; Tregaskis, the lead man on the night shift, was a good miner. He had left a deep, clean corner or vertical niche in the left half of the face, into which Tretheway's shift-end round could move the next block of ore. (Few of the uninitiated realize it, but when rock is blasted there must be space into which it can move freely in order to gain the maximum effect.) There were no humps. indicating holes which missed fire, or conical "gun pocks" of overloaded holes. Tregaskis apparently had informed himself, too, of the assay results, for the corner was perceptibly to the right of normal, indicating that the drift was being prepared to be bent toward the more profitable side of the orebody. Finally, the extreme right of the face was almost free of loose muck, allowing Tretheway and Bolitho to set up for drilling immediately. It was a real pleasure to follow a good crew; some, whom Tretheway would not have named, would have buggered up the whole job, either out of slackness or merely in order to put more ore in the box than their due share and so leave a rough setup for the other shift.

"Eh, then . . . ." Tretheway's voice was pleased. "T'will be a good spell. Yon Tregaskis h'is not so bad h'as Saint Just men go. Riley, 'ee h'and O'Leary clean op 'ere first so Bill h'and me can set she bloody column. Bolitho-lad, bring op h'air 'ose h'and then fetch usn's water bucket from they station. Now 'ere's 'ow we do she. . . ." In a few words Tretheway outlined the order of business, using a prospect pick to sketch the drilling pattern on the face of the quartzite. The vein matter was distinct in color and texture from the country rock, looking somewhat like a band of coarse, crystalline sand that had been halfheartedly cemented together. Very close inspection would have revealed tiny bits of brassy mineral scattered throughout the ore. This was the pyrite, carrying very small—indeed, microscopic—grains of gold. The problem was that the valuable minerals were not at all evenly distributed throughout the quartzite but at this level tended to be confined to an indistinguishable "shoot," or zone of higher concentration roughly centered along the lower edge of the vein matter. The assays indicated that this ore shoot had here begun to veer somewhat to the right. The miners must bend the drift to follow it or else shortly be loading marginal ore.

Tretheway and Bolitho wrestled with the brutal weight and awkward length of the drill column, setting it upright with

141

wooden blocks above and below and then extending its jack screws to wedge it solidly into position. Wood fibers crunched, and the men panted as they heaved on the bars in the jackscrew capstan holes. The steady scrape of scoops over sheet iron indicated that Riley and O'Leary were fanning the muck pile. From time to time one team or the other needed additional help, and it was given ungrudgingly. It required three men to set the Burleigh on the column; O'Leary dropped his scoop and stood beside Bolitho. Their arms strained at the machine as Tretheway set up the bolts on its arm. A few minutes later he abandoned his machine to give the muckers a hand with rerailing a loaded ore car. Nursing the top-heavy car, loaded with one ton of rock, onto the rails from the turn sheet was a job that three could do better than two. Riley departed, pushing the car to an assembly point, where the trammer and his mule could pick up a train of five and haul them to the transfer raise to be dumped. Down at the foot of the raise was an ore pocket tended by a chute puller. When the skip came down, he would load five tons of ore directly into it by gravity.

Escaping air hissed sharply as the high-pressure hose was connected to the Burleigh. Bolitho slid a short, stumpy steel into the chuck and heaved on the chuck wrench. Tretheway pun the crank of the machine's feed screw, and the starter slowly inched forward to touch the mark for the first hole, a high, deep, top edger, angled decidedly out and away from the axis of the drift. Young Bolitho set down a battered water bucket beside the pile of changes that his father had leaned up, bits down, in a sheaf against the face. Just as Tretheway was ready to turn on the air, there was an interruption. The shift boss, old Chenoweth, gray-bearded and pot-bellied, tapped him on the shoulder. "Be 'ee ready to go, John?" he asked. Not waiting a reply, he glanced keenly at the face, the setup, the general situation in the working chamber. Chenoweth had mined tin as a lad in Cornwall, copper at Houghton in his middle years, and western gold in his gray hairs. What he did not know about mining was not worth knowing, and good man though Tretheway was, he stood respectfully before this fountain of wisdom. Tretheway was aware, however, of the hard, racking cough that plagued the shifter. Chenoweth had miner's consumption, knew that he had it, and knew that no man recovered from it. But with the fatalism of a soldier he would work uncomplaining until he died.

"Deep enough," Chenoweth at length pronounced. Tretheway had anticipated his wishes well, and Chenoweth had less expert crews to supervise. Producing his dog-eared notebook from the side pocket of his jumper, he licked the end of a pencil stub and laboriously scribbled therein. The three-hundred-level crew was present and fit for duty, the work was going well, and he cabalistically noted Tretheway's representations about the general worthlessness of the toplander. Chenoweth privately decided to give the lander his time and send him down the hill talking to himself, but not for another day or two. He also decided to commend this crew to young Smith. About Smith, Chenoweth had professional though not personal misgivings. It was unnatural that mining should be learned from books and test tubes instead of the end of a doublejack, but in his heart of hearts Chenoweth admitted that Smith had somehow done wonders for the development. Perhaps the lad had a touch of Cornish blood. Now that would explain it! The old shifter padded off, his candle flame bobbing atop his hard hat.

Tretheway sighted along the piston drill and turned on the air. The relative silence heretofore was now rent by the harsh, ear-jarring chatter of steel ramming into hard rock, a hissing clatter that would continue for hours. Bolitho stood forward of the machine, four-pound hammer in hand, to knock the steadily rotating, spark-throwing steel loose if it showed any tendency to hang up in the hole or to rap it back in line should it drift off sideways before it got properly collared. Tretheway delicately played the feed crank, relying upon feel, sound, and experience to keep the bit well up to its work without crowding. The octagonal drill stock appeared to shorten as the hole deepened. In a short while he turned off the air and retracted the machine, and Bolitho unbolted the chuck. A somewhat longer and more slender change steel with a slightly smaller bit was inserted and clamped tightly. While Tretheway cranked the machine forward, Bolitho bent

143

down and tossed water from a rusty can into the hole, dampening down the silica dust generated. The air was turned on again, and the clamor recommenced.

For the next three hours there was little variation in the work pattern. Riley and O'Leary filled car after car as Tretheway and Bolitho drilled. Hole after hole was sunk into the face and cleaned, and the machine was moved to a new point lower on the column. The men perspired heavily and paused to unbutton the necks of their union suits, pushing the tops down to work naked to the waist. Young Albert Bolitho came and went, bringing this and taking that; he received only $1.00 a day, in contrast to his seniors, who received up to $3.50, but he was also learning a trade. Since the boy seemed interested and willing, it would not be long before Tretheway would let him get the feel of the Burleigh, and, strictly as a great personal concession, Riley allowed the boy to muck one carload for himself. Tretheway's stomach told him that it was approaching croust time.

Suddenly the noise of the machine changed timbre. Tretheway frowned. He spun the hand crank forward, then backward. Bolitho stepped up with the hammer, but the machine man shook his head and turned off the air. The panting muckers leaned on the handles of their scoops as Tretheway began to back the drill out of the low-set hole.

"Shanked th' steel?" O'Leary asked. (In that age of rule-of-thumb metallurgy and tempering with the unaided eye, broken drill steel was common.)

"Nay. Feels like she vug. Bolitho, do 'ee put they next change in she noisy old bitch." When this had been done, Tretheway probed forward with the feed crank and then made a measurement with his eye. "H'about two hand spans deep. H'about a foot down they 'ole."

"No vug h'im rock like this," Bolitho objected.

"Then maybe the Little People done it," Riley offered. The debate, however, was a cover for deep collective thought. A geode or natural cavity in a stratum such as this is almost always lined with crystals of some sort. Usually these are beautiful but worthless glass-clear quartz. If there is appreciable iron and manganese present, the quartz might be lavender to deep purple shot with red glints, and thus be semiprecious amethyst. But this vug was within the invisible portion of the ore shoot and occasionally, just *occasionally* . . . .

Tretheway made up his mind. "Be h'a bit of h'extra work, but are 'ee game?" There was a general nod. Tretheway contemplated the drilling pattern. "'Elp me put a 'ole 'ere, Bill, and t'other, 'ere. Riley, do 'ee go back an' fetch one stick of powder, two caps, h'and h'about h'a fathom of fuse. Tell they tool nipper to keep 'is eyes h'open h'and 'is gob shut." The men went about their labors in a new and faster rhythm. Two short holes were hastily collared and drilled with O'Leary's help. The muckers assisted a quick take-down of the machine and column, piling everything breakable into the car, while Tretheway and Bolitho busied themselves at the face. Bill Bolitho broke the stick of powder in two and slit the paper wrapping of each half, while Tretheway crimped blasting caps with his teeth on each end of the fathom of fuse. Each half stick was primed and prodded into its hole with a wooden loading stick and quickly stemmed with a handful of damp drill cuttings. Tretheway cut into the center of the fuse to expose the powder core. "Push they tool car back summat," he commanded, "then go h'eat." As the car and men retreated up the drift, he held his candle to the exposed powder in the safety fuse. In a few seconds it spat a stream of sparks and then began burning both ways. Satisfied, he rose and stalked down the drift after his men.

They had not quite reached the level station when there was a light double knock, followed quickly by a low boom. The candle flames wavered momentarily. In silence the men reached for their lunch buckets and removed their drink containers from the burning snuffs that Albert had lit at the beginning of his sentry-go. The Cousins started work on their tea and pasties, while the Irishry enjoyed coffee, boiled potatoes, and roast-beef sandwiches. These were consumed while the men were seated on the reclining planks that were the station's furniture. Afterward, as the comfortable rumbles of digestion began, the men would stretch out on the planks, using timber blocks as pillows. They were the very picture of honest industry as the cage stopped at their level.

145

Old Chenoweth stepped off, indicating with a lordly gesture that the cager should hold the cage for him.

"Knew h'I 'eard a small shot," the shifter remarked, sniffing the fresh powder smoke in the ventilation draft. He did not have to add that an explanation was in order and that it must be an uncommonly convincing one.

Tretheway, however, was already prepared for this. "Damn change fitchered," he said, affecting irritation. "Couldn't knock she loose, so put down two short 'oles to blow she out."

Chenoweth's eyes narrowed slightly, but he retained his air of benevolence. "Aye." A change of steel firmly jammed into its hole could be a decided nuisance *if* it was in a spot strategically essential to the blasting sequence. Usually, though, the machine could be moved a trifle, a new hole driven alongside the lost one, and the steel would come out none the worse with the shift-end round. Tretheway was too good a lead man to go to a good deal of extra trouble without some cogent motive. Chenoweth's mind was working rapidly, and he noticed that the crew was unusually silent. Too late, Riley and O'Leary began a political wrangle. That settled it. The gray shifter took his leave, with the intention of returning just as soon as he could. The last words he heard as he stepped onto the cage were, ". . . an' th' best way to settle the Irish Question is, as everyone knows, simply to let us Irish do as we please." The old shifter snorted cynically. In his opinion it would serve the Paddies right to give Ireland back to them.

" 'Yon old bugger'll be back in 'alf-h'our," Bolitho predicted sourly. " 'E smells more'n what's in yon candle box."

Tretheway shrugged. Some problems simply had to be waited out. He relaxed on his plank, allowing knotted muscles to smooth out. Alertness returned abruptly. What was Riley up to? The mucker was talking to young Bolitho in a persuasive tone, O'Leary chiming in at intervals. "Then ye see, me lad, how it is. Th' grease is needful, and Oi have none by me. So do you ride up with th' cager and go to Murphey, him who's in the timber yard, and ask him for a bucket of mucking grease f 'r th' turn sheet."

"Do that indeed," O'Leary urged. "T'is dreadful hard wurrk itherwise, but th' grease makes the muck-sticks slide easier.

Haven't ye seen how we've sweated over th' muck pile without it? An' Oi can't think f'r th' life iv me why even a Galway man like Riley, which iv'ryone knows is stronger in th' back than in th' head, would be after f'rgettin' our muckin' grease."

The boy was taking all this in, evidently impressed. He turned to Tretheway, and, as he did, Riley raised his head to deliver a massive wink at the lead miner. Tretheway thought it over and looked at Bill Bolitho. Bill shook his head imperceptibly. "Tomorrow, Riley," Tretheway decided. " 'Ee h'extra work'll learn 'ee not to forget she again. Bolitho, lad, 'op h'out h'and start they car down to face. Usn's'll catch op with 'ee in a bit."

As soon as the tool nipper had gone, Tretheway rounded on Riley in controlled anger. "Damn 'ee, ye Galway loon! Such a prank might be h'all right at grass. In the wheals, no! A few of such, and yon lad'll not believe a word 'ee say. Nay, nor usn's neither! Then, come fire or fall, 'e'll take 'is time to summon aid, and mayhap usn's all be dead then. I would not 'ave h'it on my 'eadstone that I be killed by a Paddy's witless pranks!" Riley offered to object, but thought better of it after a look at Tretheway's stern expression. As a good leader should, Tretheway refrained from rubbing it in worse, but changed the subject. "Time's op. An' smoke h'is clear. Let's see what usn's 'ave before they shifter stops off again."

There was some coughing as the crew arrived at the face, but the men ignored the sting of the powder smoke as Tretheway hunkered down over the small heap of muck blasted out by the two holes. He turned over ragged chunks of quartzite, finally coming up with a piece whose concave side was lined with tabular crystals of metallic-silver luster. "White iron!" Bolitho cried in disgust. Arsenopyrite is a worthless variety of fool's gold.

"Nay, bide a bit," Tretheway cautioned. Knocking a single crystal free, he weighed it in his palm and then brought it closely to his eye, turning it this way and that. As Bolitho continued to grumble, Tretheway slyly asked, "Then can h'I 'ave 'ee's share?" Bolitho's mouth snapped shut, and his hand came out. The crystal felt remarkably massive. Embedded in one silvery plane were minute, rather smeary golden-yellow squares whose edges lay

askew to the over-all structure.

"Ah, John, 'ee knows ore!" Bolitho exclaimed in admiration. The muckers crowded up, passed the specimen among themselves, and grinned broadly. The arsenopyrite was rich with native gold.

"Now, haste, before Chenoweth comes!" Tretheway warned. The men fastened upon the small pile, sorting with the speed of avarice. Tretheway snatched off his hat and laid it crown down on the turn sheet as a receptacle for the high grade. Leaving the men to sort the muck, he took hammer and moil and went to work chipping out the surface of the portion of the vug that remained at the bottom of the conical hole they had blasted out. He brushed and scraped until the chief part of his chippings had fallen into the sagging hat. Handing it by the brim to the tool nipper, he said, "Bolitho, lad, back to 'ee level station and dump she in my lunch bucket. Get 'ee gone, now! And now usn's set up and start they hole again. And, Riley, pat down this muck and get 'er in car and covered h'up in a 'urry!"

As the men panted in their haste, Bolitho asked, " 'Ow much may she go, John?"

"Mayhap fifty dollars each, give or take summat. H'I'll carry she to h'Upton's assay 'ouse—'e don't ask no questions. Take h'up on yon bolt!" Albert Bolitho scurried up and clapped Tretheway's hat on his head, while the muckers frantically fanned broken ore into the car to hide the evidence.

Sighing in relief, Tretheway was actually turning on the air to the Burleigh—a minute of drilling would destroy the last vestiges of the vug—when Old Chenoweth strolled into the chamber. He was grinning. Tretheway gritted his teeth and started the Burleigh pounding anyway, but Chenoweth held one gnarled index finger under his nose in the traditional sign from doublejack days to stop drilling. Silence fell. The shifter said nothing but held his candle to the blast hole. Satisfied, he then stooped and slowly waved his light back and forth across the particles of rock lying on the turn sheet. O'Leary sighed audibly.

Unable to stand the continuing silence, Tretheway murmured, "One share?"

Chenoweth shook his ancient head, coughed, and asked, "Going to give 'ee tool nipper a share?"

Tretheway had not even thought of Albert, but in circumstances like this the Old Rule has always been share and share alike. "Aye."

"Then h'I'll take only one quarter. A good crew like 'ee be hard to find."

O'Leary sighed again, but with a measure of relief. Official detection in high-grading meant instant dismissal, perhaps even a brief term in the slammer. Chenoweth had them over the barrel, and a meaner man would have hogged a half of the booty. In any event the shifter was in it with them now, and could ensure that no lunch bucket search would be made at the end of the shift. While the mine-run ore of the Molly Pitcher was too low to incite systematic high-grading—barring freaks of nature such as they had just encountered—the crews were forever carrying off bits of material and equipment that the spot searches were intended to discourage.

"See 'ee on top at tally, John," Chenoweth concluded, the negotiations ended. "We walk down to h'Upton's together." It was not that the shifter did not trust Tretheway, but two old hands could strike a better bargain than could one. Riley opened his mouth, evidently intending that Ireland as well as Cornwall be represented. He closed it again as it occurred to him that three men from the same shift—two from the same level, for that—entering Upton's seedy assay house in company would provide evidence from which camp gossip would draw swift and accurate conclusions. The old shifter nodded to all and took his leave.

The work commenced again. The men had lost time and still had much to do. The hole was bottomed, the column moved back, and the lifter hole in the series drilled. While hunkered down, cleaning the hole with his miner's spoon, Tretheway heard the mucking cease simultaneously with the sound of strange voices. A quick stab of anxiety ran through him, particularly when a glance over his shoulder revealed young Smith, the mine superintendent. Smith was holding a lantern to the face, while beside him stood a newcomer, writing in some sort of notebook. The visitor

151

was a short, pouter-pigeon-shaped man clad in a new jumper, fine broadcloth trousers, and unmuddied boots. He was cocking an ear to Smith's earnest explanations. Since these were conducted in scientific—as opposed to working—mining talk, three parts of it were pure gibberish to Tretheway.

He continued to scrape with the spoon while sorting out the possibilities. The visitor was not the law, that was sure. He was not fat, nor did he cultivate the luxuriant side whiskers affected by promoters and financiers. Few or none of these came underground anyway, preferring to stope people's pockets, mucking off mahogany. The wee man seemed to understand what Smith was saying, and his moustache was trimmed closely in outland fashion. A "professor" therefore, or mining expert of similar kidney, was Tretheway's conclusion. He could therefore dismiss the visitation as a mere coincidence.

A moment later the professor opened his mouth to emit a stream of incomprehensible questions, phrased in the stuffiest of old-school-tie British-English. Smith did not appear to resent being patronized, but Riley and O'Leary stiffened and looked at each other significantly. Here, delivered up unto them, was a living, breathing specimen of the very class which every expatriate Irishman itched to lay hands upon! His presence here was also now explained. Some British syndicate was perhaps negotiating to buy footage in the Molly Pitcher, and the professor had been retained by them to examine and evaluate the mine. Since the development was a sound one, Tretheway did not doubt that the Britishers would get their money's worth. On the other hand, they would probably not see one cent of profit. The English, so miserly at home, seemed obsessed by the idea that they could pay nearly what the mint and smelter returns on the blocked-out ore of an American mine would bring, and yet somehow still hoist and concentrate it at a profit.

The two muckers had vanished—up to no good, Tretheway did not doubt. As the expert began to question him, speaking as though Tretheway were a lower form of life, he suppressed his irritation. He answered briefly, aware that the questions made sense—the professor certainly knew something of mining. By the

152

time the inquisition had ended, the muckers had reappeared. They began to scrape noisily, the picture of angelic innocence to anyone who did not know Riley and O'Leary. Tretheway hoped that what they had arranged would not maim the Britisher too badly or involve Smith too deeply. Full of book learning he might be, but a fair boss, thoughtful of his crews—and also there was Mrs. Smith. Hardly more than a girl herself she was, but with a new little Smith pretty far on the way, he had heard.

The crew pitched in to realign the column and machine for the third series of holes. They had hardly got the Burleigh nursed up into position when Smith and the expert turned to leave. O'Leary almost dropped his end of the machine, but Riley stepped forward asking, "Muster Smith, sor, and can Oi have a wurrd with ye?"

Smith turned back—he was the sort of superintendent who would listen to any of his men—but the professor sniffed and continued up the drift. Irish muckers were obviously far beneath his notice. Riley launched into a long-winded complaint about something the cager had done or had not done three days ago. Smith listened in patience, but as the tale wound around, clearly getting nowhere, he frowned. "Riley," he said, cutting off the petition, "take it up with Chenoweth. If he can't straighten it out, then see me. On your own time."

"Yus, sor. Oi thank yer honor," Riley replied meekly. So whatever it was, Tretheway deduced, it would not be far away, and Riley's sole motive had been to ensure that the professor was alone when it happened. At that moment, the distant lantern described an arc and went out. There was a pause, and then a cry of anger and disgust echoed up the drift. Smith turned and broke into a run, his lantern bobbing.

O'Leary and Riley were leaning against the wall, convulsed with silent laughter. "Ah, shut 'ee gobs and bear a 'and," Tretheway commanded. Their sides still heaving and their faces red, the two muckers resumed work. After he had clamped in the starter, Bolitho could no longer restrain himself.

"What t'ell did 'ee two bog trotters do?" he demanded. Amid much snickering the story came out.

"Do yez mind that step, back about a hoondred feet?" O'Leary

153

asked, referring to a minor fault heave in the footwall. Tretheway was familiar with it. A man walking back down the drift would see it and plant his right foot carefully down on one given spot beyond it. The muckers had recovered something repugnant from the dirt box in the level station and had carefully planted it on the strategic spot. "An'," Riley continued, chuckling, "th' poor, dear man's foot may have slipped in it, an' he fallen, bedad."

"An' to ease his fall, f'r we would not wish even a black Protestant devil to hurt his swate self," O'Leary concluded, "we laid another pratie right where he would sit. Like a downy cushion, as it were."

"Why, 'ee foul-minded papist bastards!" Tretheway began, but started to laugh helplessly himself. Although technically an Englishman, the lead man had no more love for public-school condescension than did the Irish.

"Ye moight say th' gentleman has a bit of the Auld Sod on his boot, an', with inny luck, th' seat iv his foine pants," Riley pontificated.

" 'E'll stink op they drift till 'ell wouldn't 'ave it," Bolitho muttered. "And what will Smith say to usn's?"

The crew sobered. "Do Smith come back in a minute," Tretheway said gravely, "usn's best roll op h'our bindles and catch they first freight h'out of Phonolite." The muckers decided to concentrate on their scoops. A moment later, the din of drilling began anew. By the time Tretheway had worked through two changes and was ready to lower the Burleigh, Bolitho commented, " 'E ain't come back."

"Then 'e won't. Mayhap Smith had a laugh, too. 'E didn't care to be called 'my man.' "

" 'E may change 'is mind h'after smelling yon stink another h'our h'or two."

"Smelling another man's dirty breeks is a pleasure," Tretheway said philosophically.

Out of the crew's sight, loaded ore cars rolled through the other levels to the hoist shafts, were raised to grass, and were dumped in ore bins or spilled over the edge of the waste dump. Stamps chanted in the quartz mill, and at their feet tables shuffled in an

endless sideways, crablike dance, sorting out brassy-black concentrates from pulverized quartz. Cages rose and fell, signal bells
clanged peremptorily, and the great beam and bob of the Cornish
pump bowed to each other like two Japanese gentlemen as they
raised the water from the depths of the capacious sump. The sun
had long since crossed the whirling sheaves at the top of the
headframe, while the desert flat to the northeast of Phonolite was
now fully painted gray-green and pastel pink.

On the three-hundred level the last hole had been collared and
bottomed, the Burleigh and its column had been rolled back to the
station, and the crew was now laboring with saw and dag—the
miner's short-hafted ax—over the timbers brought down by the
cager. Tretheway, Bolitho, and Riley set up the posts to true
vertical. Tretheway squinted sagely at the post, craning his neck
this way and that until Riley exclaimed, "Ain't the damn thing
plumb yet?"

"Damme, old son," Tretheway admitted, "she's a bit more'n
plumb. 'And me they bleddy dag, and I'll put they wedges to she."
The broad wooden wedges were pounded into place, and then
collar braces were trimmed and put in to take the end-on thrust of
blasting. O'Leary, working around the trio, had been chipping a
forward extension to the trackside drainage ditch; the level was
presently dry at the breast of the heading, but back toward the
shaft the schist footwall dribbled water, and, should the orebody
angle upward farther on, more water would probably be encountered. O'Leary scooped up the chippings with a few sweeps of his
muck stick and addressed himself to flattening somewhat a few of
the more obtrusive humps along the line where a new section of
tramming track would extend.

Riley voiced discontent. "T'other shift do nothing but drill,
muck, and shoot," he growled. "We do as much an' have to stand
timber as well."

He was complaining just to be complaining, as Tretheway well
knew. In about two more days, the way the advance was going, it
would be the turn of Tregaskis' crew to timber for a while. An
overly smart lead man could arrange the work of his own crew so
that the other would have the additional labor for a fortnight or so,

155

while he himself basked in praise for dumping the more pay dirt. Would bask, that is, until the other shift had had enough of that nonsense. Then reprisals would follow. Tretheway knew that simple fatigue was partly behind Riley's attitude; he was feeling the continued strain of the labor himself. Part, too, was a dryness in the throat and visceral discomfort that could be alleviated only by draining the contents of certain bottles at shift end. He himself would not mind a drop, now that he thought of it—a proper ration of one gill of whisky followed by a bottle of Pilsner to stem the shot. Then perhaps another to give him an appetite for supper. Yet Tretheway and the other Cousins always marveled at the way the Irish could pour raw whisky down their throats. Nothing short of intemperate they were.

Old Chenoweth was back again. He looked about, approved the workmanlike progress, and said, "Time to tally and load," partly in reminder and partly in commendation. Drawing Tretheway aside, he announced, "Young Smith told me 'ee keep a dirty drift. 'Ad London perfessor with 'im 'oo fell h'and besmirched 'isself sadly. Smith h'about fell off 'is chair, laughing. Said, do h'it 'appen once more, give 'ole bloody crew their walking papers. Now 'ee be cautioned, John." He nudged Tretheway. "I'd of given my share to been 'ere when h'it 'appened." Chenoweth leered and left.

Young Bolitho was sent for the powder and blasting accessories, while the four men, grunting mightily, dragged the heavy iron muck sheet forward, anchored down its forward edge with a few hundred pounds of muck, and then turned back to lay tramming track. Their hammers were still clinking against the miniature track spikes when the boy reappeared with the car. Many miners carried powder, fuse, and blasting caps about in their arms, but Tretheway insisted on transporting them in the car. It was all too easy to stumble and fall with the box blocking one's view of his footfalls, and while nothing would probably happen, once in a while something did. Tretheway had a good deal of respect for the possibilities of this new powder.

The muckers finished up odd jobs, such as piling the dull drill steel into the car, while Tretheway and Bolitho began loading the holes. A slit headstick went in first, then the second—priming—stick with fuse and cap inserted and tied firmly to it with a bit of coarse twine. Next came the remaining sticks to the total number Tretheway deemed proper, to be topped off with drillings for stemming. He and his chuck tender worked swiftly and steadily by the light of Bolitho's candle hung on the wall well back from the face. Bolitho cut fuse without formal measurement, but the rat-tails hanging from the stemmed collars were nicely uniform in each series' length. Since they were slabbing sideways into the corner provided by the night shift, the rat-tails were shorter and the holes loaded more lightly on the left; rat-tails, loads, and hole depth increased steadily to the right. The right-hand edgers were exceptionally deep, angled decidedly outward, and when fired were intended to leave a deep rightward corner for the benefit of the shift to follow.

"Deep enough," Tretheway announced. "Away with 'ee, Bill, old son." Bolitho put the blasting equipment back into the car and pushed it up the track toward the shaft. In his hand Tretheway held his spitter, a length of fuse cut shorter than the shortest rat-tail on the face. With his knife he notched it to the powder core every inch or so, one notch to each hole, with two or three extra. His candle was in his hand, and a lighted snuff was in reserve behind him on the wall. He waited patiently. Up at the level station, Bolitho presumably had signaled the hoist man, following the level code with five bells in warning of imminent blasting. Presently the cage would arrive, bob up and down a time or two in acknowledgment that the hoist man would accept no other signal until the crew was on, and then await the cager's final signal to hoist them away. If some other crew beat them to it, their wait for the cage might be prolonged.

Today they were in luck. A faint hallooing indicated that the cage was waiting and that the equipment car had been rolled onto its lower deck. Tretheway held the split end of the spitter in his candle flame, saw it take hold, and shouted, "Firein' th' holes!" He grasped the upper left edger's rat-tail and, as flame spurted from the first notch of the spitter, pressed its end into the fiery notch. He waited a moment to ensure that the fire had taken hold, then released the rat-tail and moved down to the next. Although sweat beaded his forehead, he did not allow himself to be rushed. He sighed in relief when the right lifter rat-tail was alight. Straightening up, Tretheway cast a long look across the face. Each rat-tail was smoking and sparking satisfactorily. He tossed down the spitter, hawked at the growing smell of black powder smoke, and reached for the reserve snuff—the initial "spit" had, as usual, extinguished the candle that lit it. Pressing the stubby snuff into the lump of clay on the front of his hat, he marched up the drift.

The crew was on the cage when he arrived at the station. Bolitho motioned with the lantern for him to come on, but Tretheway paused for a final, all-encompassing inspection. Seeing nothing amiss, he stepped onto the deck and faced right as the cager swung down the safety bar. Everything seemed to stop momentarily, and the rustle of the hoist belt in the manway to the left was clearly audible. Then a series of sharp, spaced knocks began—the sound of the blasts transmitted through the rock—followed by and mingled with a low, growling roar. Tretheway counted intently to himself. Twelve holes they had drilled and, if he was not mistaken, eleven knocks he had heard, but one was somewhat prolonged, as though two holes had gone nearly at the same moment. Twelve, he decided, it had been. The cager at his nod gave the bell rope one smart pull. Tretheway's candle went out at once as the deck pressed up hard against his feet. As he faced the guide, he could see dimly the massive, grease-streaked pump rod, surrounded by a miscellany of ladders, guides, air lines, the rising main, and lumpy valve casings flashing by his nose.

The cage eased up to a bobbing halt at the shaft's collar platform. Even though it was nearly dusk in the open air, the light was painful to eyes that had been almost twelve hours in nearly unrelieved darkness. Swirling vapor surrounded them. The men of the crew stepped off the cage, turning back to give the cager a hand with their car. Shivering in the biting air, they pulled on jumpers and mackinaws, took their lunch buckets, and pushed the car over the sheet iron of the platform. In silence they guided it to the smithy, where the steel was unceremoniously tossed onto a clanging pile for the smith's helper to sort. Abandoning the car, they made way for another tired crew following. "Tomorrow, then?" O'Leary asked significantly.

"Mayhap. Or day after." Tretheway was abruptly conscious of the ache in his back, the tremble of his legs, and the remarkable weight of the lunch bucket hanging from his hand. The two Irishmen began the long trudge down the hill to Corktown and the nearest shebeen. After them went the Bolithos, father and son, walking companionably together. Tretheway watched them go with mingled feelings. It was a fine thing, he reflected, for a lad to be learning a proud, skilled trade under his father's eye. There was no son to follow John Tretheway. If only Rose had lived. . . . He calculated. Eighteen years now, it had been. Most men would have married again, but for him there had been only Rose.

The night shift was coming up the hill now, and there unless he was mistaken was Jack Tregaskis. "Eh, Jack!"

"Eh, John. Long shift?"

"Long enough. 'Ee left usn's a good corner. Hope we left 'ee as good. No holes missed."

"Aye. Well, *adios,* John." Tregaskis had worked in the British-owned Mexican silver mines and could never resist showing off his pidgin Spanish.

A tap on his shoulder made Tretheway start. It was old Chenoweth again, slipping up like an Indian. "Be 'ee ready to go, John? Aye? Then business first. After, I'll stand 'ee one at yon Miners' Rest. No more, though." Chenoweth bent over, coughing harshly. "Old woman won't leave me 'ave more'n one. 'Ee be'ant wed, are 'ee?"

"Nay."

"Lucky man, 'ee be. Let's go. She been a long shift." The old Cornishman began picking his way down the haulage road into the windy evening, through which the yellow gleam of oil lamps was beginning to glimmer along the valley below.

159

CHAPTER 7

1882
EILEEN BURNETT CROWLEY

AND NOW, ON RECOMMENDA-
TION of the faculty, and by virtue of the powers vested in me by
the board of trustees, I am pleased to confer upon you the degree of
bachelor of fine arts, with all rights, privileges, and immunities
appertaining thereto." In the sweltering little chapel there was a
polite spatter of applause. The graduates, perspiring freely under
their caps and gowns, rose as a body and begin to file past the
Reverend Edward Wainwright Percival, M.A., D.D., and president of Howald College for Females. The symphonium, bereft of
its best musicians by this same exercise, raised a halting, dirgelike
academic hymn. Each graduate stopped before Percival, who
lifted the ribboned diploma from the small pile, thrust it into her
extended left hand, shook her right hand, and guided her firmly
back to her uncomfortable wooden folding chair on the chapel
stage. The baccalaureate flipped over her tassel, sighed in relief,
and cautiously flexed her knees to return some circulation. Shortly
the symphonium wheezed to a halt, there was more applause, and
everybody sat down, wincing a little.

Had it been put to a vote of the parents, faculty, trustees,
graduates, and distinguished visitors and friends, the Turkish bath

Tom Phillips

would have been adjourned at once, its purpose accomplished. As it was, iron-clad tradition demanded conferral of an honorary degree upon the speaker of the evening. Tradition further demanded that the speaker be a female of some unspecified eminence. Tonight the trustees began to regret listening to Percival's rash suggestion that the speaker be one of note in the growing movement for female suffrage. Percival had accordingly exhumed Minerva Bowen McCord, a power in the vituperative congeries of covens and camorras that made up the movement as a whole. After Miss McCord was cited and nimbly invested with the doctoral hood, she set her massive chin and advanced upon the lectern flat-footed, in the manner of the Iron Brigade deploying into battle. The sight of the thick pile of manuscript she produced from the folds of her voluminous robe was depressing. It showed every sign of being a long, hot evening.

Dr. McCord was a frog-mouthed harridan with a rasping voice, which she proceeded to raise forthwith in threat, bluster, and recrimination. She admonished the new baccalaureates against the world, the flesh, and the deviltries of men, meanwhile glaring as balefully at Percival as though he had been detected selling his charges to a Buenos Aires brothelkeeper. She cast bitter insinuations upon the trustees. She reminded the husbands present that they enforced upon their wives a thralldom worse than that which Our Martyred President had lifted from the Groaning Blacks. After this ingratiating introduction, Dr. McCord cast moderation to the winds, prophesying the manner in which United Womanhood would put down presidents, legislators, judges, and whisky peddlers. Her voice croaking in ecstasy, she evoked a day when females would vote, hold public office, even the highest, put away undutiful spouses, bear only such children as they chose (this produced foot-shufflings of outrage and embarrassment), practice all learned professions, and Take Their Place Beside Men as Associates, not follow them as mere chattels. I. Thank. You.

Two or three hopelessly plain graduates seemed quite affected by these seditions, but most let them go in one ear and out the other, a trick which they had been four years perfecting with the help of the faculty. The applause that followed the harangue could be described only as dutiful. The members of the symphonium fingered their instruments while Percival pronounced the benediction and hurled themselves for the third time of the evening upon the academic hymn. Led by the senior faculty member, who bore a ribbon-decorated broomstick reminiscent of Little Bo Peep, the trustees, Percival, Dr. McCord, the eighteen members of the faculty, and the thirty-four graduates filed out the back of the chapel. As the parents, friends, and distinguished visitors scrambled after them, the symphonium emitted a death rattle like that of a bogged range steer and gave up.

The evening reception at the president's house and in his garden was a distinct improvement over the corroboree just concluded. Refreshed and flower-like in new white dresses, the graduates circulated, introduced parents to professors, parents to other parents and to best friends, threw their arms about each other, wept, autographed commencement programs, and made heavy inroads upon the iced fruit punch. They announced engagements, teaching positions, and travel to Europe or remained discreetly vague on the subject of the future. One of the firebrands loudly proclaimed that she had applied to do master's work in English at Ohio State University. No one asked her whether she had actually been admitted, just as the tourist to Europe was not asked to send back picture postcards. After four years of living in each others' pockets, as it were, the graduates knew bluffing when they heard it. Yet the sentiment was mostly genuine. Four years ago they had arrived at Howald as girls. Now all but the incorrigibles were women. Most females of their age in the United States had become mothers twice over in the same period of time.

Eileen Burnett Crowley was both enjoying herself enormously and fighting back an impulse to wail loudly. Present tonight were nearly all the people she most loved and cared for—her parents, her roommate and best friend, her favorite professors, even sweet old Dean Adkins. In an hour more they would be scattered, never to be reassembled. Eileen made the most of time between trips to the punch bowl; she had dripped so much on the stage that she felt she could never make up the liquid deficiency. During one watering halt she noticed Elizabeth Jenkins slipping up and making the secret sign. This, devised three years before, meant, "I have to see you alone, urgently!" Most often it had signaled the arrival of a cake from home. Eileen sidled into a darker part of the shrubbery.

"Eileen!" Liz whispered frantically, "I need help! Tonight! *Now!*"

Eileen could not imagine what for and said so.

"Promise you'll help me—please!"

"Suppose you tell me what it is first," Eileen replied with the caution of experience.

Liz looked around conspiratorially. Then she unclenched her hand and held it, palm upward for an instant, under Eileen's nose. The fingers closed, and the hand was gone, but the sight remained behind Eileen's eyes. Elizabeth was clutching a plain gold band. At Howald College for Females that meant only one thing.

"You *do* need help," Eileen said flatly. No female who was married, given in marriage, or circumstantially suspected of marriage could remain on the campus as a student any longer than it took old Josh, the custodian, to put her trunk into the railroad carryall. Therefore it was absolutely obligatory that any girl involved in a secret marriage must be aided, comforted, loaned money, and if necessary carried to the moon on the collective backs of the whole student body should that be the only alternative to exposure. Even tonight Liz might be stripped of her diploma and cast out if the facts became known. That such activity was Most Secret may be inferred by the fact that Liz had not even hinted of the matter before to Eileen, her roommate.

Liz poured out her story hurriedly. Visiting her aunt in Denver over Christmas, she had met a young mining engineer, evidently of brisk and forceful ways. They had been quietly married in Colorado Springs on New Years' Day. (Despite her haste and nervousness Liz's eyes got a little glassy at this point in her narrative.) Now tonight her parents had unexpectedly insisted that she summer with them in Saratoga, leaving on the east-bound early train the next day. She, Elizabeth Jenkins *Rawlings,* did not wish to go to Saratoga. She wished Saratoga was in hell! To the contrary, Elizabeth wished to take the early-afternoon train westward to Denver for reasons which required no enlargement. Now, Eileen must at once go with her to her parents and swear to Liz's lie that her Denver aunt had invited them both for the summer and that both had accepted. That Eileen would be crushed at a rebuff. That the tickets were bought. Everything!

Eileen revolved the project in her mind. She did not have to ask whether Liz's parents could be made to listen to truthful reason. Mr. Jenkins was a tyrannical ogre who would bellow like a bull calf at any initiative on Liz's part. Mrs. Jenkins was a fluttery hysteric who would scream, faint, and then babble the news to everyone, beginning with Prexy Percival. No, she decided, common honesty would not serve. Liz's politics must be continued by other means. "Liz," she asked softly, "are you . . .?"

"No, thank heaven!" was the prompt reply, though hinting that thought had been given.

That was all right, then. "Money?"

"Carl sent me my ticket. It costs sixty-five dollars."

"How much do you have?"

"Eighteen."

Not so good. Eighteen of Liz's and her own twenty-three made—ah— forty-one. Forty-one from sixty-five was, . . . well, counting incidentals . . . . "Let me do it my way then," Eileen commanded. "My parents first. Look calm."

Leading Elizabeth over to Dr. and Mrs. Crowley, Eileen placidly announced that she and Elizabeth had made plans to spend the summer with Liz's Denver aunt. She, Eileen, had accepted, and needed provision for fare and food. Would her father . . .?

Doctor Crowley smiled at the young woman who was his only daughter and was reaching for his wallet even before Mrs. Crowley could nod. Eileen was always able to manage her parents, and tonight the iron was especially hot. With her personal and economic flanks secured, Eileen turned Elizabeth around and sought out the Jenkinses. With a face of angelic innocence Eileen proceeded to lie like a Fourth Cavalry trooper. By the time she had finished, even old Jenkins had forgotten all about Saratoga.

That night, as they bedded down for the last time in the

shambles they had called home for four years, Eileen asked casually, "Where *is* Denver, Liz?"

"West. Out where it's still wild. I even saw an Indian. Right on the street."

"Are there many men?"

"Oh, lots of men. Men all over. I never saw so many men, and so few women."

"I think Denver will be a nice place to visit," Eileen remarked. "Do you like being married, Liz?"

The reply was heartfelt. Had Dr. Minerva Bowen McCord been privy to this exchange, she would have been extremely depressed. Hers would be a long, hard fight complicated by disaffection amounting to mutiny in the ranks.

While the dreamy-eyed Elizabeth and the cool-eyed Eileen are following Horace Greeley's advice, it would be germane to sketch the antecedents, education, and appearance of Eileen Burnett Crowley. The last of four children born to Margaret and Isaiah Crowley, M.D., she was preceded by three hale and active brothers, now married and busy with their families and hence unable to attend the commencement exercises. This had produced a favorable family situation, for a physician's child is exposed to table talk of exceptionally high voltage, educationally speaking. And a girl who has been reared among older brothers will nourish thereafter very few crippling illusions about men. Her mother and father respected each other and dealt kindly but firmly with their brood, and mercifully it was yet an age in which a physician in general practice could see a little something of his children in the years between their delivery and their college commencement. Accordingly, Eileen possessed few neurotic disabilities other than those the industrial revolution was imposing upon everyone within its reach. In a word, she would make some man a superlative wife, whether he willed it or not.

She had learned far more about people and things at the hearthside than at Howald College for Females, but at Howald she had perfected poise, self-confidence, determination, and social blarney, chiefly by observation of the negative examples about her.

166

Taking one thing with another, Eileen did not consider her years at Howald totally wasted, which was about the best one could expect of higher education. Her exposure to men continued with her professors and concluded with her resolve that she would die unwed rather than marry any sort of pedagogue. (Physicians, for obvious reasons, were already struck off her list.) In Greek I she had learned that "pedagogue" originally referred to a worthless, rather half-witted slave who conducted Athenian boys to and from their lessons, mostly to prevent hooky-playing, and she felt that things had not changed much in twenty-five hundred years. However, married she was determined to be if she had to marry a bear, simply because she felt that she would be missing something good otherwise.

Eileen knew that in her person she was fair to behold, save for one major reservation. Her eyes were large, wide-set and blue, her nose moderately long and thin, her lips generously full. The girls at Howald said that she was pretty, and she supposed that she would do. Before the privacy of her mirror Eileen was not depressed by the arrangements she beheld. She had longer legs and a shorter waist than current fashion decreed, but the zones immediately above were adequate in all respects. The informal dress of the period—long, full skirt and long-sleeved, high-necked blouse (coming to be called a shirtwaist) became her very well. She was healthy as a horse, and her fair complexion was almost unspotted; Liz had whispered that marriage did *wonders* for facial spots.

Eileen's inadequacy in her own and others' sight commenced about one millimeter radially from her skull and a few other scattered points. Not to beat about the subject, she was red-haired. Fortunately it was not the hideous, carroty orange that is accompanied by a horde of blotchy freckles, but red it undeniably was. As a girl she had fervently hoped that some night her good fairy would miraculously change it to blonde—even to black, in a pinch—but there was no response, and no blinking the fact that it glowed like a hearthful of embers. No red-haired girl really likes her crowning glory, but in this year of 1882 red was worse than unfashionable. It was notorious as the outward sign of heated blood, shrewishness, want of reserve, and general hellionism. The rural public believed, as firmly as it believed that root crops should be planted in the dark of the moon, that preachers' daughters and red-haired girls went inexorably from cradle to crib. The urban public was little better enlightened. In elementary school, boys had tormented her and her pigtails. At the Latin Academy, boys and girls alike had snickered knowingly. At Howald her classmates had been sympathetic, which was worse yet. Her wardrobe could contain no shade of red, orange, or pink; the dyers had nothing of these colors in their vats that did not clash hideously with what she could not amend. Eileen nevertheless carefully brushed and tended her thick, shining oriflamme almost as if she loved it, even as a mother will bestow a little extra affection upon the least-well-favored of her children. She had to live with it, and was resolved to do so. But she often wondered whether she would ever encounter a man who could tolerate that color upon a pillow. All in all, the chances seemed slender.

Denver, when she and Elizabeth at last descended from the train, was both stimulating and something of an anticlimax. Eileen had envisioned log cabins, tipis, soldiers, and buckskin-clad Fenimore Cooper scouts. But apart from the looming Rockies and the exhilarating air, it could have been any medium-sized American city. The business buildings were three-story stone, the streets were paved after a fashion, the houses were ordinary houses, and, although Eileen, too, saw an Indian, he didn't look much different from anyone else except for his black braids. Eileen would cheerfully have scalped him for those braids had she been able to think of a way to install them.

The home of Elizabeth's Aunt Martha Wilkins was another disappointment. Liz had managed, without actually saying so, to convey the impression that it was a gracious manor set in spacious and well-tended grounds. Instead it was a modest four-room frame house nestled closely among others of the same sort on a side street. Aunt Martha, after the obligatory introduction and embrace, proved to be only an older version of Mrs. Jenkins. She was a widow, and she made it clear that self-invited summer guests were expected to help with the food money and the housekeeping duties. The room she assigned Eileen and Liz was only one cut above their accommodations at Howald. Liz tried to console Eileen with the giggled hint that Eileen would soon enough have the bed and room all to herself, since she had sent a telegram to Carl that his bride had arrived. For various reasons Eileen found this not as consoling as intended. That night she toyed with the idea of boarding the eastbound train, nor getting off until the conductor put her off.

The very next morning a W.U. delivery boy left a telegram originating at a place called Black Hawk. The contents rendered Liz incapable of doing anything but sitting about and sighing like a steam engine. She broke so many dishes that Aunt Martha chased her out of the kitchen. Eileen, however, was not excused on that or any account from dishwashing, fetching in stove wood, grocery shopping, bed making, and flower-bed weeding. To her credit Aunt Martha kept pace with her, but the conversation was not stimulating. She seemed to have only three topics: the virtues of the late Mr. Wilkins, speculation about the wedded future of Liz and Carl with an emphasis on obstetrics, and detailed accounts of her own multitudinous ailments, illnesses, and complaints. Eileen quickly but silently diagnosed her hostess as a victim of chronic widow's hypochondria, stemming from the lack of a man about the place to focus her thoughts upon.

At length Mr. Rawlings appeared, drawn by a foaming steed. He gathered up the squealing Liz, whirled her around, and ordered her to pack instantly—he had but forty-eight hours to get her back up to Black Hawk, where the vine-covered cottage awaited their attentions. Liz threw clothes about with abandon, jumped on the trunk lid until it could be locked, hugged Eileen, told her she was a friend indeed, and then vanished with Carl in the manner of fair Ellen with young Lochinvar. When the uproar had subsided, Eileen excused herself and went for a long walk. She returned with the conclusion that Carl was a nice enough boy and Liz was a fortunate girl. For Liz. Yet Carl or Carl's sort was not exactly what Eileen had had in mind for herself. He was too young, too exuberant, showed few signs of original thought

169

beyond his work and the resumption of the honeymoon, and . . . .
Anyway, he was not Eileen's sort. She wondered again whether
she had not rather overdone the anything-for-a-classmate creed.

After one dull day alone with Aunt Martha, Eileen was bored.
Mrs. Wilkins told her what horsecar to take to go downtown, and
she went forthwith. She window-shopped, observed the parade of
life, compared her clothes with those of the women in view, ate
lunch in a respectable eating house, fended off three improper
advances, and was looking for the return horsecar when she saw a
small bookstore. Theorizing that she would need a great deal of
such ammunition during the summer to come, she crossed the
street and made in its direction. While doing so, she was barely
aware of the sound of horses' hooves behind her, but as she entered
the door of the shop, Eileen noticed that a man was tying a pair of
good carriage horses to the store's cast-iron hitching post. Once
inside, she dismissed the advancing clerk to make for the shelf of
English literature. History bored her, botany was an abomination,
and novels were either saccharine or crude in her eyes. The travel
books of the new author, Clemens or something, were said to be
much too philistine to be worth the reading. Eileen prospected the
slender shelf and was about to turn away when a title seemed to
leap out at her. It was nothing less than Byron's *Don Juan*! This
was forbidden fruit with a vengeance! Therefore her hand shot out
for it—coming to rest squarely upon a male hand intent upon the
same object.

Eileen pulled her fingers back hastily. She found herself looking
at the same man who had tied the team in front of the store. He
was regarding her with what appeared to be gentlemanly but
amused interest. Was her hair showing? she asked herself, and
concluded that her drawn-up back hair might indeed be. But her
hat covered it well everywhere else. This concern attended to, she
turned her thoughts outward to the man himself, a host of
impressions flooding at her. His eyes were warmly brown. His
hair was very dark, relieved by a streak of gray over the ear at each
temple. His mouth appeared mobile and relaxed over a firm chin.
His suit was conservative but in good taste for the West.

"Oh!" Eileen said.

"Pardon me," the man remarked in a soft voice that showed both courtesy and education. He gravely extracted *Don Juan* from the shelf and offered it to her across his left forearm, as a man might offer a sword. "Your book—miss."

Eileen was suddenly on the alert, a phrase flitting through her mind. "Mad, bad, and very dangerous . . . ." It had been attributed to Lady Caroline Lamb after her first meeting with Byron. From the discreetly edited *Life and Selected Verse of Byron* in the reading room at Howald she had gathered the impression that Lady Caroline had met Byron, had encouraged him to write despite these misgivings, but had been forced to sever company from him before his wickednesses (carefully left unspecified by the editor) reflected upon her reputation. In Eileen's opinion Lady Caroline Lamb had been deplorably unenterprising. A mad, bad, and dangerous man might repay a little cultivation. Her mind completed the circle. This man, still patiently holding out the book to her, looked neither mad nor bad, but he did seem capable of being dangerous. Would she, Eileen, tiptoe in where timid Englishwomen evidently had feared to tread? But, after all, what had she come to Denver for?

"Thank you very much," Eileen replied, extending her hand for the book.

"Do you like Byron?" came the logical and inescapable next question.

"I've read only *Childe Harold* and a few other selections."

"Then I'm sure that you will enjoy a complete edition of *Don Juan*," the man said soberly. He reached into his card case while Eileen hastily foraged in her reticule. He read, "Eileen Burnett Crowley." She read, "Richard Drexel Jellison. Huggins, Casey & Jellison, 117 Fremont Street, San Francisco."

You are a long way from home, Mr. Jellison," Eileen remarked before the meeting could die of malnutrition.

"So are you, Miss Crowley. The eastern fashions haven't arrived at the shops yet. How do you like Denver?"

After that things became a bit inevitable but very pleasantly so. Mr. Jellison took charge of Eileen, overrode her protests and objections, helped her into his carriage, and as the horses began

172

clip-clopping about the Denver streets, he pointed out places of interest. He considerately took her to her residence so that she could tell Aunt Martha that she was dining out, and change into afternoon clothes. Mr. Jellison fed her very well at a hotel dining room and had her on her doorstep before dark. He found out a great deal about her, had said little specific about himself, although he had managed to imply that he was not married, and at the door had asked her earnestly whether he might call on her again. With her emotional feet on the ice and picking up speed rapidly, Eileen had managed to agree calmly that perhaps he might. Tomorrow? Tomorrow would be very nice.

The following afternoon Mr. Jellison reappeared, to Eileen's carefully suppressed delight. She introduced him to Mrs. Wilkins, who brought out tea and cookies over which Eileen had labored all morning. They had a nice, formal visit. Jellison asked her how she liked *Don Juan,* and Eileen replied, very much. (She had slept little the previous night and had not even unwrapped the thing.) They discussed the Denver climate until the subject was in tatters. Finally, as the teapot emptied and the cookies showed signs of depletion, Jellison got down to business. Denver, he said, had many excellent evening attractions that he would be honored to show Eileen. Did she happen to have a chaperone available?

Mrs. Wilkins was of no assistance whatsoever. She was a widow woman, she complained, had few clothes beyond the ones on her back, and was poorly anyway. Eileen reflected to herself with some bitterness that Elizabeth, now that she was needed, had made herself unavailable. Not only was she in Black Hawk—wherever that might be—but she had not even troubled to send Eileen her address. And Eileen suspected that, even if she could summon Elizabeth, Elizabeth would not respond. She was a stranger to Denver, having no social entree or letters of introduction. It appeared to be an impasse.

"I know of a very fine lady," Jellison suggested. "Mrs. John Maynard Dawson. She is the wife of a business acquaintance here, and I have reason to believe that she finds time hanging rather heavily—J. M. is gone a lot. It would be improper for me to make such an introduction, and I feel certain anyway that you would

173

prefer to make your own inquiries. As soon as you and she are introduced, she will let me know. I am at the Oxford Hotel. Then perhaps we may enjoy an evening at the Tabor Grand Opera House. Too bad we missed Mr. Oscar Wilde's lecture there two months ago, in view of your interest in English literature."

Having done all that a gentleman could do, Jellison presently rose, thanked Mrs. Wilkins, said farewell to Eileen, and left. "He seemed like a real nice man," Aunt Martha remarked, observing his departure past a fold of her window curtain. "Very proper and mannerly." Appraising his team and rig, she added, "Not poor, neither, unless it's a livery hire."

Eileen was plunged in intensive calculation. "Who's your doctor, and where is his office?" she demanded.

"What's the matter, dear? You feeling poorly, too? Sometimes this high altitude . . . ."

Eileen was not feeling at all poorly, unless one counted a slight tendency to tachycardia induced by the presence of Mr. Jellison. Also she demonstrated one or two other mild reactions which she did not care to analyze. But even though the afternoon was getting on, Eileen made haste down the street to a frame house whose extended ell bore the shingle of a physician and surgeon. She had barely started on the ancient *Atlantic* on the waiting-room table when the doctor appeared and ushered her into his consulting room. "What is the problem?" he began, dipping his pen.

"Social, not medical," Eileen replied. She introduced herself, mentioned that her father was a physician back East, and appealed as a friendless stranger to that freemasonry which binds together all physicians and their families.

The middle-aged doctor put away his pen and a good part of his professional manner. "Well! I thought you looked a little too lively to be ailing. So you're a doctor's daughter? Mind a question?"

Eileen did not mind.

"Suppose we have a well-nourished mature female in her twenties. She comes in complaining of enlarged and tender mammae, recent cessation of menses, and nausea upon arising. What's the tentative diagnosis?"

"Six weeks pregnant," Eileen snapped back.

174

"You're a doctor's daughter all right. Now what can I do for you?"

"Do you know a Mrs. John Maynard Dawson, and would she be a suitable chaperone?"

"Old J. M.'s wife? Amelia? My word, yes! With her chaperoning you, you could . . . well, never mind. But there would be no scandal. I'll get my wife to write a letter of introduction right now. Take as directed," he concluded with a smile. "I wish all my patients were as easy to fix up." Then his manner changed, and he smiled differently, almost wistfully. "Do you know why I gave you those particular symptoms?"

Eileen decided to play innocent. "No, doctor."

"Your eyes were mighty bright when you came in here. And you evidently meant business. I have the feeling that if what you have in mind works out—and I hope it does—you'll be wanting to review those symptoms for yourself within a year."

Eileen blushed profusely, but her respect for the powers of the healing art were increased.

With the enlistment of Amelia Dawson an enthusiastic relationship commenced. Whether seated at the Tabor Opera or climbing Pike's Peak on riding mules, Dick and Eileen were conscious only of each other. They were cheerfully content to allow their long-suffering chaperone to enjoy the music or the marmots as she pleased, as long as she kept station at a reasonable distance. Over the course of a few weeks Eileen discovered that she felt extraordinarily alive in Dick's presence and that his absence was productive of great discontent. He talked to Eileen without condescension, listened to her with genuine interest, and appeared neither scornful nor patronizing about her education at Howald. Had he been a girl, Eileen decided, Dick would have been her best friend; intellectually they were a good match. Otherwise, . . . gentleman or not, she detected Dick once or twice regarding her in a manner to which she reacted with a weird mixture of flush and shiver. With any other man she would have resented this deeply. Since Dick was involved, she fought down an urgent temptation to speculate on cause and effect.

They came close to a quarrel only once. Riding out toward the

175

mountains one afternoon, Dick, Eileen and Mrs. Dawson approached a construction gang which Dick explained was improving a culvert on the D.&R.G.W. Impulsively Eileen turned her horse toward the activity, intent upon a closer look. Jellison abandoned Mrs. Dawson to catch up with her. "Better stop," he advised. "Looks like they're ready to shoot."

Eileen saw no guns in evidence. "I want to see," she insisted.

"No. It's dangerous," Dick replied, in a flat voice.

A devil awoke in Eileen. Whether Dick was right or not, she was suddenly overcome by the temptation to see how far she could go with him. She nudged her horse with her left boot heel.

Dick cut in beside her. His left hand seized and pulled the reins. As they halted, his right hand took Eileen's upper arm. She was astonished and a little frightened by his hard expression and the strength of his hand. He was not hurting her, but her arm felt as though an iron band was encircling it.

"No," Dick repeated. "Get off that horse. Now!"

Anger seethed through her. "I won't!"

"Get down!" Leaning sideways, he practically lifted her from the sidesaddle. "Dismount, Mrs. Dawson!" he called back over his shoulder. The moment Eileen's boots touched the ground, Dick swung out of his saddle and came around the horse, heading for her with bleak eyes.

"What do you think you're doing?" Eileen demanded in outrage. Before Dick could reply, there was a thumping blast from the work area ahead. Dick nudged Eileen against the side of the horse, folded both of his arms around her shoulders, and leaned his head against hers. There were whizzing sounds in the air just above them, and Mrs. Dawson's mare snorted as something flicked it.

Fright mingled with unaccountable warmth surged through Eileen. Dick's arms tightened about her as her knees buckled slightly. She realized that she had been a fool. Dick's anger had been fully justified. And she felt somehow infinitely protected with his arms about her. Eileen had no desire to move or speak, but with a wrenching effort she tilted back her head to look up at him. The hard flatness in his eyes was gone, replaced by deep concern.

"I'm sorry, Dick," she whispered penitently.

He returned her gaze for a long moment and then lightly touched his lips to hers. Eileen's toes curled inside her riding boots. She clung to the stirrup leather for support, following Dick with wide eyes while he assisted the white-faced Mrs. Dawson back onto her nervous mare. Eileen's mouth opened slightly as she stared at his hands, expertly stroking and soothing the mare's twitching neck. Her faintness was replaced by bitter resentment that he should abandon her for a horse. She felt that if he did not return to her instantly she would shriek at him like a fishwife. Then Dick turned back, and joy raced through her.

"Do you feel like going on?" he inquired softly.

Eileen wanted desperately to lie down where she was, but she tightened her grip on the stirrup leather and managed to say, "Yes. Yes, let's go on, Dick."

His gentle smile seemed to tear at her, but she resolutely let him help her remount her horse. He led the way back to the road, she following meekly. It was just as well that Jellison did not happen to glance back at her, but Mrs. Dawson saw the expression on Eileen's face and found reason to busy herself with her hat and veil.

During the days when business kept Dick away, Eileen occupied herself by writing to her parents. She assured them that she was in good hands, making friends, and enjoying her stay in Denver immensely. She made no direct reference to Liz, since there was none to make. Some intuition impelled her to be equally reticent about Dick Jellison. Eileen told herself to count no chicken before it hatched, although the incident with the explosion had changed her attitude from one of interested speculation to one of a determination so intense that its savagery nearly frightened her. Apparently Dr. and Mrs. Crowley obtained no hint of this in her letters, for in mid-July her father wrote her that a teaching position at her old academy would be open to her, that it seemed a good opportunity, and that acceptance or rejection must be in hand by August 1. Eileen replied neither yea nor nay. Neither did she say anything about it elsewhere, having decided to keep it as a hole card in case a little pressure became necessary to help someone make up his mind. She was very glad that she had done this when Jellison mentioned casually that in about a month his business in Denver would be concluded and that it would be necessary for him to resume his travels.

There were a few pieces of grit in the loaf, nevertheless. Try as she could, Eileen was not able to ascertain exactly what it was that Dick did for a living. He was not evasive, but he was certainly vague. Once she asked point-blank, "What do Huggins, Casey & Jellison *do*?"

"Why, we mostly buy sound locations, develop them, and float the footage. If it looks very good, we may keep some or a lot of the feet. Now, what do you say to seeing this program?" It sounded to her as though he were some sort of land salesman. But "feet"? Mrs. Dawson, that patient and indefatigable chaperone, was equally vague. She gave Jellison a sound bill of health as an eligible bachelor, said that her husband's dealings with him had been satisfactory, and wished Eileen well. A little light was shed when she discovered that J. M. Dawson was a mining expert. By extension this implied that Jellison's business had some connection with mining. This, though, merely pushed the question back one step instead of answering it.

Also Liz and Carl remained invisible and impalpable. Eileen began nursing a decided grudge against her former best friend and roommate. She had come all the way to Denver at Liz's behest, only to be summarily abandoned to her own devices. To herself Eileen complained that she wished Liz would get out of bed long enough to come back to Denver and at least see what Eileen had hooked by her own efforts. Maybe Liz might even help hold the net.

On July 30, Eileen arose in that state of mind in which Bonaparte had awakened in the foggy dawn of Austerlitz. This evening Dick was taking her to a dinner garden. By midnight, she swore to herself, it would be a peerage or Westminster Abbey (she had not done remarkably well in European History II). As evening approached, she girded herself for battle, putting on the whole armor of femininity. She slipped the letter about the academy position into her evening reticule. Mrs. Wilkins flut-

Tom Phillips

tered about, sensing her mood, but Eileen spoke to her as Napoleon had spoken to Soult, bidding her have patience just a bit longer.

Presumably the dinner garden was delightful and the meal delicious; Eileen neither knew nor cared. Mrs. Dawson, alerted by feminine intuition to the onset of battle, retired after the ice to clear the line of fire. Just as Eileen leaned over the table, fumbling in her reticule to bring her batteries forward and to action front, Dick Jellison sent out a white flag. Outmaneuvered and outgunned, he reached into his coat pocket to produce a small jeweler's box of unmistakable import. The letter remained buried; Eileen gasped, voiced fear and alarm, and mentioned her father's lack of consent, and only after fifteen minutes of nonstop forensics on Dick's part did she timidly extend the ring finger of her left hand. Onto it he slipped a small but exquisite square-cut emerald. Mrs. Dawson, off to the flank, smiled and waited a few moments longer before rejoining the couple to help settle the definitive terms of capitulation.

Mrs. Wilkins was waiting up for Eileen, prepared either to staunch tears or get out the dandelion wine, as circumstances indicated. Sitting with her were Liz and Carl, of all people! Eileen was too happy even to reproach Liz for her desertion but observed as they talked that Liz had already noticeably begun that retreat from previous associations and interests which marks the closing out of one life and the commencement of another. Would she herself do the same? Eileen imagined that she probably would.

Carl Rawlings had little enough to say, apart from dutiful congratulations—this was an exclusively feminine scalp dance. He had no idea who this Dick might be who was dropping through the trap, but two months of married life had taught him better than to intervene with stupid questions at a time of jubilation.

"It's going to be in two weeks!" Eileen proclaimed to the accompaniment of cheers. "Dick says he has to be out in the Rocky Mountain Territory by then and afterward go back to San Francisco. I am *not* going to go back home and teach school for a year and maybe let some—some woman—get her claws into him, and I told him so. Two weeks is enough time for my parents to come out and give me away, and he'll have Dawson or somebody stand up with him, and, Liz, you will be matron of honor. We'll be married in the Episcopal Church here—we're both Episcopalians—and I'll go with him then to Phonolite, wherever that is, and we'll have our real honeymoon after we get to San Francisco."

Carl could not restrain himself. "Phonolite? That's the Molly Pitcher. Huggins, Casey and—what's his name—Jellison."

"Silly!" Eileen exclaimed. "That's who I'm marrying. Dick Jellison."

"Dick *Jellison?*" Carl's voice rose. Mrs. Wilkins, Liz, and Eileen turned to him. Eileen suddenly felt sick. The tone of Carl's voice seemed to bode no good. Eileen knew with the clear-sighted realism of an intelligent young woman that she was preparing to entrust herself to a man about whom she did not and could not really know anything until it was too late. He might—any man might—be a brute, a drunkard, a good-for-nothing, or conceivably something much worse. But better, far better, to find out now . . . .

"You mean you don't know who Jellison is?" Carl persisted, turning the dagger another twist in Eileen's soul.

"Please," she replied faintly. "I *think* he's a fine man. A gentleman. I hope."

"Why, he's going to be a millionaire in a few years," Carl proclaimed, ignorant of the havoc he had momentarily created. At that instant Eileen became weak with relief. At another time the word "millionaire" would have inspired deep interest in her, but at this instant it was quite enough that Carl had not accused him of bigamy, bank robbery, or being a squaw man to half the Indian nations. Carl babbled on. Jellison was coming up like a sky-rocket. Eileen was a very lucky girl. Maybe some day she could even mention Carl's name to him. Huggins, Casey & Jellison had the reputation of being one of the fastest-growing and squarest development firms in the West.

"Developing *what?*" Eileen demanded in exasperation.

"Why, mines. Gold mines, silver mines, copper mines. What other kinds of mines are there?" Carl asked.

"Coal mines?" Liz ventured.

Carl spoke to her with the infinite patronization of the man who knows to his poor, pretty, ignorant little wife. "That's not mining— that's *digging*," he said, in cutting professional scorn. "Well, here's to the bride-to-be! The future Mrs. Dick Jellison!"

When the thimbleful of dandelion wine had been ceremonially sipped, Liz decided to deliver her own news. "We came down," she said demurely, "to tell you that we're going to have a baby. I think."

Eileen had had enough. Inconvenience! Desertion! Wanton cries of "wolf!" And now, Liz deliberately horning in on her moment of glory! "That's lovely, dear," Eileen said sweetly. "I hope you won't be too big to get into your gown for the wedding."

At this point love stories usually conclude with a few remarks about the bride looking radiant, the bridegroom appearing as though he had been kicked in the head by a tramming mule, and the matron of honor (Eileen had deliberately chosen a morning wedding) a touch green about the gills but holding on for dear life. The reception was laid on by Mrs. Dawson and attended by half of Denver; Eileen thought she saw "her" Indian at the punchbowl but wasn't certain. Toward quitting time, as tradition requires, the bride and groom retired to change into traveling clothes, departed in a shower of rice, and entered a private railroad car on a Denver siding, and the I.F.R.&P. pulled away into the night.

In the interests of completing the record, it should be added that, as the private car was bumping out of the Denver yards, Colonel Jellison gently brushed the rice off the attractive shoulders of his bride and turned his back for her to reciprocate fondly. They kissed warmly. Then Dick drew away and said, "Now that we are married, Eileen, would you do something that would please the bridegroom very, very much and require very, very little effort on your part?"

In her present frame of mind Eileen was prepared to do just about anything, but felt impelled to ask, "What?"

"Would you please take off that feathered monstrosity and

pitch it out the car window?"

"My hat?"

"Your hat. If that is what it is."

"But it cost twenty dollars and . . . and . . ."

"And what?"

"And it hides. My. Hair." Eileen's tone was despondent.

"That is why." Colonel Jellison was getting that dangerous look in his eyes again.

Eileen raised her face to him expressionlessly. "But I have red hair . . ."

"I know. I also know you've hidden it under some peach basket or another all the time we've been in Denver. But Eileen, I *like* red hair. I *love* red hair. I particularly dote on *your* color of red hair. Can't stay away from it. Why do you think I followed you into that bookstore? I saw it halfway down the block. Some men like one thing, and some like another, but I am enraptured by red hair on a girl named Eileen Crowley."

She sighed happily. In a wifely voice she corrected him. "Eileen Jellison, you mean, dear." The huge hat sailed out the car window like an ungainly bird, was caught by the wind of their passage, and whirled out of sight.

"I am a man of settled habits," Dick whispered into her glowing, high-piled locks. "I have *always* preferred red-headed girls."

CHAPTER 8

1885
H. OSBORN ELLIOTT

OLICEMAN WILLARD AMES was making his nightly rounds through Phonolite when he came upon a strange, skeletal horse cropping the weeds in a brush lot. Connected to the horse with knotted and decayed harness was a wagon in the last stages of dilapidation. Ames held his lantern higher. In the wagon bed was what appeared to be a load of miscellaneous furniture and iron junk. Tangled in and about it was a sleeping man, snoring vigorously. The air within four feet of his open mouth was heavy with the odor of spoiled grain. Since there was little point in attempting to question the newcomer, the policeman followed his standard procedure for such cases. Taking Old Famine by the bit, he guided the tatterdemalion rig down the street toward the lockup. Ames tucked the sleeper into bed and then led the wagon around to the corral behind, where stray stock was impounded. Ames was so impressed by the horse's mere ability to put one leg in front of the other that he doled out some oats and shook down a little hay.

By dawn's early light Ames returned to his charge. He fed the pale horse again and opened the lockup door. The sleeper still slept. In the growing light he could be seen to be wearing a

gentleman's gray suit. Its condition suggested that the suit had served gallantly if hopelessly from Ball's Bluff to Appomattox with Hood's Texans. The wearer—a match for the horse in skeletal angularity—also possessed ragged boots and a paper collar and shirt-front combination of astounding grime. A brilliant silk cravat bearing the history of his eating habits completed his dress, although a battered plug hat had been retrieved from the wagon by Ames and tossed onto the floor, where it still lay. The guest's open mouth was adorned by the customary handlebar moustache of extraordinary length but with the scantiness and droop of a grandfather rat fallen on bad times in the old sewer. Some tobacco-yellowed teeth were readily visible. Ames's attention was now directed toward the hands of the sleeper. The fingertips were in plain sight, dyed a dead-black. Just to be sure, the policeman raised his head to look out the lockup's back window. In the rear of the crazy wagon he saw the outline, like that of a truncated guillotine, of a Washington flat-bed hand press. Journalism had come to Phonolite.

Ames stepped out, returning soon with a tin cup filled with water. Holding it over the sleeper's face, he tilted it gently. The dribble soon produced the desired consequences, and when the man seemed sufficiently conscious, Ames asked his name.

"H. Osborn Elliott," was the reply, delivered upon a breath that would have appalled anyone less professional than a policeman. "Publisher and editor of the—what in hell's the name of this camp, anyway?"

"Phonolite."

". . . the *Phonolite Tribune*. Finest weekly in the West. Two cents an issue, two dollars a year, cash only in advance. Job printing done accurately, promptly, and reasonably. Where can a man get a drink around here?"

Ames proffered the half-empty cup. H. Osborn Elliott took it, looked carefully into it, and handed it back. He rose somewhat shakily, unconscious of the large damp patch on the front of his trousers. "Where's my plant?"

"Out back in the corral."

H. Osborn Elliott looked and was satisfied. "I think I'll go sell

186

some local advertising. Where's the nearest saloon?" He leaned over for his hat, groaned, put it on his head, and stalked out of the lockup in the direction that Ames had indicated.

By devices privy only to masters of his craft, H. Osborn Elliott secured a breakfast at the free lunch counter of the Miners' Rest, obtained an eye opener to steady his hands at the Shamrock, and, thus refreshed, went forth to do battle. By sunset, and by equally arcane means, he had secured the tenancy of a vacant store, transferred his cargo into it, and had hung out his sign. Like the logotype of his paper, it read only the "The Tribune" in battered gilt Gothic—a shift that produced great economy in logos, signs, and stationery as a newspaper moved from camp to camp. Although he had spent scarcely fifty-eight hours in the camp, the first issue of the *Phonolite Tribune* was being hawked upon the evening of the second day. A discerning eye could have noted that, apart from a reset dateline and a spread-eagle editorial of self-welcome, it was printed entirely from the same galleys that had constituted the last edition at whatever place Elliott had come from.

Phonolite bought the *Tribune* all the same. Aside from gossip and word-of-mouth news brought in on the narrow gauge, the camp lived in considerable ignorance of both its own and the world's doings, an ignorance which now seemed in a way to be remedied. The consensus was that a newspaper was just what Phonolite required. Policeman Ames, who had entertained some private doubts about his wisdom in not putting Elliott on the outbound train, was reassured by the mayor. And in an outburst of civic pride the city council even gave Elliott a contract to print one hundred copies of the ordinances, heretofore entered in the back of an old ledger as they were enacted. After a week or two it seemed as though the *Tribune* had always been in Phonolite. H. Osborn Elliott was an indefatigable jackdaw where news was concerned. He pilfered shamelesssly from *Mining and Scientific Press* for the benefit of his overseas and national desks but made the local rounds as regularly as Ames, pencil and notebook in hand. He printed police news, social news, church and fraternal news. It was said that he opened the office of the Molly Pitcher in the morning and closed it up at night. Elliott even arranged matters so that his serious drinking started on Friday night, safely after the week's issue had been printed and had hit the streets.

In an oak-paneled Board room in San Francisco, certain grandees became aware that beautiful letters now prevailed at Phonolite. George Huggins, who had voted for Jim Blaine only because Cato the Censor had not been the Republican nominee in "Eighty-four growled that things had come to a hell of a pass when newspapermen and dogs were let run around loose on company property. But Frank Casey soothed him. "These old newspaper-men," he observed, "are all alike. Lying Jim Townsend never hurt anyone but his creditors, and them not very much. If Bodie could take Jim, Phonolite can bear up under this one."

"I'd still have him run out. Look at Greeley." But this shot was merely fired for the honor of the flag before it was hauled down.

It is difficult, then, to state exactly when the trouble started. Perhaps as good a choice as any was the evening in October when H. Osborn Elliott's inroads upon the free lunch at the Miners' Rest began to irk the proprietor, Jack Spargo. Ordinarily Elliott ate half his dinner at the Miners' Rest and the other half at the Shamrock, thus keeping the stresses within limits of tolerance. But on this day Spargo had acquired an exceptionally tasty wheel of cheese, a conclusion with which Elliott evidently agreed. Spargo began to glower as Elliott continued stoping it without pause. He told himself that Elliott spent only half his money at the Miners' Rest and concluded that it was more than time for Finnegan at the Shamrock to bear his share of the burden. Elliott, however, blandly ignored Spargo's coughs and bar-rag flourishes.

" 'Ere, now!" Spargo finally burst out. "Save some of yon cheese for they day shift, will 'ee?"

It was a mild-enough rebuke, but Elliott put down the cut he had been foraging upon and looked Spargo straight in the eye. Spargo stared back and felt a sudden mislike of what he saw. Elliott's eyes were an unwholesome flat green, and there was a look in them that was worse. Before Spargo could speak again, Elliott had turned on his heel and was gone.

The proprietor of the Miners' Rest had nearly forgotten the

incident when the next issue of the *Tribune* came out. On the front page was a police news item:

DISTURBANCE AT LOCAL OASIS?

Policeman Willard Ames has denied reports that there was a serious affair at a local watering place a few nights ago. This newspaper has learned, however, that when our Cousins take a few too many aboard they are inclined to get pretty rowdy. We would understand it if Ames were outnumbered, but this sort of thing will not improve our fair city nor the reputation of those concerned. Is there not an ordinance requiring a saloonkeeper to refuse service to the inebriated?

Spargo read it a second time in disbelief. Without naming names, Elliott had defamed him, his saloon, the Cousins, and Ames in one fell swoop of innuendo. There had been *no* fight, nor even any unseemliness. What was Elliott thinking of—revenge for a piece of cheese?

When Ames came in, Spargo made to show him the item, but the policeman shook his head. "I read it, too. Half a dozen people showed it to me. Yes, he asked me a night ago if there had been a fight here. I told him, no. Maybe he just needs something to print. Best forget it, Jack."

Spargo was not allowed to forget it. The next *Tribune* carried a long, heated editorial condemning an unnamed local saloon as a haunt of rowdies and a disgrace to a decent camp and suggested that the proprietor move over to Bancroft, where they appreciated these things. Spargo started to hurt. Scenting action, a number of the tramp miners began to come in and behave as they would at Bancroft. Worse, the news stories following a couple of real fights began to drive away Spargo's steady customers. Brendan Finnegan of the Shamrock came over to review the situation. "For it's your growler trade and your old regulars I'm gettin', Jack—and I don't want them. Cousins and Harps don't mix, and I'm fearin' that I'll have a big fight some night and my place broken up. Looks like it hasn't done you any good, the tramps coming in, neither."

"It's all h'a damn lie!" Spargo exclaimed in frustration.

"Ah, there I can't be helpin' you. The wimmen read that paper, an' they believe every word. Could you have Ames talk to the man? Maybe he could be made to see reason."

Ames, when asked, said he would try. In the editorial sanctum, however, he had hardly said ten words before Elliott began to smile crookedly. Realizing that he was telling the editor nothing that he did not already know, Ames gently changed his tune. "If Spargo's hurt your feelings some way," he hinted, "could he make it right with you?"

"Absolutely!" Elliott responded. "Free drinks from now on, and no bellyaching about the free lunch."

This was too unreasonable for the policeman to treat as anything more than a diplomatic gambit, opening the way for serious negotiation. He decided to enter into the spirit of things. "You'd drink his profits up that way. And we have a city ordinance about no free drinks. How about one round on the house and a handshake?"

Elliott turned on him savagely. "Spargo is a leech, an ignorant, tight-fisted clod of a Cousin whisky seller!" he stormed. "This camp would be better without him, and I intend to see that he goes. And as for you, Ames—take thought for yourself. Who do you stand with, me or Spargo?"

"I'm with nobody," the policeman replied, somewhat puzzled by the outburst. "Just trying to patch things up."

"Ames, you need a lesson," Elliott murmured, his green eyes flickering. "Take your choice, me or Spargo."

"I don't have to make a choice," Ames said carelessly. Feeling that nothing had been gained, he left the newspaper office without saying anything else.

In the next issue of the *Tribune*, the campaign against the Miners' Rest continued, but a new item attracted much attention. Written in a coy manner, it ran:

WHO WILL WATCH THE WATCHER?

The *Tribune* has learned that a local functionary, whom we will not name, really should spend a little more time guarding the sanctity of his own home as well as that of others. A couple of nights ago we thought we observed a shadowy form slipping into the back door of a local home, whose Lord and Master was about his official business elsewhere. It is not for the *Tribune* to lecture other people on their private business, but it is said that the last person to know is the one most injured.

When Ames stalked into his house, he found his wife weeping bitterly, a copy of the *Tribune* clutched in her hand. Ames's own face was crimson with fury. "The dirty-mouthed little bastard!" he growled.

"You don't believe it, Willard?" his wife sobbed.

"I don't believe a word of it. But those who want to, will. And there's a lot of those."

"Don't hurt him, Willard," she pleaded.

"How can I?" he said bitterly. "I'm a policeman."

In Elliott's office Ames asked pleadingly, *"Why?* Why go out of your way to hurt a woman who never hurt you?"

"Who has hurt anyone, Ames? Why come to me? Did *I* say the shoe fit? And don't blame me if your neighbors have dirty minds. All I do is report the news."

"News you made up out of your filthy mind."

"So you say. So you would like to believe. But who was there—you or I?"

"You could put it right with a word, Elliott."

"Words are like anything else, Ames. They have a price. Remember—I asked you to choose between Spargo and me. Well, you made your choice."

"I made no choice at all."

"Yes, you did. Those who are not for me are against me. That makes the price go up." The editor leaned back in his broken chair and placed his fingertips together—black against black. "Now if there was to be a *real* fight in Spargo's place . . . ." His green eyes glowed. "You could bring over eight or nine of those tough boys from Bancroft. Give them a couple of dollars apiece. Tell me the night, and I'll be standing outside, waiting."

Ames' forehead wrinkled in thought. "Then you're hurting my wife to hurt *me*, so I'll help you ruin Spargo?"

"For a policeman you think clearly. Here—I'll give you a push. If you don't, maybe in my next issue I'll name a man. I'll even let you pick one out. Then you'll have to kill him. It will give me a good story. Or maybe he'll kill *you*. That would be a better story, plus, of course, the bereaved widow's tears. Builds circulation like a house afire."

"I could kill *you* here and now," Ames said softly.

"Why, so you could. And go to territorial prison for twenty years. Or even hang. I'm not armed, you see, and I'm not at all afraid to die. That gives me an edge on you."

Ames turned to leave. "Next issue, Ames," a mocking voice behind him said. "I'll choose him if you don't."

Ames went to the mayor and poured out the story. The mayor, who was a good-enough man with a length of dry goods, was out of his depth. "Good Lord, Ames!" he objected. "I can't do anything. He hasn't *said* anything! Sure, it's a lie maybe, but he can lie all he pleases, so long as he doesn't get caught at it. And," he concluded reflectively, "I don't know as I could do anything even then. You could sue him, maybe. But you can't shut him up."

When Ames got home, he found his wife in tears again. Their two young daughters had been chased home from school by a gang of roughnecks, throwing mud and rocks. The girls were too young to know what the shouted words meant, but they could repeat what the boys were yelling. After they had been soothed and sent to their room, Mrs. Ames said quietly, "The ladies from the church committee were here after you left. They hemmed a lot, but they asked us not—not to attend for a while. I asked them if they believed it, and Mrs. Clark said that where there was smoke there was fire. And I asked if what they were doing was Christian charity. Mrs. Clark said that charity was one thing but the reputation of the church was something else."

Just as quietly Ames whispered, "I am going to kill him."

"No, you are not, Willard!"

"He said that next week he'll name a man. Then I will have to kill *him*. It's either that bastard or an innocent man."

"It's no such thing!" Mrs. Ames stood up with an air of determination. "I don't know why all this got started, but I know how to stop it. We're leaving Phonolite tonight."

"It's running away!" Ames protested.

"It's the only sensible thing. You can get work somewhere else.

Come on, Willard. Think of our girls, not of your pride."

That evening at seven o'clock a good policeman and his family left Phonolite on the narrow gauge. When he learned of it, H. Osborn Elliott laughed in hilarity and got fairly drunk. Even while his head was still aching the next morning, he started on his next campaign.

The power of the press is almost as great as its most febrile servitors claim. Elliott had quietly built up a corps of spies and delators in Phonolite, paying them in whatever coin (money aside) they most desired: a favorable mention, suppression of an embarrassing item, an innuendo about an enemy, or merely the delicious joy of seeing one's name in print. He had discovered a major secret—the informer lays information as much to revel in a momentary sense of importance, or out of a simian curiosity to see what will come of his tattling, as of a desire to hurt an enemy or gain an advantage. Elliott knew where to go for the most profitable hunting: the part-time undertaker, the milliner, the church sextons, the depot baggage smasher. Such people saw much and deduced more, but were invisible to the casual eye. He courted the ugly, the vain, the fanatical, the censorious, the thwarted, the failure. He primed drunks. He knew that children love to talk to an interested adult, even if they know not what they say. And he was brilliantly aware that with a germ of truth and the fertilizer of innuendo one can make mighty oaks sprout from very meager acorns. The more he learned, the more power he had; the more power he had, the more information he could extract. And so he decided, for no good reason, that his next target would be the Reverend Mr. Algernon Parley—who had declined to become an ally in Elliott's permanent campaign against Jack Spargo and the Miners' Rest.

It was so easy as to be almost unsatisfactory. Mr. Parley was married to an ambitious, cold, and malignant wife. His choir director was a young matron, enormously impressed by the youthful, ascetic-looking pastor. Even without exact information Elliott could have done it in three weeks. As it was, he required only one issue. Twelve hours after it had been printed, Mr. and Mrs. Parley were gone from Phonolite. So was the young matron.

Her husband stayed on, however, for he had shot himself. Elliott ran his obituary with great glee. "Died of a gun accident," his black, nimble fingers flipped from the case into the stick. He knew that the whole camp knew the true details, so why not be reticent?

Target after target he stalked and smote down. A satisfactory near-riot between the old Irish patrons and the incoming Cousins turned the Shamrock into a shambles of broken glassware and splintered furniture. Spargo was talking of selling out. A campaign of innuendo against the Molly Pitcher had the miners growling that the directors were saying, "Men are cheaper than timber." The schoolteacher left in midyear. Elliott was turning Phonolite into a madhouse. He sincerely hoped that it was not love's labor lost, inasmuch as he was after much larger game than the mere ruin of a few inconsequential lives. He would have been delighted had he known that in San Francisco a heavy-set man with large shoes was even then handing a very thick envelope to Colonel Richard D. Jellison. "It's here, sir," the man was saying. "Or as much as you asked for and probably need. Our man was put on at the Molly Pitcher—no trouble, he's a good miner—and he's kept his ears open. We've also traced the subject back to other camps and have information from those places as well in that envelope."

"Thank you very much," Jellison replied. He wrote a check on his personal account to a famed private detective agency and handed it over to his visitor.

"Much obliged, Colonel. Anything else you want us to do?"

"No, or at least not for the time. I think I'll try to handle this one myself."

"I'd be careful, Colonel," the man cautioned. "He's turned at least four other camps into a living hell for the people there. I'd call him dangerous even if he doesn't use violence."

"I wonder why he does it?" Jellison reflected. "Well, possibly I'll find out."

So it was that a week later Jellison stepped off the narrow-gauge day coach at Phonolite. There was no reception committee, since he had not told anyone but his clerk of his destination. To Eileen, now glowing with her second pregnancy, he had said merely that he was going away for a few days to look over some property. She smiled at him, being rather used to this by now, and reminded him to return to her promptly. He earnestly replied that he would indeed. Now he picked up his small valise and made his way up the hill to the boarding hotel. The proprietor looked closely at Jellison, made no comment when he signed the ledger as "Richard Johnson, Salesman, San Francisco," but nevertheless assigned him to the first table in the dining room and roomed him in the big front suite on the second floor, normally reserved for visiting magnates of the very first chop. At dinner Jellison was aware that his incognito was severely bent, if not broken, but none of the men at the table did more than nod to him and resume discussing their own affairs among themselves. After the pie he laid up on the big brass double bed, rereading from the envelope. It contained clippings, copies of legal documents, depositions, agents' reports, and a long summary by the chief of the San Francisco bureau. By the time he had skimmed most of them, it was coming on to dusk.

Jellison put on his coat, boots, and hat and unstrapped his valise. Under his shirts were three objects. One was a thick packet of United States twenty-dollar gold certificates, the bank wrapper still about it. The second was a stubby double-barreled shotgun of the sort favored by peace officers and Wells Fargo guards. Two blue shells with "00" stamped on the end wads accompanied it. The third was a large flask covered with fine leather. It contained a quart of the best whisky obtainable in San Francisco, a city that prided itself on its cellars. Jellison did not hesitate over his choice. He closed the valise on the money and the shotgun, tucked the flask into an inside coat pocket, and left the hotel.

On the steps of the veranda he tried to orient himself. To his left the street ran downhill, terminating in the railroad line and the dry bed of the creek. A quarter-mile away to his right front and at a higher elevation was the incline headframe and, a quarter-mile beyond it, the shaft headframe of the Molly. Jellison walked uphill to the corner, turned left, and walked west along the unpaved street. He seemed to be searching for something, ignoring the buildings but concentrating on the lay of the land and the eastern ridge line. At last he stopped and crossed the street to the north. Here was a large unkempt stable or barn or some such, closed up and apparently untenanted. Under it or approximately so he estimated was the grave of Bill Penrose. "Wish me luck, Bill," he whispered. "I could sure use a good man like you tonight. Sleep tight." He paused, head lowered for a moment, and then retraced his steps to the hotel. He continued down the street to the creek bank. Water Street, here paralleling the stream bed, displayed on its east side the fag ends of the business district, whose brighter and busier portions prevailed a block or so farther north.

Jellison strolled along the board sidewalk until he came to a small frame building through whose front window the glimmer of an oil lamp was visible. In the back of the room a thin, angular man was engaged by its light in some sort of activity. His left hand, held close to his waist, supported a flat container into which his right hand was flipping tiny objects plucked one by one from the innumerable small pigeonholes of the tall wooden case that he faced. The hand moved with incredible speed, but the man did not seem to be watching very closely what he was doing. Once he carried the container over to a long table, emptied it with great care, fussed about, and then returned to his pluck-and-push work. When the man paused for rest, Jellison tapped at the door glass.

The man set down the container, picked up the lamp, and walked over to regard Jellison by its light. Following the inspection he unlocked the door and, opening it, remarked, "Come in, Colonel Jellison. Welcome to the editorial sanctum of the *Phonolite Tribune.*"

Jellison betrayed no surprise, for he was not surprised. He entered, removed his hat, and replied, "I am glad at long last to meet you, Mr. Elliott. As you know, I have come to talk with you." He did not offer to shake hands.

The man's cadaverous face did not change, but he nodded gravely. Removing his ink-stained apron, he said, "We would be more at ease at the Shamrock."

"I don't know," Jellison said. "You have a table, chairs, a light—and I have *this*. You will find it perhaps a cut above even the

196

Shamrock's better sort."

The man regarded the big flask fondly as Jellison set it down in the center of the rickety, proof-strewn table. "I—ah—have no suitable glassware."

"The cap itself is a cup. It unscrews." Jellison demonstrated. "The cork comes out—so. One pours." He tasted the whisky. It was very good indeed. "Your health, sir." Jellison drained the very small serving, wiped the cup with a clean handkerchief, and pushed it over. Elliott poured a long one, leaned back in his chair and tossed it down. He paused with a look of surprised appreciation.

"It is the best I have ever tasted. You millionaires do yourselves well." He correctly interpreted Jellison's casual wave as an invitation to pour himself another. Sipping at it, he remarked, "I am coming up in the world's estimation, I see. A policeman visited me first. Then a mayor. Then a priest. Then a mine superintendent. Now, I am receiving a millionaire."

"I didn't know about the priest. That would be Father Feeney?"

"Yes. Typical of his breed. He offered nothing, made no threats, merely whined little pieties. I heard him out before showing him the door."

"Did you say 'threats'?" Jellison asked in concern.

"Of a sort. Your superintendent threatened me with *you*. And here you are. Are his threats good, or are they merely bluster?"

Jellison reflected. "As I recall, when the boards in those other camps had had enough, they merely sent a detective. I can imagine what was said. But, you see, I myself came here."

"I am honored, sir," the editor said sarcastically. "All it would require would be a word from you, the man who really rules this camp and every soul in it but mine. Perhaps even your silence at a critical moment would be enough. Let Richard Drexel Jellison in his San Francisco office merely say nothing when some man cries, 'Will no one rid us of this villain editor?' and a hundred would race to burn this building and worse. I am genuinely puzzled that you have not done so—yet."

"Who is remembered the longer, Henry II or Becket?"

197

"Becket, of course."

"Would it have been so, do you suppose, if Henry had kept his temper—and his own law?"

Elliott considered. "Probably not."

"There is your answer, Mr. Elliott. Making a martyr is an unprofitable day's work at any time. Not to mention the law, for which I have a high regard."

"Surely you are not serious? About the law, I mean. How could a man gain your wealth without trampling over its spirit and its letter?"

"I could try to reply, but it would divert us from the point at issue. Go ahead—have another. It lubricates debate. Now the issue. You came here uninvited. You were made welcome. People treated you with charity, kindness, even respect. In this past year you have repaid them by a wholesale poisoning of this community. Good people have been driven away. Lives and reputations have been ruined. One man I know of is dead at his own hand because of you. I thought at first that someone or something *here* had given you cause to hate. But I find that everywhere you have been since 1866 it is the same story. Elliott and his *Tribune* enter a camp, and presently it is a purgatory of fear, hate, strife, violence, death. Phonolite is just another story, not a unique one. One by one, the other camps drove you out, but not before their social fabric was rent beyond repair. By *you!*"

"True, true," Elliott nodded genially. "All true. But they, you see, represented failure on my part. My purpose was to bring myself to the attention of the moneymen who owned them." He sighed. "They were shortsighted, even stupid. They saw only a source of irritation, and took the shorter way with it. But perhaps at last I am talking to a man who can see somewhat beyond the next dollar. A rare thing—a millionaire with imagination."

"Imagination enough to see that you are venal enough to be bought, Mr. Elliott. Would you care to name your price?"

"Price?" Elliott asked. "Of course. There is always a price. In this case . . . you have much money and great influence, Colonel Jellison. If you asserted yourself, you could as good as name the territorial governor."

"Whom do you have in mind?"

"You have heard of the Honorable Mirabeau Marat Ransome?"

Jellison stared in disbelief. "Who hasn't?"

"Don't you think he would be a fine appointment?" Elliott smiled insinuatingly.

"Excluding even the fact that he is a stupid demagogue, the cats-paw of fanatics, and would be beholden to *you*, I can't imagine a worse man. With him at Meade, the whole territory would become bedlam."

"But you miss the point, Colonel. It would give him a seat by which to command national attention. Supported by your money and by my pen . . . ."

Jellison's heart began to skip. Pieces of a puzzle were coming together rapidly. "I think I can perceive dimly what you may be driving at, Mr. Elliott. A man does not do as you have done—and wish to do—without some very compelling reasons. Suppose you tell me your story. I might perhaps be much more understanding."

"Delighted—as long as you're buying."

Jellison pushed the flask over to him. Elliott applied himself directly to it and kept it under his hand. "Years ago," he began, "I was a young editor of a county newspaper at—well, near the Ohio River. I was full of idealism, zeal, conscious that a free press was the guarantee of our liberties as a people. I could bring the light of culture. Uplift the people. Tell them the full story, so that they would make up their minds and vote for the better cause, the better man." He lifted his flat, green eyes to Jellison's. "A free press is the vision and voice of a free republic. Napoleon said that he feared one unfettered newspaper more than thirty thousand bayonets . . . ."

Elliott's eyes dropped. "Then came the war. An unjust war. An unconstitutional war. An immoral war, unresolved by the Congress, unadjudicated by the courts. A war fostered by a clique of rich men, wishing to be richer, led by a sly demagogue."

"Which side do you mean?" Jellison asked.

Elliott stared at him. "I am talking about that baboon, Lincoln," he snapped.

"Pardon me. Please continue."

"From the moment it began, I opposed it. I told my readers that secession was justified in law, in precedent, in morality. That it was the plain duty of honest men to let them go in peace. Mind you, I hold no brief for chattel slavery. But was that *my* business, what they did with their own? I fought the calls for volunteers. I called for opposition to the draft—the draft!" He laughed bitterly. "The war was put forward as a great sacrifice for freedom, while boys from my county too poor to purchase exemption were dragged away to die like slaughter cattle."

"You were a Copperhead!" Jellison exclaimed.

"We had other names, and better, but we would not deny that one. However, one epithet we did deny, that of 'traitor.' How could we do treason when there was no declared war? The Constitution says so."

"You are quite certain?"

Elliott drew back, affronted. "Of course!"

"Since you seem to stand upon the strict letter of it," his guest remarked, "I shall argue from the strict letter of it. Article three, Section three, reads, 'Treason against the United States shall consist only in levying War against them, or in adhering to their Enemies, giving them Aid and Comfort.' I stipulate that you did not carry arms. But out of your own mouth you admit to giving considerable aid and comfort to those who did so levy war. The common expression, 'To give aid and comfort to their enemies *in time of war*,' is popular but erroneous. It is entirely possible to be a traitor in the absence of a congressional war resolution. I cite the Whiskey Rebellion cases, or, if you please, *United States versus Burr*. But as you were saying. . . ."

"Yes, uh, well, I opposed the draft. I incited desertion, helped deserters get away to Canada or out to the territories. I supported Vallandigham, Milligan, Bowles—all the men of peace and good will and libertarianism. I was warned many times that I was inviting retribution. Finally it came."

"You were arrested?"

"Lincoln was too subtle. Some were arrested, yes. His sending

200

Vallandigham to the Confederacy was a master stroke, I grant you. But I was not important enough to merit his august attention."

"So?"

"He let human depravity take its course. A mob came. It was right after that barbarity at Atlanta had driven all the bloodthirsty beasts wild with glee. They wrecked my paper. Then—have you ever seen a man who has been tarred and feathered and ridden out on a rail? Look!" He pulled up his ragged coatsleeves. Wide, pale blotches were visible on his sleeveless forearms. "I am like that all over. They said they would make the tar hot enough for—for traitors and liars."

"To this point," Jellison interjected, "there might be some discussion about political interpretations, yes. But lying?"

Elliott drank deeply and then stood in a posture as though addressing a multitude, though his voice remained low. "When you control completely the written word," he began, "the truth is what you say it to be. Who can contradict you? Should you assert that black is white, a few men more intelligent than most will mutter, but what can they do? Tell their families? Let them! But the Word *is* truth to the ignorant, the unperceptive, those already well disposed to believe, and they will persuade or coerce the rest. Black, then, *is* white. I do not even have to erect plausible excuses. My column head screams it, and it is so! Let me tell you of my greatest feat. You are too young to remember it well, but you must surely know the name Gettysburg—that place of blood. Who won that battle, Colonel Jellison? Who won?"

"The Union, of course."

"Not in my paper! Not in my county! It was a dazzling triumph for the Confederacy! Four boys fled to Canada after I had done. The telegraph reports began to come in slowly on the second of July. I posted them up in my window as they came, for they said nothing, really, but of confusion and slaughter. By the fifth I *knew* that it had been a Union victory of sorts. But did I say so? I reasoned that victory or defeat is really a device to influence the minds of men. The victor asserts, 'I won,' and men do his bidding. The loser says, 'I lost,' and men desert his cause. But the real test is

201

not who won the field. It is who won the victory over men's minds as the consequence?"

Elliott began to pace about in excitement. "I wrote three full columns for my extra edition. I described the Confederate advance into Pennsylvania. Surprising! Stunning! After two years of bloody war and countless assurances from Lincoln to the contrary, the South was attacking. *On Union soil!* Then, the battle. Longstreet smashes the Union left. Hill rolls up the Union right. Pickett pierces the Union center. Is it not true? Every word of it? I describe the toll of Union dead, the confusion at headquarters, the consternation in Washington. Then—the Confederates show mercy. They are not conquerors. They only wish to negotiate what is theirs by right. They draw off at leisure and unmolested, leaving Meade to lick his ghastly wounds. Who can defeat a battle captain like Lee? What can defeat the Army of Northern Virginia? They are just men, fighting with *élan* in a just cause. 'Peace—now—at any price,' I cry. No more pointless slaughter. No more disasters like this of Gettysburg." Elliott pushed his face down, almost into Jellison's. "Have I said a word of untruth? One single *word*?"

"You did not tell all the truth," Jellison objected.

"An editor is not a sworn witness in a court, sir. It is his privilege and right to omit—shall we say, nonessentials—from his story."

"You deceived."

"It was in a good cause. My end justified any means, but I did not even lie. I merely exercised . . . editorial discretion."

"You lied by omission. Sooner or later you would be found out."

Elliott's shoulders drooped slightly. "It would appear that you are right. The tar was exceedingly hot. It burned more than my skin—it burned my soul as well." He sat again, staring out the window into the night. "On a night as dark as this, far out and away from that place, I took stock. I decided that God must be distant indeed to permit the wrong to triumph and liberty to die. That this nation and its leaders had been given over wholly to the devil. That the American people—barring those miserable

wretches in the South, persecuted, impoverished, treated worse
than this territory treats its felons for the high crime of asserting
their just cause—that the American people were damned. The
country I had believed in and the dream I had dreamed was dead
and stinking. What remained was only a carcass, fought over by
bloated vultures. To the hell it deserved with it and with them!"

Elliott pulled long at the flask and set it down with a thump. "So
I assist them to hell in my small way. I destroy their faith in
themselves and in each other. I set husband against wife, child
against parent, Cornishman against Irishman, worker against
capitalist. They love war—I give them war. I bring it home to them
as Sherman brought it home to the poor South. I can create chaos
at my pleasure. And I do! I do!"

"You are mad!" Jellison exclaimed.

"If I am mad, then so was the John Brown you extol, and for the
same reason." Elliott's voice changed then. "But even so, there is
hope."

"Hope?"

"Yes, hope. I have a plan—a great plan. Perhaps tonight I can at
last begin bringing it to fruition. Ransome, on whom I pin my
hopes, needs a fulcrum to begin making his mark again. He has the
voice to rally the discontented, the impoverished, the restless. He
can raise them, forge them into an army. Today—Meade.
Tomorrow—Washington itself perhaps. Ransome has no ideas of
his own, but he has that voice that can compel stones to move, and I
can supply him with more ideas than he knows what to do with. I
can guide him to power as a man guides a horse. All that is needed
is money. And given power . . . ." Elliott stared into the darkness
with the expression of a prophet who has been given a glimpse of
his heart's desire.

"Given power?" Jellison prompted.

"Why, given power, wrong can be righted, the wicked
chastised, the strong put down, and the weak exalted. My great
dream can be achieved. My dream of a pure, sweet nation, a
beacon of justice and charity to the world, restored to God's favor
and the light of the Constitution as it was." He raised both
clenched fists above his head. "They know not good from evil, but

203

I—an ink-stained scribbler—can show them the way!"

"I was under the impression," Jellison said mildly, "that, constitutionally speaking, the majority was rather supposed to run things."

"But, you see," Elliott pleaded, "you of all people *must* see, they are wrong. How can majority rule mean anything when they are *wrong*?"

"And you are right. But tell me, how do *you* know you are right?"

Elliott raised his chin in pride. "I know. It was shown me by a higher reason than a ballot box. We—all of us—all the Knights of the Golden Circle—agreed. We had the right of it. You cannot argue down the right. It simply *is*!"

"And I come in at this point?"

Elliott sighed in relief. "I knew you were a better sort than those others. I have already said. Ransome must become territorial governor. With money, ideas, his voice . . . . What more is needed, other than time and perseverance?"

Jellison appeared to consider. "Ransome—yes. He can do it. I heard him once, speaking against the Chinese in San Francisco. You—yes, I believe. Tonight you have convinced me that you are a master of your craft. I would say, a genius." Jellison nodded. "Elliott, had you served Napoleon, I think we would be speaking French today."

The editor bowed slightly in acknowledgment.

"Forgive me for asking, but what is in it for me? You can threaten me with the destruction of Phonolite and the Molly, but I can tell you frankly that I have other and larger interests. Letting the Molly go would hurt me, but not fatally and not for long. The stick is inadequate—show me the carrot, as well."

"Why, whatever you wish!" Elliott exclaimed. "Greater wealth. Beautiful women. Luxury. And the greatest prize of all—power itself! Power for its own sake, if you will. Power to do great good, I hope. Mankind would be the better. What more *is* there?"

Jellison drummed his fingers on the table. "I really do not care for greater wealth. What I have seems now to grow of itself, and I have to spend more time dealing with it than with the activities I care better for. Luxury? Colonel Casey warned me to be abstemious. Rich men, he said, tend to kill themselves with their teeth. Women? I am already married to the most beautiful woman in the world in my eyes." He smiled. "It is really all I can do to keep up with her. Power?" Jellison leaned back and put his feet on the table. "Elliott, I must be deformed or wanting in some respect. I hear men speak of power as men spoke of the Holy Grail back in the Middle Ages. But to me it means nothing. I say to one, 'Come,' and he cometh, but I *feel* nothing save anxiety that the work be not done well."

"Then for the good of mankind!" Elliott demanded.

"I am a bit uncertain about what that might be. To that extent I envy you your dream—but only slightly. You might as well speak of blue to a blind man." Jellison put his feet back on the floor. "Well, I have heard you out. Let us examine the alternatives, Mr. Elliott. Will I assist you? The answer is—no. Never. I would see you and Ransome in hell first."

"Along with Phonolite," Elliott snarled.

Jellison continued as though the editor had not spoken. "I will not use or permit the use of violence against you, for I do not hold that the end justifies the means."

The editor smiled thinly and nodded.

"Legal devices are fruitless. Freedom of the press is your constitutional right, however you misuse it. You have steered clear of slander, though you needed not. What have you to levy upon to satisfy a judgment? No, the law stands helpless."

Elliott nodded again.

"Bribery. Your price, I will tell you, is far too high. I would free Phonolite momentarily from a plague, only perhaps to deliver the entire nation to a worse plague. If it were just a sum of money, now?"

Elliott shook his head decisively.

Then Jellison's eyes opened wide. "Of course!" he exclaimed. "I was stupid not to think of that!"

"Of what?" the editor demanded, leaning forward.

"Of the ideal, which is to say the effective and ethical solution to

205

you and your viper's tongue and that obscene ambition that you call your dream." Jellison nodded to himself. "I think I shall start on it tonight. The telegrapher should still be at the depot."

"Summoning your bullies and your bravos?" Elliott sneered. "Admit defeat, then?"

"Oh, hardly," his visitor said carelessly. "You know, Elliott, I might be doing you a favor. Stupid as you are, if you did try to rise from your gutter, you would probably be crushed like a worm. My wife alone has more brains than a hundred of your sort."

"You're bluffing," the editor asserted, although a tinge of anxiety was perceptible in his voice. "I call."

"I think my hand might be two pairs—kings over knaves. In other words, Mr. Elliott, I think that what this camp needs most is *two* newspapers."

The editor sat as if frozen, an expression of horror slowly crossing his face.

"Yes," Jellison continued, almost gently, "print whatever you please. Anything whatsoever that emerges from that sewer of malice and ambition that you call your mind. Within twenty-four hours, a stronger voice will give you the lie. I am sure I can find some young journalist who would be glad of a chance to do just that."

"To act as your paid panderer, you mean!" Elliott stormed.

"I doubt that would be necessary. I shall simply choose a good young man, grubstake him, and say, 'Print *all* the truth. Show Phonolite what a good editor and—forgive me for mentioning the obvious—a sober and honest one can really do.' "

"You cannot! You *must* not! I—I forbid it!" Elliott nearly screamed.

"Freedom of the press, Mr. Elliott. It is quantitative as well as qualitative."

The gaunt man whirled around, moaning like an animal. "My work!" he whined. "My *dream*!" He darted back to the composing table and with a sweep of his simian arm dashed the galleys onto the floor.

"Calm yourself, sir," his visitor's voice cut through the clatter. As if pronouncing sentence, Jellison continued, "I am not done with you yet. Stay here if you will and fight it out if you can, although I doubt that you have the courage. If you decide to leave rather than face the people you have bespattered—and I suspect you will leave this very night—I will have the detective agency keep an eye out for you. If you start your tricks in another camp, I shall know of it soon. And what I shall do here, I shall do *there*."

"It will be costly," Elliott said faintly.

"It will be well worth it. If a man will not give even a little money to preserve common decency from the likes of you, what hope is there for any of us?"

"Well," Jellison concluded, rising, "thank you, Mr. Elliott for a most rewarding conversation. I can't say I've ever heard a better—of its sort. You may keep the flask with my compliments." He bowed. "Good night and good-by, Mr. Elliott."

Much later that evening a skeletal horse pulled a dilapidated wagon down the valley. In the back of the wagon was a collection of furniture and what looked like a truncated guillotine. Driving and nearly sober was H. Osborn Elliott, fleeing from the only thing in the world that he feared with all his heart—competition.

CHAPTER 9

1900
DR. ELBERT MACKENSEN

THE BAGGAGE SMASHER of the I.F.R.&P. depot at Phonolite was proud of his ability to figure out the business of the passengers who alighted from the day coach coupled to the end of the morning freight. Those he knew by sight didn't count, but strangers were usually identifiable. An engineer, for instance, looked, dressed, and talked like other engineers and did *not* look, talk, and dress like a tramp miner or a visiting dignitary. He could even make a fair guess of a tramp's trade, if not by his manner, then by the tools he carried. Now this man, getting off on an April morning at 10:55 (the freight was only twenty-five minutes late, hence virtually on the advertised) was a lead-pipe cinch. The wing collar, Prince Albert coat, black fedora, and thin watch chain were such that the baggage smasher did not even have to look at the black leather bag in the pilgrim's hand to make assurance doubly sure. Therefore, when he saw the steamer trunk stenciled "Dr. Elbert Mackensen," he automatically put it on top of the carryall and told the driver to take the new arrival up to the Molly headworks. They'd take him from there.

After the driver had gee-upped his horses, the baggage man relaxed in the sun. It was a comfort to have a genuine sawbones in

TOMPHILLIPS

the camp again. Old Dr. Mulligan had been good enough until he went crazy back there a couple months ago, like so many of those old Civil War contract surgeons had a habit of doing. Maybe it was the horrors they had seen that did it, but it sure happened often. Here, now, years after the war a doctor would be doing fine—oh, getting pretty gray, of course—then suddenly up and declare that he was the Holy Ghost or General Sherman and start running around naked, like as not. They always put them in the asylum, and they died after a month or so. Mulligan wasn't dead, the last he'd heard, but the baggage man figured it was only a matter of time. So, apparently, did the people up at the Molly office.

The carryall driver found his passenger uncommunicative. The doctor was looking around in a peculiar manner as they passed down Water Street and turned up Casey Street to begin the long haul up to the mine office. He could not know that Dr. Mackensen was inspecting Phonolite as a newly imprisoned convict will first examine his cell after the door is closed upon him. Or that Mackensen's motives were similar, for he was going to be here for a very long time. Mackensen still writhed inwardly at the cold realism of the chief of the surgical service during that last interview, less than two weeks ago. He had known what was coming but had somehow hoped for better than what he was going to get—and had got.

"Doctor," the chief had said grittily, "if that incident, as I shall call it, had not received so much publicity, I would be inclined to pretend I had heard nothing and suspected nothing. But you could not resist ensuring that everyone within earshot, from staff to patients, knew the full details. I give no recommendations but truthful ones, and a truthful one on you now would be worse than no recommendation at all. Every hospital in this country is as good as barred to you and will stay barred. Perhaps you might be shown some sympathy, but I will have other young men to recommend, and I will not compromise their chances in the future in order to work you off on some institution now. The truth would come out anyway, sooner or later, and reflect upon this hospital, and me, hence upon them. And all because of your damnable childishness

210

in defending the indefensible at the top of your voice."

The chief paused for a moment. "What's done is done. What you are—is what you are. Have you considered going to Vienna? They are breaking new ground there on problems such as yours. Can't say as I see much to their methods, but if it works . . . ."

Mackensen shook his head.

"No? Well, I thought not. Pity, though, to throw away your talent and your training. I'd say, become a ship's doctor, but that would be virtually a waste. Medical missionary? No, I don't think so. Here." He sorted through the papers littering his desk. "A letter from the—ah—," he adjusted his pince-nez, "the Molly Pitcher Mining Corporation. They want a resident G.P. with surgical training at, yes, here, Phonolite. Lots of nasty accidents around mines. General practice in the community. They offer a fair salary and side fees, and if you got into more difficulties there, they'd probably have to overlook anything but the most egregious. I advise you to accept it."

"You're throwing me out!" Mackensen choked.

"That was the purpose of this interview, Doctor. I just don't want you to land directly in the gutter. Now I will write to this company, telling them that you are an excellent surgeon, which you are, but couldn't quite complete your formal training, which you haven't and won't. Doctor Mackensen, you are not a disgrace to the profession exactly, but you would bring grave discredit upon it in a hospital. Perhaps it is not your fault—perhaps it is the fault of people in general and their prejudices—but a hospital *is* people. Now this is my last word. Do you want this situation or no situation at all?"

"Do I have a choice, Doctor?" Mackensen asked bitterly.

"No, Doctor." The chief laid the letter to one side. "Now some advice before you leave, which will be as soon as you are packed. Learn to control that arrogance and defensiveness. Learn to live with yourself as you are, and you will at the same time learn how to live with others. If you feel compelled to steal more chickens, go as far away from Phonolite to do it as you can. If you do half as well professionally as I know you are capable of doing, you will get all the acclaim you want. They will not be interested in your habits, if you don't throw them in their faces, as you did here. There you can find real toleration, for they will have to be tolerant toward a man who makes himself essential."

"It's a sentence to life imprisonment, Doctor," Mackensen said, a sense of the hopelessly inevitable descending upon him.

"Why, so it is. But everyone of us is serving a life sentence of one sort or another. It is part of the human condition, Doctor, and the only release is death."

Upon arrival at the cast-concrete mine office, Mackensen was taken in tow and brought in to the assistant superintendent, a long-jawed individual named Wilkinson. He was seated and given a swift résumé of his duties and responsibilities, being informed that the red-cross-marked one-story building he had seen near the entrance was the dispensary and would be his domain. "Today," Wilkinson continued, "you will inspect it, note what is needed, and give me your requirements in writing before quitting time tonight. The dispensary is also open to the townspeople, so be prepared for anything from delivering twins to sewing a man's head back on. You have a private room in the building, and you can take your meals wherever you please—I suggest the boarding hotel a couple of blocks down and over. You will have a mailbox in the front of this office, and your paycheck will be in it on the first of every month. Office consultation fees are free for Molly employees' families, one dollar for house calls, whatever you think reasonable for others. You should buy miner's clothing, hat, boots at one of the general stores. They will tell you what you need. Any questions?"

"Time off?" Mackensen asked.

Wilkinson laughed, in no great amusement. "The Molly runs twenty-four hours a day, seven days a week, so your time off will be every day—or no day. You will never be out of earshot of the headworks whistle without making prior arrangements with me. A series of short blasts continuing for some time is the general alarm. Night or day, awake, asleep, or dead, you will be at the dispensary within ten minutes after you hear that alarm. We'll also try to work out a special doctor's call if you find it necessary. I suggest you have morning office hours and make house calls in the camp in the afternoon. Dr. Mulligan said it worked best that way. But your first duty is here. I want it clearly understood that, no matter what you may be doing in the camp, you will be here within ten minutes after you hear the general alarm."

"What if a life is at stake?"

The assistant superintendent spread his big hands slowly over his desk top. "Doctor, that whistle will not blow unless a life or many lives are at stake up here. How fast can a man bleed to death?"

"If a major artery is severed, in about thirty seconds."

"In view of that, we think ten minutes is pretty generous. Sometime today, you will visit the drafting office and begin studying the maps and the model of the workings. The timber foreman will then take you on a tour of some parts of the mine tomorrow morning at seven—be at the shaft headworks then, with the oncoming day shift. He'll repeat the tour in about a week, then again until he certifies that you are familiar with the active portion of the mine. We have found it best for our doctor to know as much about the layout as he knows about—about the human skeleton. And for the same reasons."

Mackensen was not so certain about that but held his peace. The assistant superintendent appeared to be a man not easily gainsaid, and, since it was probable that he was to be Mackensen's administrative superior, it would be best to go along.

"Now, finally. Your dispensary attendant is old John Tretheway. Good miner in his day. He may startle you somewhat at first—some of these accidents leave a man in bad shape. I'll tell you the bad about him first. He's independent as a hog on ice, opinionated, and pretty nearly illiterate. But until you learn your way around, it would be best to listen carefully to his advice about miners and the mine, since he knows both, inside and out. When you have to go down, he'll go with you or ahead of you. If he says to move a man, move him. If he tells you, 'Get out!' then leave fast—no matter what. If he should say, 'Stand still on one leg and hold your breath,' I'd advise you to do it. He's a company pensioner—but he earns his pension, every cent of it."

"What if he and I should disagree?"

213

Wilkinson looked off into the middle distance. "We think very highly of old John, all of us. He knows practical mining as few men do, and he saved the lives of a whole crew, the time he was hurt. *After* he was hurt. And Dr. Mulligan taught him to help in the dispensary afterward, though I have no doubt you could teach him more."

Wilkinson's voice was soft, but Mackensen sensed that a remarkably pointed hint had been directed to him. He felt both anger and resentment at being told to submit to the whims of an illiterate against whom he apparently could not invoke standard medical discipline. However, there was more than one way to kill a cat, and Mackensen had learned some tricks himself. There would be ways to get rid of his assistant in good time.

After the orientation he made his way to the dispensary, finding his trunk in the sleeping quarters. The waiting room, consultation room, ten-bed ward, surgery, and examination room were both clean and orderly, but Mackensen shook his head at the contents of the instrument cases and the medical supplies. There was little of what he needed, and entirely too much that was out of date. He found a wastebasket and began tossing things away. Periodically he ceased the purge in order to sit down and work on the long list of supplies to be ordered. The wastebasket was presently overflowing, and as he sought around for another, the back door opened. Entering without knocking was a bent caricature of a once-powerful man, clad in decently clean working clothes like those Mackensen had observed on the men in the mine yard.

"Dr. Mackensen?" the newcomer asked in a respectful voice. "H'I'm John Tretheway. General flunky 'ere, sir."

At least he hadn't proclaimed himself hospital superintendent and head surgical nurse, Mackensen thought. As he shook the gnarled hand, he mentally catalogued what must have befallen Tretheway. The distorted, caved-in appearance of the left cheekbone and mandible appeared to match comparable rib-cage fracturing, suggesting massive trauma. The dragging gait and high shoulder pointed strongly to spinal injury, skull fracture, or both. No, it was his left side that was injured, and the dragging leg was on the left. Brain damage ruled out; spinal injury it had to be. It did not then occur to Mackensen to consider what might have been the proximate cause of such a wreckage, but it was evident that Tretheway was lucky to be alive and semiambulatory.

"Glad to meet you, Tretheway. Have you another box or wastebasket for this junk?"

The old man nodded and left, offering neither argument nor opposition to the passing of the old order. The requested box appeared, and the filled wastebasket was removed. The purge continued in silence, while the order list expanded to four closely written pages. At noon Tretheway silently re-entered with some sandwiches and coffee. Mackensen ate with one hand while he continued to write with the other. He was nearly done, he felt, when Tretheway looked at the clock and announced, "Two h'o'clock, Doctor. Drafting office say 'ee can step h'in now."

"I'm busy. Tell them I'll be along."

Tretheway then did the unexpected. Placing his huge old hand down on the stack of pages, he said firmly, "Molly Pitcher be like h'a ship, sir. H'orders be h'orders. H'if 'ee was sewing h'up h'a man, h'engineer would bide 'is time. But 'e ain't, so 'ee must go—now. They be busy men, too."

"Damn it, no!" Mackensen's voice rose a tone. "I'll come when I'm ready." He was determined to check this sort of behavior at the outset, teaching Tretheway—if he could learn—that orderlies never, under any circumstances, did more than do what they were told, when they were told, without question or comment. He lifted Tretheway's hand aside and continued writing. Surprisingly enough, the old man said no more but retired to the ward, where he busied himself with mop and pail, apparently in clear conscience.

Some time later Wilkinson strode in. Mackensen looked at his face and laid down his pen. "Tretheway, have you something to do outside?" Wilkinson addressed the old man. Tretheway hobbled out, closing the door discreetly behind him. Then the assistant superintendent spoke with crisp, controlled authority. "Doctor, you were told to familiarize yourself with the maps and model of this mine. The drafting office sent for you," he glanced at the clock, "twenty-two minutes ago. Tretheway delivered the

215

message. Why are you not there?"

"Because I have more important work to do. You asked me for this," Mackensen waved the order lists, "by the end of the day. And because that old orderly presumed to tell me what I must do and what I must not."

"What did he tell you to do and not to do?"

"He said I must stop doing this and go to the drafting office. I do not accept orders from a glorified janitor."

Wilkinson's eyes widened slightly. "Doctor," he said with emphasis, "it is of the highest importance around a mining operation that an order—any order—*every* order be obeyed fully and at once. The man who gives an order is authorized to give it. Tretheway was only acting as a messenger, and you know it. Now, listen to me carefully, for I shall repeat this only once. I am assistant superintendent of this mine with authority to discharge instantly anyone but Superintendent Siebert. But if a cager—who is in total charge of his cage—tells me to stay off that cage, I stay off. If you should tell me to help with an injured man, I'd help. And when the drafting engineer tells you to come to his office—you *go!* Now, get off your high horse and get over there. For if you don't, you'll be off this property and out of this camp in five minutes. Understand?"

Mackensen suddenly realized that he had been foolish—again. For reasons that were not immediately plain to him, this place was run like an army. Or a hospital. Or any other place where lives hung on a word, correctly spoken and instantly obeyed. And it was also apparent to him that the company physician occupied a rather different place in the scheme of things than did that same physician in, say, a hospital. He, Mackensen, was no longer at the center of things but was rather a sort of auxiliary. Under the circumstances there appeared to be but one sensible thing to say.

"Yes, sir," Mackensen replied, rising.

The maps in the drafting office were a collective nightmare. The many-paned glass model box was interesting, but as bad in its way as an unlabeled pathology specimen. Wriggling lines drawn in various colors went every-which-way without apparent rhyme or reason. Words were casually tossed out by the brisk young

216

engineer in charge: "adit, level, winze, mill hole, transfer raise, crosscut, exploratory drift, stope, incline, shaft . . . ." It reminded Mackensen of the time he had first leafed through his new copy of Gray's *Anatomy* and realized that, while he recognized nothing, he must in one short year of study absorb everything. "I'm lost," he confessed frankly. "There must be a good reason to show me this, but what is it?"

The engineer stared at him. "You'll be going down there now and then," he replied. "It'd be better if you knew about where you were and how to get a man out the quick way. Or if you can't, not to try."

"Do you mean to say that I must work on men down *here*?" His finger traced a deep-lying dark blot on the nearest pane of glass.

"That's where accidents often happen, Doctor."

"But won't the men help me?"

"Gladly, when they can. But sometimes they can't very well. And, after all, you'll be giving the orders then. Oh, cheer up; it isn't as bad as all that. Took me a while to catch on to the Molly, too. Same with every mine. A few tours with the timber foreman will do a lot for you. Nothing like actually seeing it. Now, I'll go over it once more. Then I'll call the concentrator, and they'll send someone over to take you through there."

"Concentrator?"

"Over there—the big building with the tanks. They have accidents, too."

"Is there any place around here where there *aren't* accidents?" Mackensen demanded.

"I'd stay away from Bancroft," the engineer grinned. "That place is really dangerous."

Of his first trip through the Molly, Mackensen remembered every step—and absorbed almost nothing. From the moment he stepped off the cage on the seven-hundred level, he was totally lost. The foreman led him down long passageways festooned with rusty pipe and floored with miniature rails. Side passages—some gaping darkly and others closed off with heavy wooden doors—appeared at unpredictable intervals from unexpected directions. At one point there was a cozy, well-lit hardware store, presided over by a friendly sort of clerk. There were curious huge rooms filled to the top with deck after deck of plank flooring supported by great timbers, laced by ladders and chutes, and completely deserted. In other places gangs of men were making a hellish noise, tangled up with hoses of all descriptions. He passed ominous wooden boxes labeled "Explosives—Keep Out." A small mule gently explored the pockets of his borrowed jumper with a warm and friendly nose. Surprisingly, he felt no claustrophobia at all despite the endless series of heavy wooden sets he marched past.

Mackensen learned to keep his foot out of the ditch, look away from his lantern, and follow my leader with great care. He was firmly and repeatedly cautioned to touch nothing. And he was astounded at what miners could do with a can of paint, a board wall, and an idle moment. It was now clear to him why women were not permitted in mines. Some of the frescoes would have embarrassed an obstetrical nurse. But the miners themselves seemed genuinely friendly and obliging, eager to demonstrate their work and proud of it. Mackensen began to look forward to the next tour—he had imagined deformed gnomes toiling bitterly under unspeakable conditions but instead found himself somewhat envying the pride and the competence of the miners.

The week following was devoted to the hard, routine work of opening the shop for business. Business lost no time in appearing. He was assisted by Tretheway, who acted as receptionist, anesthetist, bill collector, and ward nurse. Also blessedly the camp enjoyed the services of two midwives to take the burden of the midnight summons off his shoulders, for without them he would have been as drugged for lack of sleep as he had been during his time in the hospital emergency room. One of the grannies was pretty good; the other, barely capable. But the one called him when in need, and the other when in doubt—he saw to that. People took care of their own medical nursing at home; it meant afternoon house calls, but Phonolite was small, and the exercise was good for him. In any event, no aspect of the healing art was getting rusty for lack of use—"general practice" evidently *meant* "general practice."

To his surprise and annoyance Mackensen began to encounter

218

a number of syndromes with which he was either unacquainted or with which he was at a loss to come to grips. One, confined to adult males over age thirty, was characterized by a dry, hacking cough that was unproductive and unaccompanied by fever. It was evident that a greater or lesser portion of the lungs was calcified or ossified beyond redemption and equally evident that, while the complaint superficially resembled tuberculosis, it was not genuine tuberculosis. Tretheway came to his rescue here. The condition was "quartz lungs" or "miner's consumption," a disease with a half-dozen names. It was caused by inhaling quartz dust over a long period of time. There was nothing that could be done, Tretheway averred. Privately checking with the Meade Department of Public Health, Mackensen found that Tretheway was absolutely correct.

Upon another occasion Mackensen was confronted with an adult male who demonstrated serious deterioration of the reflexes, timidity, irritability, and—was this significant or only a coincidence?—marked loss of teeth for so comparatively young a man. Inclined at first to think that his patient had been unlucky in love over at Bancroft, Mackensen was gently interrupted by Tretheway. "May h'I butt h'in, Doctor?"

Mackensen, engaged in thumbing his *Practice of Medicine,* laid it on the desk. "What is it?"

"Yon Willett, 'oo h'I saw coming h'out h'a moment h'ago. 'E's h'a concentrator 'and. Works h'on they table line. 'E's got they quicksilver shakes."

"The what?"

"Quicksilver shakes. Willett cleans they h'amalgamation tables h'and puts h'on they fresh quick. Poison, quick be, h'after h'a time."

Mackensen picked up his text, thumbed the index to toxic metals, found the section on mercury, and discovered himself reading an account of Willett's symptoms that he himself could have written, word for word, after the examination. The loss of teeth was indeed characteristic. Mercurialism was sadly prevalent in the industries that used quicksilver, and the only palliative was laid down with brutal frankness. The affected person must be removed at once from the poisonous environment. No treatment or cure was known.

"How did you know, Tretheway?"

The old man shrugged his good shoulder. "H'everyone h'in mining should. Willett, 'e should. But 'is 'ead h'is h'a touch mazed, like h'as not."

Mackensen wrote a note to the concentrator superintendent recommending the instant transfer of Willett to a job far removed from mercury and, for good measure, moving machinery. Mackensen now realized what Tretheway might be good for. He was able enough around the dispensary, competently discharging a dozen jobs some of which were fairly revolting. The miners appeared to trust him; an order relayed through Tretheway would get a man's pants down in a hurry. Now it appeared that he was a walking directory to the complaints, injuries, illnesses, and hazards peculiar to miners. Tretheway indeed knew the Molly inside and out. Well, every hospital had at least one old nurse who knew as much as most of the staff and rather more than a few of them did. Such were respected and catered to, for the obvious reason that no member of the staff knew when the old battle-ax might save him from some perfectly obvious—and perfectly ghastly—blunder.

"Who taught you your work here?" Mackensen asked with interest.

"Dr. Mulligan, sir. 'E saw me through h'after h'I was 'urt. When 'e learned h'I couldn't mine no more, 'e said, 'Tretheway, h'I'll make h'a Sanitary iv ye. H'I turned jailbirds h'and bandsmen h'into 'ospital 'elpers back h'in they old Second Corps, h'and to h'a good miner h'it h'ought to be h'easy. 'E knows they best 'alf h'of h'it h'already.' "

"Was he a good doctor?"

"Not so strong h'on books as 'ee be, Doctor, but 'e'd do. 'E could take h'off h'an h'arm h'in thirty seconds. But 'e 'ad lots h'of practice h'in they war."

Mackensen was just beginning to let his weight down when the first bad one hit. At the moment the whistle began to yammer, he was listening to the chest of an adolescent girl whose mother had brought her in saying she was "poorly." The whistle's blatting

annoyed him so that he frowned and concentrated the harder. There was a pounding on the examination room door, and Tretheway's voice boomed, "Grab 'ee bag, Doctor! Trouble at they incline 'eadframe!"

Mackensen whipped around, dropped his stethoscope into his open bag, and bolted out, leaving the wide-eyed girl sitting on the examination table. Despite his disability Tretheway kept pace with him, a folding canvas stretcher over his lame shoulder, the box of emergency medical supplies in the other hand. A group of men in front of the incline headframe were beckoning and shouting "Over here! Over here, Doc!" All made way for him but two, who were kneeling over a recumbent figure. As Mackensen came closer, he saw that there seemed to be a tremendous tangle of greasy wire rope around the spot, as well as a great deal of blood. Men were scurrying about elsewhere, but he paid them no attention.

At first glance the man on the ground looked as though a determined enemy had had at him with a straight razor; in the hospital emergency room Mackensen had dealt with razor fighters brought in by the police, but never one so thoroughly worked over. He first took care of a spurting artery in the left arm and then scissored open the man's tattered clothes. Wickedly exposed loops of gray-pink intestines protruded through the slashed abdominal wall. That could wait. There were compound fractures on both left extremities, but no signs of spinal damage. However, the man was going rapidly into shock. "Got to move him," Mackensen decided. "Stretcher, Tretheway! You men, give me a hand!" The victim, remarkably silent, was worked sideways onto the stretcher and taken off at the trot by four workmen. Mackensen followed. He would have to do a lot of fast work in the next hour, more work at more deliberate speed in the hour after that, and then he would see.

After a great deal of suturing, splinting, and cleaning up, the man was finally tucked away under blankets, surrounded by hot-water bottles. Mackensen tried to estimate how many sutures he had tied but finally gave up. More than two hundred, certainly. Many more. "What happened to him?" he found leisure to ask

Tretheway, who was engaged in the removal of blood from many objects.

"Skip 'oist rope broke," Tretheway replied. "Bloody wires fanned h'out h'and nipped 'im. H'often nowt 'appens but h'a busted skip h'and mayhap h'a few timbers h'and rail to fix. '*Im*," he indicated with a nod at the still figure on the bed, " 'e was crossing they yard when she broke. Lucky, 'e was."

"How so?"

"Could 'ave cut 'is throat. H'or taken 'is 'ead clean h'off. H'I've seen h'it."

"Any way to prevent it, Tretheway?"

"They try. But skip rope leads h'a 'ard life. Was '*is* fault, really. Never go h'about rope what's 'oisting h'a 'eavy load."

"How about the man in the hoist house?"

"No trouble. 'E'd 'ear 'er go h'and duck down be'ind 'is 'oist drum. No rope'll cut through h'a five-foot steel 'oist drum."

Presently it did not appear that the injured man was so lucky after all. A vicious combination of exsanguination and shock began to drag him down rapidly. Mackensen discontinued the morphia and started stimulants to try to bring him out of it, but to no effect. About two o'clock the next morning the man quietly stopped breathing.

"Accidents come in threes," was the old saying, and the company doctor was presently convinced that, superstition or not, there might be something to it. On the same afternoon he was summoned from a house call to deal with an injury caused by ordinary simple-mindedness. A chute puller down on the eight-hundred loading level had allowed a tramming mule to pull away a loaded car. The car wheel had passed over the foot the man had carelessly left on the rail, thinking no doubt that he was in a saloon. This one was delivered to the dispensary, swearing bitterly. Mackensen was able to save the foot, but little else—there were possibly only five or six orthopedic surgeons in the country who could have reconstructed the splintered complex of bones. The chute puller would stump about on a crippled foot the rest of his life. And the doctor did not care to think much about the third accident, for which he could do nothing but write up the death

223

certificate. A man who pushes an ore car into the shaft at the five-hundred assuming that the cage is at his level, whereas . . . .

Mackensen had begun a profitable acquaintanceship with the youthful civil engineer who was in charge of the drafting department. After the weekly tutorials they would have a cup of coffee together and discuss matters of moment. Carlson, the engineer, was fresh out of school, glad to be with the Molly, and as much at home as Mackensen would have been, had he been offering the coffee to Carlson in the residents' lounge of the hospital. Carlson was as curious about things medical and physiological as Mackensen was about mining. He disposed of Carlson's peculiar ideas concerning Oriental women, just as Carlson disposed of his suppositions concerning the danger and frequency of cave-ins.

"In the first place," the engineer declaimed, lighting a noisome pipe inlaid with a block-silver "CCM," "they aren't 'cave-ins.' The men call them 'falls' or 'rock falls.' They occur mostly in coal mining or tunneling work in heavy ground, anyway. Here they give so much advance warning that a man would have to go out of his way to get caught in one. Which is not to say that individual blocks don't want to fall from time to time, but the men take care of that—it's their necks a block would fall on, so they don't spare the timber in blocky ground."

"Most of the accidents I see seem to arise from mishandling machinery," Mackensen ventured.

"They do that. The bigger mines are starting to hire a special engineer just to handle that problem alone."

"I wish we would."

"We're not big enough, and everybody on the staff makes it his business to work at it, anyway. But we're a medium-sized mine at best, so we have to double up on a lot of jobs. We're lucky we have as good and big a staff as we do—you know the Molly is owned two-thirds by Willie Huggins and one-third by Colonel Jellison, and they don't see eye to eye on much of anything. Jellison would buy Willie out if he would sell, but he won't. It's all the Colonel can do to make Willie toe the line and let us run it right. Wish Willie would either shoot or give up the gun."

"I didn't know Willie owned us."

"Thought everybody did. Where do you suppose his money comes from?"

Mackensen looked blank. "I thought—well—railroads, lumber, that book company of his . . . ."

"Nope. Some comes from right here. Plus Arizona copper, Coeur d'Alene lead-zinc, and I guess Comstock silver back in the old times. Old George Huggins and Frank Casey started way-back-when in mining. They took in Jellison, oh, about thirty years ago. Huggins died and left his third to his wife. Then Frank Casey died—he was a bachelor—and left *his* third to Mrs. Huggins and Willie jointly. Then when she died a few years back, Willie got all of both shares. Jellison took his third and went his way—not that he's about to go to the county poor farm, either. But I guess they meet only once a year at the stockholders' meeting, if they meet at all and don't just send their lawyers to jaw at each other. Funny damn story, though. . . . You know it, about Willie?"

"No, I don't."

"It's common knowledge, but don't say *I* said it. They say Willie is the spit of old Frank Casey. Got his brown eyes, bullet head. Looks just like a Turk, in fact."

"Casey? I don't understand. That's Irish."

"Oh, you didn't know! Casey was half-Turkish or something. His dad married some girl from the Levant. Hell, his middle name was Mohammed. But Willie doesn't like to be joshed about it, believe me. He was kicked out of Yale for beating hell out of some upperclassman who ragged him about it."

"Well, well." Mackensen concluded that inherited wealth often led to some peculiar problems, as witness all the American heiresses marrying into the European nobility. Both sides, he surmised, would have some rude awakenings. He wondered whether their children would ever amount to a hill of beans. He rather doubted it.

"Hey!" Carlson snapped. "Quick! How would you take a man out from stope E if the shaft was blocked? Don't look at the model! Look at me!"

"You're a hard teacher, Carlson," Mackensen protested.

225

"You told me the other day that you doctors were hard losers. Stope E—fire in the shaft!"

Mackensen closed his eyes. "Stope E is—ah—west of the haulage incline. Turn north, go through the crosscut to the winze. Down the winze to the eight hundred, and you're on the haulage level. Go south to the incline. Put him in the skip. Uh—the skip . . . ."

"You're doing fine. What about the skip?"

"What if the skip hoist rope breaks?"

"It isn't likely to if all you have in it is an injured man and the mine doctor. You'd weigh a lot less than five tons of ore."

"What if the skip is loaded and the rope breaks?"

Carlson looked off. "Why, I guess the pump man in the sump rings three-three-three."

"What does that mean?"

"Hoist recovered bodies."

The conversation somehow marked the distinct break between Elbert Mackensen, M.D., and Doc Mackensen of the Molly Pitcher staff. The once-anonymous faces around the headworks now bore names, personalities, trades. The weekly tours underground were officially concluded when the timber foreman and Carlson pronounced Mackensen familiar with the active levels. Since Mackensen had acquired something of a taste for these, however, he pressed Tretheway into service as a guide to the older, higher abandoned stopes and levels. On one such ramble on the old three hundred, Tretheway pointed down a dark passageway and remarked, "H'I was working there back h'in 'Eighty h'or thereabouts h'under old Chenoweth. 'Ad a good crew— Bolitho h'and 'is son, h'and they two h'Irish devils, Riley h'and O'Leary. Played h'a rare prank h'on h'a British perfesser, they did. Them h'and their 'orseplay . . . ."

"Are they still here?" Mackensen asked.

"Chenoweth—'e's h'up *there*," Tretheway pointed upward. "H'a fathom h'under grass h'in they burying ground. Quartz lungs. Bolitho, h'I dunno. Nor Riley h'and O'Leary, neither. Miners come h'and go, like. But we'uns was h'a good crew."

And very high up they entered the one-hundred-level station, so near to surface that the shaft had sunlight in it. Tretheway led the way up a gentle incline, which he called "the old exploratory." At its head they turned left into a small crosscut and walked south past decaying timbers and small falls of rock until at last they halted before an infilled access portal. " 'Ere," Tretheway pointed. " 'Ere was they Penrose Shaft. First 'un sunk on they ore h'in she Molly. Colonel Jellison 'imself 'elped sink 'er, so 'tis said."

"Why do they call it the 'Penrose'?"

"Dunno. Mayhap a director or summat. H'I never 'eard. Colonel Jellison, 'e would know, but 'oo's to h'ask? Look 'ere." He pointed to an indentation on the rocky wall. " 'Ere's h'a double-jack steel 'ole. We drilled by 'and then. Black powder h'and 'and steel. Not h'a h'air machine h'in they West. See 'ow big it is? We 'ad to drill big to 'old h'enough powder."

"What are all those timbers set sideways above us?"

"Them's stulls. They stoped she h'outcrop to surface. Put h'in stulls to 'old they ground h'open. Then backfilled with waste. Afore my time, too. She Molly be h'old—thirty years h'or more."

"Who first found her?"

"Dunno that, neither. Well, Doctor, best we go back. 'Ee's seen h'all there h'is to see, h'up 'ere. H'another day, we look over yon sump h'and they machinery."

Mackensen was nearly content with the physical arrangements of his life. Tretheway conjured up morning coffee and biscuits—good smithy coffee, black and hot as the forge fires. Lunch was equally satisfactory: more coffee and big, thick roast-beef sandwiches, obtained from some mysterious source and at infinitesimal cost. He ate his dinner at the boarding hotel in order to avoid becoming a complete hermit. At night his dispensary quarters awaited him. The paycheck arrived promptly and was as promptly mailed to the bank at Meade, where his account was growing admirably, since day-to-day expenses were more than met by his private fees. Molly employees were treated free, but otherwise office calls were one dollar and house calls two dollars, with prescriptions thrown in. After a few years he would have money enough to leave the Molly, open a private practice in some city, and be done with the past—if he wished.

Mackensen was eating dinner in the boarding-hotel dining room, dissecting his second porkchop and looking forward to the berry pie, when the headworks whistle's staccato beat filtered into the noisy room. Everyone fell silent. Mackensen rose and picked up his bag. Someone said, "I've got a horse out on the street, Doc. Take it." Mackensen was not a good rider, but he took it, and the horse seemed to sense that it was better to cooperate than to object. The animal got him up to the headworks, where Mackensen abandoned it and followed the general gesturings toward the shaft headframe. They were holding the cage for him, with Tretheway and the extra equipment already on it. The cager slammed down the bar and pulled sharply at the bell cord, and the cage seemed to drop out from under them. "What is it?"Mackensen panted.

"Something on they seven hundred. Don't know 'oo or 'ow many," Tretheway replied. "Goddam' tellyphone don't work 'alf they bloody time. They rang 'er up h'on they 'oist bell." This was in reference to the new but very undependable mine telephone system installed shortly before. The damp air of the upcast shaft played hob with it; telephones might be very well for city offices, but they had a long way to go before miners would place any great reliance on them. Mackensen noted that the hoist engineer was giving them an old-fashioned sleigh ride and hoped the brakes would take it when he slowed the cage.

At the seven hundred the cage bobbed to a halt, and a glance around the station showed surprisingly little confusion or bustle. But a level boss was waiting, and as he led the way, he barked over his shoulder, "Bad one. Bill Collins. Stope K. Shanked a stoper steel, and it got him."

That could be very bad. The man had evidently been using a stoper—a slender, elongated air machine that drilled upward into the back of the stope. As the steel pounded up into the hole, the man rotated the machine bodily by means of an outward-sprouting arm. As the hole deepened, he would press a button on the handgrip of the arm. This bled a brief shot of air into the space above an extensible foot, extruding it downward to keep the steel up in the hole. Stopers were very useful machines, but if the steel

228

was shanked, or snapped by the pounding, the broken portion could recoil downward with unpleasant velocity. Other things could happen with stopers, as well . . . .

Collins was lying on his back on the top-level planking of the stope sets. At first glance he seemed to be merely resting, his machine beside him. As Mackensen's eyes accommodated to the gloom, he saw the bright tip of a star bit protruding out of the hollow where Collins' right shoulder joined his neck. Mackensen sucked in his breath. The steel had speared Collins, slipping in between the clavicle and the scapular and diving almost straight down. Mackensen had once seen a picture of a Roman statue, *The Dying Gaul* or some-such title. The barbarian, supporting his dead wife, was committing suicide by thrusting his short sword down into his thorax in almost the same place and manner that the drill steel had got Collins. It was a world's wonder that the man had not died instantly.

Mackensen bent over the man. "How deep is that thing in him?" he demanded.

The level boss looked at the stump protruding from the stoper's chuck and eyed Collins. "About *here,*" he said, indicating a point on Collin's chest an inch or so below the sternum.

Mackensen pulled his hypodermic needle from the basiliar vein in Collins' left arm. He then knelt down to estimate the lateral angle of the steel—it appeared to run at an appreciable if small angle from right to left, the tip somewhere about the midline. He then lay almost flat to sight as best he could along the axis of the steel, attempting to correlate its direction of entrance with the innumerable organs, blood vessels, and nerves it might have struck. If anything, the direction was ventral, rather than dorsal. The lungs and bronchiae were apparently untouched or nearly so, for there was no bloody froth on Collins' lips. The great arteries and veins must have been missed, or Collins would be dead. "Has he vomited blood?" Mackensen demanded. Heads shook, no. Had it missed the stomach, too? "Could we move him?" Mackensen demanded of Tretheway.

The old Cornishman shook his head. He displayed the broken shank of the steel, now freed from the stoper chuck. The steel had

229

snapped at a decided slant to the axis. The broken edges were short but razor-sharp. "We'un's try to move 'im, yon steel'll wiggle about 'and cut 'im to pieces h'inside." That was true. Collins could not be moved, be it ever so little, with that thing inside him.

"Give me a big shot, Doc, an' let me go," Collins pleaded in a whisper.

Mackensen gently probed the belly with his fingertips. There was little or none of the dull tautness associated with internal bleeding. Collins' pulse was stronger than reason dictated it should be, and his color better. Ruptured diaphragm? Perforated gut? Probably, if not certain, but not immediately fatal. Was it possible that the steel had missed everything vital within the chest cavity? A long-dormant memory recurred to Mackensen. Was it Paré who had said of a somewhat analogous case, "I told the physicians that, since they accounted him a dead man, I proposed to treat him as a dead man"? One final glance at the entry wound in the trapezius. There was blood there, but not *much* blood.

"This steel has got to come out now," Mackensen said flatly. The miners glanced at each other, shuffling their feet as spectators in a courtroom would stir while sentence of death was being passed. "Tretheway, it must come out exactly the way it went in," he continued, sitting down, careless of the havoc the planking and grime was playing with his suit. He adjusted himself so that he was facing the axis of the steel, his left foot in Collins' left armpit, his right leg angling off. Mackensen hitched himself around until the steel appeared lined up with his own hands and his forward-flexed spinal column. The position was damnably uncomfortable, but there was no help for it. "You two—kneel down at his right side, and support and brace that steel as best you can while it's coming out. If you let it move around at all, it may cut a . . . . something."

As the two indicated men edged into position, Tretheway contributed more help. " 'Ere, you," he said to a third miner. "Get around and brace Doctor's back and arse, so 'e'll 'ave h'a good purchase. Sit down h'opposite 'im, h'and lean back h'into 'im. Give forward as 'e comes back. You two—h'as they steel comes h'out, 'ook h'a couple fingers h'under 'er. She'll be greasy, but 'old 'er steady h'as a brimful glass h'of whisky or 'e'll die."

Good idea! Mackensen thought, feeling the solid weight of a miner settle against his lumbar region. These men knew how to nurse heavy objects into exact relationships with each other and required little instruction. " 'Arris," Tretheway snapped to the level boss, "grab h'and steady 'is feet." The level boss nodded silently and knelt down, clamping a big hand around each of Collins' ankles. Eyes met eyes around the circle of men, and there were imperceptible nods. Despite the morphia, Collins' eyes were open and fixed on some invisible point of the stope back overhead. His lips moved soundlessly for a few seconds.

Laying his fingers about the lumpy bit, Mackensen tested it gently, got a good grip, and gradually increased the tension of his forearms. At one point of strain, the steel stirred faintly. He increased the pull a bare fraction. The steel began to creep toward him, a hair's breadth at a time. Mackensen cursed himself for not having a dressing ready to cover the wound and then reflected that if they were lucky there would be time enough later to put one on. If they were unlucky, no dressing would be required. It was infernally hot in the stope, and everyone seemed to be sweating freely. Mackensen blinked his eyes but kept the steady tension on the steel.

One of the kneeling miners reached over with his left hand and gingerly slipped two fingers under the steel shank, bracing his elbow with his right hand. Mackensen felt a tiny increment of upward pressure, but no more. The miner was awkwardly bent and extended, but as the steel emerged further he moved with it to make room for his fellow. The man beyond—no, Tretheway himself—would have the hard job of keeping the sharp end steady as it emerged. Mackensen maintained his tension—thank God, the steel had not pierced any major musculature, which would clamp tightly about it. Hair by hair . . . millimeter by millimeter . . . the miners were incredibly patient despite the awkward strain they were feeling. Tretheway simply knelt in passive silence, waiting his turn, although sweat beaded his craggy, distorted old face.

The air in the stope was foggy with condensation, giving the

231

candles on the men's hats halos of light. The flames barely wavered as little by little the steel yielded. Now the second miner was leaning forward, his work-scarred hand extended. Again Mackensen felt the least addition of upward pressure. Blood trickled slowly from the fleshy meniscus of the wound, kissing the steel as though reluctant to let it go. Mackensen wanted desperately to call a halt, to ease his shrieking back and nerves, to see how far the steel had emerged. He caught his lower lip between his teeth and bit hard. None of the six men could stir a quarter-inch until it was over, one way or the other.

Mackensen had fallen now into a pattern of movement; the steel was gliding steadily toward him. Peculiar how red it was—as red as though it had been used to stir paint. Mackensen was accustomed to the thin, pink films on shining carbon-steel blades and suture needles, not this dark heavy coating over a cold octagonal bar. The two miners swayed very gently to their left, keeping pace with the snaillike creep of movement. The level boss was staring over Mackensen's head. Suddenly Tretheway bent forward. His huge, gnarled hand went out over Collins' throat with almost feminine delicacy. His fingers eased down, the back of his hand supported on the tendons of Collins' neck. Mackensen was panting with tension, and he blinked again to clear the stinging sweat from his eyes.

"Clear!" Tretheway said softly. The steel vanished. Mackensen craned his aching neck to inspect the wound. The hole was now contracted—it looked barely the diameter of a lead pencil, and it was not spurting like a fire hose. Rising to his knees, Mackensen bent over Collins again. There was still no bloody froth, no sucking of a punctured lung at the wound, no new evidence of internal hemorrhage. Collins was in as good condition as wild optimism could hope for. "Collins! Collins!" Mackensen commanded. "Do you hear me?"

The miner opened his eyes and his lips formed a silent, "Yes."

"We got the steel out. And you look good. We're taking you up now. Hang on, and if you feel anything happening, let me know at once. I'll be with you every step of the way. Understand?"

To his amazement Collins slowly winked one eye. These miners! The crew eased him over onto the stretcher, each man taking a handle. Harris put the broken steel on with Collins.

"What the hell did you do *that* for?"Mackensen demanded in the flareup of anger that follows the relief of excruciating tension.

"He'll want it. To show off in the Miners' Rest and brag about."

"Let's go!"

The operation that followed was an anticlimax. Collins' diaphragm required some cursory repair, and he exhibited one small nick on the superior surface of the transverse colon. A suture there was hardly necessary, but as long as Collins was open . . . . Despite odds of ten thousand to one, the steel had missed the great arteries and veins, the lung, the entire closely packed contents of the upper thorax. A brilliant anatomist could hardly have duplicated the feat at his leisure upon a cadaver, assuming he wished to try for some reason. Mackensen left Tretheway tucking up Collins in the ward and wandered out through the examination room and into his consultation room. He lit the desk lamp and fell into his chair, too exhausted even to think of sleep despite the late hour.

Presently Tretheway entered, carrying a glass and a bottle of dispensary brandy. " 'Ere," he said, pouring a generous dollop and sliding the glass across. " 'Ave h'a short 'un. Then go to bed." He corked the bottle firmly and returned it to the locked supplies closet. Noticing that the glass remained untouched, Tretheway commanded, "Drink h'up, Doctor."

Mackensen sipped and then tossed the rest of the brandy down his throat. He wiped off his mouth. "Now I know why some surgeons get to drinking too much," he muttered. "The tension . . . ."

"Aye," Tretheway nodded, sitting down. "Old Dr. Mulligan, 'e got so 'e couldn't 'ardly leave yon brandy h'alone. 'Ad to watch 'im h'all they time, h'I did. But 'e was good, for h'all that. 'E thought nobody knew h'about h'it. But this here's h'a little camp, Doctor. Nobody's got no secrets. So we 'ave to live with h'each h'other, 'ee might say."

Was Tretheway trying to tell him something? Mackensen wondered. He thought it over, felt the brandy begin to blur and slow his mind, and decided that perhaps the old man was. And, as well, that it made no great difference. "I think I'll go to bed now," he announced.

"Best 'ee do, Doctor. I'll call 'ee if need be. Goodnight." Tretheway rose and stretched awkwardly and shuffled out toward the ward. After a moment Mackensen turned down the lamp, watched the flame fade, then sought his own room. It would seem, he reflected, that the hard-hearted old chief of surgery had had a point or two. And as for his original plans to be rid of Tretheway—Mackensen laughed a little sourly at himself. One might as well scheme to be rid of one's father. As he sank into sleep, Mackensen was wishing that he had had a father like old John Tretheway. Well, better late than never. . . .

Upon a morning in late summer a mother brought in an eleven-year-old boy whose looks Mackensen did not greatly care for. The boy exhibited two degrees of fever and a cough and complained of headache and nausea. The mother explained that this had been going on for a week, getting somewhat worse each day. Examination revealed little besides a slightly enlarged spleen. After ordering the mother to keep the boy in bed, feed him very lightly, and to call him at once if the boy took a turn for the worse, Mackensen dismissed them. No, he decided, he did not like it at all. The usual run of childhood diseases developed far more rapidly and spectacularly. After wishing that he had put in more time in the children's ward at the hospital, he sought assistance in his *Practice of Medicine.* It proved of no great help.

Three days later he was called to the house. The boy's temperature was now 103°, and there was flux and a heavily coated tongue. The child was irritable and exhibited a peculiar, rather vacant, expression. Everything pointed to a massive infection of the intestinal tract, possibly typhoid fever, except that typhoid almost never appeared in a single case. The rest of the family was in good health, and Mackensen had encountered no similar problem at the office. He spent some time questioning the mother, urged great nursing care, and resolved to drop in daily. When the definitive abdominal rose spots appeared, nailing it down as typhoid, he was not at all happy. He was so far from being happy, in fact, that he made an appointment to see the Molly superintendent, Siebert, as soon as possible.

Siebert, a grim veteran of the mining wars, had Mackensen come in immediately.

"We have one case of typhoid in Phonolite," Mackensen announced shortly.

"I've seen typhoid epidemics," Siebert replied. "What's to be done?"

"I don't know. We have one case—no more. Mr. Siebert, there's a focus of infection in this camp. It's given us warning. But I have no more than that to go on. Usually they come in a bunch, and by process of elimination you can find the one thing they all have in common. Some one food. Some one water source. But we are sitting on a time bomb, and I can't tell you where it is."

"You are sure the source is here, Doctor?"

"The first thing that occurred to me. Neither the patient nor his family has been away from the camp for months. They have had no outside visitors. No incoming packages of edibles. They use the camp water supply. There is a chance in a million that it came from outside, some improbable chain of circumstances, but . . . ."

"It's like smelling fuse smoke in a drift you think is deserted," Sibert nooded. "I see. What do you need?"

"Word from you that I am to have full cooperation in a lot of prying into people's affairs. Somewhere, somehow, that boy put something in his mouth that no one else has—yet."

"Why not ask him?"

"He's delirious, for one thing. For another, he won't snap out of it for quite a while, and for a third, his mind may be clouded for a longer time yet."

"Should the health department at Meade be told?"

"By all means. It may mean quarantine—an embargo on the camp."

"That's all right."

"And I'll be out of my office a lot."

"That will be all right, too. Just cut that fuse, Doctor. My wife and I lost a baby to typhoid at White Pines."

As a *de facto* surgeon Mackensen had not entertained inordinate respect for his colleagues in public-health work, tending to regard them as practitioners who had resorted to the public trough for lack of greater skill and diligence. His opinion began to change drastically as he went about the wearying and painstaking business of reconstructing contacts, activities, conversations, while sifting mountains of laboriously gathered verbal chaff for a few grains of specific information. Incidentally, he got a great deal of exercise walking. Fortunately he was armed with Siebert's patronage and was girded with his own considerable (if he privately felt, undeserved) reputation as a first-class *gris-gris* and voodoo special-ist, as capable of conjuring a drill steel into a man's belly as of extracting it subsequently. In consequence, even the former loyal Croatian subjects of His K.u.K. Majesty, Francis Joseph, resentful as they were of all forms of constituted authority, offered deference, glasses of *slivovitz,* and what cooperation they could. All to no purpose. There was sickness enough in Phonolite but no signs whatsoever of typhoid except for one miserable boy, now reduced to a feverish, muttering rack of bones. Siebert, thank God, did not hound him or volunteer well-meant suggestions. The superintendent seemed to hold the opinion that Mackensen wanted to solve the mystery as badly as he wanted it solved and would do best if left alone. For which attitude there was much to be said.

Eliminating the public school (it had been in summer recess for nine weeks), church school (no refreshments or picnics), the candy and tidbit counters of the stores (the boy had no unusual or exotic tastes in these), the family itself (fecal examinations, negative), there remained to investigate only the boy's gang of friends. These were rounded up and separately questioned. Promising with great oaths that there would be no reprisals, Mackensen elicited the story that about three weeks previously the junior banditti, including the typhoid victim, had gone up to the head of the reservoir for a day of aimless pottering about. Carrying their rations, they had built a dam in the creek bed, demolished it, staged several satisfactory rock fights, built a fire, extinguished it in the traditional manner of boys, and gone swimming—all contrary to strict orders. One tow-headed lad then remembered that the sick Jimmy's lunch sack had fallen, or maybe been thrown, into the water on the way to the swimming spot, whereupon he himself, out of the purest motives, had shared his own sandwiches with Jimmy.

There was a delay while more fecal examinations of the tow-headed boy and his family were conducted. Results: negative all around. Recalling the boy, Mackensen praised his manly fortitude and truthfulness and began to ask more questions. Had Jimmy drunk any creek water? No. Put any rocks or debris in his mouth? No. Eaten anything on a dare? No. However, the lad was stimulated to the observation that Jimmy had fished out his water-logged lunch, discarded the soggy bread of his sandwiches, and eaten the sliced meat therein. Had he shared this second repast with anyone? No.

"Let's go for a walk," Mackensen decided. The young imp led him up Hayes Street and its continuation, the dirt service road that extended around the northwest of the reservoir. Turning off the road, Mackensen was guided through briars and mud to a small indentation on the marshy shoreline. "Here's where the lunch fell in?"

"'Bout here."

Mackensen took a sample of the water and turned around. "What's over the rise?"

"The baseball park."

That was so. There was no room in the narrow valley below for a diamond, but up here beyond the engineers' homes was a suitable stretch of flat ground. "This is where the big kids come in the evening to hug and kiss," the boy volunteered unnecessarily. In the course of his practice Mackensen had long been aware of this. "The Bancroft team beat us here the last time they played," the boy continued. "I was in the privy when they hit that durned old single that McLaughlin muffed and let them score on."

"There's a privy?"

"Sure—a six-holer. People used to have to come down here

between innings, but they built it last summer after old Mrs. Skinnaway complained."

Mackensen reflected that privies, water, and typhoid went together like biscuits, ham, and eggs. But the privy was over the rise and on the reverse slope behind the nearer wooden bleachers. Drainage could not run uphill. Glancing back across the thin, weedy soil that covered the granite, Mackensen thought he detected a faint but continuous line. A fissure of some sort? "Time to go back," he told the boy.

"Is Jimmy going to die?" the boy asked in interest.

"I don't think so." Privately, Mackensen was not so confident. There was no specific for typhoid, and Jimmy's fever, which should have broken by now, continued unabated.

Two days later Jimmy died. The day after, the Meade Public Health Department reported the water specimen positive for *Eberthella typhosis*. A gang of men from the Molly blasted open the mouth of the fissure, dammed it with concrete, and dumped calcium chloride in the privy vault. Mackensen was busy dosing the boy's mother with sedatives and handling a backlog of patients. He decided that he felt like hell, and his face must have reflected it as he answered Siebert's summons. The superintendent did not attempt to cheer him up directly but did say, "It's funny how the easy looks spectacular to laymen, who don't appreciate the professionally tough jobs. You cut the fuse, for which you have my eternal gratitude, but all the camp talks about is how you pulled that steel out of Collins. I even hear from other places about it."

"Good luck—nothing more," Mackensen said. "In fact, inevitable. I would go so far as to say that the men themselves could have done just as well, once an intelligent shifter realized that there was no other course. Collins might even have done quite well without the trifling repair I did later. 'I dressed his wounds—God healed him.' "

"Ambrose Paré," Siebert cited. "Just as we miners are always quoting Agricola—wish someone would do a *good* translation of him some day. However. Only a few people appreciate or even know about your stopping this typhoid before it contaminated the whole reservoir. We would have had to drain it down, close the mill, lose six months' production at least. Don't know about lives—we chlorinate the camp water, but someone might have gone swimming. . . . Too bad about little Jimmy, but we all know you did the best you could."

"Thank you."

"Now." Siebert began in a more official tone. "Ordinarily, I'd recommend you for our standing innovational merit bonus and give you a few days to go to San Francisco to collect it. Provided you could arrange for a relief for yourself, of course. In fact, I will, but not for another few days. Colonel Jellison is coming here next week and wired that he particularly wants to meet you. Funny thing. Willie is majority stockholder, gives orders right and left—and we just ignore him. The Colonel asks a small favor as one gentleman to another, and we turn ourselves inside out for him."

Mackensen understood. "I'll be happy to meet him. He must be a very unusual man."

"He is that. Not at all what you might expect in a bloated capitalist. Well educated, deeply respected, married to the most beautiful woman you ever saw, *if* you like red hair, which he apparently does, very much. He is a gentleman in the old-fashioned sense that he leads his own life and is content to let others lead theirs, their own way."

Was this another hint?

"Well, you'll see for yourself." The interview was now obviously over. "We owe you a lot, Doctor. Thank you again."

Mackensen had nearly forgotten the approaching visitation when Tretheway, ushering out a patient during morning hours, came back in and said, "Colonel Jellison's h'outside, Doctor. Says 'e 'ates to take h'up your time, but 'e 'as to leave h'on they h'evening train." Without waiting for a reply, Tretheway ushered in a slender, gray-haired man whose face was remarkably unlined for one his age. After a brief but decent commendation Jellison made an unusual request. "Would you listen to my chest, Doctor? As long as I'm here, I may as well secure a second opinion."

"Take off your coat and shirt, please." Mackensen applied

himself to the task. It did not take long. The lub-dub was textbook-clear. "A scarred mitral valve," Mackensen offered, knowing perfectly well that Jellison knew it perfectly well. "Watch your weight, avoid undue exertion, go to bed early, and you may live to be a hundred."

"Some of that is self-contradictory," Jellison said with a smile. Then Mackensen remembered. Mrs. Jellison was both beautiful and red-haired, by repute still as enamored of the Colonel as he was of her. Some people had all the luck, ticky heart valves or not. Jellison chatted idly as he dressed and then took the chair, evidently prepared to get down to business. "Doctor Mackensen," he said gravely, "Siebert speaks most highly of you and your ability. The men think you are a miracle worker. Why does a first-class surgeon bury himself here when Johns Hopkins—the Massachusetts General—even Vienna perhaps—would be glad to have him?"

"Personal reasons," Mackensen said shortly.

"So I suspected." He pulled a long envelope from his coat pocket. "Once—long ago—I found a viper in my bosom, as it were, and learned from that to take nothing for granted. So I had certain inquiries put afoot in regard to you but then thought better of it." He handed the envelope to Mackensen, who read the detective-agency return address on the corner. "This is sealed—as it was when I received it. You'll wish to burn it, I imagine." He leaned forward. "I know for certain only that your hospital would not recommend you for any position but the one here. You were beached, in other words. Would you pardon an old man's garrulity for a moment?"

Mackensen nodded silently.

"Once I was asked to use my influence to end—an embarrassment. I refused point-blank. But it occurs to me that I could use influence here to very good effect. You are worthy of much better than Phonolite. If you desire, I can give a—an endowment—to your hospital. It would be substantial enough to sway even the man or men responsible for your predicament. The money would do much good directly and would restore you to the mainstream of your profession. I have no doubt that you could be a credit to it. All you have to do is say the word."

"Why?" Mackensen stammered. "What's in it for you?"

Jellison smiled reminiscently. "It would be idiotic to deny that self-interest was involved. The fact is that I knew an old Jew once—knew of him, rather—who did something similar. Being very young, I asked why, and was told that he did it for the satisfaction of it. I was scarcely able to comprehend it then, but, as we age, we gain perspective." Jellison smiled again, almost boyishly. "I would not like to admit to my conscience that Moses Finkel went me one better in that department."

You don't have to be charitable to me!" Mackensen insisted vehemently. "I am responsible for my—own condition."

"That is my reason, in a nutshell. I don't *have* to and you *are* responsible for yourself. If I thought otherwise, I should not have put myself to the trouble. Yet why should I selfishly keep you here when a little money spent on a good cause would restore you to your own? I am no man's jailer, and I refuse to be maneuvered into that position. The cell door is open—*vaya con Dios.*"

"What of the Molly? The people here?"

"The Molly was here before you came. I doubt if we shall close it down because you left." Jellison lifted one shoulder briefly. "Some people would perhaps—perhaps—die sooner, but, I assure you, none would begrudge your good fortune. These miners are much like soldiers. They know that some will die, they hope it will not be themselves, but they come to the headframe regardless. Not so much for the money as out of a sense of duty. They chose their profession, and they follow it where it beckons. If I sent them away, they would just go to another mine. Failing that, I honestly believe they would start their own. Some men are born to be miners, so miners they must be."

" 'They were born to be miners, so miners they must be'," Mackensen repeated. "And by what standards do you judge them?"

Jellison raised his eyebrows. "By the only standards they or I can set. Are they good at their work? What else could matter?"

"And the standards of a surgeon?"

"You sink, drift, and hoist after your own fashion, too, Doctor.

Apparently you do it very well."

Mackensen laughed softly. "Why, so I do. Thank you, Colonel, thank you very much."

Jellison nodded, then continued, "I'm not certain I have ascertained your wishes, Doctor."

" 'Relieve suffering, cheer the patient, console the family,' " Mackensen quoted. "I can do that as well here as anywhere. Perhaps a little better, though, if you would hire an experienced surgical nurse for us. Even Tretheway can't be everywhere at once or make these miners behave as well as a nurse could."

"I'll speak to Siebert." Jellison rose, extended his hand, and said, "It's been an honor meeting you, Doctor Mackensen. If my wife should be here when her time comes, I'll have no qualms about calling you."

"You are expecting a child?"

"Our fourth. I suppose if we are here then, you will extort a hospital from me next as your delivery fee."

"I must confess I had something of that sort in mind. We really need a children's and an obstetrics ward. Oh yes—and pay Tretheway one dollar as you leave, Colonel."

"One dollar?"

"Since medical care is not deducted from your paycheck, that makes you a Phonolite resident. Office calls, one dollar."

Jellison chuckled silently. "I knew this visit would cost me money, one way or the other. If you physicians don't look out, you'll be pricing yourselves out of business. Good-by, Doctor." And he was gone.

243

CHAPTER 10

1912
SPRAGUE L. SIEBERT

ON THE EVENING OF APRIL 16 the lights in the engineer's clubhouse everlooking the Phonolite reservoir were reflected in the water with exceptional brightness. This was literally true: the Molly Pitcher had been shut down for forty-eight hours, and there was juice to spare from the big D.C. generator at the powerhouse. Ordinarily everyone in Phonolite who boasted an electric bulb knew it when the incline hoist operator swung over his control-box handle to start five tons of ore up from the twelve-hundred level. The carbon filaments would dim almost to redness and then gradually grow brighter as the skip began to pick up speed. Few resented it; the dimming represented work, security, prosperity, not to mention the light itself, which made reading or sewing much easier on the eyes. So taken were people by electricity's advantages that there was talk of building an electric interurban line to Bancroft—even maybe to Meade.

There had been so many changes in the last twelve years, changes so miraculous that some of the older people felt that they could hardly keep up with the world. A road now roughly paralleled the I.F.R.&P. right of way, a road scraped out by men and mules and looking like it, too, but adequate most of the year for

Tom Phillips

the brass-radiator Model T's, of which Phonolite boasted no less then four. There was a telephone central, too. Any day now the subscribers were going to be assigned numbers. Some rejoiced at and some regretted an end to twirling the magneto handle, hearing receivers being lifted down the line, and finally asking Miss Burchard for the desired party by name in the full assurance that the whole camp would be listening in to the conversation. The old one-room school had burned and had been replaced by a four-room'er, staffed by a male principal and three schoolma'ams from Meade Normal College. These last seldom made it to their second school year, being grabbed and married by the younger engineers at the Molly almost as fast as they arrived. Water Street was paved, and Hayes Street, and Casey Street leading up to the headworks. One could go on and on.

Social changes were in the air as well. The Cousins and Irishmen were now mostly gone from the Molly payroll, having been replaced by Italians, Austro-Hungarians, and Swedes—the management held out resolutely against Finnlanders, who were notorious for the social vice of alcoholism and the more fire-breathing dogmas of socialistic syndicalism. A Japanese family had moved into camp; Nakamura seemingly spoke no tongue but that of the delicious vegetables which he could apparently grow out of solid rock, but the Nakamura kids were in the school, where their devotion to scholarship was the envy and despair even of the Gold children, offspring of one of the storeowners. The schoolma'ams spit on their hands and did their level best to inculcate intelligent, critical participation in democracy, having it held constantly before them that school was not preparation for life, the school was life itself. After one year of the child-centered curriculum, the ma'ams usually called it deep enough and succumbed to wedded bliss with a will.

To the citizenry, tonight was a particularly special night—hence the preparations for festivity at the clubhouse and some unusually active business at the saloons. All the executives and engineers of the Molly had been invited to be present with their wives to celebrate the twentieth anniversary of Sprague Siebert's appointment as general superintendent. And, just as significantly, the gathering would commemorate the realization of a twenty-year dream of Siebert's own. He had come to the Molly in 1892 aflame with an idea. It had required two decades of his own labor and that of innumerable others to translate it into reality. Had a stranger then asked what that idea was, he would have been told, "Listen!"

And after listening to the night wind blowing gently down the valley to the basin country, rustling the new green leaves on the cottonwoods, the visitor would have replied, "I don't hear much of anything."

Whereupon his host would have said, "That's it! You don't hear *any*thing." For the first time in nearly forty years Phonolite was genuinely quiet. After the last New Years' Day the stamps in the concentrator had been hung up for good. There had been people who had entered the camp comparatively young, lived to a reasonably old age, had died and been buried with the chant of the stamps never out of their ears. For that, in the last three months, quite a few citizens had been heard to complain that they could not get to sleep without the comforting, drumlike thud to soothe them into dreamland. Well, there are railroad towns where the discontinuance of the 5:15 A.M. freight and its accompanying grade-crossing whistle has produced grumbling.

In a word the Molly was going on cyanide. Cyanide was magic, almost the philosopher's stone. A very weak solution of sodium cyanide leaching finely crushed ore in the huge redwood vats sited where the Frue vanners and Dorr cones used to stand, would dissolve virtually every atom of gold and silver contained therein. This ore was physically reduced in quiet, clean little ball mills, instead of as before pounded into dust under the old stamps. The technique was of tremendous moment, for it meant a new extension for the old gal's life, hence for the camp of Phonolite.

Examining the Molly's stope sheets back in 'Ninety-two, Siebert had come to the conclusion that, upon a given day in the future, and barring a dramatic improvement in the state of the art, the Molly would have to close down. The rising costs of deeper stoping and the gradually thinning values in that same deeper ore produced two curves that ultimately crossed on his time-base graph. At the crossing point (about mid-1915, he estimated) the Molly would be no more. To be sure, there would still be gold in the deeper ore horizons; it simply would cost more money than it would bring in to hoist it. Cyanide, just beginning to be spoken about in the technical journals, appeared to be the breakthrough he needed. Under the very best conditions the old concentration was unable to prevent milling losses of about five dollars a ton in the tailing. Cyanide theoretically could recover most of that five dollars. Every time the skip dumped into the ore bin, cyanide would put the Molly twenty-five dollars to the good and at a lower cost to boot. Its active life could be extended perhaps another twenty years.

Easier said than done, of course. The process itself took time to be perfected to the point where it could be moved from the laboratory to the field. It took more time to adapt it to the Molly's particular ore. It required the effort of years to persuade Willie Huggins that it could be done and ought to be done and the money somehow found to do it. Willie had other sources of income and other fish to fry, but had finally come over, whereas Colonel Jellison had been strongly in favor of the change from the moment Siebert had first broached it. Pilot experiments had had to be run, blueprints drawn, machinery ordered and installed.

As long as they were about it, Siebert and his staff drastically revised the Molly's internal arrangements, having the end in view that the ore must move from stope to mill without being lifted by any hand whatsoever. Even the spent tailing from the cyanide vats would be returned whence it came, piped down to refill stoped-out areas to the very top, improving the looks and the safety of the Molly to a great degree. When time and capacity permitted, even the old tailing heap and waste dump would be levied upon and returned to the depths of the earth. Siebert predicted a day not far off when the sole key to a mine's character would be the headframe, a day in which the waste dump and tailing heap that made a mine impossible to mistake for anything but what it was would not be there any more.

More by luck than by planning, his twentieth anniversary so nearly coincided with the cyanide mill's going on line that the staff decided to make a double-header of it and had planned tonight's dinner by way of celebration. There had been talk of a surprise party until Siebert displayed signs of knowing too much. Wilkinson, in charge of arrangements, managed to coax old J. M. Dawson to come down from Denver to make the obligatory address. Dawson was going on seventy; for that, he was an active engineer when John W. Mackay had hit the Consolidated Virginia orebody back in, oh, 1875. Yes, say, fifty-five and twelve was as close to seventy as made no difference, Siebert reflected, knotting his best necktie around his stiff collar. Dawson was retired now, but they said he still went to his office every day, writing up his memoirs. Siebert grinned at his reflection in the mirror. Would Dawson write about the time that smart Mexican had salted the Oro Perdido and sold it for a hundred thousand on the strength of Dawson's report thereon? He rather doubted it. No man would relish relating how he had been fooled by an obliging Mexican, who furnished him dynamite loaded with salt gold dust. And Dawson was a remarkably self-opinionated old goat. British-born, though you wouldn't know it.

Waiting for Melinda to finish dressing, Siebert considered that the guest list for tonight's party would be confined strictly to members of the fraternity and their wives, excepting Doctor Mack. But Doctor Mack had been around so long that he was virtually a member, *honoris causa*. Mackensen might have made a good engineer if he hadn't gone to the dogs of medicine, but then we can't all be lucky, Siebert reminded himself. Willie Huggins had been invited pro forma and to everyone's relief had declined. He was too busy working on the renomination of Colonel Roosevelt, coming this summer at Chicago. And, if Siebert was any judge, quietly intriguing for a stand-off between Roosevelt and Taft, hoping that a worn-out and despairing convention would buy Willie as a compromise candidate. Hell, if that happened, Siebert would jump the party and vote for Champ Clark or whomever the Democrats nominated. Anybody but Willie!

No invitation had been sent to Colonel R. D. Jellison and family. Dick and Eileen were unavailable, and their older children were well scattered about the country. Even as were Siebert's own children. Which led him to the thought: If they could invite all the dead who had ever been interested in the Molly, who would come? A whole crowd of people he himself had known, headed by George and Cecelia Huggins and Frank Casey, hell, even down to poor old Dr. Mulligan and big John Tretheway. There would probably be an even bigger bunch of total strangers to him. All sorts of people . . . Spaniards, Indians, old-time prospectors. They'd all enjoy christening the Molly's new life.

When Melinda finally announced that she was ready to go, Sprague offered her his arm, and they strolled down toward the club from the head of Hayes Street at the curve where it turned south. As they came near, it was apparent that the younger crowd had been there for a while down in the basement rathskeller, nor wasted their time. There was some hilarity, though no one was getting out of line. Wilkinson had J. M. in tow, performed the introduction, and went one way while Melinda went another. The conversation instantly became professional. Yes, Dawson pontificated, there was no doubt that copper had displaced gold as the king of metals. Now that flotation was practicable and the grip of the English patent monopoly on the process loosened, copper was bound to boom even more. Dawson had high regard for Anaconda at Butte and for the United Verde in Arizona. In his opinion, however, the Keweenaw was playing out, and he had got rid of his interests there long ago. Mexico had looked good, especially what Colonel Greene had been doing at Cananea, but with the political troubles there under this Madero fellow . . . . He spoke feelingly of a strong foreign policy under a strong president. To Siebert's relief Melinda caught his signals of distress and finally came over to relieve him.

Doctor Mack was looking a touch lonely, and Siebert went over to chat. "Happy anniversary, Sprague," Mackensen greeted him. "Congratulations tonight, and tomorrow."

"Long, hard pull," Siebert admitted. "And there will be trouble when we go on line—there always is. Just hope we can find it and fix it before the next problem crops out. How are things at the hospital?"

"About as usual. We keep busy. Some time I'm going to take three months off and just hide down in the pump chamber. How's Melinda?"

So it went until they filed into the dining room and Siebert found his way to the head table. Dawson sat on his right, Melinda on his left, with Wilkinson and his wife beyond, and so Siebert was forced to listen to more bulls, encyclicals, and pastoral letters. He began to form an opinion about why Dawson's wife had quietly taken to her bed and died some years previously. In the egotism department J. M. was right in there with novel writers and painters, although in all justice he still had some way to go to catch up with Willie. Siebert had the malicious thought that, had Willie been here, he would have put him and J. M. together and alone at the head table and watched with enjoyment as they battled it out.

When the dessert plates were cleared, Wilkinson tapped his glass with his spoon and rose. Fortunately, Wilkinson believed in great works but few words. He named the occupants of the head table, announced the purposes of the dinner, and then dug down for a small gift-wrapped box which he handed, amid applause, to Siebert. Sprague opened it. It was a dandy gold watch with a nice inscription—very welcome too, since the old Hamilton he had carried for thirty years had been taken down with quartz lungs or something. He thanked them one and all, said they were a good bunch, and sat, Melinda hugging his arm warmly. Wilkinson then introduced J. M., referring to a scrap of paper containing personal information he had stoped out of J. M. earlier. It was obvious that Wilkinson was saying more than he wanted to but considerably less than J. M. had fed him. Why, Siebert thought to himself, do these old fossils want to dwell so on every last detail? Enough to say that Dawson had received the gold medal of the A.I.M.E. a few years back. Even Doctor Mack would by now have a fair idea of its significance and implications.

Dawson rose, evidently prepared to make an evening of it. He did begin with a surprise by announcing that it was he himself who back in 1874, at the request of Huggins & Casey, had examined the Molly Pitcher and predicted that the relatively narrow outcrop

251

would expand into the substantial orebody they were now working. He had other connections with the Molly as well. His late wife, Amelia, had acted as chuck tender in the courtship of Colonel and Mrs. Jellison, and had given their wedding reception for them. Therefore, he said with diplomatic hyperbole, he felt right at home here tonight.

Having got through the personal references to Siebert and wishing all success to the new mill, Dawson launched a set-piece oration, "The Future of the Engineering Profession." It was soon evident that the speech had seen much prior use and would undoubtedly serve again later—Dawson's acceptance speech for the A.I.M.E. medal? Siebert reflected that a title on the order of "The Rise of Engineering from Hiram, King of Tyre, to J. M. Dawson" would be more appropriate, since Dawson started with the invention of fire and worked forward through history, evidently taking aim squarely at himself. After Stephenson, Brunel, and Roebling, however, Dawson put his helm over and took an unexpected tack, actually doing some predicting. Engineering, he declaimed, had proved its ability to do the job—any job—in the last hundred years. It was now becoming evident that it should cease to be the mere handmaiden of society and begin to assume a role of economic and political leadership, should assume the planning function, in other words. He, J. M. Dawson, ventured to predict that, within the lifetime of most of those present, an engineer (he hoped it would be a mining engineer, but any good C.E. would do) would be president of the United States.

The people, he continued, were ready to acknowledge this in view of the magnificent accomplishments of the profession. The practical application of electricity, the perfection of the internal combustion engine, mastery of heavier-than-air flight, the taming of Niagara Falls, the Salt River Project in Arizona Territory— pardon me, the *State* of Arizona—all reinforced the point. Now, he repeated, it was time to assert the leadership that was being virtually thrust upon otherwise unassuming men. Why, this very night the largest, safest ship of all time was undoubtedly docking at New York City at the conclusion of its maiden voyage. Public attention was fastened upon it, and it should give them all valuable publicity. Kings, prime ministers, and heads of state were receptive to the advice of engineers. Therefore, Dawson concluded, it was time to lift one's eyes from the drafting table and fasten them upon the objective of directing the destiny and economic betterment of all mankind! I. Thank. You.

Siebert returned silent thanks—that it was over. There was a flurry of handshaking and congratulations, with the women cooing over Melinda. Then the younger crowd vanished incontinently in the direction of the rathskeller. Soon the sound of a gramophone playing some disreputable music drifted up the stairs. The young wives did not drink in public, thank God, but they seemed to feel no inhibitions about shaking a leg in one of these new dances about which Siebert entertained the gravest doubts. The older and considerably less dance-mad generation sought out settees and easy chairs to allow the processes of digestion and conversation full play. Just as he was settling in, Siebert saw a young man—by his dress, a depot employee—enter the club, glance around, and head directly for him. The superintendent knew trouble when he saw it. He walked casually over, led the messenger outside to the veranda, and asked, "What is it?"

"This just came in on the telegraph, sir. I thought you would want to see it, but I waited outside until the speech was over."

Thoughtful of him, Siebert reflected; also, it apparently had nothing to do directly with the Molly. He unfolded the train-order flimsy and read:

> Marconi, Cape Race, Newfoundland via NY. SS Carpathia reports RMS Titanic in collision with iceberg off Tail of Grand Banks midnight Sunday. Carpathia steaming to assistance.

"You know what's in this, son?"

"Yes, sir."

"All right. If any more news comes in, bring it up to me here or to my home." Siebert walked slowly back into the club. Since Dawson was momentarily free, Siebert drew him aside and held out the flimsy. "Here, J. M., what do you make of this? What are

253

her chances?"

Dawson read the message twice over and then handed the flimsy back. "I wouldn't worry too much. You know somebody aboard her?"

"I'm not sure. Dick and Eileen Jellison took their youngest girl to Europe last fall to put her in a Swiss boarding school. They stayed over for the London season. They planned to come back this spring. If they came now, they'd book on the *Titanic* for sure. Every American millionaire in Europe is sailing on her, if half what they say is true."

"Any way to find out?"

Siebert shook his head. "Ordinarily I'd wire our San Francisco office or the White Star office in New York. But they're closed now in San Francisco, and I bet the telegrams are pouring into New York by the bushel. But you're the traveler—is it serious?"

Dawson in turn shook his bald, massive head. "At the worst— the very worst—she'll dock in New York a day late with a stove-in forepeak. Somebody will catch hell, maybe lose his ticket. There wasn't anything else, was there?"

"No. But I asked the depot to send up anything more that came in."

"Don't expect much. It's nearly forty hours—no, forty-four, since it happened. However, . . . can you keep a confidence?"

"I try." Siebert's tone was a touch frosty. The ability to keep information to oneself was as vital to mining men as the ability to read a stope sheet. That Dawson, of all people, should ask such a question . . . .

"I have friends in the London clubs," Dawson plowed on. "The *Titanic* was built with an Admiralty subsidy like all the big liners, for conversion into an auxiliary cruiser if need be. That means she has very elaborate bulkheading. As I understand it, there are twenty watertight compartments, ten to a side, divided by an axial bulkhead running down the centerline from bow to stern. She'd have to flood ten to lose all buoyancy, or four on one side to lose stability. But hitting an iceberg would flood only the two bow compartments in the forepeak. They're the smallest of the twenty, and behind them is the collision bulkhead, the strongest of the lot.

254

Sprague, the *Titanic* could ram Gibraltar at full speed without doing herself mortal harm."

"I see. No wonder they've billed her as unsinkable."

"Well, 'unsinkable' is a pretty big word. An armored cruiser squadron or one of John Fisher's battle cruisers could do her up, provided they could catch her. But normal peril on the sea . . . ." Dawson shook his head again.

"Glad you say so. I'm not only worried about Dick and Eileen, but I was thinking about your speech tonight and the faith the public has in the profession. After the way the *Titanic* has been bragged up, it would be a nasty jolt for all of us if she were to go down."

Dawson looked concerned. "So it would. Remember when the Quebec Bridge fell, back in 1907? It ruined Ted Cooper and set us all back a bit. But at least it wasn't opened for traffic, and a couple of train loads of millionaires killed. I'll admit, now that you mention it, that presenting the *Titanic* as unsinkable was overdoing it gratuitously. There's nothing that can't be smashed if you put your mind to it."

"Could it conceivably happen?"

"Let me think. Where can we talk over a piece of paper? The dining room's cleared out now." Dawson led the way to a table, where he and Siebert sat together. Dawson produced a pocket notebook, flipped to a clean page, and sketched a plan of a ship's hull, subdivided by one longitudinal and nine lateral lines. "Here we are. Forepeak, forward hold, boiler rooms one, two, three, four, engine rooms, what-not. She can lose any five scattered at random, or three together on one side. Any more than that, she's in trouble. But there's no way, short of tearing out her whole bilge, to open her up from the bow clear back into the boiler rooms, or to breach them on one side."

"Why can't you breach the boiler rooms?"

"Hell, Siebert, no ship can steam sideways. She couldn't even drift sideways into a berg with enough force to hurt herself."

"Um, . . . I just had a thought. What if this Irish independence gang smuggled some bombs aboard her?"

"I'd discount that. Not even the Sinn Fein would murder

255

women and children on a liner. If they had the money for dynamite, they'd spend it on whisky. And the message said an iceberg."

"Are those bulkheads solid, or do they have doors?"

"Doors, of course."

"Suppose they failed to close them or the collision racked the ship so much that they couldn't be closed? You know how earth movement can throw things out of alignment in a shaft. Say, she hit somewhat at a tangent and then was heaved strongly up and over?"

"I'm no naval architect, Sprague. I'd guess they'd allow for that, but if they didn't, you're right, there could be problems. But she couldn't sink like a stone even so, and they'd have ample time to get off in the boats."

"Yes, of course. And don't those big liners have to have lifeboat capacity for everyone, including the ship's cat?"

Dawson started to nod, then reflected, and finally coughed in embarrassment. "As a matter of fact, they usually do . . . ." His voice trailed off.

"Usually? Are you telling me the *Titanic* doesn't?"

"There are—ah—certain underwriters' minima. I'm sure she meets them. Would have to, of course, to get insurance."

"J. M., you're dodging the question!" Siebert bored in.

"Ah—Sprague, I don't know. From the newspaper pictures I saw, and compared to other ships I've been on . . . the fact is, I'm not too certain."

"Good God Almighty!" Siebert was stunned.

"As well-built and thoroughly bulkheaded as she is," Dawson ruminated, "and lifeboats cost a great deal to no economic return . . . . And the shipping business is highly competitive . . . ." He brightened somewhat. "Besides, she's in or was in the center of the main North Atlantic shipping lane. Other ships all over. If she fell into collision, logically it should have been with another ship, not a berg. In any event assistance would never be far away, as witness the *Carpathia*. A few hours' steaming at most. No matter what, she'd last long enough for another vessel to come alongside and transfer everyone in both ships' boats."

256

The Molly's superintendent flushed a dangerous red. Barely controlling himself, he said softly, "Dawson, you're making apologies for indefensible optimism. Would you permit a mine to be operated on the basis of wishful thinking like that you've just described?"

"Look, Sprague, I'm not exactly defending it!" Dawson's voice belied his words, however. "Truth is, I'm just as unhappy as you. But cheer up. Worse comes to worst, the first-class passengers are always sent away before anyone else. You know—women and children first."

"That's a contradiction in terms. Damn it, J. M., there's second class and steerage women and children. I know Dick Jellison, and I know he'd stand back for them."

"Well, certainly Eileen would get off."

"No, she wouldn't! I know that woman! If Dick couldn't or wouldn't get away, she wouldn't go without him. That is one couple who would far rather die together than either one live on without the other. Oh, God!" Siebert's distress was acute.

"Do you really mean that?" Dawson asked gently. "Women are the realists, however much they—and we—try to pretend otherwise."

"Of course I mean it. A woman will kill for her children—but theirs are grown or provided for. And those two are like a pair of Canada geese. Just as smart and just as devoted to each other. With most people, marriage after a while cools down to—to a necessary and convenient companionship. Affection, habit, inertia. But not with Dick and Eileen. They've been married thirty years. Four children. He's close to sixty-five. She must be a bit over fifty. Yet two years ago in San Francisco I saw them at a party holding hands like newlyweds. Why, if I looked at Melinda the way Dick was looking at Eileen, she'd faint or run. But Eileen just smiled back at Dick, and they left the party right then. Both strutted out like peacocks, and you knew darn well what they had in mind."

"It's said that in his bachelor days he was something of a rounder," Dawson ventured.

"He hasn't been since," Siebert smiled. Then his smile faded. "No, if he went, she'd go with him. Just as he'd go with her. I don't

257

believe they'd even discuss it. And maybe after all it would be what they'd want. Suppose Dick died of something—where would that leave Eileen? She'd mope around for a few months and then go to bed and die, too."

At that moment Mackensen walked into the dining room. Seeing the expressions on Siebert's and Dawson's faces, he asked, "Something in my department?"

"Excuse me. J. M., this is Doctor Mackensen, our surgeon. Doctor Mack can keep his mouth shut," Siebert hinted.

The message was displayed, and Dawson demonstrated again the improbability of the *Titanic* being in serious difficulties. Mackensen was inclined at first to be more concerned about the Jellisons, but the problem evidently began to intrigue him as much as it did Siebert and Dawson. Mackensen stared at the little diagram and then asked, "Hypothetically, what if she lost all engine power off a rocky lee shore?"

"She has two engines, three screws," Dawson answered. "Doesn't go near such shores. No land at all, for that, off the Grand Banks. But hypothetically, nothing man ever built could stand *that* treatment, I grant you."

"An iceberg is a rocky shore when it comes down to it," Mackensen offered.

"Oh!" Dawson's old eyes opened widely. "So it is! But I was just saying, the *Titanic* would have to hit it hard, sideways, which you just can't do with a ship. And the berg certainly couldn't hit *her*, they move only a knot or two at best."

"Maybe she lost all power—her engines are new, I suppose—and the berg did hit her while they were stopped."

"Your sawbones can use his head, Siebert," Dawson said with approbation.

"We are aware of that, J. M."

"Should have been an engineer."

"We've told him that, too. But not too much, or he'd quit sewing us up and be down trying to boss a stope."

"Right spirit, anyway, Doctor. Oh—oh!"

"What?" Siebert asked.

Dawson smiled. "Forgot my basic physics. If the berg is moving with the current, so is the ship, stopped or not. Theoretically, the berg can't possibly hit an object floating in the same current. Practically it might—greater moment of inertia—but it would just nudge the ship. Scrape some paint. No, we must do better than that."

"I have it!" Siebert announced. "Mackensen has one element— loss of engine power—and another, the lee shore. A full gale could drive *Titanic* down against the berg a lot faster than the wind would move the berg itself. The North Atlantic is stormy this time of year."

Dawson nodded with approbation again. "Very good. However, speaking as an official shellback, I would say that the odds are really much longer than that. The storms blow from west to east. *Titanic* would have to be west of the berg—have passed it, in fact—*then* lose engine power at just the right second to lose headway, be caught and driven down on it, and that before the crew had time to rig a sea anchor, put up some sort of jury sail forward, what-have-you. Frankly, it won't wash. Too many improbabilities."

Siebert tried to relax, but unease gnawed at him. He smelled disaster despite Dawson's facile and sound reasoning. His engineer's instincts told him that something, somewhere, was wrong. Some factor was at work that no one present had yet mentioned, though Mackensen's comparison of a berg to a rocky lee shore was close to the issue. "What have we missed?" he asked helplessly.

Dawson smiled, but Mackensen did not. "The same thing comes up often in my line of work. Things look open and shut, but there is something just the least bit wrong. At that point, we reconsider. Get a second opinion. Hold off a moment. You have this feeling . . . ."

"Gentlemen!" Dawson intervened. "One would think we were trying to sink that vessel, and we don't even know yet but that she's tied up to the pier in New York. I grant you it was a blunder of the first magnitude to call her 'unsinkable,' but these newspapermen have no shame."

"It was hubris all the same," Mackensen said soberly. "It was asking for it. . . ."

"Are you superstitious?" Dawson inquired with a faint sneer.

"Call it what you will, sir. But we're all human, hence capable of error. I patch up a lot of men who merely did the wrong thing at the wrong moment of time. And there are some I can't patch up. You tell a man a hundred times, 'Do that and that in an emergency,' and when the emergency comes, he panics and does exactly the opposite. There are men on the bridge of that ship, too. All we've considered are two masses, one of steel and the other of ice. Professor Dawson, if it were just those, I'd say no more. But we've ignored the *men*. If there's a way to mess things up, some man will do it every time."

Melinda came in then and broke up the trio by suggesting that it was really time for Sprague to take her home. She sensed that something was not well, but, seeing who was involved, concluded correctly that the men were having the blues about something abstract, hence something that could wait. It was time for the married couples to clear out and let the bachelors have the club. Siebert rose, thankful that he could avoid the high jinks. At his age moderation in all things was—regretfully—a necessity rather than a virtue. He did not have to concern himself with Dawson's welfare; J. M. had preferred to put up at the boarding hotel rather than stay at any of the executives' houses. He said good night and walked Melinda back up the street to their home. Once he was inside his door, restlessness seized him again. "You go to bed, Melinda," he remarked, looking at his new watch. "I think I'll go for a walk around the reservoir or something."

"Good night, dear," she replied, leaning over for him to kiss her cheek. Siebert did so with a twinge of regret for youth long past. Twenty-five years ago . . . . He went down the street a second time but as he passed the noisy club, he saw a red cigar coal glowing on the veranda.

"That you, Sprague?" It was Dawson.

"Yes, I felt like a walk."

"I'll go with you. You're heading toward my digs in any event." The two men strolled along the reservoir and then down Hayes to Water Street. Just as they turned the corner, a voice asked, "May I join you?" It was Mackensen, apparently also a prey to restlessness. The three men said little more, though as by common consent they headed toward the depot. A single bulb was lit in the central office cubicle. To Siebert's mild surprise quite a few men were present. They were gathered outside talking quietly among themselves but made way for Siebert and his companions with nods of recognition.

The green-eyeshaded operator looked out his open window, recognized Siebert, and shook his head negatively. The three men seated themselves on the bench below the window on the depot platform—the wooden slats were warm, and Siebert knew that the bench had been vacated at his approach but thought, what the hell? Rank hath its privileges. From where he sat he could hear the

telegraph sounder, amplified by the traditional Prince Albert tobacco can slid in behind it. From time to time the sounder clicked sporadically, but there was no urgency to it. Nevertheless, the Molly's superintendent got a mental image of ten thousand such depots scattered all through the nation, each with its operator and a similar silent gathering, waiting in patience. Craning his neck, he saw that the office clock showed 10:45. Soon after, there was an incoming message, a short one, to which the operator rattled off a brief reply. "Number two entering the Bancroft yard," the telegrapher said loudly enough to be heard outside. Dawson, sitting at his right, stuck a cigar in his mouth and lit it by striking a wooden match with his thumbnail. Mackensen simply sat relaxed, possibly catnapping.

About 11:06 the clicks grew in number, bursts rattling briefly and then falling silent before another sequence began. "Message coming in," the operator said. Siebert stood up and turned around, looking almost directly down at the desk. The operator shifted in his chair and reached for the order pad and his pencil. There was silence for a time. Then the clicking resumed, a steady unhurried chain of sound. Reading upside down, Siebert saw the words forming:

> New York. RMS Olympic reports RMS Titanic sank 2:20 am four hours after striking iceberg. 866 survivors rescued by SS Carpathia about 1250 missing. Carpathia expected New York momentarily with survivors 30.

Somehow Siebert had known it. He stood silently while the operator read the message aloud. Dick and Eileen were gone; he knew it as surely as he knew anything. He felt regret but asked himself, how can you be sad for two people who made a free choice and preferred each other's love to the alternatives?

The crowd was dispersing now. "So it's true," Dawson muttered. "Both of you were right. How could you know?"

Siebert and Mackensen looked at each other. Mackensen shrugged. "Perhaps it comes from running a working operation," Siebert ventured. "After so many years I can often tell when there's something happening or getting ready to happen. The rhythm of things changes. Mackensen here has the feel, too. More than once I've seen him running to the headframe even before the telephone rang. How do *you* do it, Mack?"

"I don't know. I know only that it's time to get going. Tretheway, God rest him, had it also."

"Um." Dawson drew on his cigar as they continued down Water Street to the east. "Very unscientific. Very. But if intuition works, don't knock it. Reminds me of John W. Mackay and the Consolidated Virginia. Old Philipp Deidesheimer—do you know he's still alive?—said there was an orebody there. But no one believed him, including—ah— me. No evidence at all. Then Mackay got the same idea. Went after it, and there it was. I suppose you know that, if he'd started his exploratory drifting on the level he wanted to, he'd have missed it; it was in the hanging wall, not the footwall like all the others. But Ralston made him use the eleven sixty-seven of the Gould & Curry, and the rest is mining history. And, speaking of history, I suppose you two know that we heard it being made this evening?"

"Yes." Mackensen kicked a pebble absently. "Can't say I enjoyed it."

"Nor I either." Dawson shook his massive head. "I think—I think we witnessed the end of an age. What I said tonight . . . . the age of the engineer. We thought we'd laid the foundations well and truly. Now, I don't know. I don't know at all. We built something close to a religion. Call it the First Church of Applied Science. Have faith and come unto Us, all ye heavy laden, and We shall give you a full belly and an end to working like animals in the field. And we did it. For a good many, at any rate, and they believed. But now that that ship's gone down, they'll begin to wonder. *I* start to wonder. And the moment you start to wonder, the magic is lost for good. Like Luther, speculating on indulgences. One minute he believed, though he didn't want to. The next minute, he questioned—and the rock of a thousand years began to crumble. Is the *Titanic* the first crack in our foundations? I hope not, but I'm full of forebodings. Well, Siebert?"

"You've studied history, J. M. I haven't. But I know we can't call up the newspapers and say, 'Look. Nothing on God's green earth can stand up to *every* stress. We build to economic and structural limits. They're big limits, but they're still limits. Exceed them at your peril. Somehow, some way, the limits on that ship were exceeded. It's not *our* fault.' "

"They would give us the horse laugh," Dawson agreed. "Mackensen, you doctors are lucky. You can bury your mistakes. Our mistakes bury us."

"It's not quite that simple," Mackensen replied with dignity. "Never so simple. We try to keep it within the family, I admit. But sometimes that's worse. Far worse."

"Here's where I turn up the hill," Dawson noticed. "Good night, Siebert. It was good meeting you again. I'll leave on the morning train. Would have liked to see the new mill go on line, but know you'll have your hands full. Give my respects to Mrs. Siebert." They shook hands. "You going up this way, Doctor?" Dawson asked Mackensen.

"Yes. I live at the hospital, and I have to check a couple of patients before I turn in."

"Good night, Sprague."

"Good night, J. M., Mack."

Sprague paced swiftly back up Water Street and then up Hayes. What an evening, he thought to himself. The culmination of twenty years' work, and, instead of being happy, I sincerely and truly wish I was back starting at the beginning. And what are those young yahoos up to tonight?

The noise from the club was clearly audible on the sidewalk. Siebert walked to the veranda and opened the front door. He was met by a blast of sound coming up the stairs from the rathskeller. A piano was being played, not inexpertly. Someone lifted voice in verse:

> Godiva was a lady who through Coventry did ride,
>   To show the royal villagers her white and perfect hide.
> The most observant man of all, an engineer, of course,
>   Was the only one who noticed that Godiva rode a horse.

A bellowed chorus cut in with the roar of an electrically fired round.

> We are, we are, we are, we are, we are the engineers.
>   We can, we can, we can, we can demolish forty beers!
> Drink rum, drink rum, drink rum, drink rum, and come along with
> us,
>   For we don't give a damn for any damn man who don't give a damn
> for us!

Sprague Siebert sincerely hoped that all the ladies had gone home, for the tenor immediately went on from bad to worse.

> She said, "I've come a long, long way, but I'd go to the Moon,"
>   "With the man who takes me off this horse and into a saloon."
> The man who took her from her steed and led her to a beer,
>   Was a bleary-eyed survivor and a drunken engineer.

"Bless their hearts," the superintendent of the Molly thought. "They may never run the world, but they'll build the roads it runs on."

> The Army and the Navy went out to have some fun.
>   They went down to the tavern where the fiery liquors run.
> But all they found was empties, for the engineers had come,
>   And traded all their instruments for gallon kegs of rum.

The piano segued, evidently to permit the taking of additional refreshment. The tenor then hurled down the *defi*:

> MIT was MIT when Harvard was a pup,
>   And MIT will be MIT when Harvard's busted up,
> And any Harvard bastard who thinks he's in our class,
>   Can pucker up his rosy lips and kiss the Beaver's ass!

Smiling broadly, Siebert softly joined in the final chorus:

> We are, we are, we are, we are, we are the engineers.
>   We can, we can, we can, we can demolish forty beers!
> Drink rum, drink rum, drink rum, drink rum, and come along with
> us,
>   For we don't give a damn for any damn man who don't give a damn
> for us!

CHAPTER 11

1932
KENNETH CARVEL

THE TRUCKER EASED on his brakes and pulled the old GMC over a foot onto the narrow shoulder. "Here you are, buddy," he announced confidently.

Ken Carvel looked around the bleak expanse of sagebrush and desert flat, wondering whether the trucker was having some kind of joke at his expense. The trucker seemed a fairly good Joe, having even given Ken half a sandwich from his own meager lunch sack fifty miles back. He didn't seem the kind to dump a man out in the middle of nowhere for the enjoyment of it, although Ken had learned that some people were capable of that and worse. "Nothing much here," he finally replied in a neutral voice.

"Over there." The trucker jerked his thumb to the left. "Follow that dirt road and the old railroad line to them hills and on up the creek. Don't know how far it is, but I've heard not too far. Good luck."

"Thanks. And much obliged for the lift." Ken shook hands, stepped down from the running board, and stood aside, holding his blanket roll, while the trucker pulled back onto the highway and started running up through his gears. Across the gray hardtop was the dirt road, marching straight across the flat to the west and to a

TOM PHILLIPS

low range of hills, where it seemed to terminate at a notch. Ken estimated the distance to be five or six miles—two hours' hike. He adjusted his blankets for easier carrying, and began to put one foot ahead of the other. After about a mile he was reassured by the sight of an old right of way littered with jumbled, rotting crossties, curving in from the left. The trucker had apparently given him the straight goods. Furthermore, the road he was on seemed to have been recently used.

As he entered the valley notch, road and right of way blended, crossed, and crossed again, generally paralleling the stream bed. Signs of former human habitation appeared in the shapes of rusty iron and odd junk. A mile or so in, Ken came to a wooden sign, its paint rendered nearly illegible by weathering. It said "Phonolite. Molly Pitcher Mining Corporation. Population 1,500." Someone had crossed out the "1" and the two zeroes with black paint of more recent vintage. Encouraged, Ken stepped up his pace for a few hundred feet, hoping to see the town come in sight shortly. Then he abruptly halted and looked around. He was inside Phonolite without having realized it. Underfoot was cracked and weedy paving. Nearly hidden by new brush to his right were the low stone foundations of small buildings. Over to the left was what must have once been the railroad depot. Fire, decay, and vandalism had reduced it to a few charred boards and a chipped concrete platform. For that, Carvel was standing at the ghost of a street intersection.

Since the road going uphill from where he stood appeared to have been used, Ken turned right and began to trudge upward for a few blocks; it was hard to think of the intervals as blocks, since everything was so grown-over and dilapidated. Fairly soon he entered a flat, comparatively open area of gravel that had obviously been an industrial site. Battered concrete or rusty corrugated-iron-sheathed buildings were visible, the windows systematically smashed. They bore weather-peeled signs: Blacksmith Shop, General Offices, Power Plant, and so on. Inside they were empty of everything but dust and litter. Directly ahead of Ken was a massive steel headframe, stripped of all but its concrete bins. The machinery was gone from the hoist house leaving only dusty patches of hardened grease. From the looks of things—and Ken had become an expert in judging such matters—the mine had been closed down and stripped between five and ten years before. Closer to ten than to five, he decided. Quite sometime before the Crash, the watershed by which all recent history was calculated.

To the west on a lower and artificial plateau was a large building, likewise sheathed in rusty elephant iron. Big circular tanks were still in place beyond it, evidently being not worth salvage. Rusty iron piping and warped, leaky wooden troughs ran here and there, some of them terminating abruptly in empty air. The only sound was of the wind and the crunching of gravel underfoot. The only point left worth investigating was a smaller headframe perhaps a quarter-mile farther east. Ken headed for this, his worn work shoes making a gritting noise that seemed very loud. Again he began to wonder whether the tip of a job to be had here was right. So far the information had been accurate. He was in Phonolite (or what was left of it), there was or had been a Molly Pitcher mine, but there could be no work without people, and up until now the only signs of life he had seen had been the jays and a few ground squirrels. He consoled himself again with the thought that the road at least looked as though it was in use.

Ken sighed in relief when he came in sight of an inhabited house near the eastern headframe. It had obviously been brought up here from the town and put down on small, store-bought concrete piers. It looked neat and clean, with washing on the line, a small old solid-tire truck parked under cover, some chickens in a pen, and even a garden behind. Ken paused to look it over. A man could tell a lot about people just by using his eyes. There was no ramshackle collection of junk or heap of refuse or outdoor museum of mineral specimens, but petunias grew in a whitewashed planter, and the place looked as though it was kept decently by decent people. As he came closer, he heard the drumming of a gasoline engine. Outside the front gate—a gate in good repair—he halted and, as politeness required, called, "Hello, the house!"

Reaction was immediate. An uproar of dogs surged around the corner and hurled themselves at the gate, bellowing blood and slaughter. Though they could have jumped the fence easily, they contented themselves with threats until Ken stepped inside the yard, whereupon they instantly fell silent and began sniffing at his ankles and crotch. Ken waded through them, heading for the front door, but at that moment a big girl appeared from out back, arms full of clothesbasket. She put the basket down and walked forward, estimating him as women did. He stood quietly, legs emerging from the sea of dogs, knowing that she saw a lean man in his mid-thirties, wearing jeans, shirt, hat, and work shoes and carrying a blanket roll. In that year the West had a half-million men exactly like him. God only knew how many more there were in the rest of the country.

"What do you want?" the girl asked in neither curiosity nor hostility.

"I heard there was work here," Ken replied in a tone to match the girl's.

The girl said "Wait," and returned to the house. After a minute a woman who was evidently her mother came out. She was about Ken's age, a pleasantly round-faced woman with a few freckles, slightly buck teeth, and unbobbed brown hair, wearing a plain homemade dress like the girl's. What Ken especially liked about her, apart from her candid manner, was her cleanliness. Not scrubbed to death by any means, but the cleanliness of Mormon ranch wives. He hoped these people weren't Mormons—they wouldn't hire anybody but their own, though to their credit there were none of them on relief, either. Then he thought, Mormons don't mine. He took off his hat and repeated his request.

The woman nodded. "I don't know. I'll get my husband. You want a drink—it'll be a couple of minutes. Joanne, take him back to the pump." The girl quit hanging clothes and led him behind the house. As he drank thirstily, Ken could see the woman walk to the headframe and pull on a rope. After a wait a bell rang. The woman disappeared into a shed. The gasoline engine changed its sound, and the one sheave wheel atop the big headframe began to rotate; it seemed like a very large wheel for so slender a rope. Soon a cage appeared at the platform, and the man in it raised the bar to push off a rusty mine car. His carbide light still burned, but after leaving the car he removed his cap to reveal white hair and turned off the light. He walked over to the pump where Ken stood. Ken could see that, despite his easy walk, the white hair and lined face placed the man as fifteen or twenty years older than his wife.

"How do," the man said, sticking out a hand. "I'm Tom Pritchard."

"Ken Carvel." The gasoline engine had cut out completely, and the woman joined them from the shed. Looking at her husband, she bobbed her head toward Ken. "He said he heard there was work here, Tom."

The man looked down, somewhat embarrassed. "Where'd you hear that?"

"At Meade. Man I met at a truck stop there said there might be work here."

"Meade? You come all the way from Meade?"

"I hitched a couple of rides."

"Who was the man talked to you?"

Quick at sizing things up, Ken decided that the woman wanted to give him a job, the husband was weighing the situation. "I don't know his name. Tall man. Light hair. Driving a Reo truck."

"Oh, that's Fred Somerset," the woman put in.

"Well, the fact is," Pritchard began slowly, "we could use help, and I guess Fred knows it, but we can't pay nothing. No money, that is, only food and room. And the work is hard."

Ken had already been told as much. "What kind of work?"

"General mine work. Mostly brute strength and awkwardness. Mining's a two-man job no matter how you look at it. And lots of other things. Machinery repair. Gardening. Handyman work."

"You do it by yourself?"

"I have to."

Ken reflected some more. "If you took me on and got some money, would you pay me what you could then?"

"That's only fair, but I can't promise nothing."

Ken looked around. He liked what he saw. There was not a hell of a lot here, but these people seemed to be making out with what they had plus hard work. The woman was kind-spoken, and Pritchard himself was polite even to a hobo like Ken. Hard work alongside nice people was a lot better than an easy job around bitter or stupid folks. "I don't know much about mine work, but I generally catch on. That bad?"

"I can teach you what you have to know. But are you up to it?"

It was Ken's turn to look down. "Well, I was—hurt. I can do a pretty good day's work, but no company wants you if you've been hurt. Afraid you might go sick and then try to come on them, I guess."

"How were you hurt?"

"In the Argonne—Blanc Mont."

Pritchard raised his eyebrows. "What outfit were you with?"

"Second Engineers."

"We heard of them. Machine gun?"

"Gas."

"Guess you can handle a shovel. And it's not very damp around here except in spring." Pritchard was evidently coming to a decision, unaware of his wife's eyes on his face. "Are you game?"

Ken picked up his blanket roll. "These days, any job is a good job." So saying, he went to work at the Molly Pitcher.

For a few weeks it was pretty hard, mostly because he could barely get the hang of any one task before he and Tom Pritchard had to jump to another. That first day, after a noon meal, he went back down in the cage with Tom—Mrs. Pritchard ran the hoist engine—to help him scoop broken, chippy rock into an endless succession of old mine cars. One man would fill a car while the other took a full one up in the cage, pushed it over to dump it into a bin, and then went back down with the empty. They did this until suppertime, and Ken's back and leg muscles knew it when he sat down again to eat. But Pritchard seemed pleased and kept saying that two days' work had been done in one afternoon.

Mrs. Pritchard served the supper. How she had cooked it while running the hoist Ken couldn't figure, although she had the girl to help her. They all ate together, the Pritchards, the girl Joanne, and two younger boys about twelve and ten years old. The food was plain but good and plentiful, with vegetables from the garden. Ken was too tired to make much of anything but the meal itself.

Afterward they fixed him up a place to sleep in a lean-to shed. Pritchard apologized a little, but Ken knew there was no place to sleep inside except in the boys' room, and he'd just as soon not do that. The lean-to wasn't bad even so, and, after washing up some, Ken went right to sleep.

The next morning Ken and Pritchard went over to the ore bin and started tapping the ore down a chute into a little cast-iron crusher. Some rolls like a washing machine mangle reduced it further, and the pulverized ore ended in a set of steel oil drums, arranged in a sort of stairstep fashion on scaffolding built of salvage lumber. Tom added some chemicals to each and then carefully put in a small measure of white powder taken from a steel drum marked "Sodium Cyanide" (Ken knew what cyanide meant and kept his distance upwind without need for urging). Then they had to fill more drums with water at a little homemade reservoir down at the creek and bring them up in the truck. Ken was struck by the way Pritchard had laid things out to let gravity or machinery do most of the work for them. It was while they were filling the water drums that Tom pointed out a high concrete dam, perhaps a quarter-mile upstream. "Wish the highway department hadn't blown the gate on it," he remarked. "We could pipe our water then and save this work."

"Why'd they do it?"

"Well, I couldn't promise to keep day-and-night watch on it, and they were afraid it would go out sometime. The water would shoot down the valley here and maybe wash out the highway and kill somebody. So they drained it down and blew the gate out. But she was a big one." Tom waved his arm at the valleyside beyond and to the west. "Used to be some fancy houses up there. Mine superintendent, engineers, all that."

"You work here then?"

"No. I came in here with the crew that was pulling out the machinery. Talked with one or two of the old-timers that were still around. I figured it would make me a living, and I had a stake, so I bought the rights and talked them into leaving me some of the machinery—cage and a little compressor, and so on. Stuff that would cost more to ship than it would fetch as scrap or salvage.

They were pretty decent about it."

Upon their return to the drum line Pritchard parked the truck uphill and showed Ken how to siphon the water into the drums, using old compressed-air hose. Then Tom connected some iron piping and went off to start the compressor. Presently air began to bubble at the surface of the liquid. "What are we doing?" Ken asked.

"Cyaniding the ore to get the gold out. We'll let it steep a few days and then run the liquor down into those wooden boxes there. They have zinc shavings in them, and the gold will come out as a black sludge. About once a month we clean the sludge out real careful, drain it good, and put it into a drum. Fred Somerset comes by in his truck and takes it into Empire to ship to the smelter in Pueblo. The smelter sends us a check and fresh zinc when I ask for it. Then I can pay Fred and the railroad and get food and supplies, and we go at her again."

Since the next day was a Sunday, there wasn't much for Ken to do but work in the garden, do some outside painting and repair on the house, move supplies around, help Tom set up for the next day's work down on the level, wash his work clothes, make his room in the shed a little more homelike, and pitch in with the gasoline engines' maintenance. It was while they were cleaning the spark plugs of the hoist engine that Ken asked, "How come you're making a living here when a big company up and quit?"

"Oh, shoot," Tom replied. "They had five hundred men on the payroll and had to hoist close to a thousand or more tons of pay ore a day to stay in business. But they ran out of that kind of ore eight, nine years ago. What's left is mostly in the footwall. That's that schist we've been hoisting. Didn't pay them to take out more than a foot or so of it, but the gold runs in as deep as five, six feet. We're grabbing that. A ton of it averages out about ten dollars by assay. We can get a little more than half of it with this old setup. Sounds like clear profit, but it costs like hell for food and gasoline and haulage and everything. Billie June could tell you—she keeps our books. If we get back enough from Pueblo to keep going another month, I'm happy. But in another couple of years all the ore in the three-hundred footwall will be gone."

"Then what?"

"Could do a lot of things, but it would cost more than we would make. Like go down and do it over on the four-hundred level, but it and everything below it is flooded. Probably wrecked, too. They pumped her with electric, but the powerhouse is cleaned out, and the public service company isn't about to put in a seventy-mile line just to please old Tom Pritchard. But maybe in a couple of years the country will be back on its feet again. Then I can either sell out to some mining company with luck, or just quit here and get a job with a going mine. How did things outside look to you?"

Ken shook his head. "I didn't see any signs. People are getting pretty desperate. I'm just thankful to be here."

"How come you aren't drawing some kind of pension?"

Ken hesitated—truth or lie? Tom would likely swallow a lie, but there seemed no reason not to tell the truth. "I'm kind of on the run."

"Law trouble?"

He shook his head. "Woman trouble."

"Sometimes that's worse. But it's none of my put-in."

"Maybe do me good to tell it. I got married just before we left Hoboken for France. Came back, and we found out we'd made a mistake. It just wouldn't work nohow. So I left. She could trace me if I put in for a pension, so I didn't. She'd just take it all anyway."

"Any kids?"

"No, thank God. She didn't want none. Now I'm glad—it made leaving easier. She either went back with her folks or got work. But she wouldn't work unless she had to. I think sometimes she hoped I'd get killed in France. It would have been ten thousand clear to her."

"What was her trouble, Ken?"

"Maybe hers, maybe mine. She had big dreams. Wanted everything. I honest to God hope she found some man who's well off and can give her what she wants out of life. I couldn't."

"You're a good worker."

"Thanks. But that's all I am or want to be. She wanted

something more. A man ought never marry a girl who wants him to be more'n what he is. Just makes both of them miserable."

"Guess I'm lucky with Billie June, then. Here, hand me that knife. These points are about three million miles too wide. No wonder she's been missing on that cylinder."

Monday was drilling day. They hung a big old Ingersoll from the bar and started sinking short blast holes in the schist footwall. The rock drilled easily, which was good, since the compressor did not deliver much air. Nor did the rock dull the steel much, which was good, too, since Tom said sharpening drill steel was quite a chore. And they could pour water into the holes to keep down the dust, since they had no piped-in water to wet it down through the steel. Still it was tough work, and Ken wondered how Tom had managed it singlehanded. Once he asked.

"Shoot," Tom replied, "you got a wife and three kids depending on you, you do just about anything. But I admit having a partner to help is a blessing. Makes everything go four times as fast and eight times as easy. Maybe we can make enough to pay you something, for you are sure as hell worth it to me."

"You always worked this alone before?"

"I'd have busted a gut before now if I'd tried. But men come and go. Seems like the good men I can't keep—don't blame them for going, with no pay—and the bums I have to kick off the place. Last helper I had was O.K., but he would *not* take a bath. I finally told him we'd have to feed him outside, so he told me what I could do with it. Also, he was stupid."

When they had finished drilling and it came time to load the holes, Tom insisted on doing it alone. When Ken wanted to know why, Tom asked, "Don't tell Billie June? Fact is, the company left me nearly ten tons of powder in the magazine east of here. It sure ain't getting any younger, but powder costs like hell. So I use the old stuff. Oh, I'm careful, but old powder is old powder—sensitive and touchy. I turn the cases I can reach and wet 'em down good before I move or open them, but you never can tell. No sense to us both getting hurt, and I'm more used to handling it than you, Ken."

"But I'm the hired hand," Ken protested. "They trained us to do it in the Engineers. You got a wife."

"Did you hire out to argue, or did you hire out to work?" Tom demanded. "Now you go up and tell Billie June I'll be shooting in about an hour and not to go falling asleep over that hoist." Ken left, shaking his head.

Ken apparently was not the only person troubled by this, for a few days later they had a visitor. A small truck with the state seal and "Bureau of Mines" on the door drove up and parked. A man dressed in neat khakis and wearing a wide felt hat waded through the dogs, who were greeting him like an old friend. Tom introduced him as Verne McCloud, a deputy mine inspector. "Glad to meet you, Mr. Carvel," the man said, shaking hands. "I've been a little worried about Tom, here, trying to do it all by himself. Now I'll feel easier in my mind." He glanced around and then continued, "Tom, are you still using that old powder?"

Pritchard nodded stubbornly.

"Now you know I wish you wouldn't. But I admit I don't know what to do. You bootleg miners violate every law on the books, but if I closed you down like I ought to, it'd just be more people on relief. You a miner, Mr. Carvel?"

Ken shook his head. "No, sir. But Mr. Pritchard here, he's learning me a lot."

"He's a good worker, Verne."

"No insurance, you know," the deputy persisted.

"I know, sir. But Mrs. Pritchard is a good cook."

The deputy inspector tilted back his hat. "Don't tell me you're working for board?"

"A man that can't afford to buy new powder for himself can't afford to pay wages," Ken affirmed. "It suits me."

"What in hell is going on in this country?" the deputy demanded of the world at large. "Two good men working like dogs in a dangerous hole like this . . . ."

"It's honest work, Verne," Pritchard said slowly. "You know any mines hiring?"

"Nobody's hiring on, Tom."

"Then I'd rather use old powder here than be hanging around Meade six days a week to stand in line for relief on Fridays."

"What about Billie June and your children?" the deputy asked, in a manner which indicated that he and Tom had gone over this ground many times before. "Do them any good if you blow yourself to kingdom come?"

"Mr. McCloud," Ken interjected, "in France I saw a lot of men get themselves blown to kingdom come for something maybe not as good as wanting to keep their families from having to go on relief."

"What the hell do you have against relief, apart from stubbornness?" the deputy asked in exasperation.

"Verne, if you got to ask that, there's no way I can answer you," Tom replied. "But I'm a fair-minded man. You talk Billie June into it, and I'll close the Molly down and go into Meade like you say."

"He doesn't have to come to me—I'm here," a new voice spoke. The three men turned to face Billie June. "Mr. McCloud," Billie June began, "now I'll say it. I know what he's doing. And every time he spits those fuses, I'm scared to pieces for him and my children and me. And I wish before God he had a safe job in town or in a regular mine. But there aren't any jobs, Mr. McCloud. *None!* And I married a man, not a lazy house cat to lay around the house all day. It would kill him to take relief, and if it would kill him, it would kill *me.* I don't want to spend twenty years looking at a man I helped cut, like you'd cut a bull calf. Yes, and have him looking at me and knowing I helped do it to him. And why do you have to come out here and start trouble? And . . . ." Billie June buried her face in her apron and fled into the house.

McCloud slowly replaced his hat. "You got quite a wife there, Tom," he said, in grudging admiration. "And you're a stubborn old bastard, and, speaking unofficially, I wish there were more like you. Maybe we wouldn't be in such bad shape. But you're not nursing some idea about making a big strike here, are you?"

Tom shook his head, clearly glad to change the subject. "The Molly's pretty nearly played out, and I know it. I give her another two years. If gold went up and somebody came in with a quarter-million dollars, he just might get his money back. But I think she's about dead. It's just a way to make a living."

"Good luck to both of you," the deputy said, "You need it. Anything I can carry into town for you? Mail? No? Well, good luck. Glad to meet you Mr. Carvel. 'By, Tom." He stopped in the midst of his escort of dogs to scratch one or two behind the ears, got into his truck, and started down the hill.

"Does he aim to make you trouble?" Ken asked in anxiety, as the truck went out of sight.

"Verne? No—just a good man trying to do a tough job. He knew there wasn't any use before he came out here."

"Then why did he come?"

"Mostly for mileage. Deputy state inspectors don't get paid much, either. Verne's got to eat, too." Tom turned away. "Time to go run off a batch."

They decanted the cyanide liquor through rubber hoses into the zinc boxes and made another trip with the old truck for rinse water. Working side by side, the men overturned the drums to dump the spent tailing sideways and down the slope. It was then necessary to go down to the level and continue the wearisome job of mucking the schist. Ken stood at the foot of the muck pile, heaving the schist up to an iron mucking sheet, from which Tom scooped it upward again into the car. It seemed to Ken that every piece of ore had to be lifted three times by hand, and again he wondered how Tom had done it alone. "You know," he remarked during a breather while they rolled Bull Durhams, "ignorant as I am, it seems there ought to be an easier way."

Tom smiled tiredly. "Plenty. In a real mine they don't lift anything by hand any more. All done with loading machinery or chutes. Even an old-time hand miner would laugh at us, knocking ourselves out this way. But this is Depression, boy, and all we got to invest is our labor."

By the time Ken got used to the work and was toughened enough not to go to sleep any more over the supper table, he looked around and saw trouble coming. It was Joanne, the girl. She was fifteen, looked nineteen, and was obviously restless. He had a fair idea of what was likely to happen, and though he seldom spoke to her, he knew she was watching him, sizing him up, and waiting for the right time. It came on a hot night in August, as he was

smoking a good-night cigarette on his bed out in the shed. Joanne slipped in and put it right to him. She offered Ken anything—she made it plain what she meant—if he would take her away from here. The girl was full of adolescent boredom, rebelliousness, ambition, and she reminded him in a sorry way of a similar girl who had said similar things outside Camp Dix, fifteen years back.

"Joanne," he replied quietly, "you think it's wonderful because you haven't had to live in it. I have. Plenty. And I'm glad to be right here. It sure beats freezing and starving. Best a girl like you could do is work five-and-dime if you're lucky. Even the—the bad women are having a tough time of it."

She then went for his jugular as only a desperate girl-woman could. "If you don't," she hissed, "I'll tell my folks you Did It to me. My dad will either kill you or run you off. Either way, you lose." She meant it, and he knew she meant it.

He tried another angle. "Suppose I said, sure I did, and say I'm willing to get married?"

"Then I'll tell them that you—do nasty things."

This girl has got an evil mind, Ken thought, but where did a country girl learn tricks like that? He tried yet another angle. "Look—if you hooked up with me, you'd never get anywhere. I'm a bum, and I'll stay a bum. You need me like the country needs Hoover. If you're bound to go—go. You'll go faster by yourself than with me along. I'm broke, old, and no good to you. Just hike down to the highway—the first trucker going south will give you a lift."

"No. I know what that trucker would do. And the ones after him. I need somebody to look out for me until I learn town ways. Then you can go."

The smart little bitch! he thought in reluctant admiration. She's got it all figured out, and figured right, too. With a sense of weariness that was not fatigue, Ken realized that he was boxed. "You planning to take off tonight?" he asked with what he hoped was the right tone of resignation. He reached down for his work shoes.

"No, stupid! We'll need money. The smelter check will come

tomorrow or the next day. When Mom signs it, I'll carry it out to give Fred Somerset to mail—only I'll switch envelopes. Then we'll leave that night, hitchhike to Empire, cash the check at the bank, and get a bus. To Los Angeles."

"You'd steal from your own folks?"

"I'd steal from God to get out of here. Guess you want a down payment now," Joanne said, her fingers going to the neck of her dress.

"Too tired. I'd need to rest up a few days." Ken faked a cough that turned into the real thing.

Joanne seemed convinced. "Don't you say a word, or I'll tell," she repeated.

Ken nodded, his eyes full of cough tears. After Joanne had gone, he grimaced to himself. Kids! They thought they knew it all. Joanne would have gotten away with it if Ken had been her own age. A boy would have been so excited by terror and lust that a hard-headed girl who knew exactly what she wanted could make him stand on his head. But not a tired man who had seen Paree, not to mention the Argonne Forest, with a depression and a bad marriage thrown in for good measure. The moonlight was bright enough for him to write a short note to Tom and Billie June, explaining how he was sorry but he couldn't work without wages any more. Not their fault, but he thought he would go north to try his luck up there. Good-by, and it was nice knowing you folks. Yours respectfully, Kenneth Carvel. He propped it against the base of his coal-oil lamp and then, with economy of motion, rolled up his blankets and tied them. Outside the dogs were puzzled by his moving around, but they were quiet as he scratched and pulled gently at their ears.

Walking down the hill in the moonlight, Ken felt as though out of the corner of his eye he could see the camp as it had been—the houses, business buildings, even the depot and rails beside the creek bed. As he turned left, the illusion was lost. He hiked down the valley and by midnight was at the highway, turning south in the direction of Bancroft and whistling "The Wreck of the Old 97" to keep himself company. He knew that no trucker would stop for a hitchhiker in the darkness, but that was all right. After another hour or two, he curled up in the ditch for a nap. Awakening at light, he started off again. All the traffic was north-bound; there was nothing going south nor would be until about noon, he estimated.

It was still morning when Ken heard the unmistakable sound of the old chain-drive truck behind him. He cussed Tom a little for wasting the gasoline and then stopped and waited, wondering whether Tom would shotgun him, cave in his head with a drill steel, or just beat hell out of him with his fists. On balance it didn't seem to make a great deal of difference one way or the other. He'd been beaten up before, and he'd seen too much death to be very afraid of it. But Ken knew he would have to take it and keep his mouth shut, mostly for Billie June's sake. Tom would never believe ill of his daughter, but Billie June was a woman, hence wise to women's ways. No use splitting her from her daughter just to save his own worthless hide. The truck pulled up beside him amid a hideous squeal of unlined brake shoes.

"Hi, Tom," Ken said, trying to keep calm. He didn't see a shotgun or a steel on the wornout seat cushions.

Tom killed the motor and slid over. "Hi, Ken." He pulled out his Bull Durham bag and a paper of ZigZags, rolled one, and passed the makings over to Ken. They sat together in the shade on the running board and smoked companionably. After a while Tom flipped the butt away and got down to business. "I come to bring you back. I'll tell you, it was something this morning. But Billie June slapped it out of Joanne, the whole story. I still don't know how Billie June knew. I'm sorry, Ken. That girl about had me convinced there for a while."

"It's O.K. Man's got to stand by his kids. No hard feelings, but I still better go. Joanne will hate the sight of me now, and pretty soon there'll be choosing up sides."

"We'd been talking it over, and we were getting ready to start paying you some wages. Last smelter check was bigger. Two men do four times the work of one."

"No need, Tom. But I want you to know I was happy with you folks. Now you can buy Billie June a Monkey Ward dress or two. Kind of grinds a woman down, never having nothing store-bought to wear."

"Sure you won't come back? Ken, we need you bad . . . ."

Then Ken had an idea. "What you were going to pay me? Would it send Joanne to town, to high school?"

Tom considered. "She could ride in to Empire with Fred. Board there pretty reasonable if she helped with housework. That would help a lot of ways, but why should you pay to send my girl to school?"

Ken laughed, one hard bark. "Won't cost me much. She'll be married to some boy there before Christmas."

Tom nodded. "That's the truth. She may be my own daughter, but I feel a little sorry for that boy."

"Don't be too hard on her, Tom. Loneliness is tough on girls. Agreed?" They shook hands, climbed in the truck, and Tom cut it around to head back north to the Phonolite road.

Joanne was not visible when they got up to the Molly, and Billie June welcomed Ken back without saying very much. The incident was tacitly shelved, but Billie June moved Ken's place at the table to put him between the two boys. Tommy and Steve were noisy little hellions, but they had taken to Ken and he to them. After a while they hardly played more than one prank a week on him, while Ken taught them to fake bending a teaspoon double, and caught Tommy with the old "hot" pie trick. Ken stayed in his shed the day they put Joanne in Fred Somerset's truck to go into Empire. Hardly was she gone before Billie June redded out Joanne's room, proposing to move Ken into it.

She ignored his protests. "Winter's coming on. Can't have you freezing out in that shed. Whenever she comes back, you can sleep on the kitchen floor by the range."

The work came more easily now. Ken was tougher, and he and Tom now knew which one wanted the ball for a shot without taking time out to talk things over. The smelter checks stayed higher. Ken guessed this from hints and occasional words but, since it was none of his business, didn't try to pry. On the other hand, the schist ore was shrinking steadily. There were times when Tom would pace off the remaining part of the level and talk about pumping out the old four hundred so they could have a try at that, but both knew that the insuperable obstacle was power. Gasoline pumping was out of the question, as was a power highline, both for reasons of cost. "If we only had a steam engine, now," Tom would say. "There's enough old timber for fuel to pump the whole mine dry. But who has a second-hand steam engine these days?" So they let it drop; it was just talk anyway.

The Monday before Thanksgiving, Tom and Ken finished the blast holes, rolled the old Ingersoll back, and then went up, Ken to get the fuse and caps, while Tom walked the quarter-mile east to the powder storage magazine. Meeting back at the headframe, Tom took the blasting materials down, while Ken went to the hoist house to take another lesson on the controls from Billie June. It was fairly simple: there was a hand-brake lever, a clutch lever, and a floor accelerator stolen from the same old Chevvie that had contributed the hoist engine. When hoisting, one stepped on the accelerator to bring the engine up to speed and then eased on the clutch while releasing the brake. One foot movement, and two opposing arm movements did it, though Ken suspected that it would take practice to do right. He was following Billie June in a dry run when the hoist bell rang once.

"He sure got them loaded fast," Billie June remarked casually. "Now watch me again." She went through the movements smoothly, but when the cage appeared, there was nothing on it but a few tools. "Now what is that man up to?" she asked.

"Just a minute," Ken intervened, thinking he had seen something but hoping he hadn't. "Hold it there." He trotted around the hoist, out the door, and over to the shaft platform. The floor of the cage held a bright-red puddle. Ken flung up the bar, stepped on, and jerked once at the bell cord. Billie June's face, framed in the hoist-house window, made O's of eyes and mouth in surprise. Ken stabbed downward with his thumb urgently. Her shoulder went forward, and the cage dropped. Ken pulled off his cap, turned on the water of the carbide light, and when the pungent reek of acetylene came to his nose, spun the lighter wheel. A tongue of white flame illuminated the cage just as it stopped at the level.

Ken stepped off cautiously, looking around. Virtually at his feet was huddled a heap of what appeared to be paint-stained rags. A whiff of powder smoke was now perceptible. Ken knelt, gently turning the bundle over. He felt bile surge into his mouth, but calmed himself by looking away for an instant and telling himself that he had seen much worse. He looked back. Only the white hair made what was left above the collar identifiable as Tom. One arm, upflung above his head, lacked a hand. He had obviously had a hole nearly loaded when the old powder went. Tom was dead.

Ken felt an urgent need to reconstruct what had happened after the blast. Shocked, blinded, Tom had evidently got his bearings and crawled toward the station. But why had he not merely crept onto the cage and then pulled the bell cord? Looking down at the big red pool on the sheet-iron flooring, Ken saw a soaked shoelace. One of Tom's shoes lay back a way, open and laceless. Tom had clearly used the lace as a tourniquet for his spurting wrist. He had crawled to the shaft, struggled erect—then what? An unverifiable suspicion began to form in Ken's mind. Tom must have realized that he was blind, maimed, merely an object of horror and charity if he were to live. Therefore, had he merely taken the bell cord in his good hand, worked off the tourniquet, and, as he finally collapsed, given it the one tug that would bring the cage up empty? It would guarantee him the three or four additional minutes for the rest of his life to drain away. But why pull the cord at all? Miner's instinct, perhaps. A man in his condition could not be expected to think rationally.

Up top, Billie June must be waiting in terror. No time to fool around further. Ken dragged over an empty car, managed somehow to get Tom's body into it, and found some old canvas to cover it. He didn't want Tom to be visible when they got to surface—Billie June would perhaps faint, and he didn't want her to do it while her hands were still on the brake and clutch. He didn't think she would, but there was no use taking chances. Tugging on the bell cord, he thought, it's going to be one hell of a Thanksgiving.

The rest of the afternoon was a daze to Ken; it was like when your platoon sergeant was hit, but you just kept on with the job anyway. First he got Billie June to bed and hunted out the pint of bootleg whisky he knew Tom kept somewhere in the kitchen. He

285

fixed a strong drink and made Billie June drink it. She tried to be sick over it but finally kept it down. He built a fire in the range and was frying some eggs and side meat, for the boys would be coming in from the school bus soon, and kids had to eat. Something had to be done about Tom, and the law in Empire had to be notified, but the living took priority over both. Then the boys came in, screeching and hungry, and although they sensed at once that something was wrong, Ken made them eat before he told them what had happened. For boys their age they took it pretty bravely and nodded when he said they should comfort each other and he would keep them company but they shouldn't stir up Billie June. He had to do everything from feed the dogs and the chickens to wash the supper dishes, but he could think and work things out while he was busy. He fetched the laundry off the line, made Steve blow his nose, and after dark put them to bed, hearing their prayers. Billie June was asleep when he looked in on her. Ken finally sat down in the silent kitchen and took a long look at the pint of bootleg, but decided against it. Anything they didn't need right now was a drunk hired hand.

The next day, Tuesday, Ken got up early, roused Tommy and sent him down to the school bus with a note for the law in Empire. By the time he had finished the morning chores, Billie June was awake and working in an absent-minded fashion. Ken hated to do it to her in her state, but he had to ask, "Did he have any insurance, or do you have money put by for—for a funeral?" She shook her head. It was as he had suspected, anyway, so he got himself pulled together for a fight. It came in the late afternoon when a sheriff's deputy drove out from Empire in response to the bus driver's note. The deputy looked at Tom's body where Ken had laid it out in the shed and went down the shaft with Ken to see the site of the accident. After he was satisfied, the deputy popped the question, "Which undertaker do you want?"

"She," Ken said with a nod in the direction of the house, "doesn't have any money, any insurance. I reckon we'll bury him ourselves."

"County'll do it."

"Where? Here?"

"Bancroft cemetery. She'll have to apply for a pauper's funeral."

"We'll do it ourselves. Hell, she doesn't even have a way to get in to Bancroft until Fred Somerset comes by."

The deputy shook his head. "We got laws in this state. Got to have a burial permit, licensed funeral director, embalming."

"How much is a county funeral?"

"We allow sixty-five dollars."

"How much would it cost the county to put me on trial and send me up for breaking that goddam law?"

"Hard case, aren't you, buddy?" The deputy tried to look as menacing as possible, but Ken stood his ground.

"I been in the mill before, and I can go in the mill again, officer. Nothing says you can't report he was blown to pieces. Save the county money both ways, and I bet the supervisors would be kind of happy with you."

The deputy looked unhappy nevertheless. Ken suspected that on the one hand he could use the five dollars he would get from the undertaker he would have touted, but on the other hand would like a pat on the back from his superiors. "You'll do it decent?" the deputy asked.

"He was her husband. My best friend. A good miner. We'll do it decent as we can."

"Well, O.K. Only don't use the old Phonolite cemetery over on the west side of the creek. Now and then there's a body moved or something—they'd see a fresh grave, and my ass would be in a sling."

"That's fair." After the deputy had left, Ken went scouting for a good gravesite. He finally found what he was looking for on the east slope, up a few blocks from the creek. It was a good spot, right where the evening sun would hit it, more or less overlooking the valley, and a trifle below the lower end of the old mine yard. Billie June came out with him and approved of it, and Ken got a pick and shovel and went to work, while Billie June did what she could for Tom—Ken had taken the precaution of bandaging what was left of his face and the mangled arm, so she wouldn't have to have the sight burned into her memory. The ground was hard and full of chips, and once Ken came across a piece of rotten board and a couple of old-fashioned nails, nearly rusted away. He wondered whether someone else had been buried here long ago.

On Wednesday morning they put Tom on the bed of the old chain-drive, and Ken and Billie June and the two boys drove him over and laid him in the grave. Ken had a Bible, and he read some from it, and they said the Twenty-third Psalm together, and it was done. Then they drove back to the house, and Ken went down into the mine and spit the fuses on the holes Tom had loaded. He also shoveled a little loose muck over the now-blackened spots on the iron level sheet while he was waiting for the cage, reflecting that it seemed lonely and confusing to be working without Tom. And when he got up top, he could tell by the look on Billie June's face that she felt the same way. It was at that moment he knew that he was going to have to make a decision sooner or later, and he knew that he would put off making the decision for as long as he could.

The day after Thanksgiving things began to slide downhill. If Billie June and the boys hadn't needed him and if cold weather hadn't been coming on fast, Ken would have left right then. As it was, he found out fast that Tom had been right: mining without a partner went four times as slow and eight times as hard. The good November smelter check would see them through December, but after that it would be like bailing out a leaky boat—they had lost a week's work from Tom's accident and nearly another week plus some money waiting for Fred Somerset to bring out new powder from town. Billie June had put her foot down on that matter, crying, "I don't care about the money! If Joanne has to leave school and come back here, all right, but I won't let you commit suicide, too!" Since she ordered it and her money paid for it, Ken couldn't see any way to stop her.

Mostly by brute strength and awkwardness Ken managed to cyanide two more batches of ore before the combination of a hard freeze and bone weariness forced him to quit. Then he hung storm sash, bucked timber into stove lengths, and made himself as useful as he could without being inside the house too much. For one thing, he remembered Billie June's remark about not wanting a

288

lazy house cat of a man under foot all the time. For another, it was getting a little trying for him to be around Billie June herself, and he didn't want to have to look at her or talk to her too much. Sometimes, despite his fatigue, he couldn't sleep very well for thinking of her. Once in a while during the night he would hear her crying softly or turning over, and he wondered if she knew he was awake, too.

They were now too much like a real family, he thought. Even at meals he ate at the head of the table facing Billie June, with Tommy and Steve at either side of them. He didn't want to sit in Tom's place, but it would have been silly to crowd in beside one of the boys, leaving it empty. And he was a man and hadn't been with a woman for God knows how long, and Billie June was as nice a woman as he had ever seen. As long as Tom had been alive, he couldn't think of her as a woman—only as Tom's wife—but now that Tom was gone, matters were different.

Ken admired Billie June. She never slopped around, was always clean, wore a dress, had her hair combed. She didn't tease him or nag at him. She was a God-fearing woman, too, without being grim about it, teaching the boys to say their prayers, and if she had been able, she would have gone to church every Sunday. Sometimes Ken speculated just what she'd do if he simply got up some night and came into her room. If she was the way he hoped she was, she'd tell him quietly to get out and the next day ask him to leave. And if she wasn't, Ken didn't want to find it out. He wasn't exactly in love with her in the way the radio crooners sang about, and he doubted that she could ever love him, but they got on well together, and he was fond of those two boys of hers. A couple of times they called him Uncle Ken, just to devil him, and he'd chased them around threatening to paddle their pants, with them laughing like hyenas and Billie June trying to look disapproving.

Christmas, when it came, was glum. Ken brought in a scrubby little tree, which Billie June and the boys decorated with what they had, putting a carbide light on top for a star. The boys got new overalls, new clodhopper shoes, and two-bit cap pistols. Ken found a new pair of work jeans for himself under the tree, but he felt like a dog, for he hadn't got anything for Billie June, not that he could have paid for it, even if he'd remembered to ask Fred to get something. The day was improved (or worsened) when an old sedan drove up with Joanne and a boy from Empire in it. The boy was clearly under Joanne's thumb, and she showed him off about the way a fisherman would show off a fourteen-inch trout.

290

Mercifully, they left soon after, and Ken entertained no doubt that his guess about Joanne getting married soon was close to the mark. He silently wished them both luck on the grounds that they would need all of it they could get. What in hell, he thought, are these kids coming to? Then he reminded himself that he hadn't been any smarter at that age, and the thought made him, if possible, even more morose.

It must have shown on his face, for after supper, when the boys had finally quit and gone to bed, Billie June said, "Ken, you look a little blue. Why don't you have a drink of that whisky if it will help?"

He shook his head. "It don't work for me like that, Billie June. Just makes me sadder."

"I know how you feel. Sometimes I wish they would hold Christmas only for the children. Spending it away from your family and all."

He shook his head again. "My folks are gone, and I don't have any more family than you and Tommy and Steve." Since this was verging on dangerous ground, he rose from his chair and said, "Think I'll turn in. The more I loaf, the tired'er I get. Merry Christmas, Billie June."

"Merry Christmas, Ken."

He put another chunk in the stove, stepped outside to the privy, and then went into his cold bedroom. Taking off his new jeans, he thought, where was I last Christmas? He searched his memory and seemed to recall that he spent it in a boxcar outside Omaha or somewhere interesting like that. Hell, he chided himself, I got a roof over my head, three meals a day, work to do, and I'm still feeling sorry for myself. Last Christmas, freezing in that boxcar, I'd have thought this was heaven. And what about that Christmas of 'Seventeen in France? Or the one after that in Coblenz? Some people are never satisfied. But I wish, he thought, God, how I wish Billie June was in here to comfort me. But Tom's been dead only a month, and I got no right to ask, anyway.

If the weather was too cold to work outside, Ken could work down on the three-hundred level, but there was no denying that things were steadily going from bad to worse down there. He

291

could not seem to get the hang of sharpening steel: his bits either broke and were ruined or went dull so fast that they just pounded away to no purpose. He forgot to lubricate the Ingersoll and had to waste a day taking it apart and getting it working again. Setting up the bar by himself took forever, and getting the machine up on it was a nightmare of struggle. Air hose blew out, and rope parted. His shins were a mass of bruises and abrasions. The amount of ore he finally managed to hoist appeared ludicrous when compared with what he and Tom used to break out together. The last straw was the compressor. One windy, damp March day when his lungs were troubling him anyway, the thing quit delivering the air. The gas engine ran fine, nothing seemed frozen or stuck, but the air would not come. Then Ken discovered that the compressor exhaust valve was broken. The compressor was an antique, and no automobile part could possibly be substituted. He threw down his wrench, looked around the yard in despair, peered at the tiny heap of ore in the bottom of the bin, and then strode into the kitchen and took a chair.

Billie June glanced up from the potatoes she was peeling and asked quietly, "What is it, Ken?"

"We're done, Billie June," he replied grimly. "The compressor went out, and I plain can't fix it. I don't think they even make them any more. Don't know where to get parts, even if they do." He stared at the floor in defeat. "Tom was the miner, not me. I don't know anything."

"How much would a new one cost?" she asked.

"Too much." Ken took off his cap and scratched his head. "I can scrape out enough ore for one more cyanide batch, if I got to pick it out by hand. That batch will fill up a drum of sludge for the smelter. Then that's it. The end of the line. Only a real miner could keep it going now, and we can't hire one to come here."

She reached over and patted his hand reassuringly with potato-damp fingers. "Don't take it so hard, Ken. Even Tom said the day would come. Guess it just came a little earlier than we thought."

"That ain't what bothers me. I could roll my blankets and be down on the highway hitching a ride in a couple hours, but this is

292

your home—you and the boys will have to leave it and go away too."

It hurt him to see Billie June's face at that. "Why can't we stay here?"

"The mine was what fed you, not that garden and those chickens. Only now it won't any more. Come fall, you'll be out of money and have to go anyway."

He could tell she was doing sums in her head, and at last she nodded. "So you think we'd better leave as soon as we can?"

"The way I see it. Better to go with money in your purse. I'm sorry, Billie June. Terribly sorry. I done my best, but it's licked me."

"The dogs? The chickens?"

"Eat the chickens. I'll . . . I'll take care of the dogs." She knew what he meant, for the dogs couldn't be taken and couldn't be left to starve, either. "Better give thought to what we can load on the truck, and let's hope it takes us to Meade. Then I'll look for a job or we can apply for relief."

"Do we really have to?" she asked wistfully. "Women hate to leave a place after they've put years into it. Couldn't the boys somehow look out for me?"

He shook his head firmly. "The court would take them away from you, even if they tried. When they grow up, they'd leave anyway. And you have to leave, too, or stay on here and go crazy. I've seen some of these old people who wouldn't leave a dead mine. They have dogs and garbage and dirt up to here, and they're crazy as jaybirds. You don't want to be a skinny, crazy old woman, sleeping on the floor at night with ten dogs to keep you warm, and dying all alone some cold spell."

"I'd have to leave . . . Tom."

"Billie June," he persisted gently, "comes a time when we all got to walk away for good from a grave." He shuffled his feet on the scrubbed, worn linoleum. "Billie June, it'd be better for all of us if you and I got married when we got to Meade. But you know, I guess, I was married once and never got a divorce."

She dropped her eyes into the potato bowl and began peeling a fresh one with great concentration. "Tom told me about it. How long ago was it?"

Ken thought. "Over ten years."

"Where is she now?"

"Still back on the East coast for all I know."

"Do you still love her?"

He shook his head. "It's just like it all happened to somebody else. I don't feel anything, one way or the other."

"Are you offering out of pity for me and the boys?" she asked, her eyes still down.

"I like them boys a lot. Hope they like me. And, no, Billie June, I'm sorry for your bad luck, but it isn't pity. Pity is nothing to ask a woman to get married on."

"Tommy and Steve do like you," she mused. "And you were sensible with Joanne and tried to spare our feelings." Womanlike, she went off on a tangent. "That girl is my own flesh and blood, and I can't abide her!"

"She'll get better as she gets older. Kids generally do." Ken grinned slightly. "Bet you'll be a grandma this time next year."

Billie June snorted and carved deeply into a potato. Then she tossed potato and knife into the bowl together. "Kenneth Carvel," she said in determination, "if you don't ever mention that wife you had, afterwards, I won't." At his nod, she twisted off her wedding ring, turned it over in her fingers, and handed it to him. "Here, you keep this until we get to Meade. Oh, I don't know *what* I'll tell the boys tonight!" she concluded in exasperation.

"Something I'd like to know," Ken said diffidently. "It don't make no difference, but . . . well, Billie June, can you still have kids?"

Billie June colored slightly, but snapped, "I'm only thirty-three years old and not ready for a wheelchair yet."

"That's good!" Ken said happily. "That's real good." He reached for his cap and carbide light. "Now if you'll send me down, I'll try to scoop enough of that ore to help get us to Meade."

Billie June threw on a sweater, and companionably arm-in-arm they walked together to the headframe, the last crew of the Molly Pitcher, going to work on the last shift.

EPILOGUE

PHONOLITE IS NOT TO BE found today on any road map of the state. Having looked up its site on the maps in the archives of the State Historical Society at Meade, the visitor must drive through Empire to Bancroft, and at the junction just beyond take the secondary highway that curves off to the north. At 69.3 miles he should slow down and watch for a cattle guard to his left. This is the point at which the old haulage road terminated. From this point the notch in the skyline of the Mineral Mountains is visible. Unless the visitor is an experienced and dedicated hiker or is operating a four-wheel-drive vehicle, he would do well to go no farther.

A few local ranchers are better acquainted with what was once the Molly Pitcher and Phonolite. During the white-wing dove season in autumn they ride jeeps or horses up the trail from the highway to the outwash fan at the throat of the notch. From there they make their way on foot, shotguns at the port. Should hunting be poor or should they get their limit soon, they may poke about the meager remains in view. These are few enough in all conscience. During World War II, scrap salvagers made off with the old headframes and the sheet iron, camping in Tom Pritchard's house, which they set afire when they left. Upstream the hunters can see the remains of the high dam. There is occasional local talk of applying for a federal loan, rehabilitating the dam, and creating a fishing and recreational lake. Such talk is not taken very seriously even by its advocates. Who would travel seventy miles to fish, when TV is at hand?

On two occasions after Ken Carvel and Billie June Pritchard and her sons left, the location was reprospected. During the uranium rush of the late 'Forties men waved Geiger counters and scintillometers over the remains, but the instrument readings were far too low to be worth any sort of consideration. Fifteen years later still, the demand for such exotic elements as germanium, niobium, and cesium inspired mineral corporation geologists to take more dump samples. Once more the assays—taken in manners and run in fashions that would have baffled Matt Wheeler and Ben Roderick—proved much too lean to be of interest.

There is really little enough for even the dove hunters to see now. The valley is much more tangled and brush-grown than it was when Matt Wheeler first laid eyes upon it. The old Phonolite cemetery on the west side of the creek is neglected, invisible even at close range. Up the hill on the east the incline and shaft collars appear to be only wide, rock-filled pits, a yard or two deep at the center. Ends of reinforcing rod and rusty segments of corrugated iron protrude at odd angles from the broken waste. The concrete work is rotten and crumbling badly. Only the jays, the ground squirrels, and the aspens flourish.

Ironically enough, Bancroft lives and thrives, unconsciously maintaining the tradition of a century. Truckers and tourists are advised when leaving Meade to get fuel and service at Empire and to pass on through Bancroft without pause except for the obligatory halt at an unexpected and well-camouflaged stop sign. Failure to do so will result in instant arrests and levying of memorable fines. Bancroft has more saloons than its proportions appear to warrant, a few tourist-trap stores, two filling stations, and a truck stop. Only the rowdier and more adventurous truckers pull their rigs off the road here. Staid and experienced drivers

297

watch their speed carefully and sigh in relief when they have left the corporate limits.

Fuel prices in the Bancroft filling stations are rigidly fixed at precisely fifteen cents the gallon higher than at Meade, ten cents higher than at Empire a mere twenty miles back. It is Bancroft's pride that a local gas pumper who knows his business can walk casually around a tourist's car and in twenty seconds leave it totally disabled. An unaccompanied woman or covey of vacationing schoolma'ams who allow him to lift the engine hood will be more swiftly and certainly undone than if they allowed him to lift their skirts: the turnover in fan belts, tires, radiator hose, and batteries is phenomenal. One genius recalls in pride that he sold her own transmission twice to a touring English teacher—once on her way north and again when she stopped by on her return to thank him for his remarkably fine repairs.

Of the inanimate relics of the Molly Pitcher the best preserved of all is to be found within a low, fortresslike building in Kentucky. Its specific location is vault B, the second layer from the bottom, third row from the front, seventh place from the left. Its stamped inventory number is 1048457; its fineness number is 9996. Since it is surrounded by its fellows, it reposes in as total darkness and silence as did its component atoms before they were first shot down in the stopes of the Molly Pitcher. Peculiarly enough, it has never been minted, never adorned fair women, never been looted in war. On six sides of it is gold of Alexander, Montezuma, Ghengiz, gold of Guinea, of the Yukon, of Siberia. If gold could speak with miraculous organ, the vault would resound with unbelievable tales of the glory, the villainy, the ingenuity of all mankind. Amid such company what tale could the gold of the Molly Pitcher tell that would be worth the hearing?